Praise for T. Jefferson Parker

"Parker ranks as one of the top contemporary suspense writers."
—*Publishers Weekly*

"A pro, that's what T. Jefferson Parker is. His plots are intricate, keenly crafted, clearly mapped."
—*Los Angeles Times*

"If there's a better mystery writer around . . . well, there isn't."
—*The San Diego Union-Tribune*

Praise for *A Thousand Steps*

"A compelling coming-of-age thriller that will entrance you with its sixties vibe and backdrop, and captivate you with its engaging storytelling and a believable cast of characters."
—*USA Today*

"A unique thriller and also a coming-of-age story: the not-so-sentimental education of an impressionable teen."
—*The Wall Street Journal*

"As powerful as a riptide in summer."   —*Los Angeles Times*

"Parker already has two or three titles on my all-time best-ever list . . . and now comes *A Thousand Steps*, which might be his crowning achievement."   —Lee Child

"Parker is one of the greats, and has been for years."
—John Hart, *New York Times* bestselling author

A THOUSAND STEPS

T. JEFFERSON PARKER

TOR PUBLISHING GROUP
NEW YORK

A THOUSAND STEPS

Copyright © 2021 by T. Jefferson Parker

All rights reserved.

Designed by Gabriel Guma

A Forge Book
Published by Tom Doherty Associates/Tor Publishing Group
120 Broadway
New York, NY 10271

www.tor-forge.com

Forge® is a registered trademark of Macmillan Publishing Group, LLC.

The Library of Congress has cataloged the hardcover edition as follows:

Names: Parker, T. Jefferson, author.
Title: A thousand steps / T. Jefferson Parker.
Description: First Edition. | New York : Forge, Tom Doherty
    Associates Book, 2022.
Identifiers: LCCN 2021033433 (print) | LCCN 2021033434 (ebook) |
    ISBN 9781250793539 (hardcover) | ISBN 9781250793546 (ebook)
Subjects: GSAFD: Mystery fiction. | Suspense fiction.
Classification: LCC PS3566.A6863 T49 2022 (print) | LCC
    PS3566.A6863 (ebook) | DDC 813/.54—dc23
LC record available at https://lccn.loc.gov/2021033433
LC ebook record available at https://lccn.loc.gov/2021033434

ISBN 978-1-250-89021-4 (trade paperback)

Our books may be purchased in bulk for promotional, educational, or business use. Please contact your local bookseller or the Macmillan Corporate and Premium Sales Department at 1-800-221-7945, extension 5442, or by email at MacmillanSpecialMarkets@macmillan.com.

First Forge Paperback Edition: 2023

Printed in the United States of America

0 9 8 7 6 5 4 3 2 1

For brother Matt Parker—artist, inventor,
and inspiration—thank you for the years, the letters,
and the laughs. And for the way we write our histories.

Laguna Beach
June 1968

New morning on a waking city and a heaving dark sea. And on a boy, Matt Anthony, pedaling his bicycle up Pacific Coast Highway.

His fishing rod, strapped to the rack behind him, whips and wobbles in the air. A tackle box rattles and bounces beside it. He's pedaling hard for Thalia Street, where the cop cars and a fire engine and an ambulance are clustered, lights flashing.

He skids to a stop on the sidewalk and props his bike against the wall of the corner surf shop. Hustles past the vehicles to the stairs leading down to the beach. Jams his hands into his poncho against the chill and joins the T-Street Surf Boys, who have gathered to watch the cops. Matt recognizes two of the surfers as just-graduated seniors from his high school— cool guys, friends of his sister—but they ignore him, wet suits slung over their shoulders and boards at their sides, all their attention on the dark beach below. The waves break almost invisibly, with overlapping echoes that end abruptly then repeat.

It's hard for Matt to see what's going on down there. But he's a curious sixteen-year-old, so he clambers down the stairs to the beach, his rock-worn sneakers slapping on the concrete then thudding in the sand. He gets up close. Where he sees, through a knot of Laguna Beach cops standing in a loose circle, a pale girl lying faceup on a slab of rock. Her arms are spread and her hair is laced with seaweed. A black bomber-style jacket covers her middle.

Matt's ears roar as they do when he sees something that causes strong emotion. It's like rushing water.

A young officer jogs past him, his holster and duty belt clanking, and a blanket tucked under one arm. One of the other cops yanks the blanket from him and spreads it over the girl. Then he looks over at Matt. He's Bill Furlong, the big LBPD sergeant who badgers and busts the hippies in town, cuffing and herding them, sometimes six or eight at a time, into a windowless white prisoner van the locals call Moby Cop.

The ambulance team trudges across the beach with a stretcher, pausing for Furlong, who advances on Matt with all his large authority. He's got straight dark hair, heavy brows, and tan eyes. There is something bear-like about him.

"Matt," says Furlong. "Is that who I think it is?"

"That's Bonnie Stratmeyer," says Matt. He feels as if the blood has drained from his face.

"How long have you been here?"

"Since just now."

"How'd the fishing go?"

"Two bass."

Furlong almost always asks about the fishing, and about Matt's mother, brother, and sister. Less so about Matt's father, Bruce, a former cop himself. Now Matt hears the waves slapping and watches the ambulance guys lift Bonnie Stratmeyer onto the stretcher. Facing each other they rise together, balancing their load.

Another wave pops sharply and the blanket slides off. Matt sees Bonnie's yellow bikini and her hair spilling over the stretcher like a drowned animal. Two uniforms put the blanket back over her, then lay the black bomber jacket on top to keep it down. The roar in Matt's head is back.

"She's been missing almost two months," says Furlong. "Did you know that?"

"Everybody knows that."

Matt has seen her posters in the shop windows, read a story

about her and other runaways in the *News-Post*. He's never talked to her and now he realizes, with a strange recoil, that he never will. Bonnie was a brainy one, like his sister—honor roll students.

"Is Bonnie the type to go out swimming in the dark alone?" Furlong asks.

"I don't know. She's two years older than me."

"Was she in-crowd, or more to herself?"

"Herself."

"Was she a head?"

"I don't know."

"But do you suspect she used drugs?"

"I don't know, sir."

"Matt, I want you to look behind you up at the landing where the surfers are standing. And tell me, do you think if you jumped from there it would kill you?"

Matt turns and considers. "If you hit a big rock I think it could."

"Well, just yesterday a hippie chick tripping on LSD thought she could jump from the El Mar Hotel balcony, fly all the way across Coast Highway, and land on the sidewalk. She's in the hospital now with more broken bones than you can count."

Matt doesn't know what to say. He purses his lips and nods.

"You still delivering the newspapers?"

"Every day."

"How's your brother doing over in the jungle?"

"He's still alive."

"Say hello to your mom, Matt."

Matt nods. Years ago, divorced Furlong tried to date his mom, but Julie Anthony would have none of him. Matt thought it was uncool to treat his mom like a potential girlfriend. Any mom. Furlong wears a wedding ring now. Matt has never liked nor trusted the man, and senses the sergeant knows this.

"I saw Julie out in Dodge City yesterday," says Furlong.

Dodge City being a nickname for a few narrow streets out

in Laguna Canyon where the rents are low and the hippies and artists and surfers and young freaks have taken root. The houses are mostly small and rickety, clustered amid the eucalyptus trees. At school, Matt hears tales of drugs being smuggled in and out, and of cops and the FBI staging stings and raids, making arrests, shooting at smugglers running into the canyon brush. He's heard there's a monkey chained to a tree. Dogs running wild and children running naked. The newspapers he delivers have Dodge City stories all the time.

LAGUNA POLICE RAID DODGE CITY
Pot, Hashish Recovered

So, naturally Matt wonders what his mom was doing out there.

2

At home, his mother sits at the dinette in a green silk kimono, working on her morning coffee. The smell of weed has wafted in from under the closed door of her bedroom because Julie Anthony will not be seen smoking grass by her own children. Matt wishes she didn't get high so often.

Home is a clapboard bungalow that huddles in the shade of the phone company building at the bottom of the Third Street hill. Three tiny bedrooms. It was built just after World War II as a summer home for a Pasadena banker. Or so says the landlord, Nelson Pedley, who sometimes tries to shame Julie into paying her rent on time by complaining to Matt about people meeting their obligations first and their pleasures second. Pedley claims to be the banker's son-in-law. But, a banker's second home or not, this is a drafty and uninsulated one-bath box held together by loud plumbing and temperamental electricity, dwarfed by two-story apartments on three sides, and the looming General Telephone & Electronics building across Third. The rent is remarkably cheap, for Laguna. Julie gets the tiny "master," while Matt's sister Jasmine gets one of the bedrooms, and Matt—beginning with high school two years ago—has moved from his and brother Kyle's room to the garage.

"Honey!"

"Hi, Mom."

"How'd you do?"

"Two good bass. Bonnie Stratmeyer washed up on the beach early this morning, Mom. She's dead."

"Oh my goodness," she almost whispers. *"Why? How?* Was she swimming?"

"It only just happened. Nobody knows anything yet."

"What a terrible thing. Jasmine is going to be seriously blown out!"

Matt says nothing. He dislikes his mother's sometimes antic behavior while high.

Matt puts the bass fillets in a baking dish and pours in enough milk to cover them. It isn't a lot to eat but it's fresh and free. He sets the fishy newsprint in the trash can outside and washes his hands in the groaning kitchen faucet.

"I'm freaked out," says his mother. "Bonnie's been missing two months, now this? Her mother will be so *totally* bummed."

"Probably her dad, too."

His own dad being a sore spot around here, Matt dries his hands on his shorts and goes to wake up his sister, maybe break the bad news about Bonnie, and see if she's up for the beach later.

No Jasmine, which is a bit of a surprise. First time she hasn't come home after a night out, Matt thinks. She left last night in Julie's old hippie van. Which wasn't in the driveway when Matt left to fish early this morning, and isn't in the driveway now.

In her room he looks at her senior portrait, crookedly thumb-tacked to the wall above a big psychedelic pink-yellow-and-orange Dr. Timothy Leary lecture-in-Laguna poster. Flanked by her Buffalo Springfield and Sandpiper nightclub flyers. On the bedstand is her diary and *The Tibetan Book of the Dead.* No cans or bottles in the wicker trash can.

Jazz. They're close in the friendly-enemies way that brothers and sisters are close. If Matt had to answer Furlong's nosey questions about Bonnie Stratmeyer on behalf of Jazz, he'd have to say his sister is more in-crowd than a head, though he has seen empty beer cans in her trash. She's also an effortless straight-A student, a former cheerleader, wiseass, and an all-around bitchen teenager. Plays a ukulele and writes her own songs. She makes ugly faces that crack him up.

Back in the dining room, little more than a windowed alcove off the kitchen, he asks his mother where Jasmine went last night.

"Miranda's, I think. She took the van again. We, um, had some words about her attitude towards her mother."

Not the first time for that, thinks Matt. "She's never not come home."

"She's also just graduated and blowing off steam," says Julie. "She was angry. Feeling her oats, though I'm not sure what 'oats' are in this situation."

Out in the garage Matt stashes his fishing gear and takes off the poncho for the warming June day. He leaves the big door up to let in some sun. The garage has two windows, the heavy spring-loaded door for cars, and a narrow convenience door for people.

His mattress, sleeping bag, and pillow are on the floor. There are orange-crates stacked for his books and painting supplies, a desk and a chair. One overhead light operated by a wall switch. There's a pulsing blue lava lamp, a gift from Jazz. His current painting is a mess of a seascape, half-done if that, propped on a wounded thrift-store chair. Matt keeps his garage clean but creatures get in under the doors, mice sometimes, earwigs and spiders, and once in a while, a scorpion.

Now his mother stands just outside the garage, framed in sunlight. Julie's wearing her Jolly Roger Restaurant waitress uniform—a red wench's blouse with a plunging neckline and off-the-shoulder sleeves, black pantaloons, red socks, and hideous black buckled slippers. Her dark hair up. Matt thinks she looks too young to be his mom.

"I'm off to work, Matty. Are you copacetic with what you saw?"

"I've never seen a dead person before."

The dead frogs in biology were bad enough. The smell of formaldehyde. Bonnie looked so cold.

Julie strides into the garage and throws her arms around her son. "I know, Matty. I know."

Then she backs away, takes both his hands and looks up at him with teary eyes.

"You said Miranda's," Matt says.

"Miranda's?"

"Jazz, Mom. You said she went to Miranda's last night."

"I think that's what she said. Miranda lives on Cress."

Matt has delivered newspapers to Miranda Zahara's driveway every day for two years and four months, so he knows exactly where she lives. He knows exactly where hundreds of Laguna Beach's thirteen thousand people live. He also knows which customers give him bonus money at Christmas. Which last year helped to get him the new black Schwinn Heavy-Duti delivery bike with the cantilever frame, heavy-duty saddle, drop-forged crank, and pannier rack.

"Matt, don't worry about Jazz," says Julie. "She's just testing her freedom. And me. She'll be home any minute with a big old hangover."

Julie lets go of her son and heads down the driveway, the buckles of her slippers twinkling in the sun.

Cress is a short bike ride. Miranda's mom says that Miranda was supposedly at *his* house last night. Matt thinks of the double-reverse play in football. Very much like his sister to pull something like that over Julie's eyes.

"Miranda came home late," says Mrs. Zahara. "She's still asleep."

"Do you know where they went?"

"The Sandpiper maybe? That singer they like was there last night, and the bouncers usually let them in."

Matt nods. He knows what singer she's talking about and doesn't like him. Jasmine has a crush on him. He also knows that Jasmine's fake ID is pretty good because he made it for her, carefully doctoring the date of birth and expiration date numerals after she had reported her CDL stolen and gotten a replacement. The fake is pretty obvious in sunlight but indoors or by flashlight you had a chance of getting away with it.

"Is everything alright?" asks Mrs. Zahara.

He thinks of Bonnie Stratmeyer but nods anyway. Wonders why moms don't keep track of their kids better. "Pretty much."

She says that Miranda would probably be out of bed by the time Matt came back here to deliver the paper. He could talk to her then if he wanted.

3

Matt sits on an upended red bucket in his driveway, folding and rubber-banding the *Register* afternoon final editions, two heavy bales of which have just been muscled to the ground by his supervisor, Tommy Amici. Tommy brings the papers no later than one o'clock and they must be delivered no later than five. If he delivers the papers later than five, he'll get complaints, which make collections harder. Matt is enrolled in a shortened day work-study program at school to make this possible. The route earns him twelve dollars and fifty cents every other week.

Collections are the first and third Sunday mornings of the month. Sundays he doesn't deliver: the *Register* morning final is too heavy for kids on bikes to throw.

And, Matt has learned, the houses that complain are less likely to pay a Christmas bonus. So he tries his best to porch the papers. Just last week Mr. Coiner had cussed Matt out for a late delivery. *Ten minutes after five!* A month ago, an older teenager had told Matt that his dad was sick of his paper being late, then beaned him with an orange.

Matt has come to understand that people—especially older people—want their news like, immediately. Just hours after it happens. They don't want to wait for the evening TV. So, newspapers aren't just important, they're vital. And when they're late or soggy or come apart and get blown around, the paperboy is the one to blame.

Tommy kneels, cuts the twine ties with a pocketknife, and Matt carries a thick load of papers back to his bucket.

Tommy asks what he always asks. "Jasmine home?"

Matt answers what he always answers, that he doesn't know where she is. He sits again and begins folding today's papers, twice over, and slipping on the rubber bands. After doing this every day for two years and four months, he barely has to think about it.

Tommy is recently arrived in California from New Jersey. He's not one of the hippie freaks who've been pouring into town since last year's Summer of Love in San Francisco, the ones Matt sees tripping on acid on Main Beach, or hitchhiking Laguna Canyon with joints in their mouths, or washing their skinny white bodies with people's garden hoses, or hanging around the Mystic Arts World head shop, or scoring drugs across the street in front of Taco Bell, freaks for sure, all hair and tie-dye, sandals and headbands and dope, dope, dope. No, Tommy smokes cigarettes and has the Jersey accent, wears his T-shirts tight with the sleeves rolled up, and his hair in a pompadour. Drives a white Chevy Malibu with a *Register* logo on the door. Stares at Jazz like a hopeful dog. He's at least ten years older than his sister, which Matt thinks is too old.

"You hear about the high school girl dead on the beach?" Tommy asks.

Matt feels so bad about Bonnie he can't put her into words. "No."

"Bonnie Stratmeyer," says Tommy. "This morning the cops said she probably got caught in a riptide and drowned. Then washed up. Later they said she didn't have any history of taking early morning swims in a cold ocean so they weren't ruling out a fall from the cliff above where they found her. No witnesses. She'd been an official missing person for two months. The autopsy will give them a lot more to go on."

Tommy stands and slips his knife back into his pocket then wraps the cut twine around one hand. "I got another call from Mrs. Coiner," he says. "Try to keep the paper out of her sprinklers."

* * *

Matt powers his *Register*-burdened Heavy-Duti south on Glenneyre, hitting his targets like a quarterback—the Raiders' Daryle Lamonica maybe, his favorite—throwing four quick completions to the Heun, Parlett, Cabang, and Rigby houses before heading up Legion, around the high school, and onto Los Robles with four more completions, one of them a bomb to the very tough Murrel house, hidden behind a defensive front line of blooming bougainvillea.

Between throws he's off the seat, zig-zagging and grinding up the hills, wiping his sweaty forehead on the shoulders of the canvas delivery bag that holds the papers. He breathes hard, his skinny legs strong as pistons from doing this for 850 straight days. Eight completions so far, forty more to go.

At the dreaded Coiner home he skids to a stop, kickstands the bike and hand-carries the paper all the way to their porch, the sprinklers watering his legs and their poodle Gigi barking furiously at him through the screen door. Then runs heavy legged back to his bike.

He works his way uphill and takes a break at his highest house on Bluebird Canyon Drive. Pants and rubs his face with a shop rag from the carrier. Heart thumping like a marching drum. Far below, the Pacific is a spangled silver mirror in this afternoon light. A distant barge and small sailboats look like toys on glass. He'd like to get that in a painting. Painting is difficult and expensive. His paintings are all ugly and he's never actually finished one. Paints them over until he has to stop. He uses discarded house paint they save for him at Coast Hardware, ghastly colors not found in nature.

By the time he gets to Miranda Zahara's house she's outside washing her red VW Beetle. Brown bikini, brown skin. He stops behind the car, one foot on the ground and one on the pedal. His T-shirt is soaked through and the nearly empty canvas carrier feels like a sopping hot jacket.

She gives him a gloomy look then continues spraying the

hose water along the rounded Beetle roof. "Did you hear about Bonnie?" she asks.

Matt nods, lobs the Zahara's paper almost to the porch. "I saw her on the beach this morning."

Miranda looks at him, the hose water sparkling into the air. "What . . . how did she . . . *look*?"

"Well, she was lying on one of those big rocks down off Thalia. She had a cop's jacket over her and her hair had seaweed in it and she was dead."

Matt feels important giving Miranda this terrible news. He doesn't know why.

"She was cool," says Miranda, redirecting the water to the roof. "Not stuck-up at all. I think it's very suspicious that she would be at the beach that early, swimming. After running away from home, or whatever she did."

"It weirds me out, too."

"Want a drink?"

He brings the hose to his mouth at an angle, feels the cool water rushing in, gulps it down and hands the hose back.

"Where did you and Jazz go last night?" he asks.

"The 'Piper, to see Austin Overton."

"Good show?"

"Far *out*. New songs. He's such a god."

Matt had snuck into an Austin Overton set at the Sandpiper a few months ago. Didn't like his music and didn't like him, but the girls in the audience sure did.

"Where'd you go after?"

"I left early and met some friends at Diver's Cove. Jazz wanted to stay. My mom said your mom called and Jazz didn't come home last night."

Matt nods, wondering if one of the Sandpiper owners—brothers Chip or Chuck—might have seen Jazz leave. And if so, seen whether she was alone or with somebody.

Miranda gives Matt the hose again and he takes another long drink before handing it back. She watches him drink. "You know, that Phisohex soap works good on zits."

He averts his eyes. Dr. Bill Anderson has recently recommended the same expensive acne cleanser. And reassured Matt that his long-aching joints are only growing pains.

"Thanks, Miranda."

"I mean, you hardly have any, but—"

"Yeah, right on."

Miranda folds the hose over and holds it with both hands, pinching off the flow. "Sorry. Look, Matt, we were just groovin' to Austin Overton last night. We had a couple of beers is all. Whatever she did after, I'm sure was cool. Maybe she went down to Thousand Steps with the gang. If so, she's probably back home by now."

"I hope you're right. But it's the first time she's not come home."

"You're worried."

"Seeing Bonnie made me worried."

"It would me, too."

4

The Sandpiper on Coast Highway is dead at five when Matt pushes open the heavy, decal-plastered front door. Chuck says Matt can only stay a minute, being way under twenty-one. Says Furlong could bust him for this. The club is small and dark, no windows, and it smells of cigarettes, beer, and bleach. The stage is stacked with amps and the walls are crookedly tacked with carpet remnants for better acoustics, giving the room a teetering, ship's-hold kind of feeling.

Chuck wants to talk about Bonnie Stratmeyer but Matt does not, so he pretends he hasn't heard. Chuck fills him in: Bonnie was found naked and possibly murdered below the Diamond Street stairway to the beach and she was probably a federal informant and that the cops were covering it all up. She'd been missing for nearly six months, says Chuck.

Of course, almost everything Chuck says about Bonnie is wrong. Matt thinks it's funny how quickly the under-thirty Lagunatics like Chuck blame the cops, the government, and the very right-wing John Birch Society for whatever goes wrong in their town. And how the cops, the government, and the John Birch Society think the young are all drug addicts, draft dodgers, sex fiends, and communists. Matt wants to side with the young and free, of course, but he's not sure how. Smoke pot? Wear that lame tie-dye hippie stuff?

However, Chuck did in fact see Jasmine last night, had served her and Miranda soft drinks and allowed them to hear Austin Overton. Why? Because Chuck had heard a "confirmed rumor" at Mystic Arts World that Sgt. Bill Furlong and most of the LBPD would be conducting another Dodge City raid last night, rather than busting underage drinkers around town. Jasmine had left after the last set, sober and apparently happy. Chuck gives Matt a conspiratorial look.

"Who with?"

"Austin Overton."

Shit, Matt thinks. He knows the anger is showing on his face. He doesn't care. Chuck tells him that the singer hangs out at Mystic Arts World, if Matt wants to find him.

"I know where he hangs out."

Matt has seen Overton at Mystic Arts World more than once. He's one of the celebrity acid-heads who spend a lot of time there—Dr. Timothy Leary and Johnny Grail being two others. Leary being the former Harvard psychology professor, and Grail being the founder of the Brotherhood of Eternal Love, which owns Mystic Arts World. Which Furlong says is nothing more than a drug emporium disguised as a head shop.

Matt hangs out at Mystic Arts World too, because he likes the artist who runs the MAW art gallery in the meditation room. Christian Clay not only lets Matt loiter around and paw through the expensive art books MAW sells, but also lets Matt help him hang the gallery paintings. Gives him a tattered demo book once in a while.

They talk about art, art, and art. Matt knows that Laguna was founded as an art colony and he wonders if growing up here led him to art or if he would have found art anywhere. Clay's reputation is as a "psychedelic artist," but Matt thinks his paintings and sculptures are much more than that. In those heavy art tomes, Christian points out influences on his work, some going back centuries. Matt wishes he had one-tenth of the talent Christian has. A hundredth.

He walks into Mystic Arts World at sunset, entering through a wall of incense smoke that thickens toward the ceiling.

The light is dim. A chorus of *oms* drones from the meditation room in back. The main room has shelves of books on mysticism, spirituality, metaphysics, philosophy, Eastern religion, illustrated sex texts, mind-expansion through drugs; separate stands for the bestselling quarterly *Psychedelic Review*, hardcover and paperback volumes of Timothy Leary's *The Psychedelic Experience*, and Aldous Huxley's *The Doors of Perception;* long glass cabinets and lacquered burl tables stocked with recreational drug paraphernalia; bins of bootlegged tapes from the Dead, Hendrix, Cream, Jefferson Airplane, the Beatles, and Dylan; potted plants growing lush throughout—ferns, ficus, creeping Charlie, and philodendron.

The store is crowded with shoppers, most young and well-haired, wearing loose clothes and smothered in bags—bags with straps over their backs or shoulders or around their waists, bags in their hands, bags on their arms and at their elbows—sewn bags, knit bags, woven bags, bags featuring feathers and seashells, wooden amulets, ceramic zodiacal symbols, and beads, beads, beads. Matt's young instincts tell him that this world of mystic arts is funny and crazy and maybe a little dangerous. He feels an undertow of arousal every time he walks in. Jazz once described MAW as "horny."

To Matt, the Brotherhood of Eternal Love is cool, generous, and secretive. Christian has told him that lots of young men claim membership but only a few actually are. It is widely known that the BEL is a legally registered church in the state of California. And that they make no secret of worshipping Jesus, God, Buddha, LSD, and marijuana. They want to buy an island and create a utopia on it. Forever stoned to see god. Forever free to make love. Matt has heard that the island is already paid for.

Matt has also heard that the BEL makes large amounts of money smuggling hashish into Laguna from Afghanistan. He has seen that they are flagrant and prodigious drug users. Surfers. Motorheads. Petty criminals. Street fighters from inland. All on a mission to bring freedom, love, and LSD to the people. One day Matt saw Johnny Grail speeding down Pacific Coast Highway in a white convertible Cadillac Eldorado

with the top down, screaming happily about love and tossing hundred-dollar bills in the air. Matt got one. BEL. Acid
church. Religious cult with an eye for profit. A going concern.

But no Austin Overton here at Mystic Arts. Matt figures it
might be too early for a popular rock musician to be showing
himself in his adopted hometown. Probably eating, which reminds Matt how hungry he is, nothing since the peanut butter
and jelly burrito before his paper route.

He stands near the entrance of the meditation room, looking
in. One of Christian Clay's huge psychedelic paintings, *Cosmic
Mandala*, hangs illuminated on the far wall. It's an awesome
circular swirl of colors and shapes that explode outward from a
coupled yin and yang, depicting—according to Christian—life
from the beginning of matter to the end of time.

Seated cross-legged on a table beneath the painting is a
large, dark-skinned, long-bearded man in a crimson robe, eyes
closed and both hands resting on his knees in *Gyan* mudra—
thumbs and index fingers forming loose circles. Matt knows
the *Gyan* mudra from his mother, who took up meditation just
recently and thinks the incense she burns while meditating in
her room cancels out the marijuana she's been smoking more
and more frequently.

Except for the crimson-robed leader sitting on his table,
everybody else in the meditation room is facing away from
Matt. He studies the back of each hairy head for Austin Overton but doesn't see him. What exactly would Matt ask him?
Didn't the singer have the right to go out with an admirer
after his show? A small part of Matt thinks he might even
find Jasmine here with Overton, both of them exhausted and
meditating together soul-to-soul after having sex all night.
He hates that idea because Overton is too old. Matt knows
Jazz has had sex because she told him. He disapproves though
knows it's not his business.

Now Matt feels a grumble in his stomach and a lightness
in his head. Bonnie Stratmeyer weighs on his thoughts, even
more heavily now than she did this morning. In Matt's mind,

Jasmine's failure to come home is darkly related to Bonnie—absurd and irrational as he knows this is. Bonnie as warning. Bonnie as fate.

Stepping outside Mystic Arts, Matt breathes the cool salt air and rubs his fists over his smoke-stung eyes.

He has a sudden hope that Jazz will be home when he gets there. Like Miranda said. Be so great to see her. So great to know she's alive and well. To see there's no connection to a girl who went missing two months ago in the same small town and was found dead on the beach just this morning.

He can cook up the sea bass fillets and hear about whatever she did last night, and where and who with.

5

But no.

No sun-faded two-tone tangerine-and-white van in the driveway. Jasmine's room is empty and his mother's door is shut. When she's "sleeping," Julie hangs a puka shell necklace on the knob, but Matt sees that her light is on. He hears music inside.

He cooks and eats the fish, cleans up, and sits on the lumpy living room couch, looking out the window. Sets a soft drink can on the wicker trunk that serves as their coffee table. There's a streetlight directly across Third that sends down a misty cone of light that reminds him of Hopper. Hopper was the first painter he liked, years ago as a fifth grader, courtesy of a book in his classroom at El Morro Elementary. Hopper made it okay to be alone.

He hears the music stop and his mother's door open, the puka shells tapping against the wood.

"Hi'ya Matty," she smiles dreamily. She walks through the living room into the kitchen, wearing another of her silk kimonos, the orange one, her hair up in chopsticks, something in her hand. "I didn't hear you come in. No Jazz, huh? I called all her friends soon as I got home. Nobody's seen her."

"I thought she'd be here."

Matt hears her open and close a kitchen drawer. Utensils rattle and clink. He smells a different odor in the little bungalow. It's not the usual skunky green odor of pot, it's sharper and darker smelling.

The refrigerator clunks open and shut and Julie comes out

with a white sack in one hand and a fork in the other. She sits across from Matt on a blue vinyl chair, part of the furnishings when they moved in.

His mother's voice sounds thin and somehow distant. "I'm going to talk to the police tomorrow if she's not home tonight. I think she's still mad at me."

He knows that Jazz chides Julie for smoking dope and drinking too much wine. That Jazz can get under her mother's skin quick as a bee sting. And seems to enjoy it, sometimes.

"I'll wait up for her," says Matt.

"Great, honey. It's only nine. I promise you she'll be home tonight."

She pulls a cardboard canister of Jolly Roger leftovers from the bag and goes to work on the noodles. Matt smiles at this tableau, his mother in a kimono with chopsticks in her hair eating noodles with a fork. She looks up and smiles back.

Watching her eat makes Matt hungry again. His hilly paper route leaves him consistently famished on the scant twenty-five dollars a month. The home fridge and cabinets are poorly stocked due to what his mother calls budgetary concerns, and her free take-home food from the Jolly Roger rarely lasts the night. She's admitted to Matt and Jazz that she eats her way through her shifts, trying to preserve the home foodstuffs for them. Thus for Matt: fishing the rocks for the plentiful bass, halibut, and perch; occasional handouts from a friend who washes dishes at the swank Hotel Laguna restaurant on Pacific Coast Highway; stolen neighborhood oranges and occasional avocados; and embarrassing runs to the Assistance League Food Exchange. He's never full for long. He's skinny. Jazz told him he probably has a tapeworm.

"Have you heard any more about Bonnie Stratmeyer?" asks Julie.

Matt shakes his head. "Just people making things up."

"I see you got another letter from your father. Did he have anything good to say?"

"What he always says. For me to come out and live with

him. Hippies and queers are ruining the country and that's all there is in Laguna."

"Is he still in Nevada?"

"Oklahoma now."

Matt knows that his mother knows where Bruce Anthony is and what he's up to. Bruce had been an Orange County Sheriff deputy, handsome and hard-drinking. Matt got his thick blond hair and gray eyes, but not any handsome part that Matt can tell. Jazz got the hair too, not Julie's dark curls.

Matt was ten when his dad left for Texas with a woman from county payroll, in order to take a cop's job that didn't pan out. He'd come to hate California, especially Laguna Beach, which was the stated epicenter of Bruce Anthony's vision of Armageddon. When he left the family, Julie cut him off—no calls, no letters, no contact at all. Threw his things in a church dumpster and set them on fire. She sent his first few letters back to sender, then they stopped coming altogether. Matt and his father have traded occasional letters and postcards for four years now, and Matt knows his mother reads them by the careless way she leaves them on the counter then pretends not to know where Bruce is, like tonight. When he analyzes his mother and father as individuals, they seem like vastly different people, almost fated to despise each other. His father gasoline; his mother a match. Or maybe the other way around.

"I don't know why he always picks such rough places to live," says Julie.

"He thinks California is soft and spoiled."

Julie shakes her head with a soft catch of breath, sets the white container on the coffee table. "I know he thinks I am."

"He doesn't say that. I think those places he lives make him feel tough. They seem more like him than here does. His guns and the hunting and fighting. The survival stuff."

She smiles slightly. "Remember the bomb shelter? In case the Russians dropped atom bombs on us?"

Sure he does, and it wasn't that long ago. The bomb shelter house is up in Laguna's Top of the World neighborhood. Its three-room basement had been fortified by his father and his ultraconservative John Birch Society friends, who added extra thick sheetrock and insulation, an industrial-grade AC/heater, and powerful air and water filters. This was all to protect against a communist nuclear attack or a race war, both of which the Birchers thought possible. It was provisioned with enough canned food and bottled water to last six months, Bruce claimed. Matt remembers helping Jasmine arrange the shelved cans in alphabetical order so you could find exactly what you needed, quickly. Hundreds of them, and jars too, of peanut butter and pickles and jellies and jams and tomato sauce. And big locking plastic bins of spaghetti and bow-tie pasta. The game freezer for meat. Two electric can openers; five manuals. And, of course, the noisy generators to keep the bunker going when the end came. Now, he wishes he lived around that much food, wonders why his mother doesn't seem to mind.

Matt had never thought the basement was that funny until last week, when he'd told Christian Clay about it at Mystic Arts World. Something in the telling brought back all sorts of details. Christian said the household bomb shelter was one of the funniest concepts he'd ever heard, and he got Matt to repeat the story to BEL founder Grail and Tim Leary, who were back in the MAW office awaiting a rumored delivery of forbidden products from Oakland. Matt's story elevated his status around Mystic Arts from a mere sixteen-year-old paperboy to someone who had survived the Establishment, seen the folly of materialistic, soul-dead, military-industrial America and cosmically advanced to a higher level of consciousness. They'd offered him a hit off a huge joint—the first he'd ever taken—and by the time Grail grinned and popped the roach into his mouth, Matt's face was melting and his thoughts were being heard by everyone in the office. When the weed first hit him he was suddenly scared of everything and his feet and hands went cold. Then, not long after, he was laughing like a tickled child. It was the last time he'd smoked dope, on purpose.

"I liked our basement days, Mom."

Julie yawns, covers her mouth. "Your dad felt obligated to protect us. Maybe overprotect us. Like a lot of cops—you know—they'll do anything to protect you. Even if it's half-crazy like alphabetizing the cans in a bomb shelter. It seems so long ago." She yawns again, then forks up another load of noodles. "Kyle has forty-three more days in Vietnam. That'll put him home the last Friday of July."

Matt knows this. And he knows his mother obsesses about Kyle even more than he does. Together, they watch the news almost every night, dreading the Vietnam War coverage, during which they stare in wide-eyed silence, waiting to see Kyle being carried from battle or maybe *in* battle. Matt has seen bloody young men who look like Kyle, tattered and dying or even dead already, right here in his own living room, on the crummy black-and-white RCA.

There's a calendar on the fridge and she X-es through every day that passes. Kyle's letters have been coming more often now that he's getting "short." Matt hears the fear creeping into them, but what really worries him is brother Kyle's spooky idea that short soldiers have a better chance of dying the closer to discharge they get. It's a common superstition, Kyle has written. Matt can't remember seeing anything like fear or resignation in his brother, ever. Kyle, a natural athlete, a four-sport varsity player and champion at high hurdles. With enough balls to bodysurf the Wedge up in Newport, which has the scariest waves that Matt has ever seen except in *Surfer* magazine. Kyle has shot river rapids in a kayak. Caught rattlesnakes in Laguna Canyon. Killed a bear with his father in Montana. Enlisted in the U.S. Army.

Matt looks out at the streetlight across Third, watches a hippie girl with her dog. The dog is an Irish setter with a red bandanna around its neck. The Irish setter is the hippie dog of choice. It lifts his leg on the lamppost, produces a well-lit stream. The lamplight cones down through the dark. A Hopper in Laguna, Matt thinks. The hippie puts a lighter to something in her mouth and a puff of smoke rises into the damp night air. Matt wonders if she knows that the cop house is less than a block away. He thinks about those bomb shelter days when they were all together. Lots of fights between Mom and Dad. Terrible words. Threats and thrown objects. Jazz cried more than he did. But good times too. A driving trip to the Grand Canyon in the red Country Squire station wagon with the fake wood trim. Mom and Dad at his and Kyle's Little League games up at Thurston, and Jazz's synchronized swim meets over in Tustin. Helping Dad at his workbench and Mom in the kitchen. Christmas Eves with the Calhouns.

When he looks at his mother, she's asleep sitting up, head back against the well, the chopsticks pushed forward like antennae, almost far enough to fall out. She's mouthing something, softly. Matt picks up the container, bag, and fork. Touches her shoulder and startles her awake.

"Oh, jeeeez," she slurs. "Weird scenes in my head."

"Time for bed, Mom."

Julie rises and drifts back to her room. The door shuts and the music comes on. In the kitchen Matt tosses trash, rinses the fork and checks to see what she put in the drawer: a small pipe, glass and stainless steel, thick with residue. Puts it to his nose and gets that strong pitchy reek that's new to him.

He sets it back, next to a wrinkled foil package about the size of a Ping-Pong ball. Inside is a crumbling half sphere of what looks like black mud wrapped in a thick gray skin. The smell is heavy and strong. He's heard that the Brotherhood of Eternal Love smuggles hashish to Laguna from Afghanistan, pounds of it at a time, some as dragon balls—powerful hashish frosted with opium from the famous Afghan poppies. He's never seen one until now, if that's what it is. People say that dragon balls are the best euphoria possible. They say that Orange Sunshine, the BEL-supplied LSD, opens your mind to new realities. But dragon balls make you feel like you're floating on a cloud having orgasms one after another. Matt imagines that. Bums him out that his mom is using this stuff. He's tempted to flush it down the toilet.

He shuts the drawer and resumes his vigil on the living room couch. Dozes awhile. Has strange dreams: a pale girl in a yellow bikini standing on a rocky beach and waving at him while an enormous wave comes at her from behind; the Mystic Arts World meditation room in flames and he can't find his way out; Kyle gaunt and bearded, with the body of a dog. Matt wakes in a sweat, ears thrumming.

Listens at his mom's door—music off now.

Considers his sister's quiet bedroom.

Looks into his and Kyle's old room. Wonders if he should move back into it. Keep a little closer eye on Mom. But with Kyle coming home in a little over a month he'd have to move back out. Too cramped in here for both of them, and no space at all for his art supplies, records, and books. It was always more Kyle's room than his, anyway. On the dresser is a photo of Kyle in his U.S. Army dress uniform. Matt knows it's only in his own head but the closer Kyle gets to coming home, the less confident that face in the picture seems to get.

From the garage he fetches a sketchbook and a piece of charcoal, takes it back to the living room. Dashes off a sketch of Furlong questioning him down at Thalia. More caricature than portrait; but the details are telling. Then of Miranda washing her Beetle.

Matt stares out the window a moment, then starts in on the streetlamp, tentatively at first, then begins to feel it and speeds up until he's slashing that hippie girl into being, then her dog with its lifted leg, even the pee dancing off the pole in the lamplight. He carves darkness in around the cone of light and the two figures, so everything is black except for them. His strokes are angry and hard and the drawing is a violent mess. He's tempted to rip out the page, wad it up and chuck it, but there's the clean backside and you can't waste supplies. He tosses the sketchbook onto the blue chair.

Around nine thirty, Matt quietly panics, suddenly sure that Jazz isn't coming home tonight. What can he do but go get her and bring her back? She's only been really missing for less than twenty-four hours but his heart tells Matt that she needs him.

Right now. He's sure of it. She needs him.

Back in her room he takes his pen-and-ink sketch of her off the wall, puts the thumbtack back in its hole, and folds the drawing into his back pocket.

Start at the Sandpiper, Matt thinks—the last place where anybody he knows has seen her.

He'll pick up her trail and follow where it leads.

6

Which is easier said than done because they won't let him into the nightclub this late, fake ID or not.

Chuck just shakes his head and points Matt back outside. Coast Highway is buzzing with cars, windows down and their tape decks blaring against the music throbbing from the 'Piper.

Four very loud Harleys with four gnarly looking riders fart past in an accelerating wake. He's heard about a new motorcycle club in Costa Mesa, just a few miles from Laguna—badass guys who stand up to the Hells Angels. Matt sees the vest patches on the men as they disappear south.

Sidewalks still busy. Moby Cop, the white prisoner van, comes north toward the police station and all the people gathered outside the Sandpiper wave and yell fuck you, Furlong, pigs eat shit! though Matt can't see if he's in there or not.

He shows his sketch of Jasmine to the people loitering at the nightclub door and to everyone coming out, but nobody saw his sister last night. It's a good likeness of her, too, but most of the folks he talks to weren't even here the night before.

Until two older T-Street Surf Boys spill out and come his way. Matt recognizes them from this morning, two of the surfers gathered at the top of the Thalia Street steps looking down on Bonnie Stratmeyer. They're talking as surfers do, their voices slow and their words drawn out as if their lips are numb. They don't even stop walking as Matt approaches, holding out the pen-and-ink sketch. But the taller one takes it and Matt falls in beside them.

"I know Jazz," says the surfer. "Total fox. She left the 'Piper last night with Austin Overton."

"Which direction?"

The surfers finally stop and the taller one hands the drawing back to Matt. "They ran across the traffic about right here. Holding hands. Overton had his guitar case, like *The Sound of Music*. Headed downtown, the last I saw."

Matt runs back to his bike, pushes it across Coast Highway to a chorus of horns, then pedals to Mystic Arts World. But it's closed. Loitering near the entrance, a woman in a tattered Stars and Stripes T-shirt with a big beaded bag over one shoulder offers Matt a joint and he says no thanks. Realizes how hungry he is again. He shows her the drawing and she shakes her head.

Then north on Coast Highway to the crowded White House Tavern, where a loud Buffalo Springfield–like band strums away, guitars jangly and loose. The food smells more than just good. The bouncer won't let Matt in but he snatches the drawing, studies it, and shakes his head. "Familiar," he says, "but tonight or last night? No. Beat it."

Just a few blocks up at the Jolly Roger nobody has seen Jasmine in over a week. Matt doesn't even need to show the picture because of Julie's long tenure here. They all know who he is and Matt detects concern in the way they look at him. A waitress passes in front of him, hands and arms laden with plates. Matt's gut rumbles and turns. Even the parsley looks good.

Then down to the Marine Room Tavern on Ocean Avenue, where another stout bouncer studies the drawing and shakes his head.

"She might have been with Austin Overton," Matt says, trying to prompt the big man's memory.

Of course, Matt knows that his sister and the singer could have simply gotten into his car—or Julie's battered van, parked right there on PCH across from the Sandpiper—and driven anywhere in the city or beyond. He's heard that Overton lives with other musicians in the big yellow house on Bluebird Canyon, a few blocks beyond his paper route. There're always music and parties. Everybody just calls it Big Yellow.

Matt jay-cycles to the Hotel Laguna, where nobody in the restaurant or bar has seen his sister or even recognizes the girl in his drawing. The bartender orders him out.

He walks his bike around to the back door of the restaurant kitchen, where one of his friends, Ernie Rios, washes dishes and takes out the trash. And gives him food. Matt prizes Ernie for more than just the table scraps. He's goofy and open about his dead-end crushes and fruitless romantic blunders. He can laugh at himself.

Looking through the heavy screen door, Matt sees wiry Ernie in big rubber boots, rinsing a plate with a big commercial sprayer hose, water pouring down into a huge metal sink. Matt bangs on the screen and Ernie comes clomping to the screen, a white dish towel in his hands. "Can you believe about Bonnie Stratmeyer?"

"No. I saw her dead."

Ernie twists the dead bolt and opens the door. Matt follows him through the big fragrant kitchen, his stomach grumbling, explaining what he saw that morning. Ernie wants to know what Bonnie looked like and Matt endures that memory for what feels like the thousandth time.

"Have you seen Jazz?" asks Matt.

"Not tonight."

"Last night?"

"It's been a week or two. You hungry?"

"I'm starved."

Matt takes his usual place in the corner, on a folding chair pretty much hidden from the rest of the kitchen by stainless steel shelves laden with foodstuffs, and the walk-in freezer. It's where Ernie eats when he's off the clock. Matt feels the humid kitchen warmth and smells the miracle of cooking food and thinks again how cool it would be to have his own restaurant. Ernie has offered to get him on washing dishes here but the weekly take-home is about the same as his route and the hours way longer. His mom's income, his newspaper money, and the Food Exchange are keeping the Anthony family fed. Barely. Although you can't eat newspapers and rubber bands, he thinks.

Ernie brings him a foraged plate with a lightly eaten T-bone steak, half a mound of mashed potatoes, and two uncracked crab legs. Clean utensils, a crab cracker, and a cloth napkin.

"So Jazz didn't come home last night?" Ernie asks.

Matt answers Ernie's questions between bites. Tells him about Austin Overton. Ernie is concerned about Jasmine because he's in awe of her and she's always been nice to him in her own subtle, superior way.

"Maybe she'll be home later tonight," says Ernie.

"I hope so."

But silence creeps into Matt's audible lack of hope, and Matt knows what Ernie is going to say before he says it, because Ernie has long had a crush on Bonnie Stratmeyer.

"That's a bummer about Bonnie," Ernie says. "Tonight the mayor and two of the Laguna councilmen were in, and they told Janet on station four, who told Deke the bartender, who told me, that the cops are not ruling out foul play. Because of some bruising that doesn't match up with drowning. On her ankles and the top of her head. They also said she could have just fallen over the stairway railing. The autopsy is tomorrow."

Another uneasy silence.

Matt rides south to Thalia. It's not midnight yet but a thick marine layer stands like a gray wall not far offshore.

He straddles his bike at the head of the stairway where he was this morning. A streetlamp beams down mistily. Matt looks at the faintly visible beach where Bonnie Stratmeyer ended up. Feels a fresh jab from the dark dread that hasn't left him since seeing her here.

The lights are on in one of the oceanfront homes and Matt

sees someone standing on its deck, looking down at the water. It's a wooden, ramshackle house, weather-beaten and weirdly out of kilter from Matt's point of view.

The guy turns to Matt and gives him a long look. He's a potbellied older man, forty probably, a joint in one hand and what looks like a martini glass in the other.

"What do you think you're doing?" he asks gruffly.

"Looking where they found Bonnie."

"Did you know her?"

"No."

"Last night I saw a hippie van pull up right about where you're standing. About this time, in fact. I wish I'd have waited up, seen what they were doing at two in the morning. I knew I should have, and I didn't."

"They?"

"Two people sitting up front. Not moving. Pretty dark, and the streetlight reflecting off the glass. Hardly make them out."

"Did you tell the cops?"

"This morning, hell yes."

"What color was it, the hippie van?"

"The two-tone green and white. A newer one. They're all over Laguna now. Curtains with some kind of pattern, but I couldn't see what."

Matt tries to find the rock that Bonnie Stratmeyer had washed up on or perhaps landed on, or was maybe even dragged to. Not ruling out foul play. But the fog has advanced over the beach and swallowed the homes around him and Matt now stands in a thick white cloud.

"They'll get to the bottom of this, if there is a bottom," the man calls down. "In the meantime, how about you come up for a drink and a smoke? This sinsemilla from Mexico will blow your mind."

"No, thank you."

"Suit yourself."

Matt pedals for home in the fog but by the time he gets to

Mystic Arts World the fog is so thick it's better to push the bike than ride it.

At Forest he catches the red light and walks his bike across the empty little intersection, having to veer around two girls who have decided to wait for the walk sign across Pacific Coast Highway.

With a jump of heart, Matt recognizes the Kalina sisters, Laurel and Rose. Laurel is his age and he's had a crush on her since fourth grade. He's gone to school with her all his life. Rose goes to college but Matt doesn't know where. Laurel told him once that they are part Hawaiian and part German-English. They're olive-skinned and dark-haired and to Matt, thrilling. One of his first fourth-grade cursive sentences he wrote on the lined training paper was, *She's beautiful!*, which he tore off and wadded up and put in his pocket the second he'd written it.

Now, suddenly, just seeing Laurel Kalina makes Matt feel like a different person. A more confident person. All of the worry in his heart lies down, and something like joy stands up. So, he carves his bike to a stop with one hand, in a sweeping matador's veronica. He hopes the light stays red.

"Hi Laurel! Hi Rose!"

They greet him and Matt watches them checking the crosswalk light. Laurel tells him how awful about Bonnie, and Rose says she knew her pretty well and she was a spiritual and sensitive person, not material at all.

Laurel tells him they both have roles in Laguna's popular Pageant of the Masters. Matt's seen it only once—human actors staged in famous works of art. *Tableaux vivants,* according to his English teacher, Miss Benson. It's a big deal—lavish costumes and makeup and lighting, thunderous music and narration. Hundreds of spectators pack the big Irvine Bowl amphitheater. To Matt, it's expensive and mostly for tourists.

But Laurel insists he come: she and Rose star in a totally boss Gauguin tableau, she says, the best painting in the whole show.

Matt sees the walk light turn green and tells them he'll do that, come to the Pageant and see them in the Gauguin. Pageant tickets are way more money than he can afford but he keeps that to himself.

Rose steps into the crosswalk but Laurel lags behind. Matt holds her gaze for as long as he can stand it, then follows her into the crosswalk and ferries her safely through the fog to the other side of Coast Highway.

He backtracks when the light tells him to, then swings boldly into the saddle for the short ride home.

Where, in his garage, he stays up even later, making drawings of the sisters but mainly of Laurel. They're good, even to Matt's self-critical eyes. There's an interesting connection, he thinks, between what you think of someone and how you draw them.

Still full on Ernie Rios's generous table scraps, and unable to sleep, Matt goes back to his earlier sketchbooks, where he finds three drawings of Laurel Kalina's face from when they were nine. And ten. And twelve. He's known her for almost half his life, but he's never really *seen* her until tonight.

7

Kyle's letter arrives the next day in an airmail envelope with red and blue bars on the edges. It's written in his aggressive, forward-leaning print, on flimsy field stationery.

May, 1968

Dear Matt,
  Just thought I'd drop you a line from beautiful Cu Chi base. As you know from my letters, we Tunnel Rats see most of the 'Nam from underground. But here at Cu Chi base there's fucking AC, ice machines, golf courses and swimming pools! First, we bombed them then we built this damned base, THEN we found out that the ground under it is full of tunnels and they're building more every day. The tunnels are full of VCs. Thousands of them, digging in from all over the Iron Triangle. So many Charlies, they got underground hospitals with doctors and nurses to treat the VC as fast as we can shoot, stab or strangle them down there in the cold dark. They have babies down there. If you get stuck on your way down, you can expect a bayonet up your ass. They skewered Myers with a bamboo spear last week and he bled to death by the time we got to him. They left the spear in him like savages. A GOOD GUY. It's so quiet and dark in the tunnels you can hear a man blink.

So, I got a weekend of R&R here at base, where we got most of the VC cleaned out of. Right now I'm by the pool. Play some Foosball, read magazines. Hoochie girls sneak on base but they're syphilis bombs. I think of the girls in high school. Seems like a thousand years ago. I'm not the same but I hope they are. An innocent girl is the most special thing on EARTH.

Then I go back to the tunnels. 'Rat holes leading to hell,' the colonel calls them.

What's going on with you in groovy Laguna? Mom and Jazz hanging in there? Jazz graduates soon, right? Hear anything from our asshole dad?

I'm down to fifty-three days in-country. I'd be lying if I didn't admit it's driving me fucking crazy. Everybody gets this way, even Tunnel Rats. They say we're crazy and maybe we are but we're not TOO crazy to know the shorter you get the more chance you'll catch a bullet or a knife or a spear. It's just an odds thing, like how many times in a row you can roll a six. Say the six is life. The pure odds on each roll are one-in-six that you'll roll a six—LIFE—but anybody who's thrown the dice knows that after you've thrown, say, five straight sixes, it's not very damned likely that you'll throw another one. It's proof of the law, right there, simple. So when your tour is nine months and you're down to say, fifty-three days, you've got to roll a lot of sixes to extend your life. All of which is just a way of saying I'm deep down afraid now, and the afraid gets thicker and darker every day. Which tunnel should I follow in this dark? Which one will end in the light that is my death? A surprising number of guys buy the farm their last day of tour. If that happens to me, just remember I love you and you're a good brother. If that happens to me, take care of our family.

Love,
Kyle, Rat 9

Matt writes his brother right back, as always. Toward the end he thinks of mentioning that Jasmine hasn't come home for two nights running but decides against it. He doesn't want to burden his brother in combat. What if Kyle gets deep into one of those tunnels and gets distracted about his sister back home? Takes a bullet or catches a spear? Matt doesn't tell Kyle about Bonnie Stratmeyer either.

Big Yellow is a two-story wooden home built in the fifties, up high in Bluebird Canyon. The house slouches due to a landslide that undermined the foundation. The site was dozed and stabilized, a new foundation was poured and the house hoisted back onto it by helicopters. Matt watched them do it. The city engineers signed off on the home as safe but it never did look quite plumb to Matt or anyone else in Laguna. Over the past several years it has become a notorious party house, loud and overrun with musicians, surfers, and of course, artists.

He has to walk his bike up the last hundred yards because the road is so steep. It's almost eleven o'clock, and he'll be back here in just a few hours, delivering his papers.

Big Yellow presides crookedly over the tawny dry hills and the other houses downslope. Matt can see batik curtains blowing in and out the second-floor windows, and a guy leaning on a deck railing with a guitar, no shirt, and long blond hair. A cloud of smoke hangs over him and two girls reclining on chaise lounges. Beyond, the Pacific is white-capped, blue and infinite. Matt searches the street for his mother's VW van, last commandeered by Jasmine.

On the front porch he toes down the Heavy-Duti kickstand, parks the bike, and knocks on the door.

After a long minute he knocks again louder.

Eventually, Austin Overton opens the door. He's the jeans and no shirt man from the deck, with two days of stubble and stoned eyes. Barefoot. Bigger than Matt remembered from seeing him at the 'Piper that one night. Overton gives Matt a hard look.

"You got the wrong guy," he says, with a twinkle in his blue eyes.

"I'm Jasmine Anthony's brother."

"Meaning what?"

"I was wondering if you know where she is."

"She was here, uh, yesterday morning and the night before. Haven't seen her since, though. Everything cool?"

"She didn't come home. Hasn't come home two nights in a row now."

"I guess I'm your prime suspect, then." Austin Overton's voice is strong, and sharp as a knife, and his Louisiana accent is heavier than Matt remembers.

"Suspect of what? I mean, sir, mister," Matt stumbles with his words. "Mr. Overton, did something happen?"

"Settle down now boy—nothing unusual. But your Laguna girls do run a little on the wild side. She is eighteen, right?"

"Yes, just graduated."

Overton rubs his stubble and shakes his head. "High school. Hell, Austin. Won't you ever learn?"

He walks into the house and Matt follows, closing the door.

The big living room is sparsely furnished, sofas and over-stuffed chairs, bean bags and amps and guitars. A few people sleeping. Beer cans and wine bottles and bulging ashtrays. Everywhere Matt looks there's a guitar on a stand, in a corner, up on a couch. Toward the back of the room is a grand piano with a mic on a stand beside it. Concert posters on the walls. Cats everywhere.

"Kinda dead around here this early," says Overton. "Back in the bayou they'd be guzzling frozen daquiris this time of morning. You Californians are kind of lazy to tell you the truth."

Out on the back patio, Overton reclaims his guitar and takes a hit from the joint the girls are sharing. He introduces them to Matt: Dana and Crystal. They look about his sister's age. Tie-dye shirts and sandals and lots of hair.

He nods and smiles but they seem to look more through him than at him.

"Ladies, what time did that Jazz gal leave? That would have been yesterday morning. I crashed hard around three, I think, and when I woke up about ten, she was gone. This is her brother and he's looking for her."

Dana shrugs and looks down, hair sweeping over her face. Crystal stares blankly at Matt.

"I think it was like eight," says Crystal. "I was experiencing in the big room, working up a song on one of the acoustics. She came downstairs, went outside. She didn't look at me or say anything. She didn't talk much that night. We all hit the hookah and danced, then ended up in the pool. We flopped in Austin's waterbed—your sister and me. And of course, Tarzan himself. But the acid hit me weird and I couldn't sleep."

Austin turns his back and picks his guitar.

Crystal offers Matt a hit and he says no thanks. "Your sister is one of those chicks who's too cool for school, you know? Thinks she knows everything and has everything under control. She acted kind of superior. She writes songs. So what? I think she wanted Austin for herself. Didn't she, Austin!"

He stops playing and flips her off without turning around.

"Anyway, she wanted no part of me, which Austin likes to watch. Through a window I saw her drive off in that funny old van. It smoked."

"Was she loaded?" Matt asks.

"Everyone was loaded. I don't know if she was tripping or not."

It's hard for Matt to picture Jasmine in Big Yellow, partying with the musicians and druggies. Jasmine actually *is* too cool for school—an A student who rarely studied, a former cheerleader who quit because she thought leading cheers was *asinine*, a girl with a knowing air and a sharp tongue. Maybe her better-than-you attitude had worked against her, prodded her to prove she wasn't really that way, got her stoned and into bed with a popular musician and one of his girlfriends. Pretending to be a bad girl. He remembers something she'd said just a few weeks ago, with graduation only days away:

The second I throw that cap in the air, Matt, I'll be free. And I'm going explode on the world!

"If you see her again, tell her to come home," says Matt.

"Right on, brother," Austin calls over his shoulder, still picking the guitar.

Matt is climbing onto his bike when quiet Dana catches up with him.

"Hey, Matt—Crystal's just jealous. Your sister really is cool. Good on that ukulele and she writes quirky songs. She has a sense of humor, too."

"Sounds like her."

"Look, she talked about these parties in Sapphire Cove. A house on the cliff, overlooking the bay. Fridays into Saturdays. She said the people were classy and smart, older guys, like professors and lawyers and doctors. They had money. Some Hollywood types, too. Thrown by a guy named Cavore, I think. So, I mean, maybe like, you could look there. Today is Saturday, so maybe it was meant to be that you find her there. Like, Karma."

"Thank you," says Matt.

"Give me your number and I'll call you if I see her."

"Wait right here."

He gets an old sketchbook and piece of charcoal from the basket on the Heavy-Duti, writes his mom's number on one corner of a drawing, tears it off, and runs it back to Dana.

8

L ater that day, Matt and his mother walk to the Laguna Beach police station in the warm afternoon. It's less than a block from where they live. Jazz has been missing from home for almost forty-eight hours.

Julie wears her wench's getup for her upcoming five-to-midnight at the Jolly Roger, camouflaged by a batik wrap she got at Mystic Arts World. Matt has on his *Endless Summer* T-shirt, faded blue Jams, and the same red Keds slip-ons he wears for fishing. The big nightshade in the neighbor's front yard steeps Third Street in its sweet, heavy scent.

Matt feels good but hungry. He's always hungry; always trying to figure a better paycheck. His current paper route earns him twenty-five dollars a month. But he knows that if he learns to drive better, gets his license and uses his mother's van, he can get a much larger route, make more money, and buy more food and art supplies. However, gas just hit thirty-four cents a gallon, so he'd have to factor that against his weekly take-home.

The Saturday desk officer is younger than Matt's mom. Maybe like, under thirty. He's never seen her. In fact he's never seen a female police officer in uniform other than the unarmed meter maids who write parking tickets.

Her badge says *B. Darnell.* Her blond hair is in a tightly braided ponytail, and her face is pleasant. Blue eyes and freckles on her nose. Matt sees that her arms are tan and muscled.

She holds open the countertop lift-door, then leads Matt and his mother to a small interview room. Closes the door.

Matt and Julie face Officer Darnell across a stainless-steel table bolted to the floor tiles. Matt sets his best sketch of Jasmine on the table facing the policewoman, and Julie brings one of her daughter's senior portraits from her floppy, bead-laced bag.

They talk family for a moment: Officer Darnell remembers Kyle set records at track, then was sent off to war. She does not ask about him. Darnell's own son is seven and goes to El Morro. She looks at the sketch and the photo of Jasmine.

"I've seen her around town," says the officer.

"She was a cheerleader, if you went to any high school games," says Julie.

"Yes, I went to the homecoming game last year. Artists fifty-four to zero!" A darkness crosses Darnell's formerly sunny face. She takes the pen from her uniform blouse and squares the yellow pad in front of her. "When is the last time you saw Jasmine, Mrs. Anthony?"

"I saw her before she left for Miranda Zahara's, two evenings ago now. Thursday. I loaned her my van. We'd had words. Although it hurts me to say this, I'm worried that she might not *want* to come home."

Matt's heart sinks. He's been thinking the same thing.

Julie explains that Jazz had done some "creative storytelling" about staying the night with Miranda, the reverse of what Miranda had told her mom. Julie says Jazz sometimes fabricated alibis for being out late, but had never not come home for the night, let alone two in a row.

Matt adds that his sister left the Sandpiper lounge Thursday night with the singer Austin Overton. Stayed overnight in Big Yellow and left at eight the next morning.

Julie straightens and gives Officer Darnell a brisk look, as if to underscore that she is not judgmental of her daughter for probably sleeping with the older singer. Matt has heard his mother encourage Jasmine to be open to life and love and experiences and different relationships. Like she has.

Again that darkness as Officer Darnell looks down and writes on the yellow pad.

"That's the last place any of us know she was, for sure," Matt adds. "So, that's almost exactly forty-eight hours."

The officer smiles slightly. "Don't worry about the number of hours."

An uncomfortable silence then, and Matt guesses the reason but says nothing.

"Was Bonnie Stratmeyer friends with Jasmine?" asks the officer.

"Not close," says Julie. "Different sets of friends. They were both good students, though."

Officer Darnell considers. Matt hears the voices coming from the station lobby, a door closing.

"How did her ankles get bruised?" he asks.

Julie's head pivots.

"I can't comment on that," snaps Darnell.

"And the top of her head?"

"No, Matt," says the officer. "You should not have that information. None of it has been verified or released to the public."

"Sorry," he says. "It just bothers me that Bonnie disappeared and died, then my sister disappeared kind of like, similarly."

"Yes, and we do know that Bonnie Stratmeyer was seen at the Sandpiper during the time she was missing."

Matt wonders if she might have paired off with Austin Overton. Knows that Darnell won't tell him if she knows. Makes a note to see if Overton played at the Sandpiper during Bonnie Stratmeyer's missing days.

"How about at Cavore's parties in Sapphire Cove?" asks Matt.

Officer Darnell smiles and shakes her head. "Jordan Cavore's Sapphire Cove parties? Matt, you get around."

"I just listen."

"Don't try to go to those Sapphire Cove parties," she says.

"Why?" asks Julie. "I haven't heard of them."

Officer Darnell taps her pen on the pad. "Rich out-of-towners doing bad things. Private parties, not big happenings like the hippies do. They charge money just to get in. Has Jasmine talked about them, Matt?"

"No, never," he says, neglecting to mention what Dana said.

"Does she talk to you about personal things?"

At times, his sister seems to be a warren of secrets and evasions. Others, eager to confess. "Not usually."

Officer Darnell takes down the names of Jasmine's friends and what numbers Julie has in the little address book in her bag.

When Darnell asks about boyfriends, Julie says that her daughter has had some male friends but never a steady boyfriend. She looks at Matt, who nods.

"What about her general outlook? Is she happy, angry, withdrawn, outgoing?"

"All of those things at different times," says Julie. "Mostly . . . steady. Jasmine is self-directed and in control of her emotions. Though she can be temperamental."

"Does she have a religious or spiritual side?" asks the officer.

"Not church," says Julie. "But she's always searching for meaning. She read some of the Bible, and some of *Siddhartha*, and some books about Hinduism. I think *The Tibetan Book of the Dead* is in her room right now."

"She got it at Mystic Arts World," says Matt.

"Interesting," says Officer Darnell. "Does she go there often?"

"We took a meditation class together there," says Julie. "In the private meditation room. From one of Mahajad Om's swamis-in-training. I think they're called Enlighteners."

"Have you been to Mahajad's Vortex of Purity?" asks Darnell.

"Too expensive," Julie says. "Even if you're accepted to study there with Mahajad."

Darnell examines the sketch and photo of Jasmine. "Let

me have these for posters and press releases," she says. "And don't worry, Mrs. Anthony, Matt. She'll come home or we'll find her."

Like you found Bonnie Stratmeyer? Matt wonders.

He can tell by his mother's and Officer Darnell's expressions that they're wondering too.

9

Matt sits in the eucalyptus tree behind the Irvine Bowl amphitheater, settled into a V in the big branches, looking out through the fragrant leaves at the Pageant of the Masters unfolding below.

He's done this before. Tonight he's got on his Mexican poncho against the June chill, and the half bag of peanuts he discovered in the threadbare pantry, snug under his T-shirt. The rope is looped beside him. It wasn't easy climbing the tree because eucalyptus branches start well up the trunk, but with a lucky hurl he was finally able to get the loop over and down, run the tag end through, haul it tight, and pull-run himself up the into the foliage. Then bring up the rope so as to not give himself away. It helps that he's skinny and light. The woods behind the amphitheater are high and dense and give him cover against pageant security.

Now he watches the dark stage and listens to the next painting's dramatic introduction. As everyone in Laguna is proud to point out, the voice is that of Sugar Frosted Flakes pitchman Thurl Ravenscroft, who for years—as Tony the Tiger—has been booming out *"They're GRRREAT!"* from every TV in the land.

But tonight, Ravenscroft's voice is beguiling, Matt thinks, almost godlike.

"The French painter Paul Gauguin first traveled to Tahiti in 1891, hoping to find an Edenic paradise where he could create pure, primitive art rather than the primitivist faux works being done by painters in France . . . In When Will You Marry? *Gauguin*

*creates one of his iconic island paintings, capturing a touching
and mysterious moment between two women—one of whom wears a
white flower behind her ear, indicating she desires a husband* . . .
*Ladies and gentlemen, behold this masterwork of color and compo-
sition,* When Will You Marry? *by Paul Gauguin.*"

When the lights bring the *tableau vivant* alive, Laurel and
Rose Kalina repose in a field of vibrant green, yellow, and blue.
Laurel is in the foreground in bold Tahitian native dress—red
and yellow pants and a simple white blouse. From behind her,
Rose looks over her shoulder. She's wearing a salmon-colored
Western-style dress with a prim white collar. Both have the
blended mocha skin of their Hawaiian-Caucasian parents,
lustrous black hair, and soulful almond eyes.

Laurel wears a hopeful expression and she seems focused on
some distant object, or maybe on her own thoughts. Rose's
gaze is focused in another direction altogether and she looks
wary and displeased. Is she reading Laurel's mind? Does she
not want her sister to marry? Behind them are two distant
figures and lush Tahitian hills.

The sisters are both absolutely still and Matt wonders how
they're drawing breath without seeming to move. The vibrant, strongly lighted colors shiver in the surrounding darkness of the amphitheater, right up into his eyes. Matt knows
that Christian and the other serious artists in town think the
pageant is pure kitsch, call it the Pageant of the Monsters.
Same way they call the Festival of Arts the Festering of Arts.
But Matt still likes the way a two-dimensional painting can
be elaborately staged with living, three-dimensional bodies—
only to appear as the flat painting that inspired the tableaux
in the first place! It's art in reverse, a magic trick.

But what gets to Matt the most, what gets him leaning forward, hands on two big eucalyptus branches for balance, is
how totally choice Laurel is, how boss, bitchen, and beautiful.
He could watch her forever. Maybe she'd let him paint her
someday. I'll have to get good before that happens, he thinks.
Without taking his eyes off her, Matt works the bag of peanuts

from under his shirt, snaps the boner in his pants hard with his middle finger, and cracks open a shell.

After the show he waits with his bike outside the Festival of Arts grounds, watching the tourists and pageant cast members file out. Tries to think of what to say. The tourists are decked out, especially the girls and women, and he can smell their scents on the damp beach air.

Then there she is, coming out the exit with her sister in their street clothes, looking little like Gauguin's women.

Matt walks his bike through the oncoming bodies and swings it around to join them.

"That was unbelievably cool," he says.

"More like cold tonight!" says Laurel.

"I love Gauguin and you two were perfect. I couldn't even see you breathe!"

"We *are* professionals," says Rose, giving Matt a look. "Hey, there's Cathy and Melanie. I'm splitting. Night, kiddos!"

Rose departs up the sidewalk toward her friends, turns and waves. Leaving Matt alone with Laurel, which sends a nervous tickle down his back.

"Can I walk with you?" he asks.

"Okay. What's that rope in the basket for?"

"Nothing."

"*Okay* . . . well, did you get a good pageant seat?"

"In the back but good."

"I get a cast discount if you want to come again."

Matt's thoughts skitter through his brain. Taking up Laurel on her discount offer and seeing her again would be a date! He feels excited and addled right now, this close to Laurel, in public but alone at the same time. His practical side takes over.

"Are you in the phone book?" he asks.

"Call if you want another ticket."

"Definitely."

"Good. Well, okay then, Matt . . ."

He catches her drift, doesn't want to lose her. "Can I walk with you some more?"

"Alright. I live on Brooks."

"Far out." Of course he knows this. Sometimes he takes a less direct way home on his paper route just to see her house. Not that he'd admit that to anybody, especially her. Red with white trim and roses out front. A white Volvo and a blue Volvo. The Kalinas do not subscribe to the *Register*. They are probably *Los Angeles Times* people because both mister and missus Kalina are UC Irvine professors and almost certainly liberals. Conservatives prefer the *Register*.

They cut through downtown to walk Pacific Coast Highway south toward Brooks. It's busy on this Saturday night, Coast Highway with plenty of cars and the sidewalks like escalators, moving people. A convertible Mustang with the top down glides by, the passenger yelling *foxy lady!* at Laurel. Laurel is a slow walker and when she talks to Matt she focuses her attention on him and is sometimes bumped by the oncoming pedestrians.

Her thick long hair glistens in the streetlights. She's in a summer writing workshop at UC Irvine, "totally arranged by mom." It's harder than it sounds, she says, lots of exercises and assignments.

"They won't let you just space out and stream your consciousness," she says. "They want a piece of writing to be hard and dimensional as a concrete block."

"Don't drop it on your toe!"

Matt cringes when he hears himself say this but Laurel smiles and stares at him a little sideways. For that second she looks like she did back in the Pageant tableau—focused and optimistic, maybe a little amused at her own thoughts.

"What do you think about when you're onstage?" he asks.

"I try to understand my character. What she wants and what she's feeling. She is hope. The woman behind her is suspicion. Historians say the painting foretells the loss of paradise and the inevitable slaughter of innocents."

"I thought it was about a girl who's thinking about getting married," says Matt. He's leafed through enough of the art books at Mystic Arts World to know that he almost never sees what the critics see. He's more literal, simpler.

"I remember Mrs. Herron showing the class your drawing of Johnny Tremain being chased by the British redcoats," says Laurel. "And her saying how good it was. And it was."

Matt is immensely proud to have one of his artworks remembered fondly by his longtime, secret crush.

"I remember her reading your scary Halloween story."

"Scary how bad it was!" she says.

"The witch with the St. Bernard's face and the monkey's tail," says Matt.

Laurel covers her ears and shakes her head, smiling.

Then a heavy silence as they stop at Thalia and look down where Bonnie Stratmeyer was found. Matt tells Laurel what he saw and about his conversation with Furlong. Just as Miranda Zahara and Art Rios had wanted to know how Bonnie Stratmeyer looked, so does Laurel. Matt describes Bonnie as accurately as he can but he can't keep his emotions away, and his ears roar as if waves are breaking inside. His first dead person. Bonnie. A girl he's seen hundreds of times. Her hair tangled with seaweed. The paleness of her body and the brightness of the yellow swimsuit.

"Let's keep moving," says Laurel.

Matt glances up at the cliffside beach house from which the potbellied Joint-and-Martini Man propositioned him the night before.

They head south. "I don't know if I should say this, Laurel, but Mom and me filed a missing-person report on Jasmine today. She hasn't come home two nights in a row. Tonight would be three."

Laurel stops and grabs his sleeve. Her grip is strong and her eyes are big with fright. "No! I just saw her a few days ago, down at Thousand Steps. She was doing some kind of modeling."

"Modeling?"

Laurel lets go and Matt pushes his bike along beside her.
She tells him she saw Jazz at Thousand Steps on Tuesday,
which Matt calculates to be two days before she didn't come
home from the Sandpiper. Laurel says that Jazz and "a whole
circus" of other young people were being photographed. There
was a man with cameras strapped all over him, some kind
of equipment guy carrying duffel bags, and an older, huge,
Charles Atlas–type muscleman posing with Jazz and the others. The girls were in bikinis and the boys in Jams. She recognized some locals. The muscleman wore one of those gross-out
water polo swimsuits that show just about everything. The
equipment guy was moving around these big silver reflector
umbrellas that kept tipping over in the wind. Jasmine looked
a little bummed by the whole scene. You know, bummed out
but above it all, like she is.

Matt sees all this in his mind, the young locals being cap-
tured by exotic artists. Sees Jazz posed with a muscleman in
boulder-holders. Gauguin and the natives. Slaughter of the
innocents. He wonders why his mind finds such dark paths,
here in sunny Laguna, a land of beauty and pleasure.

"What time of day?" he asks.

"It was early evening. I'd seen the photography crew at different beaches before. Here at Brooks, and Main Beach too.
Always in the evening. Shooting young people like that. But I
only saw Jasmine that one time."

They stop at the Sunshine Inn for ice cream and Matt hero-
ically offers to pay. This is not a Thrifty Drugs five-cent-cone
kind of place. It's not soft-serve either, but heavy, dense hard-
balls of frozen cream, sugar, and chocolate. Two sundaes cost
him one of his last three bucks. They look through the windows of the Stoke Sixty-Six surf shop, Matt keen on the twin-
fins—smaller, quicker boards perfect for Laguna's waves. He
likes to surf but not as much as fish. You can't eat waves. He
says nothing. He's lost to thoughts of Jazz and her adventures
as a model with a muscleman.

They walk the long gentle slope up Brooks to the red house with the white trim and the blue Volvo in the driveway. The lights are on inside and there's a warm glow to it that reminds Matt not one bit of his drafty clapboard bungalow in the shade of the phone company building.

"Thanks for letting me walk with you."

"I'm sorry if I bummed you out about Jazz."

"Not at all. I just need to find her."

"I'll make some calls. We have a some of the same friends."

"Ever been to one of Cavore's parties in Sapphire Cove?"

"No way. Creepy from what I hear. Why?"

He shrugs.

"I liked tonight, Matt. It's nice to talk to someone you've known forever but hardly said a word to."

He smiles, feels the blush on his face, thinks of his zits, doesn't care.

"You're not interested in going to one of those Sapphire Cove parties, are you, Matt? It's by invitation. All older guys."

"No way."

He hops on the Heavy-Duti and pushes off.

Circles back, flashes Laurel a peace sign, and wheelies down the hill for Pacific Coast Highway and the long haul to Sapphire Cove.

10

Where, of course, the guard sits within his guardhouse as Matt covertly watches from behind a low mandevilla-covered wall. It's almost midnight, according to his Timex Skindiver, bought cheap at King's Pawn. The guard seems to be reading. He sips from a cup. Matt's only fifty feet from the lowered gate arm but there's no way he can get past the guard without a distraction.

It's a full ten minutes before his opportunity arrives: a convertible red Mercedes with a middle-aged hippie dude at the wheel and a young blonde next to him, her hair wild and bright in the guardhouse floodlight.

Matt walks his bike up the sidewalk now, right out in the open as the guard steps out to confront the driver. With the guard's attention likely on the woman, Matt swings onto his bike and makes a hard left toward the guardhouse. There's plenty of room for a kid on a bike to get around the lowered exit arm. In a blink he's a pedaling blur on the privileged grounds of Sapphire Cove.

He keeps to the darkness of the wall and the windbreak trees. Without slowing he braves a look back: the entrance arm rising, the guard standing by, the headlights of the Mercedes just beginning to move. The car passes him a moment later, the total chop Tijuana Brass blasting. This older guy has to be taking his date to a party, Matt thinks.

Cove View is a long, curving street studded with handsome houses, some grand and some humble. Matt distantly follows the Mercedes and soon arrives at a large, modern post-and-beam two-story home backed against a rocky cliff. It's set well away from the street. He wedges himself and his bike into a hedge of oleander and watches.

To get to the house from here he'll have to go through a closed iron gate. There's a keypad/intercom box on a brick gatepost, and the driver of the red Mercedes is speaking into it.

Beyond the gate, the driveway is littered with cars parked on the downslope side. Matt doesn't recognize all of the brands, but he knows Porsche, Jaguar, and Ferrari when he sees them. Near the house a young man trots away from a valet stand where, in the lights of the porte cochere, stand two men. They have mod, over-the-ear haircuts and baggy white bell-bottom suits. Midthirties maybe. Matt wonders for the millionth time why old men are so eager to look ridiculous. The valet, keys shining in one hand, disappears into a knot of cars beyond his stand.

Matt forces his bike deeper into the hedge, clambers up the brick gatepost and drops to the other side. Scurries into the shadows as the Mustang headlights rake past him.

Closer to the house now, he hears the music, a droning Sonny and Cher song the old people think is hip. He cuts deeper into the dense garden, away from the driveway and its lights, and finds himself within a lush grove of ferns, squatting for a better look at the house. A Buddha fountain gurgles to his left. Colored lights behind the windows. Invitation only, he thinks. Old guys. Young girls the same age as his sister.

The house is a staunch-looking structure of darkly finished wood beams and posts, anchored together with metal connectors and ties. Lots of windows and sliding glass doors.

Interconnecting walkways and decks link room to room and floor to floor. A giant treehouse. The railings are lined with potted plants, the air heavy with the smell of weed and incense, patchouli, Matt thinks, always patchouli. On one upper deck a man and a woman make out—both naked to the waist.

Wow.

He hops through the islands of shadows, finds his way to a first-floor room and looks in. There's a faint red glow coming from inside but the shades are drawn. Still, pressing his nose to the glass and squinting with one eye, Matt can see a section of what's inside: a dimly lit room in which a man and two girls/women writhe nakedly on a bed.

Matt once saw a 16-mm porn movie that his friend Teddy stole from his dad and showed in his backyard for money. Teddy billed it as "Night at the Cruddies," and Matt paid his seventy-five cents. It was black-and-white and almost unbearably stimulating. He had no idea that's what people did. Besides that, he'd only seen *Playboy* magazine, a couple of racy drawings, and an astrological sex-position poster at Mystic Arts World that Furlong actually pulled off the wall and took to headquarters as obscene material.

But this live action here in Sapphire Cove is another level of excitement altogether—far more powerful and immediate. Matt feels incomprehensible currents massing against each other inside, mixing and separating and massing again.

He slumps down against a wall, hiding in a pool of darkness, making himself small, figuring what to do next. It seems necessary to continue. Cowardly to quit. What if Jazz is here and he fails her by leaving now? Worse, what if Jazz is here and he finds her and she won't come home? Why would she come here in the first place if she wanted to be home? This idea has hit him before but never this hard—that his sister has run away because she *wanted* to. In that case, he wishes she'd have taken him along. Just them in the Volkswagen van, heading up the coast to L.A. or maybe down to San Diego or even Mexico, working odd jobs and sharing their money for gas and food and cool things.

Currents massing and pooling.

He presses on.

Through another first-story window he sees more naked people, more coupling, more combinations. Lava lamps, thick smoke. Naked people on beds, sofas, chairs, the floor. Some wear masks. Some are frenzied, some slow. Young girls and mostly older men. He studies each female face but no Jasmine. Into the room strides a fully clothed middle-aged man in blue denim bell-bottoms and a long-sleeved paisley shirt open to mid-chest. A lumpy mod haircut, bangs. He's got a bong that he offers to the various fornicators. Cavore?

A woman trails him, stoking the bong dope with a fireplace lighter that throws a blue flame. She's wearing a black dress and a small black mask that covers only her eyes and part of her cheeks. White-blond hair and a wholesome-looking smile. Apple-red lips. She's one of the only women with any clothes on. To Matt she looks more like a hostess than a participant.

Possible Cavore takes a take a deep hit off the bong, then blows his smoke down the throat of a girl grinding away on top of a man.

Carefully, Matt times his sprint up the stairs to the second floor. Makes the landing unnoticed. From here he can see the twinkling black ocean and the pale curve of Sapphire Cove and a plump half-moon behind clouds.

Bent at the waist, he sneaks along a dark second-story deck, then stops short of a sliding glass door. It's been left open a crack and they haven't bothered with shades or curtains up this high. He peers in. Couches and a pool table. Overstuffed chairs and fluffy sheepskin area rugs. Smoke to the ceiling. Draped everywhere are bodies in motion, and joints being passed, and plates of white powder being snorted through red plastic straws. Beer and wine and cocktails going down. Sinatra croons at low volume. It's a big room, and as far back as Matt can see it's a panorama of humans, some mating or finishing mating or about to mate. Some naked, some clothed. Some just watch, sitting or standing or milling around like shoppers.

It's impossible to believe his sister would do this.

He, Matt, will not allow her to do this.

Again, the mod bell-bottom-and-paisley-shirt man goes from person to couple to whatever combination he finds, offering the bong to his guests, blowing smoke down the throats of the girls.

"Jordan! Over here!" a man calls out.

When Jordan Cavore begins to thread his way back out of the crowded room, Matt hustles into position on the second-floor wraparound deck. Doesn't even bother ducking out of sight as he passes the picture windows and sliding glass doors overlooking the endless dark Pacific.

He takes his sketch of Jasmine from his pocket and unfolds it. His hands tremble and his ears roar. The man's shadow is approaching as Matt steps into the light and directly into the path of Cavore, bong in hand.

Cavore comes to a stop. He's taller and huskier now.

"Get out."

Matt steps forward, knees shaking, but holds the sketch up for the man to see. "That's Jasmine Anthony and she's my sister. You need to tell me if you've seen her."

"I don't need to tell you shit."

"Have you seen her?"

Cavore looks at the drawing and the trespasser, then snatches the sketch, crumples and drops it. Matt reaches for it as Cavore swings the bong into the side of his head, which sends shards of glass into the lights. Matt hits the deck, braced on one hand and holding the other to his head. A light smear of blood on his fingers.

"You are on private property," says Cavore. "Now beat it and don't say one word about any of this. I can find you. And no, I've never seen that girl before."

Matt grabs the wadded drawing, flies down the stairs and across the property the same way he'd come in.

He stuffs the drawing in his pocket then tries to wrestle his bike from the poisonous oleander. Really has to wrench it. His rope bounces from the basket and gets caught up in the spokes. Finally, he jumps aboard and hauls butt along Cove View toward the guard booth and Coast Highway.

As he speeds around the lowered gate arm, the guard stands for a better look at him. Matt flips him off.

The next thing he knows he's down hard on the Sapphire

Cove sidewalk. He rolls twice, then pops up and runs back to his bike. The guard comes fast. Matt remounts and pedals away with all his might.

Skids into the turn at Coast Highway and heads for home, cars swooshing past him just a few feet away.

It's almost 2 A.M. when he turns on the garage lights and gets a good look at the damage: elbows and knees scraped badly, bloody at the edges, pink in the middle. His palms are gravel-ground and feel bruised. In a hand-mirror he checks his head where the bong hit him—swelling and a few nicks.

His mother appears behind him in a kimono, sleep-faced and bed-haired. "What happened?"

"Nothing, Mom. I'm tired and need a shower and that's all."

"But where have you been?"

"With Ernie at the hotel. Don't worry. I slid out on my bike. I'm fine."

"But you didn't come home like Jazz hasn't come home. I waited up and saved most of the spaghetti and meatballs for you."

"Thanks, Mom. I'll eat it later. Now leave me alone. I'll be in to take a shower in a minute."

"Did someone hit you?"

Matt is rarely angry but when he is, it owns him. It's like a switch gets thrown. His facial expression is tied to that switch and his mother knows exactly what it means. He forces her out of his garage with it.

The next thing Matt knows he's in the shower, warm water gurgling through the old plumbing while images of this night flood through him. He's short of breath and there's a clenching knot in his throat. His ears roar and his balls ache. The soap and shampoo scald his palms, knees, and elbows. While inside him, the incomprehensible currents mass and separate and mass again—Laurel and Jazz and Bonnie and everything he saw at Sapphire Cove.

11

Monday morning, as Matt browns a scrawny peanut butter and jelly burrito in a skillet for breakfast, his father calls.

Bruce Anthony's voice is soft and clear and he's developed a drawl over the years.

"How's my son?"

"Good, Dad."

Matt's mind still swarms with memories of Saturday night, and his knees and elbows are still raw and fiery. His palm heels are now showing bruises from breaking the fall. Other than that, the rest of his body and soul are starting to feel about half-right again, and the ding in his head from the bong barely hurts. But the images of that party agitate him greatly.

With the phone clamped between his head and one shoulder, and the long cord uncoiling out behind him, Matt pours the burrito onto a plate, gets a fork, and heads for the tiny breakfast nook by the window. The PB&J burrito is his invention, probably the cheapest way to fill an empty stomach, depending on how much peanut butter you've got left, and how much milk to chase it down.

"And your mother?" asks his dad.

"The same. But Jasmine hasn't been home for four days. We filed a police report."

Matt gives his father a general account of Jasmine's disappearance from home, and some of what little he knows about where she was and who she was with. No way he's going to mention Austin Overton or the water polo muscleman or anything about Sapphire Cove. Bruce Anthony has a short fuse and he doesn't take bad news well.

"It's what she gets for staying in that evil town," he says. "I'll make some calls. I've still got friends with the sheriffs. Tell me what happened again. I'm going to take some notes."

Matt repeats the story, hears the flap of paper and tap of pen.

When he's finished, Matt says he's worried about Kyle, and Kyle's idea that short-timers have a higher chance of dying the closer they are to coming home.

"That's nonsense," says Bruce. "But fear can get into a soldier's head and make bad things happen. A self-fulfilling prophecy."

Bruce was Air Force in Korea. Military police, at just nineteen. He's never talked about it to Matt like he did with Kyle when Kyle joined up.

"I'm unhappy about your sister. I'm tempted to come back and put things right. Tear that rotting town apart and get my girl. I've seen the hippies on TV in Laguna and San Francisco. You can practically smell them. The Summer of Love. Christ, what an abomination that was. Now Laguna's got the overflow, from what I read in the papers."

"It's not so bad here. The fishing is still good."

"Those were great times, you and Kyle and me. The best hours of my life. Those, and shooting doves out in Juan Acuna's groves with you boys."

Matt pictures the three of them fishing off the rocks in Laguna, or catching bass and perch and halibut off the sandy beaches when the tide was right. He was one hundred percent happy. Even had some aptitude for it that Kyle didn't. His dad called him "fishy." Juan Acuna managed an endless grove of navel oranges in Tustin, just inland from Laguna Canyon, and for a case of beer and a few dollars he'd let the Anthonys shoot doves in September. Matt was one hundred percent happy doing that, too.

Now as his mother pours coffee, he sees from her dark look

that she knows who's on the line. She takes the coffee back to her bedroom and he hears the door close. His burrito is long gone but there's no tortillas left. Milk.

"I'm still willing to send money to you kids," says Bruce.

Six years ago, Julie had torn Bruce's first check to pieces and washed it and the letter down the garbage disposal as Matt, Kyle, and Jasmine watched. And done the same with the next few, until they stopped coming. For a year after that, each of the Anthony children got occasional notes containing five-dollar bills but these ran out too, due to Bruce's financial setbacks. His stated main reason for leaving Laguna and his family was a sheriff's position in Clay County, Texas. But there was more, Matt came to learn. Such as his father's belief that Laguna Beach was not reality, that it was tempting his wife and children with a way of life they could never afford. There was also his affair, and the deputy job that had "gone to hell in a hurry." Since then, there have been yearlong spans of time when Bruce Anthony hasn't been heard from at all.

"I don't think she'll take money," Matt says quietly, thinking his dad probably doesn't have any to spare anyway.

"Too much thickheaded Irish in that woman," says Bruce.

But Matt wishes she *would* take it. He rarely sides with his father against his mother but he can't help himself now.

"It's embarrassing at the Food Exchange," he says. "Getting looks from people you know."

"They're spoiled, thankless people."

"Okay."

"I'm sorry you have to put up with that. But hang in there. Keep a sharp eye out for Jazz. Knowing her, she's spending time with people with money. She always liked nice things. The most expensive things. Exactly like her mother."

"She was twelve when you left, Dad."

"What do you mean by that? I know my own daughter like I know my ex-wife. They're both women who want better things than my money could ever buy."

Matt has heard it before but can never understand this

pretzel-shaped logic from his father. Who defines his family as something they aren't, then attacks what he's created? Who says he can't afford life in a town where he was affording life just fine?

"Okay."

"Saying 'okay' doesn't mean that things are okay, Matt. It's about time for you to stand up and become a man."

This is the first time his father has said this. It has always been *when you grow up*. Now it's *become a man*.

"Stand up how?"

"Don't be a wiseass, son."

"I'll find Jazz," says Matt. "Don't worry."

"Stay out of trouble, Matt. Say no to the drug pushers and the queers and girls who only want shiny objects and ocean-front homes."

"I will."

"You still have the paper route?"

"Yes."

"Still drawing in the sketchbooks and scrounging paint from Coast Hardware?"

"Yes, still."

He thinks of telling his father about Bonnie Stratmeyer but decides against it, knowing it would make him angry.

"Just remember, when it's time for college, pick a major that gets you into money. Life is about making money."

"I'll remember."

"If Jasmine isn't home in a week I'm coming back and taking over."

More than once, his father has proposed "taking over" as a solution to the various misbehaviors of his children and ex-wife. Which he seems to think this is: misbehavior by Jasmine.

Matt's guts tell him that Jasmine hasn't vanished because of her own misbehavior, but he doesn't have enough proof to make that argument.

"Okay, Dad. Good."

"Love you."

"Love you."

When Matt hangs up, his mother is standing in the doorway dressed for work.

"You're pretty banged up, Matt. I didn't see all that damage before. Must really hurt."

He's got on his Jams trunks and a white T-shirt with a blue competition stripe across the chest. Looks down at his Band-Aided kneecaps, which feel like they've been worked over with a cheese grater. Elbows too.

"We need to talk," she says.

She takes his fingers gently and turns his hand to see the bruised and gouged palm. Leads him into the living room trailing a wake of sweet hashish-opium smoke.

"Matt, we've had some bum trips at work," she says. "Um, the summer tourists haven't picked up because of the June gloom and all the hippies scaring them off. Of course, the hippies don't eat out very much and hardly tip at all. So, my hours are getting cut back. Not completely. But back."

"That's terrible, Mom."

"They're a little mad because I was late twice last week. After missing those two shifts the week before. For the flu."

Matt remembers those two "flu" days. She'd spent them alone in her room with the music on and the smoke thick enough to creep out under the door, the puka shell necklace over the beveled glass knob. It was the first time he'd smelled opium and hashish burning together and hadn't realized what it was until she stashed the half-smoked dragon ball in the kitchen drawer and forgotten it was there.

"And so, if dear landlord Nelson comes around complaining about the rent being late again, tell him it's coming soon. I'm doing all I can."

"I can pick up a *Times* or a *News-Post* route to bring in more money," says Matt.

"You did that once. It wore you out and wrecked your grades."

"I was young."

She smiles at this. Her expression is empty but dreamy, thinks Matt, my stoned mom dressed like a wench and on her way to work. She never seemed resigned and sad like this before. Part of it must be her daughter leaving home after an argument, he reasons.

"Weren't we all?" she asks. A long pause. "I think your sister might be in trouble."

About time, Matt thinks. "I do, too."

"So many temptations. She's a searcher. She follows things that call her. But she's not experienced enough to spot trouble."

Matt agrees with her assessment. Jazz is always the one to make the leap. Provoking him to do likewise. To catch up. Show some balls. Sapphire Cove images cross his mind in a tangled rush. Certainly, Jazz would have sensed trouble if she knew anything about what went on there. But what if she was in the mood for that kind of thing?

"Maybe the police posters will help," says Julie. "Officer Darnell told me they're ready and she'll drop some off. Imagine, my little girl's face all over town. Right after Bonnie's face all over town, and now Bonnie dead on the beach. It terrifies me."

Matt feels his mother's worry on top of his own.

"How is your father?"

"The same. He threatened to come take over if Jazz isn't back in a week."

"He's a broken record," she says. She gets her beaded hippie bag from a dinette chair, slings it over her shoulder and heads for the door.

Matt knows he should tell her what happened in Sapphire Cove but there's no way he could describe those things to his own mother. They may or may not relate to Jazz being gone. Plus he'd just be bringing those lurid, thrilling scenes back on himself.

He knows his mother knows he's not telling the whole truth. Her way is to wait and pry, wait and pry, until she finally cracks whatever nut she's working on.

"Sure you don't want to tell me what happened Saturday night?"

"It's what I said happened, Mom."

"You'll tell me when you're ready. Remember, if Nelson comes snooping around here, you tell him I'm out making the rent."

So, twenty minutes later, as Matt is finishing up the dishes, the knock on the front door sounds like Nelson Pedley's signature *tap-t-tap-tap*.

Instead, Officer Darnell is on the porch, hooking her sunglasses into the loop on her uniform blouse, not far from the *B. Darnell* nameplate.

She looks as she did before, but a little older and tougher in the sunlight. Hair braided like a rope again, and pinned up.

She gives Matt a flyer from the thick stack she's holding. It's black-and-white and the resolution is poor. They've used Jazz's senior portrait and Matt's drawing of her, side by side. Under them, her description and the LBPD number to call.

She asks for Julie and Matt says she'll be home around five.

"I was hoping to see Jasmine's room."

Matt searches Darnell's face for some indication of why she's here right now, with no prior call and no mention of seeing Jasmine's room two days ago at the interview.

"Have you learned something bad?" he asks.

"No, no, nothing like that, Matt. This is routine. Sometimes we'll find something that points to where someone has gone."

"Come in. We haven't made the bed or anything."

"Good, that's best."

"It would be cool to find a clue."

12

Darnell observes Jasmine's room through the open door, then steps inside. Turns slowly in place in her heavy-looking black cop boots, taking in the three-sixty view around her.

"What happened to your knees and elbows, Matt?"

He makes up a brief story about Saturday night, meeting up with a friend for a late dinner, catching a pothole at high speed on Carmelita and going down.

"My fault."

"As a mother I worry about boys on bikes in the dark."

"I'm pretty careful."

She looks like she's about to say something but doesn't. Looks around again.

"How angry was Jasmine at her mother?"

"I wasn't there for the argument. They argue sometimes but usually forget pretty fast."

"Sometimes or often?"

"Sometimes."

A nod. "I see she likes music and clothes."

Matt follows her blue-eyed gaze to Jazz's closet, all the way open as always and packed with clothes. The boots and shoes are piled two layers high across the closet floor. Matt knows that some of them haven't fit Jazz for years but she won't throw them away.

"I'm surprised by the Tim Leary poster and her books," says Darnell. "Not just how many books, but the subjects. Your average eighteen-year-old doesn't read *The Tibetan Book of the*

Dead or *The Psychedelic Experience*. Or *The Doors of Perception*. Or the *Upanishads*. Do you read these books too, Matt?"

"No."

"Have you met Timothy Leary?"

"I've talked to him at Mystic Arts World."

"Has he offered you LSD?"

"No. Never."

"Does Jasmine know him?"

"I don't believe so."

She studies him flatly. "Did she take anything unusual with her, the first night she didn't come home?"

"I don't know what she took. I was out delivering papers when she left in the van."

"Nothing is obviously missing?"

Matt looks around the small, disheveled room, trying to be of help.

"I just don't know. It's hard to see what's missing."

"Boy, that's the truth."

But something bothers him.

Darnell's smile is generous and uncomplicated. She goes to Jasmine's dresser and looks down on the bottles of perfume and tanning potions, a small round mirror on a stand, jewelry boxes, a small woven bowl that contains inexpensive bead necklaces and earrings and anklets.

"You know," says Matt. "There is something missing. Her ukulele. It's usually in the corner."

His first thought: she takes it sometimes for parties and cookouts. She's good on it and she has a beautiful clear voice. She makes up her own songs and her friends play and sing along. His second thought: she took it to play for Austin Overton. He tells the officer as much.

Darnell considers. "I talked to Overton yesterday after I took your report. He said what you said. That he played the Sandpiper and slept with Jasmine Thursday night. She took off in the morning around eight and he hasn't seen or talked to her since. I don't like Austin Overton, but I believe him."

Matt doesn't understand exactly why, but he likes and trusts Darnell. From the card she gave him earlier, he knows her first name is Brigit. She doesn't seem out to get everybody, like Furlong. She seems more like an ally than an enemy and she seems to care about his sister. And the truth about his Saturday night has been bellowing to get out.

"I went to one of those Sapphire Cove parties Saturday night," he says.

"I knew it. I knew you would. Tell me everything."

He does. The obscene, exciting scenes flood back on him. He's slightly proud to tell Darnell that he flipped off the guard, but also slightly ashamed that he crashed his own bike.

Darnell stands with her hands on her hips and a slight frown on her face.

"We have trouble with Sapphire Cove security too," she says. "They won't even let us in except to clean up a mess or cite a vehicle. They're not city of Laguna, so we have no authority. Matt, are you willing to make a statement I can take to a judge? About that orgy?"

"No. I just want to find my sister."

She nods briskly. "I understand. I can require you to make a statement, you know."

"Haven't I already, just now?"

"I can use what you gave me. But it has more warrant weight coming from you."

Gear and weapon clanking softly, Officer Darnell goes to the open closet, then to the window, then to a Beatles poster. Comes to a stop in front of Matt. She's close enough he can see the gray flecks in her blue eyes.

"Matt Anthony, I'm going to go out on a limb with you. Right now. This is only between us, but Bonnie Stratmeyer went to at least one of the Sapphire Cove parties while she was officially missing."

"That's bad news."

"It gets worse. Your mother's hippie van has been towed to our impound yard from Sapphire Cove. It was parked overnight without a permit, and Sapphire Cove security called us to have it towed. We're processing it now. The ukulele is in it."

"Parked *when* at Sapphire Cove?"

"We're working on that."

"But nothing about Jasmine herself?" asks Matt. He feels as if a dark shadow is crossing over some remote plain in his mind. Jazz abandon her own van? And her uke? No, clearly, she was planning on coming back for them. Clearly. So, why didn't she?

"Nothing about Jasmine herself," says Darnell.

"Terrible news."

"That's why I need your statement."

"I want the van back."

"You're not old enough to drive it."

"I've got my learner's permit. And the van is sitting there at the station, less than a block from here."

She considers him. "You need an adult in the car to drive with a learner's permit. We can get the van here together, *if* you'll sign a statement about what you saw in Sapphire Cove Saturday night."

"Cavore said he could find me."

"All the more reason to provide the statement. I'll write it up and you'll sign it."

Matt nods unhappily. "We have to do it now. I've got papers to fold and deliver. Can I have forty-eight of those posters of Jazz?"

Darnell's dubious look gives way to a smile. "To go with your newspapers?"

"Yes, please."

"Of course you can. And the rest are for your mom. Get the spare key and we'll be on our way."

Matt angles the posters into the window light. Studies his sister's portrait and his own drawing of her, side by side on the letter-sized sheet. The photo captures her conventional beauty, and his art catches something of her confident humor.

MISSING
HAVE YOU SEEN ME?
Name: Jasmine "Jazz" Anthony DOB: 5/1/1950
Hair: blond Eyes: blue Height: 5'7" Weight: 115 lbs.
LAST SEEN AT SANDPIPER NIGHT CLUB
LAGUNA BEACH POLICE ASK YOUR HELP!
(714) 497-0701

A cold, foreign feeling settles over him.

His sister on a missing-persons poster.

The next thing Matt knows he's at the helm of his mother's sputtering tangerine-and-white van, Officer Brigit Darnell riding shotgun. He signals and swings the van from the little LBPD impound yard behind City Hall onto Third Street. The van is agonizingly slow. It coughs roughly. His house is right there; he could have walked it faster.

Pulls into the driveway and parks in front of his garage.

"Thanks," he says.

"Come to the station after your paper route. I'll have the statement ready. And Matt? Say nothing about you-know-who and Sapphire Cove parties. Nobody knows that but us cops and you."

Matt bobs his head obediently and Darnell heads down the sidewalk for the station.

He opens the side doors of the van. It's a Westfalia camper van, two-tone tangerine and white, a 1958 model with windows along both sides, a pop-up top, a framed side-awning that stows along the ceiling, cabinets, a fold-out table and padded seats that convert to a bed, an ice box and sink, and curtains sewn by Julie from bongo drum and palm tree–print cotton. Matt has never quite understood how they fit this many features into a small space, but it's all functional, more or less.

He pulls a sleeping bag over Jasmine's ukulele on the bed. Remembers his sister, playing the little instrument down at Crescent Bay one evening last summer around a campfire that threw orange shadows across the faces gathered around it. Matt, lurking behind the fire and the older teenagers, watching. Jazz pretty and sweet-voiced in firelight. Seems much longer ago than just a year.

His paper route, counting the folding and rubber-banding, is four hours of zinging pain, with his raw knees and elbows and his bruised palm heels, which have turned pale blue since Saturday night.

Having Jazz's "missing" poster folded inside each and every *Register* makes him feel useful, deflecting the pain. Some. That's forty-eight subscribers who might see her and call Darnell, he thinks.

He lands the Coiner's *Register* in the sprinklers again, has to wade through those knee-high sprayers to fetch the paper and hobble with it to the porch, Gigi shrieking from behind the screen door, old Coiner hollering at the dog and Mrs. Coiner yelling at him.

When he gets home, landlord Nelson Pedley is standing in the middle of the tiny dried-out front yard, examining the sparse crop of fruit on the centerpiece avocado tree. It's a brown Fuerte, sun-starved and dehydrated because Pedley won't water it, so it produces small fruit. Pedley does not allow the Anthonys to pick any—it's an actual condition of the lease agreement. When he comes to collect the monthly rent, he sometimes brings a small paper bag into which he puts two or three skinny avocados as a gift for his valued tenants.

As he does today, handing it to Matt with a smile.

"She's not home so don't even knock," Matt says. "She's out trying to make some money if that's okay with you."

"Well, of course, young man, certainly it is."

"Okay, good. I have an errand to run, Mr. Pedley."

"It's late again, Matt. The rent."

"It's on the way. Don't worry."

"I do worry, about your mom."

Matt shrugs and walks off toward the cop house half a block away.

When he's done signing Officer Darnell's almost verbatim report of his Sapphire Cove adventure, Matt hurries back home for something to eat. He's starved, as usual, after three hours of peddling the hills and heaving papers.

The pantry has nothing but peanut butter and a can of beets, and his mother is still not home from the Jolly Roger with possible leftovers. Matt's got almost fourteen dollars, which can buy plenty at the market, but he's saving money for another expensive sketchbook and some good pressed charcoal, and something for Laurel's birthday next week. His next route collection is almost two weeks away. So he rides to the Assistance League Food Exchange, his stomach grumbling hopefully. Last time it was milk, bread, eggs, cereal, rice, and . . .

Today it's closed.

He settles for the peanut butter, the beets, and all three of Pedley's scrawny avocados. He eats in front of the TV, watching the news. Walter Cronkite has been suggesting the war will not end in an American victory, but a "stalemate." Cronkite had left his CBS studio in February and traveled to Vietnam to see firsthand how the war was going. He looked funny in his helmet. This evening he suggests that the American president has been overoptimistic about the war, in spite of the first five months of 1968 being exceptionally bloody, thanks to the Tet Offensive in January.

This evening's battle footage shows helicopters landing under fire from communist Viet Cong gunners hidden in a misty forest. The bullets zip into the choppers but you can't hear them over the rotors. The American troops come spilling out, running hard, crouched and heavily zig-zagging. Some pull up, kneel and shoot. No Kyle.

He takes his dishes to the sink. Looks out the kitchen window past the GTE building and sees that this will be a dramatic evening: blue skies, dark clouds blowing in, an orange-and-black sunset made for photography. Sunset just after eight. It's going to be warm tonight, too, for June.

Matt still feels hungry, but lucky, too, like he's going to see Jazz soon. Going to get her back where she belongs, safe from bad people and the things they do.

He loves beets. And avocados. Hates the thought of another long bike ride with his knees and elbows dipped in acid. He considers the lumpy tangerine-colored van in the driveway.

Figures the best driving route to Thousand Steps without getting caught.

Hopes to catch a glimpse of what Laurel saw there two days ago.

13

The camper van putts down Coast Highway, pulling to the right. Matt feels the gears shifting under him as he pushes the squishy clutch and moves the stick from gear to gear. His mom has coached him on timing the shift to the rpms and keeping the clutch all the way down until you're in the next gear. It feels funny to have control over this much power and weight, even though this Westfalia camper has only thirty horsepower. The non–power steering wheel is large and takes some muscle.

It gets Matt down to Ninth Street, where he finds a place to park. No driving mistakes and no cops. He's pleased to have broken the law and gotten away with it. Wonders what else he might get away with. Puts a sketchbook and a box of pressed charcoal sticks into his backpack, a burly thing made by his mother from outgrown blue jeans with surf shop patches and emblems. Slings it on and begins his long descent down Thousand Steps.

Which are actually 219 steps. Matt has counted them once every year since his ninth birthday—another day he very clearly remembers—when his mom and dad took him and Kyle and Jasmine to the big wide-open sandy beach here, perfect for surf-mattresses, bodysurfing, tidepool-combing, and getting tan. The menfolk had fished the south-end rocks that day because that's what Matt had wanted on his birthday and there weren't too many tourists. Matt, now at step number eighty-eight, remembers a keeper-sized halibut he caught that became dinner that night. Remembers the Boston cream pie his mom made and the Rapala lures his dad got him. Less than a year later his father was suddenly gone.

Now he's nearly to step number one-seventy-two. The steps are concrete, and narrow, and they are bordered closely by steel railings. The dense shrubbery of the oceanfront lots line the railings on either side. It's like being on a path through high jungle, and he thinks of Kyle on real paths in real jungle, in narrow dark tunnels filled with men and women waiting to spear or shoot you. "Sunshine of Your Love" plays on his left, and "Foxy Lady" on his right. Voices and laughter and the smell of marijuana. He remembers Kyle telling him he wasn't scared of war and he'd "kick Victor Charlie's sorry ass" or die trying. Jack Bruce sings about waiting so long to be in the sunshine of somebody's love. Hendrix sings about a sweet little lovemaker.

The beach is still crowded, the tide low. He walks into the suntanning bodies and their bright swimsuits, sees the skimboarders and surfers out in the crashing white-foam waves. Two pale jarheads throw a football, faces and backs burnt pink. Hippie girls in cutoffs and genie pants play hacky sack. Young people try to keep their Frisbees from beaning old people. Acres of sunbathers recline on their colorful rectangles, radios play, a biplane pulls a banner for Tab across the sky, and the sexy aroma of suntan lotion hovers over it all.

He stops, looking for the photo shoot that Laurel described: the bossy photographer with the cameras draped over him, the fumbling assistant with his windblown reflectors, the muscleman in his tiny swimsuit. And all of the beautiful young people as models, some of them locals that Matt will certainly recognize. But no sign of these. Not here, not south, not north.

So he heads south along the waterline toward the fabled Thousand Steps Pools, thinking that they would be a perfect place to photograph young people doing beachy things. There is also the tunnel you can pass through when the tide isn't too high, and some dramatic rock outcroppings. And the sweeping, yellow-sand beach.

The pools—big concrete rectangles built by a Hollywood movie director who lived here back in the twenties—are busy with waders and pool-gazers eyeing the swift croaker and perch. But no photographers. Matt stands on one of the walls, watches the fish surge and slash.

He finds a place above one of the big pools and sits. Lets his good strong eyes scan the beach. Maybe if he waits and watches, Jazz will show.

He gets out his sketchbook and a good charcoal stick and does another Laurel in the Gauguin painting. He does an Officer Brigit Darnell sitting across from him in the station; a decent Jordan Cavore looming over him on the Sapphire Cove walkway. He makes people he doesn't like look uglier than they are, and people he likes look better. Cavore looks pretty bad. He does another Jazz, based on his favorite drawing of her, pretty much wrecked by Cavore. At home, Matt has flattened and pressed that crumpled thing between the pages of a heavy Impressionism tome he bought at a Laguna Beach Friends of the Library sale for a nickel. The best five cents he's ever spent.

Now he tries his mom in the embarrassing wench's costume, and manages to capture her expression of whatever's been eating at her these last weeks. But what is it? Does she have a disease she doesn't know about? Or worse, she does know about but won't admit? Ernie's dad got cancer but lived.

Matt looks up to note that the evening sky is a deepening blue, and a band of low gray clouds lies on the horizon like insulation.

Which is when a man with cameras dangling around his neck, another man carrying large black duffels, and a very big guy in a maroon robe come traipsing south toward him. Camera Man wears a baggy white suit and white sneakers. A caravan of young men and women follows along well behind them, the girls in bright bikinis and hot pants and sheer cover-ups and sun hats; the boys in canvas surf shorts and colorful T-shirts or Hawaiian shirts or no shirts at all. One carries a shiny new twin-fin surfboard balanced on his head like the guys on Matt's *Endless Summer* T-shirt. Some have packs and bags or small duffels. Matt studies every one of them. No Jazz. No one he recognizes.

He watches as Camera Man stops and raises his hand like a patrol sergeant. His platoon stops too, except Robe Giant, who approaches the leader. They talk, then Robe Giant goes back to the group and returns to Camera Man with one of the young women by the hand. In her other hand she's got a pink skateboard with white daisies on it, one of the cool new models with the wheelie deck and fat wheels. She looks a little like Jasmine—a suntanned blonde with square shoulders and long legs. Younger, maybe. Matt counts nine young people against the backdrop of golden beach sand.

Camera Man turns his back to the descending sun and scans his people with a long-lensed camera.

Duffel Guy drops his bags, kneels and unzips one. Robe Giant reclines in the sand on his side before the young woman with the skateboard, his wine-colored robe parting to reveal his sculpted chest and bulging swimsuit. Skateboard Girl looks down on him skeptically.

Matt moves closer, climbs a gentle dune, and settles cross-legged into the warm sand. Opens the sketchbook across his lap and swiftly cuts in the twelve figures, using both pages without even looking at them, trying to set the scene.

Camera Man approaches Robe Giant and Skateboard Girl, kneels, and, cranking the focus, starts shooting. Matt hears the muted clicks carrying on the breeze. Duffel Guy sidles up behind Camera Man, holding a big silver fabric disc that reflects the sunlight onto Robe Giant and Skateboard Girl. Camera Man barks something that Matt can't make out, but Skateboard Girl drops her board to the sand and hops on. She lifts her arms for balance, and bends her knees as if she's riding straight at Robe Giant, who gazes up at her with what at this distance looks to Matt like a bored leer.

Matt is drawing fast, barely looking down, letting his eyes

and hand do the work, no thoughts to interfere. Turns the page without a glance. Really trying to get those faces right, not just the details but the attitudes. Can make adjustments later.

Camera Man squats and shoots, rises and shoots, circles, changes cameras, backpedals and shoots again. Skateboard Girl kneels with her arms out in a good pantomime of speed. Then squats almost all the way down and raises her hands, the wind catching her hair just right, blowing it back as if from sheer velocity.

The other young models activate. Matt watches them dig through their packs and duffels and produce treasures: a fringed buckskin vest, a pair of Stars and Stripes genie pants, a suede miniskirt quickly zipped on by a girl in a Day-Glo green bikini. Then, two tie-dye peace-sign flags with handles, skillfully deployed by a smiling redhead, as another girl pulls what looks like an enormous unmelted ice cream sundae from her bag. A young man straps a small guitar over his naked shoulder and strums a chord; Surfboard Boy approaches Skateboard Girl, stabs his twin-fin into the sand and starts rubbing on board wax in long suggestive strokes as Camera Man swivels, changes cameras and continues shooting again. Robe Giant, rising, lets his maroon cover drop to the sand, revealing his bulging biceps and armored six pack and the tiny American-flag water polo briefs that revolted Laurel. Matt realizes for the first time how tall the guy is, six and a half feet maybe, a tower of oiled muscle who now squats and lifts Ice Cream Sundae onto one shoulder where she curls her legs up like a mermaid on a rock, smiles greatly, and proffers the ersatz sundae to Camera Man with one outstretched hand.

Matt can't draw fast enough, but he gets decent faces of the photo crew. By then a crowd has gathered, so he joins them to watch this strange circus, this twisting, ever-changing double-helix of weirdness.

It goes on and on. Matt circles the action and the crowd but it's not as if different angles give him any more understanding of what he's seeing. Camera Man has given up shouting direction and the young people seem to be improvising.

By the time the photographer calls it a wrap, Matt and dozens of other spectators are loitering under a magnificent orange and black sunset. The actors and the audience all applaud Camera Man, who opens his arms and calls out.

"Thank you so very much, my friends," he says. His voice is rough and strongly accented. "Once again we have made our art with our hearts and our bodies. Some of these images will come to be in history and some will be used only to sell products. But you my friends are the soul of art. Thank you. Tomorrow is Diver's Cove at six P.M. Please reimagine your costumes and your props so that we do not repeat ourselves."

Most of the audience is still hanging around, and as Matt circulates through he realizes that most have stayed on to see about joining this strange circus.

I got a Barbarella suit that looks great on me!

What, you just do whatever comes into your head and hope the pictures turn out good?

Can me and my old lady get into this scene?

Matt's got the fresh picture of Jasmine right there in the sketchbook and he opens to it. Robe Giant eyes Matt steadily as he cinches the robe sash. Something tells Matt that these people might like him and his drawing about as much as Jordan Cavore did last Saturday night. But he holds it up to Robe Giant anyway.

"Have you seen her?"

Robe Giant shakes his great head and turns away.

So Matt joins some people taking flyers from Skateboard Girl.

"You were great," he says. "Your performance."

"Far out," she says, handing him a sheet of paper. "Here. If you come to the Evolution Ceremony tonight, I'll get you in for half price. Good food. I'm an Evolver."

"Bitchen. I'm Matt."

"Sara."

He shows her his sketch of Jazz. "Do you know Jasmine Anthony?"

Sara squints at the drawing and nods. "I saw her at a couple of these photo shoots, and I saw her once at the Vortex, pretty sure."

"Vortex?"

"Read the flyer."

"She's my sister and she's missing."

Sara squints again and shades her eyes against the lowering sun. Studies Matt's face. "She's cute, like you. I haven't seen her in days, though."

And she's gone in a flurry of breeze-blown hair, her flyers in one hand and a beaded bag for her skateboard in the other.

The flyer is glossy and expensive looking, with a pale blue background that could be a sky or a swimming pool without ripples, and puffy, cloudlike letters:

THE VORTEX OF PURITY
Presents
SWAMI MAHAJAD OM
Evolution, Enlightenment, Ecstasy
9 P.M. Tonight
1 Thermal Ridge Drive, Laguna Beach

14

The ascending series of switchbacks that is Thermal Ridge Drive brings Matt to the Vortex of Purity in the hills. The van chugs. Matt heads for the far reaches of the parking lot, away from the clot of cars near the campus entrance.

He knows this place, formerly a Catholic seminary, an art school, a psychiatric hospital, a military academy, and later the Laguna Beach Bible College, which closed its doors in 1960. He was eight when they boarded up the buildings and fenced the grounds. It took a year for the FOR SALE signs to go up. But Laguna Beach real estate was pricey even then, so little demand for a beat-up campus half-hidden in the hills, and so old that it ran on gas generators.

But Matt remembers the swanky chancellor's residence with its own blue-domed bell tower, the classrooms, a lecture hall, dining hall, gym, lap pool, athletic field, and dorms. Matt and Kyle used to prowl the weedy, debris-littered acres, hunting lizards and snakes that Kyle kept in his room in their bomb shelter house on Top of the World.

Standing in the parking lot, Matt carefully tears his new drawing of Jasmine from the sketchbook, folds it, and puts it in a back pocket of his shorts.

Then locks the Westfalia and walks across the lot toward a bright marquee where the old wooden Laguna Bible College sign once stood:

THE VORTEX OF PURITY
EVOLUTION
ENLIGHTENMENT
ECSTASY

A large, glittering gold Hamsa protrudes into the space between the words, taking up the bottom half of the marquee. Matt recognizes the Hamsa from one of the Mystic Arts World employees, Hamsa Luke Lucas, who has one tattooed across the top of his right hand. Luke calls it the Hand of the Goddess. To Matt the Hamsa is an intriguing symbol—a human right hand, open—with an eye staring out from below the fingers. It's supposed to protect you from the evil eye, and Luke swears it works. This marquee Hamsa is made of tiny gold bulbs that flicker and glow alluringly. The eye has a golden iris and a penetrating crimson pupil. Matt stands for a moment taking it in, watching the people walking around it, some of them also stopping to look. He smells food—cooked food, good food, food made with unusual spices—calling him from the auditorium.

There's a table set up at the entrance and Matt digs out a quarter for Sara the Skateboard Girl who said he was cute.

"Take any seat you'd like inside," she says.

"Thanks for the discount."

She looks him over, hands back the quarter. "You could use some food. It's after the Evolution, in the lobby."

Indeed it is: two long picnic tables of covered bowls, crockpots, and vessels, with paper plates, plastic utensils. Matt can't wait. Presiding in the lobby are some of the young people from the shoot at Thousand Steps beach, most of them dressed in loose white pantsuits, boys and girls both, all with pleasant expressions.

Matt takes a seat in the back to be closer to the food. The auditorium is almost full. He breathes the complex atmosphere of curry, incense, ocean, and hillside sage. The room is dimly lit except for the stage, which waits in bright light. The stage floor is a shiny finished maple, and the rug in its center is a rich arabesque of wine-red and blue. In the middle of the rug sits a thickly padded white leather chair with crimson piping and a small crimson pillow to support the lower back. Like a throne, Matt thinks. There's a mic on a swivel stand on one side of it.

He sees locals he recognizes, some of the older high school students and recent grads. Most of them are pretty in a wholesome, girl- or boy-next-door kind of way. Like Jazz, he thinks. The girls look eagerly toward the empty white throne, trading whispers, faces hopeful and eyes wide. The boys are more relaxed and skeptical, making cracks and smiling. Only a few in the crowd look like moms and dads.

The swami walks on. Short slow steps, arms out, palms together, fingers up. He's barefoot, the tops of his feet dark, and the soles pale pink as he walks.

As Matt remembers from Mystic Arts World, Mahajad Om is tall, weighty, and slow in motion. His crimson robe is shiny satin and reveals a wedge of gray chest. The robe sweeps up dramatically over his shoulders, buttressed by pads, Matt guesses, like a *Star Trek* villain. Mahajad's lustrous gray-black hair goes to his shoulders, the gray-white beard clear to his chest. His cheeks and forehead and eyes show no wrinkles, moles, or marks. His skin is unblemished, even with the spotlights bearing down. He looks to Matt like he could be anywhere from twenty to a hundred years old.

Now comes a ripple of applause as the swami approaches his white leather throne. Some in the crowd stand. But Mahajad Om quickly raises his hands to quell the clapping, and many of his orange-clad and apparently more experienced followers stand and do likewise to the audience. *Silence please! Silence please!*

Matt, who has risen, sits back down in the sudden silence, in which Swami Mahajad settles into his chair, reaching back to position the pillow before settling his weight.

Mahajad slowly draws in the microphone, taps it with one finger as he looks out at his audience.

His voice is smooth, subtly accented and surprisingly resonant.

"A stone falls into water and creates disturbing waves. These waves oscillate concentrically until, at last, the water returns to its condition of calm tranquility. Similarly, *all* action, on every plane, produces disturbance in the balanced harmony of the universe, and the vibrations so produced will continue to roll backward and forward . . . until equilibrium is restored."

His eyes twinkle and he looks ready to smile but he doesn't quite.

"Welcome. Peace be with you. Shantih, shantih, shantih."

Matt recognizes the last words of "The Waste Land," which was a favorite of Marybeth Benson, his sophomore English teacher. Miss Benson had told them that it was a Sanskrit word that meant something like "the peace that passeth all understanding." Matt had liked the poem, though it was confusing and scattered, like something that had blown up. Miss Benson said it was trying to capture the world after the horrors of World War I.

The swami continues in his smooth clear voice:

"The wicked man in prosperity may, all unknown to himself, be darkened and corroded with inward rust, while the good man under afflictions may be locked in a struggle of spiritual growth. No, God is not mocked; but also, let us always remember, He is not understood."

Then a pretty dark-haired young woman glides onstage from behind Mahajad. She wears a crimson robe like the swami's, and carries a sitar. It's a gleaming, intricately detailed, burnished thing, and large. She positions herself near the swami and gracefully lowers herself, resting the rounded body of the instrument on the rug.

The notes sound reluctant at first, ringing and lonely. Then the woman's fingers are traveling the neck in long strokes and the notes fall from the air like rain. The music is mysterious but inviting, and Matt gives himself over to its droning, twinkling energy.

When the music trails off, the swami speaks:

"Through evolution we become the stones that are born and reborn toward purity. Through enlightenment we become the water. Through ecstasy we become the waves that move through the water. We welcome you, new stones. You are the Evolved. You are on the path to seeing the world in a new way. Yours is a new reality."

Music again, then Matt hears the door clunk open behind him and turns to watch six young actors from today's Thousand Steps performance trailing up the aisle toward the stage. They're still in their beachwear. Three girls and three boys, one of them Sara, with her thick hair pulled back and spilling out of big plastic claw clips.

The veteran orange Vortexers stand and clap, quickly joined by Matt and the others. Swami Mahajad Om watches, still as a statue, his eyes wide and gleaming. The Evolvers line up in front of the stage, facing the audience, palms together at heart level, their expressions serious. They bow once, then head back out the way they've come in. Matt waves at Sara but she doesn't acknowledge him. The music continues and when Matt looks back, Swami Mahajad turns and small-steps his way offstage and out of sight.

Matt heads straight for the food.

15

Good thing he sat near the chow, because a lot of hungry young Vortex of Purity visitors are already having at it.

He puts the utensils in his shorts pocket, loads a plate, and heads outside. Sitting on one of the concrete benches, he remembers being here once with Kyle as they checked out a king snake they'd caught one spring day.

Now he watches the guests and followers mingling in the lobby and outside, where the night is cool. Two sharp-faced older men—in their forties, Matt guesses, and dressed in white suits over black T-shirts, their hands clasped in front of them—watch over the people like security guards. Matt catches glimpses of Sara, surrounded. The food is pretty good but it tastes a little funny, too.

When most of the audience has left, he goes back for seconds. It's picked over but there're still some noodles and vegetables. He wants to walk the grounds as he eats, see what the Vortex of Purity has done with the old campus.

Matt's ninth-grade history teacher said that the original seminary architecture is Spanish Revival. Its central feature is the bell tower adjacent to the chancellor's big residence. The tower is domed with cobalt blue tiles and often lit at night.

The buildings have their white plaster walls, rounded doors, and terra-cotta roof tiles. There are ornamental iron grates on many of the campus windows, and many painted tiles. The chapel looks like a small mission and sits in a grass meadow between the grand chancellor's quarters and the auditorium.

Matt looks out at the rolling grounds. Considers the former chancellor's residence and the blue-domed belfry on a rise at the far boundary of the property. He remembers the plywood that once covered all the vandalized windows and doors, the weeds that grew dense as ivy.

Now the central quad bustles with young men and women, most of them in street clothes but some in white, yellow, and orange pantsuits, and sandals. Some smile at him. The two serious looking men in the white suits stride by with alert expressions.

Matt walks past the former classrooms and small lecture halls, along a garden of paloverde, cacti, and happy looking succulents. He continues between two facing arcades of small apartments where he and Kyle used to chase and throw rocks at each other through the pane-less windows.

There are lights on within the arcades, and Matt wonders if the Vortex has many full-time students, or members, or worshippers, or whatever they're called. And what's the purpose of all this hospitality, he wonders. Camera Man directs his models here and Mahajad throws a banquet. Why? Recruitment? How much does the Vortex charge students who enroll? He remembers his mother's comment about how expensive the Vortex of Purity is.

Most important, would Jazz come here?

The Jazz who Matt knows, or thinks he knows, probably wouldn't have come here more than once. She is a seeker, yes, as her interest in the Bible, mysticism, and spirituality proves. An artist, too. But not a joiner. Not a follower. She's the opposite of that. Jazz the skeptical, the questioning, the unconvinced. She writes songs for herself and her ukulele, not for a band, because, as she once told him, "other people would stink them up."

But Matt knows from Laurel Kalina that Jazz has participated in at least one Thousand Steps shoot—on Tuesday of last week, two days before her first night gone.

Jasmine looked a little bummed by the whole scene. You know, bummed out but above it all, like she is.

Matt ponders why she did the photography thing at Thousand Steps. To show off? For the trip of doing something sexy in front of other people? To be a celebrity?

Which leads him to the Sapphire Cove parties of Jordan Cavore. No, Matt still can't picture her there. She would have fled, in spite of the curiosity that might have led her on, of which she has tons. In spite of what she said or didn't say to Austin Overton's friend Dana. She would have *fled* in superior disgust.

He continues past the arcades, sneakers crunching on the gravel walkway, the coastal mist tingling his skin and cooling his scabs. The old gym building actually looks good now, he thinks, with windows instead of plywood and no trash and weeds in the parking lot. The lap pool is full and lit, the surface a wobbling mirror. Bums used to make campfires and sleep there. He's never seen the place looking anything like this. Mahajad must make a lot of money.

Looking at the flat blue pool, Matt wonders where Jasmine is exactly right now. What, exactly, is she doing?

He stops at a trash can to toss his paper plate and utensils but wonders if there's any food left. Those veggies have a way of not sticking with you, and thirds would be nice.

The main parking lot is empty except for his mother's little van. But the auditorium door stands open and he sees light in the lobby.

Inside, Mahajad Om stands before a food table in his crimson robe, eating snow peas from a paper plate. A wheeled cart stands nearby, onto which the bowls and pots and the crockpots are being piled by two women, and apparently, by the swami himself. The women look Indian and to Matt's eye must be mother and daughter.

Mahajad looks at Matt, his eyes lively and his expression amused. "I am always hungry after an Evolution Ceremony. Did you enjoy it?"

"Yes, sir, I did."

The swami takes another bite then steps away and gestures to the table with his free hand. "Please to eat all you want."

With expressionless looks at Matt, the two women recede.

"Thank you, sir. I read 'The Waste Land' just a few weeks ago at school. So I know what 'shantih' means."

"It took me forty years to learn what 'shantih' means. Don't forget the snow peas. They are cooked in bacon fat left over from breakfast."

Matt fills his third plate while the swami stands and watches, bringing small forkfuls to his mouth. The women watch from a corner.

"You look familiar to me," says Mahajad. "Do you meditate at the Mystic Arts World?"

"No, but I help run the art gallery," Matt answers, suddenly very proud—in the presence of this man—to have a position other than paperboy.

"Maybe there is where I've seen you."

"Christian Clay is my boss. I don't get paid, though."

"There is greater pay than money."

"I get to read the art books and help hang the paintings."

Matt's thirds don't last long. The swami points to the table with his plastic fork, but his expression doesn't change. Deep in the thicket of hair and beard, his eyes really do seem to be laughing.

One more little plate can't hurt. They eat together standing and facing each other, Mahajad half a head taller and almost a body heavier than the hungry sixteen-year-old.

The two white-suited, black-shirted men come briskly in from outside, see that Mahajad is talking, assess Matt, and pass into the auditorium proper.

"Why did you come here tonight?" asks the swami.

"I got invited to see Sara evolve."

Matt senses that Mahajad approves his stated motive. The man says nothing for a long moment, just patiently eats with small bites, poking the fork with what looks like bemused concentration.

"But, like, actually," says Matt. "I was at the beach today, looking for my sister, Jasmine Anthony. She did the photo shoot last Tuesday at Thousand Steps. And we haven't seen her since Thursday evening. So, Mom filed a report. And I wanted to see if she might be there, again today. She wasn't. But I got an invitation to tonight. I have this . . ."

Matt puts his plate on the table and works the new Jasmine sketch from his pocket. Unfolds and holds it up for Mahajad to see.

Again, the happy eyes and expression of amusement on his dark face. Matt waits, hears the far-off generators through the night. They drone like the sitar. It's almost peaceful.

"No. I have not seen Jasmine here. My memory is very good. But I feel your love in the way you say her name. Tell me about her."

Matt isn't surprised that his sister is not a Vortex follower. Maybe Sara the Skateboard Girl got Jasmine mixed up with someone else here. He's relieved. It's okay to take a wrong trail, he thinks. It's how you find the right trail.

He describes his sister to the swami, trying to be accurate and objective, not like a brother but like Walter Cronkite on TV. He tells Mahajad Om that he doesn't think his sister ran away.

"You love her very much," says Mahajad. "You will find her soon and your family will be together as one again. I have something for you."

He puts his plate on the table beside Matt's, gets a clean one from the stack and heaps it with the last of the food. From the wheeled cart he takes up a long skinny box of tin foil, swings out a good length of it and wraps it around the heavy paper plate, twice.

"I never learned to drive a car, but one of my women can give you a ride home."

"I have a van. Thank you, swami."

"Shantih."

"Thank you, your . . . holiness?"

"Just swami."

"This is for you."

Matt has already written his phone number on the back of his new Jasmine sketch.

The swami looks at the sketch again. His black eyes are wet.

"There are many missing souls. Even in beautiful places. Bonnie, the girl from the flyers in town, evolved here. I wish I had spoken to her. Maybe I could have intervened, even if only spirit-to-spirit. One of the reasons I created the Vortex of Purity is to fill the emptiness that leads people into unhappiness and wrong behavior. To fill the soul with the enlightenment that leads to ecstasy, which is the conqueror of emptiness. And I always feed the hungry, because I am one of them. Go in peace, Matt."

Laurel's sixteenth birthday party at Brooks Street beach: a warm summer afternoon, twenty bouncy girls and skinny boys sunning, surfing, skim-boarding, sneaking beers from coolers and disguising them with plastic Coke and 7Up sleeves.

Over hot dogs and potato salad, Laurel opens Matt's gift box, which he has wrapped in Sunday's *Register* color comics page. She pulls the small framed oil painting of herself in the Gauguin tableau from the box, and smiles. His heart seems to expand. He bought new paints and worked hard to get it halfway decent.

Next, the bottle of Heaven Sent perfume he knows she likes, purchased at Bushard's Pharmacy downtown. Laurel smiles again, blows him a kiss across the loose circle of young people— some reclining in canvas beach chairs, some sitting on towels, some sprawled directly on the warm sand—all slathered in Coppertone or Piz Buin or baby oil right out of the bottle to amplify the tanning power of the sun. The blown kiss makes the teenagers cheer loudly with fake surprise. Laurel, Matt sees, doesn't look embarrassed at all.

Other gifts: a stereo LP—*The Songs of Leonard Cohen*— which is left in a bag and stashed in one of the coolers so it won't melt in the sun, a book of poems by Rod McKuen, 45s from the Beatles and Aretha, a packet of patchouli incense, a tie-dye scarf, a glass bead necklace and earrings, an anklet of small pearls—Laurel's birthstone—given to her by an obviously admiring Lance Gentry. Even as a sophomore, Lance is a varsity tennis star and a renowned surfer. He's popular and has long hair and a good complexion. He kneels before Laurel to attach the anklet, unleashing a storm of envy in Matt.

Who sits cross-legged in the sand, blanket over his legs to hide the ugly knee scabs. Furlong and his partner march six handcuffed hippies toward Pacific Coast Highway and Moby Cop. Furlong is smiling and talking to them, apparently happy with his catch.

Matt watches Laurel as closely and often as he can without her knowing. She catches him twice, which, if he's figuring right, means she could be doing the same to him. Matt's heart seems to expand, again. He's had this feeling before, in connection with Laurel Kalina. And sometimes in connection with other people, or animals. Daisy, the family puppy. Calypso, a fluffy calico kitten he found downtown on Forest Ave. one rainy Saturday. Kyle, standing in the batter's box at the high school playoffs. Jazz, playing her ukulele at the beach that night. He's pretty sure this feeling is love. It's much stronger now, the older he gets.

Toward sunset they're alone, walking the low-tide beach. He has taken Laurel's hand, which is warm and strong. Her half-Hawaiian skin is already dark, and summer doesn't even start until next week. Her shoulders are round and her arms are sleek and her breasts are all movement and intrigue within her black and yellow hibiscus print bikini. She's got her beach towel around her waist, reminding Matt of Gauguin's native islanders.

"I made those calls I told you about," she says. "To my friends, about Jasmine. I just got the call I didn't want to get. I can't tell you how I know this. There are people I have to protect, good people. But she was at Jordan Cavore's Sapphire Cove party last Friday night."

"How do you know?"

"I just told you I can't say how."

"But it's true?"

"One hundred percent. Don't ask me any more questions about it. She was *there*."

"Will you tell the cops?"

"I will not. You can, but leave me out of it. I'll do anything to help Jazz, but I can't betray a friend."

That low thrumming in his ears again. He'd missed Jazz in Sapphire Cove by one day. One day! Confirming what Officer Brigit Darnell suspected as to why Julie's van was parked there to begin with.

"I feel terrible having to tell you, Matt."

Not as terrible as you would if you knew what goes on there, Matt thinks.

"Let's find a place and watch the sunset," she says.

They find a rock outcropping shaped like a horseshoe, back near the cliff, a good view to the west. The sky has gone gray-orange and the sun is a perfect half circle above the horizon. People stop and watch, their figures almost colorless in the vanishing light.

Matt and Laurel spread their towels side by side in the little cove, and sit with their legs almost touching. His skinned kneecaps burn. He takes her hand. Laurel has sprayed on some Heaven Sent before adding it to her sister's cooler for transport back home. Matt smells it on her, a sweet, almost powdery scent that Sheila at the pharmacy said was the perfect perfume for a girl becoming a woman.

"Kind of cool tonight," she says.

Matt sidles closer and puts his arm around her. She leans into him. His knee shrieks with fresh pain. He sees his rival's pearl anklet and wishes he'd thought of that, but then, it's way more money than the perfume. He can also smell her salty hair and the Coppertone on her skin.

Laurel talks on about her friends, filling Matt in on some surprising romances he's been unaware of. His arm falls asleep but he will not remove it from Laurel Kalina's warm, fragrant shoulder. He cranes his neck so that he can see the sunset, unfolding spectacularly, and still see Laurel's profile.

She tells him about her writing assignment for the UC Irvine workshop her mom got her into: five three-page, double-spaced, typed character sketches based on people she actually knows. All five of whom were at this party today. Thus her "nosey curiosity regarding their private lives!"

Matt wonders again exactly how Laurel came to know of Jasmine's Sapphire Cove appearance on Friday night. Wonders too if Laurel knows what really goes on there. She certainly might. She's talked to somebody who was there, someone who knows Jasmine, right? One thing he's coming to know about Laurel is her fierce curiosity about the people around her. Her eye for detail and nose for facts. Like she's compiling characters for a book.

Matt realizes that he can tell Laurel very little of what he's learned or done since his sister vanished from home. Not Bonnie Stratmeyer's mysterious injuries and presence at one or more Jordan Cavore parties. Not Jazz's sleeping with Austin Overton up in Big Yellow after his Sandpiper show. Not that he'd been in Sapphire Cove Saturday night at an orgy, was hit in the head with Jordan Cavore's bong, and later crashed his bike near the guardhouse on PCH. He doesn't like lying or omitting to Laurel Kalina. What he really wants is to unload everything, every detail and discovery, so she'll have his secrets too. To have a secret sharer.

"They found Mom's van parked in Sapphire Cove without a guest permit," Matt says. "The cops towed it."

"But no Jasmine?"

"No. And I don't see why she would just leave the van for so long it gets towed. Unless, you know, she planned on getting back to it and wasn't allowed to."

"Like, prevented?"

"Not *like* prevented—*prevented*."

"That's scary."

"She left her ukulele in it. And some good eight-tracks."

Through his fallen-asleep arm, Matt can feel Laurel take a long deep breath. She turns to look at him, their faces very close. "What if she ran away from home and doesn't *want* to go back? Doesn't even want to be found?"

Of course, Matt's been asking himself those same hard questions. But he just can't make his sister's disappearance from home into something she did on purpose. Sure, she'd run away with a girlfriend when she was eleven, given all of them a scare when they rode their bicycles to a movie theater twelve miles inland and got picked up by the cops. Each girl had had a rucksack full of clothes and food, and confessed that they'd run away to see the world but maybe made a mistake and decided to see *One Hundred and One Dalmatians* instead.

But that was different. Since then, she'd never talked of doing anything like that. Never seemed sick of it all. Never furious. Never so down she couldn't function. Maybe she wasn't happy like a girl can be happy, but Jazz at eighteen wasn't a girl anymore. And so what if she's arrogant and aloof and acidly critical of herself and others? So what if she calls her mother a delusional stoner right to her face, and her father a redneck asshole, and Matt a zit-faced jack-off? And so what if she sneaks beers and throws the empties under the bed? So what if she's had sex? Her just running away still didn't add up. Wouldn't she have taken more clothes? Her suitcase and hair stuff and makeup and records and books?

Coming from Laurel, though, the idea of Jazz running away sounds more possible.

"I just don't think she ran away," he says.

Her face is still so close he can feel her exhale on his skin. Eyes like black ponds. He feels a shudder go down Laurel's back.

"I don't either, Matt. But if she didn't run away on her own, then maybe she's been *lured* away."

"By Cavore?" he says. "To his parties for rich old men?"

Again, this notion collides with Matt's belief that Jordan Cavore and his friends would truly disgust his sister. And send her running for . . . where? For who? Not back to her drafty bungalow on Third Street with the starving pantry and a bathroom shared by three—soon to be four again. No, not home, apparently. Not to a friend's, either—he's called every one of them he can think of, many of them twice. Motels and rooms for rent? Too expensive. Could Jazz endure Sapphire Cove for money? If so, then she could be almost anywhere, hiding out, impossible to find. Jazz as a prostitute is not imaginable.

"I can't picture her in that scene," says Laurel.

"Lured," he says. He hadn't thought of that word to explain what might have happened to his sister. To a fisherman it has a specific, deadly meaning.

"You can kiss me if you want," she says.

"I really want."

His first kiss, not counting spin-the-bottle at Carolyn Plath's party on Linden Street in the eighth grade.

So, he like, knows what he's doing.

Two hours later, his tongue and throat muscles sore and his balls aching mightily, Matt treats Laurel to another wallet-busting ice cream sundae at the Sunshine Inn.

Then walks her home and hugs her awkwardly good night on her front porch. The smell of Heaven Sent coming off her is one hundred percent unforgettable, he thinks.

"This was the best birthday of my life," she says.

"Me too."

"I like you. If you were a story I'd sit up in bed tonight and read you."

"I like you too, Laurel."

"You can call me anytime. I'm in the phone book, you know."

"I'll call."

"We'll get Jazz back. She's too smart to get tangled up with bad people."

Ten minutes later he's walking into the weekly program at Mystic Arts World on Coast Highway, where—as hundreds of dizzying, pink, yellow, and orange Flower Power posters hung all over town have proclaimed—Dr. Timothy Leary, pictured on the poster, smiling widely, will tonight present:

WHAT IS THE PSYCHEDELIC EXPERIENCE?

Matt thinks that his chance of finding Jazz here is one in a thousand.

He'll take it.

One of these posters is the one on her bedroom wall.

17

Mystic Arts World is dense with smoke and bodies. The smoke is mostly incense and tobacco, as Furlong and his fellow cops just yesterday busted and dragged off four hippies sharing a joint on the sidewalk outside. Matt scans the faces for Jazz but it's going to take him some time to get a good look at everyone.

Christian Clay, standing with a crowd at the meditation room entrance, waves Matt over. He's a wiry young man, with bushy hair and mustache and goatee. Something knowing in his eyes.

He sizes up Matt with his open stare, then leads him to a semiprivate corner of the meditation room, where Christian's enormous *Cosmic Mandala* painting hangs on the back wall.

"Why didn't you tell me your sister ran away?"

"She didn't run away."

"I'd rather not read it in the paper and see her on flyers around town," says Christian. "It's important to tell your friends when bad trips go down. Friends can help."

Matt apologizes then tells him what he's learned about Jasmine's whereabouts. Lets his vision drift around the crowded room in search of her. He tells Christian that he doesn't think Jazz just ran away to sleep at Big Yellow or go to Jordan Cavore's parties.

Which gets him a sharp look from the artist. "You should talk to Johnny about this. He and the brothers know the town."

Just the mention of Johnny Grail brings a subtle thrill to

Matt. Grail is the founder of the Brotherhood of Eternal
Love, which of course owns this store. Grail is borderline
worshipped by the BEL but detested by the cops and the
straights. Leary openly adores him; Furlong wants his head
on a platter.

To Matt, Grail is a contradictory knot tied with truth,
falsehood, and mystery. Matt knows from the *News-Post* that
Grail is in his early twenties, married with two kids, grew
up in Anaheim. Beyond that, Grail is rumored to be a former high school wrestler, hot-rod driver, and street fighter.
After experimenting with a variety of recreational drugs,
Grail allegedly took LSD one day and found God. Matt has
overheard Grail here at MAW, talking excitedly about finding
Jesus Christ and the Buddha through LSD, saying everyone
should take acid—free your consciousness, find your soul, and
save the world.

Some call Grail a mystic—charismatic, spiritually advanced,
and generous. Others say that he's a profiteer who distributes
LSD, as well as powerful opium-laced hashish, smuggled into
Laguna from Afghanistan by his daring BEL pirates. Matt's
heard that Grail is rich. That he gives LSD away to those
who haven't tried it yet or can't afford it. That he lives fru-
gally out in Dodge City with his family. Others know he is
amassing huge drug profits and burying cash in steel drums
out in the rough hills around Dodge City. That he's buying an
island to sail away to.

The Great Johnny Grail takes Matt into a small office
behind the meditation room. There's an old steel desk and
folding chairs, a floor safe that looks straight out of the Wild
West, metal grocery-store shelves cluttered with books and
papers.

Grail takes a hit from a cobalt-blue bong; offers it to Matt,
who declines. The dope the BEL smokes would melt his face,
as he found out once before.

They sit across the desk from each other. Grail is small but
muscular and he has kind eyes. Plenty of hair and a scant

beard. He looks impish. Christian calls him a leprechaun. He's got on a black Mystic Arts World T-shirt with a swirling white design on it—an ancient calendar, maybe, or some kind of cosmic symbol. Matt has the feeling that Grail is focused totally on him in this moment.

"I heard about Jazz running off," Grail says. "Is she back?"

"She didn't run off, I don't think."

"I put two of her posters up in the windows. That foxy lady cop brought them by."

Grail listens to Matt's account of Jasmine's not coming home for five nights running. Of her two confirmed sightings, and her mother's van found in Sapphire Cove. Of the fact that Bonnie Stratmeyer had gone to one of Jordan Cavore's Sapphire Cove parties and been found dead and bruised at Thalia not long after. He hopes Darnell will forgive him for sharing their secret about Bonnie.

Johnny Grail takes an enormous hit from the bong. From the joint he smoked with Leary and Grail and Christian, Matt remembers the smoke expanding in his lungs, and the scary sensation that his lungs might burst. He'd gagged up a river of smoke. But Grail holds it forever, then lets it out in a billowing jet. He smiles and his eyes widen. A tiny little cough.

"Man, that's a lot of bad Karma for Jasmine. I like her. She's choice and smart. She's into mysticism, and the older Eastern ways of dealing with what we think is reality."

Matt has seen proof of that: all those books on the flimsy shelves in Jasmine's room. Almost as many books as record albums. He can picture Jasmine out in the MAW book department, checking out the new arrivals. Books and music are expensive unless you buy used, which Jasmine doesn't. She doesn't have a steady job. She's done some modeling—not the phony Thousand Steps kind of modeling—but real modeling for an agency. It didn't pay much. She worked scooping ice cream one summer at the Sunshine Inn. And briefly at the Jolly Roger like her mom.

Suddenly Matt feels woozy and off-center, a contact high in a small smoky room.

Grail stares at him with kindly, wide-open eyes. It occurs to Matt that in spite of his apparent attention, Johnny Grail could actually be a million light years away from here right now. *Should* be a million light years away, given the powerful stuff he's smoking.

"She buys books here, and albums at the Sound Spectrum," Matt says. "Then, you know, clothes and makeup and music lessons. I've always wondered how she pays for things."

He wonders if this leap of conversation is logical or if the smoke has made him overly suspicious.

Grail freshens the bong bowl from a baggie in the desk drawer, then takes another massive draw. Holds it in forever than exhales hugely. Another small cough. It smells like a jungle in here to Matt: humid and green and hot. Which makes him think of Kyle. Which bums him out. Which is what happens when you're high—your mind runs off to places you don't want to be.

"We give her work sometimes," Grail says. "Nothing steady, but sometimes Jasmine makes deliveries to customers who can't leave home. Old, sick, paranoid people. Like half of Laguna! Just kidding."

"How much do you pay her?"

"Just store credit, like the art books Christian gives you."

Matt feels the dope smoke in his brain, making time pass more slowly. Hears "Mr. Tambourine Man" from out in the store. Thinks Johnny Grail really does look like a leprechaun.

"Your mom was in Dodge City yesterday looking for a place to rent," says Grail. "She put up some posters of your sister, too. And passed them out door-to-door."

"A place to rent? *Really?*"

"Yeah, really. What's wrong with that?"

"All the drugs and cops and busts. Dodge is in the paper every week."

"Yeah, man, but there's a lot of very cool brothers and sisters out in Dodge. I'm raising my two kids in Dodge and I wouldn't do that just anywhere. The papers blow everything up. It's just capitalist, bummer-driven journalism."

But what worries Matt more than the quality of journalism about drugs and cops and busts is why his mother would want to move there. She hadn't said anything to him about it. His next thought is: living in Dodge City would add another half a mile of pedaling to his paper route every day, and anytime he needed to go to town. To and from school, too. Ever think of that, Mom?

"Is anything for rent there?"

"Sure. It's who you know, and she knows half the people out there because they love the Jolly Roger."

"Did she get a place?"

"You didn't know she was looking, did you? Sorry man. I didn't mean to freak you out."

"No, I knew she was looking. For sure. Just not there."

"Well, Dodge City is as close to heaven on earth as you can get," says Grail. "A very cool place. It's all art and music and surfing. Almost everybody is young. Freedom, man. Everybody shares. No material trips at all. Establishment unwelcome. It's cheap and close to town and you can walk up into the canyon, all the way to the lakes or the Living Caves or Top of the World if you want. Deer and quail and coyotes. Raccoons and they say mountain lions but I've never seen one. And bobcats. I have seen them. Wildflowers in the spring. There's a bunch of us, we hike to the peak near Top of the World on Sunday mornings. Watch the sunrise. Chant and worship whatever gods we choose. Totally spiritual and cosmic. Take off our clothes if we want. Let love in. No egos. Stay for hours. Sometimes 'til sunset."

In Matt's smoky mind, it sounds pretty good, except for the naked part. Maybe Julie can get a place that's cheaper than Third Street, but has enough room for him not to live in a garage. Enough room for Kyle when he gets home, and for Jazz to have her privacy. Maybe two bathrooms. No Nelson Pedley!

"She was hoping to find some work out there, too," says Grail. "Something she could do from home."

"Like what?"

"There's not much. Housekeeping maybe. Tutoring or babysitting the kids. Kids all over the place out there. When I saw your mom yesterday, she had just gotten off work. And wearing the stupid pirate garb they make her wear."

"She doesn't enjoy that costume."

"Chauvinist piggish to be sure. Matt, let's go hear what Tim has to say about the psychedelic experience."

18

Matt squeezes into the standing-only crowd in the back of the meditation room, with Christian and Grail and some of the brothers. The high ceiling is pale with smoke and the branches of the potted ficus reach into it. Christian's grand, explosive *Cosmic Mandala* presides over all.

Leary stands at the podium looking not at all like the college professor he is. He may be a man nourished by knowledge and admiration but to Matt he looks more like an outdoorsman, a surfer or fisherman maybe. He looks over six feet tall and is well built. He has over-the-collar sun-bleached blond hair and amicable blue eyes. Well-tanned, with a wide-open white Mexican wedding shirt and baggy linen pants. There's a boyish merriment in his face, something of the prankster. He's quick to smile. Even amplified by a mic, his voice is earnest and pleasant.

Leary says he's a victim of the cops and the Establishment press, which gets a rowdy response from the crowd. Says he's not a pusher of LSD or anything else, except the right of any adult to choose what goes into his or her body as guaranteed by the Constitution. Whether you want to kill yourself suddenly with cyanide or slowly with cigarettes, it's up to you.

As if on cue, Furlong and Darnell come in from Coast Highway, the crowd parting for them. Furlong is scowling and Darnell smiling. Catcalls and curses and pig snorts from the audience. Someone turns the ceiling lights up high so the intruders are fully displayed. The MAW customers have been especially hostile toward the cops since Furlong pulled the allegedly obscene drawings and astrological sex-position chart off the gallery wall and booked them into evidence at the station. Christian and Matt and one of Christian's lawyer friends had gone downtown the very next day and gotten them back, made copies, and hung them in the windows facing busy Coast Highway where they could offend thousands of people a day.

"Officers!" Leary calls out. "Welcome to Mystic Arts World and to the Brotherhood of Eternal Love, and to the very first night of the rest of your lives!"

Furlong stands with his hands on his hips, facing the boos and snorts; Darnell turns in a circle, smile gone but waving. Matt wishes they wouldn't call her a pig. He uses the newly brightened lights to search the many faces for Jasmine. But she's not here, just as he knew she wouldn't be. For the hundredth time Matt feels in his gut that Jasmine hasn't just run away from home. Feels it really strong now. Something else has happened. Is it the secondhand pot making him feel this way now? Afraid and anxious? He doesn't think so. He *should* feel afraid and anxious.

The ceiling lights cut through the smoke and the *Cosmic Mandala* floats in the upper layer like an artifact from the mists of creation. Matt enjoys his secondhand high right now, decides marijuana isn't so bad. Darnell catches his eye and all he can think to do is wave to her.

"People, people!" Leary calls out, the mic close for volume. "Nobody is as far out as a cop, so let's not be critical. Officers, join us! Learn about the psychedelic experience. Don't judge us and we will not judge you."

Someone turns the lights back down and the boil of ridicule from the crowd lowers to a simmer. Matt watches Furlong and Darnell retreat from the meditation room then pass from his field of vision into the front of the store, and, he guesses, make for the exit. Chants of *aloha* follow them out.

In their smoky wake, four bikers swagger in, two of them

huge and two skinny. The muttering falls to silence. They've got dirty black jeans and harness boots, wallet chains and hunting knives holstered on their belts. Long tangled hair and beards, vests and back patches that read: HESSIANS. The logo is a skull with a sword thrust through the back and out the front, between the eyes.

"Welcome, friends," says Leary. "I've never met an outlaw I didn't like."

To Matt, they seem to be looking for someone, just like he is. He notes that Johnny has disappeared. The Hessians finally turn their attention on Leary, then they turn and walk back out.

"Brother bikers!" Leary calls out. "When confounded, go mystical! Stay and be! Rest your bodies and expand your minds! Experience!"

Nothing from the bikers but a slamming door.

Leary smiles and waves and continues his program, explaining how he based his book, *The Psychedelic Experience*, on *The Tibetan Book of the Dead*, which he and two colleagues translated into English and is *NOT* "an embalmer's guide," but a book to teach the living *HOW* to die. It is *FOR* the living. It's a passage guide, he says. A guide to attaining the next of the many higher planes of consciousness a person will experience in their several lives and incarnations. Another way of achieving this higher consciousness is through psychedelic compounds such as peyote, mescaline, and lysergic acid diethylamide, or LSD.

Leary introduces the three basic stages—"Bardos"—of the journey in *The Tibetan Book of the Dead*.

First Bardo: The Period of Ego-Loss or Non-Game Ecstasy. Second Bardo: The Period of Hallucinations.

And the Third Bardo: The Period of Re-Entry.

Matt has almost no idea what Leary is talking about, but by the silence in the room he assumes that everybody else does. He looks around at their expressions, very church-like, based on the several times his mother and father took the kids to church.

After the program, reappeared Johnny Grail invites Matt and Christian to stay in the meditation room after the crowd leaves, just hang with a few of the brothers and Tim and Rosemary, have a toke and brainstorm and experience. Matt knows that to "experience" means to "trip," which means LSD. Matt has heard that Leary and Grail ingest spectacular quantities of acid, almost a competition, and Grail always takes the most. Matt has heard them bragging how great acid sex is, especially if your old lady is tripping too.

The four men and four women sit in a circle on small, plentiful Afghan prayer rugs that MAW sells by the pallet load, perfect for meditating, decorating cribs, your dog. Matt has heard that the rugs are used in smuggling by the BEL daredevils who risk prison or beheading for importing the powerful opium-laced hashish dragon balls. He believes it, based on the numbers of rugs, and of street dealers who have recently tried to peddle him those balls. If Matt is seeing things correctly, even his mom has gotten herself hooked—or almost hooked—on them. Now she's thinking of moving out to Dodge City? What if she gets into acid?

They pass the hookah stuffed with hashish around but Matt declines. As he passes the billowing contraption to Rosemary—Tim's wife—he wonders exactly why Grail has invited him here. He's too young, not BEL or prospective BEL, just an untalented minor with a volunteer "job" helping Christian run the art gallery.

Leary looks through the smoke at him. Grins at Matt with an unlikely combination of guile and candor. He has smile lines that radiate from his eyes like a cat's whiskers.

"What did you think?" Leary asks Matt.

"Good program."

"That's what I needed to hear. You are everything, you know. You young. The hope of the world and its future."

Matt's high hasn't worn off yet, and he feels its grip of suspicion. Everybody's eyes are all pupil now and he wonders
how much LSD they've taken.

"Has your lovely sister come back home?" Leary asks.

Matt senses unanimous attention on him. "No, sir."

Even through the smoke Matt can see the small flinch of
disappointment on Leary's face. No cat whiskers now.

"My own son is about her age," he says. "Matt, I have to
say that Jazz is one of the most beautiful young people I've
ever known. Her consciousness is high, even though her ego
is very strong. I hope she's become a pilgrim, not a victim."

"She didn't run away, if that's what you mean," says Matt.

Leary asks Rosemary if she agrees.

Matt looks to Rosemary, seated to his left. She's whole-
somely elegant, dark haired, and has a winning smile. Beautiful for someone over thirty, Matt sees. She's got to be almost
as old as his mother.

"Anyone can be born with a lovely exterior," says Rosemary,
setting her hand on his knee. "But you have to be skeptical in
this age of brainwashing and Establishment lies."

"Right on," says Johnny.

"I saw her two weeks ago here in the store," says Tim. "She
was packing up a big box of books to take to a customer too ill
to come here on his own. I admired her generosity."

"She was getting paid for it," Matt says.

"In books," says Grail.

"Beautiful," says the former Harvard psychologist. "She'll
be back, Matt. She will be back."

Shades of Mahajad, thinks Matt. All these wise old men
who think they can predict the future. And old women saying she'll be back, but thinking that maybe she ran away on
purpose.

Matt stands. Wobbles. He's higher now, after another jolt of
secondhand smoke. "Thanks. It's late."

Grail rises to walk him out, steers him through the main
part of the store, the door key jangling on a piece of driftwood

in his hand. Stops at the main cash register and picks up a book from a stack of books with notes rubber-banded to them. Sold copies, Matt surmises. Hold-for notes or delivery addresses attached.

"I'd like to ask you a favor, Matt. We have a very good but very ill customer up on Diamond—Patricia Trinkle. She's ordered a book, but with Jazz not around, it's just sitting here. You wouldn't mind, would you, on your paper route tomorrow? Just set it on the porch? She leaves a box outside for deliveries."

Matt studies Grail's happy, trusting face.

"Diamond isn't on my route, Johnny."

"Oh man, I thought it was! I totally spaced. So sorry. I'll deliver it myself. But look at this thing!"

He pulls the note off and hands the book to Matt. It's a black leather-bound *Tibetan Book of the Dead,* with gold foil filigree on the cover and beautiful embossed gold letters. It's wrapped in thick clear plastic.

The idea comes to Matt—maybe because he's stoned—that this favor might, in some cosmic way, bring him closer to Jasmine. Bring him onto her plane. He, doing something that *she herself* has done. He might even ask the sick woman about her. Maybe Jazz had disclosed something important to her . . .

"I'll do it."

Grail takes the book with an impish smile, slides the index card under the rubber band and gives the heavy volume back to Matt. Gives Matt a grinding little laugh that sounds conspiratorial.

"I really dig this, Matt. Thanks and bitchen. I'll give you some store credit as payment. You're helping out Jazz, too. Sending some good Karma her way."

"Okay, cool."

"Anytime tomorrow is good. You'll see a blue plastic milk crate on the porch. That's it. Just knock three times on the screen door and she'll know the book is there."

Matt walks north on PCH in the foggy night. Stops at Fade in the Shade to look at Jasmine's MISSING poster in the window. He thinks she looks afraid, but he knows it's just himself. He tries to clear his fear but the hash smoke packs a wallop. He still can't believe that he can see pictures of her all over town but he can't see her actual, breathing, present self.

Third Street is just a few blocks from Mystic Arts World. So he takes the shortcut, Park to Mermaid.

Where, as he approaches the base of the Third Street hill, he sees the girl running up Third toward him.

She reminds him of Jasmine, but a lot of girls remind him of her.

It can't be.

It's the damned hash.

But really, it *could* be.

Then he *knows* it's her, zig-zagging weakly up the middle of the street, breathing hard, barefoot, in a billowing orange dress. Her blond hair is flying.

"Jazz!"

She looks in his direction, stumbling and searching for him as if she's blind or confused or not sure where to look.

Suddenly: headlights in pursuit behind her, catching up fast. The high-rev whine of a small engine. Matt squints into the brights, sprinting for Jazz. But the vehicle overtakes and passes her, then skids to a stop.

Jasmine is almost to their house when two men barge from the car and into the headlamp beams. Within a bright cloud of the tire smoke and fog, one of them lifts Jazz off her feet, as if she's no heavier than a scarecrow, and locks his free hand over her mouth. The vehicle idles in the exhaust and fog and the two men carry struggling Jazz back into the darkness.

Matt hears a door slide open and slam shut, then the high-pitched scream of acceleration.

He dodges hard to his left as the car comes at him, the headlights nearly blinding him. He leaps onto the sidewalk in front of the phone company building. Suddenly, the vehicle carves a U-turn across Third and goes whining away from him, toward Laguna Canyon Road.

Matt sees that it's not a car at all but a late-model Volkswagen van.

He pushes off from the building and runs after it with all his adrenalin-crazed might. Long strides, fists up. But the van doesn't putter like his mom's. Matt can see as it passes the cop house streetlamp that it's a newer model, with probably twice the horsepower as the Westfalia. You can't kidnap Jazz Anthony in front of the cop station, he thinks: you cannot do this.

The van goes left on Ocean, toward Pacific Coast Highway. So Matt cuts left at Forest, which runs parallel with Ocean and will hit PCH at a signal a hundred yards up, where it will have to stop if the light is red.

Forest is a crowded retail street—boutiques and galleries and restaurants and Bushard's where he got Laurel's Heaven Sent, and the stationers and the donut place and the jewelry stores and his art supply store. Matt flies past them all, dodging the occasional tourists and locals out with their dogs, his lungs swelling and emptying, his legs working, the damned *Tibetan Book of the Dead* still in one hand, its protective plastic slick with sweat.

Out ahead he sees the signal at PCH—red! He forces his young body into another gear, his highest, his fifth, to get to the light before it changes and he can catch the van and . . . and . . . do what?

Matt angles across Forest to save a few steps, gets honked at, and he's still a hundred feet from PCH. The traffic light goes to green and the late-model hippie van—which Matt sees is a two-tone white over green—passes through.

He runs south on PCH at the light, watching the van trundle past Park with its precious cargo, taking away his last real chance to catch up. It accelerates away.

Matt stops at Park. The van is out of sight and he's so winded he has to drop the *Tibetan Book of the Dead* to the sidewalk, put both hands on his stinging knees and breath as fast as he can. Two-tone white over green, he thinks, panting:

two-tone white over green. The same vintage and color VW van that Joint-and-Martini Man saw down at Thalia the morning Bonnie Stratmeyer was found. Still panting, he realizes he was too addled by adrenalin and caught by the headlights to get a good look at the license plate.

You blew it, he thinks. You had her, you had her, you had her.

Matt looks up Coast Highway at the cars and the traffic coming at him. Picks up the book and runs for the cop house.

19

Hounded and haunted by images of Jasmine running for her life, and vowing never to be outrun by a hippie van again, the next morning Matt drives illegally to the DMV and passes both the written test and the actual driving test.

Now he heads toward home, his first journey as a fully licensed driver. Inwardly, he berates himself for not having done this earlier. He could have caught up with Jazz driving Julie's van, right? But he didn't have the guts to take the driving test until it was too late.

Back home he finally manages to get his father by phone. Matt tells him what happened and Bruce goes quiet for a long moment. Always a bad sign.

"Expect me," Bruce says.

"You've said that before."

"I've got a few things to nail down first," he says.

And hangs up.

Matt helps Tommy load his papers onto the driveway behind the Westfalia. He can't stop thinking about what he saw last night. Still can't believe that the desk officer on duty thought he was somehow mistaken. He'd asked if Matt had been smoking dope or maybe tripping. When he had finally gotten home early in the morning, wholly unable to sleep, Matt had furiously sketched out what he'd seen with his own good eyes, in twenty-ten vision, tested by the school nurse, best in the ninth grade at LBHS.

"Now that you got your license, you want a vehicle route when one comes up?" Tommy asks.

"I'd like to make more money."

"More papers, more money, Matt. But it means wear and tear on this old van, and insurance and gas. Up to thirty-six cents a gallon now."

"Sign me up for a car route."

"There's a wait. Heard anything out of Jazz?"

"No, Tommy."

"I worry about her. Back home in Asbury Park, Elke Meier ran away from home and never came back. And she was really clean-cut and smart. Like Jasmine. Maybe the posters will help."

"Jasmine didn't run away."

Matt does not recount last night's event for Tommy. First of all, Darnell asked him not to tell the press or anybody else about it. The cops want to work this white-on-green VW van lead quietly for now, and if the bad guys know their vehicle has been seen, they just might leave it in the garage for a good long while. Second, Matt's exhausted after going over Jazz's abduction with the doubtful desk officer, and later with Darnell and later again with the very skeptical Sgt. Furlong, who asked pointedly if Matt had been smoking dope with Johnny and Tim and Christian last night before he and Darnell had come in. You look a little dazed to me, Furlong had said. Matt said no, he'd tried pot months ago and didn't like it—a half-truth only.

"You know, we've got a story in the paper today, about Bonnie Stratmeyer's autopsy," says Tommy. "They're saying she drowned. An accident maybe. But maybe not. And she had drugs in her that the coroner could not identify. So the FBI is helping."

Bad news is failing to surprise Matt. It's everywhere he goes.

But his route goes without a hitch, even with the rod and tackle box strapped behind him. He just pedals harder, takes the corners easier. No dogs today, the Coiner paper perfectly porched, nice words from Miranda and Mrs. Zahara. They're worried sick about Jazz, and Matt can tell they both feel somewhat responsible, since Jasmine's disappearance commenced in the wake of hers and Miranda's connivance. He actually finishes his deliveries early.

He arrives at the two-story home of Patricia Trinkle, the MAW customer on Diamond Street. The house is surrounded by walls of bougainvillea in eye-shimmering violets and hot pinks. The hedge has a cutout for a gate. When Matt opens and closes it behind him, a bell chimes brightly.

The front yard is a square of healthy green grass and three bird baths, all with gurgling fountains. Two doves in the far bath look up at him then go back to their drinking.

The walkway is brick and the house a Craftsman style, with pillars and a raised wooden porch. Matt takes one more look at the heavy, handsome *Tibetan Book of the Dead* and sets it in the blue milk bottle crate near the screen door.

In the blue crate, propped up on the far side to face him, is a square white envelope with the letters M.A. typed on.

Matt lifts it out and feels it, sensing a cash tip.

Inside is a once-folded twenty-dollar bill, crisp, dry, and new.

A fortune.

Too cool for words.

By five thirty Matt has caught three good calico bass off Moss Point. He's about to land a fourth but he slips on a slick sharp rock and goes in. He feels the power of the surge and the bouyant lightness that is his body, a speck in the vast Pacific. He hangs on to his rod, though, waits for the surge to lift him up, clambers back onto the rocks and up.

That hasn't happened in a while, he thinks.

His knees are freshly banged up now and there's a new scratch on his shin that bleeds weakly but at least it's a warm day.

He works out his wallet to make sure the twenty isn't too badly soaked. Jackson is damp but fine. His new driver's license is pretty soggy.

Later Julie makes dinner for Matt and Laurel Kalina. His mom is supercharged with energy to rescue Jazz from her tormentors. She took the day off from work to put up more posters around town, and made still another trip to the police station to convince them that Matt's story of her abduction is true. Then spent the rest of the day cleaning the house, playing a dreadful Tom Jones album that Matt had given her last Christmas, straightening Jasmine's room and changing the bedsheets. As if a clean house will draw Jazz home. Jazz, kidnapped not a hundred feet from where they now make dinner. Matt, unable to help her. It makes him feel sick.

In the kitchen Julie has a little trouble with the fish so Matt takes over at the skillet and gets the fillets done but not too done. He mixes the last of the dressing into the salad, puts a piece of bread on each plate.

This is the first time Laurel has been in his house, and he's aware of its age and smallness. When Matt walks toward her with her plate she's like a vision of paradise here at the yellow chrome dinette for four. Gauguin's vision, maybe. She seems inordinately large. Her sleek black hair moves upon her brown shoulders, her red lipstick matches the red in her cherries-on-white dress.

"I have some very good news for you, Matt," says Julie. She smiles at Laurel, too. "We'll be moving from here to somewhere better, out in Dodge City. It's got enough rooms for you and Jazz and Kyle. Just one bath, but the neighbors will let us use theirs when we need to. Lots of very cool people around. As you know, my first room in Laguna was there, in 1946! The neighborhood wasn't called Dodge back then. It was mostly colored people. So, this will be like a homecoming for me. Roosevelt Lane. Pretty name, isn't it?"

Matt feels like a housefly flicked off a table by a giant finger.

Today of all days, Julie announces they're *moving*? With Jazz kidnapped and Kyle on his way home and the fridge always empty and her sucking on the opium pipe like some kind of oxygen bottle?

He also wants to throttle his mother for bringing this up in front of his girlfriend. His *first* girlfriend. He's been to Dodge City and he doesn't like Dodge City and he doesn't want to live in Dodge City, his own room or not.

Matt can't believe his mother is selling the house out from under her own daughter. "What about Jazz?"

"What do you mean? We'll have a nicer home to welcome her back to!"

"I hope she knows where to find it, Mom."

A look from her. "Please try to be okay about this, Matt."

"I'm sick of being okay with everything," he says, looking away.

"That is exciting news," Laurel says quietly.

"And that's not all," Julie says. "No more of me being a serving wench! I've got myself a job right in Dodge. I'll be canning tomatoes they grow in the community garden. I still have my canning skills from being a farmer's daughter. Remember the jam I used to make? We use organic tomatoes grown in the canyon, right off the vine. They sell them at the roadside stand and farmer's markets. Doesn't pay a ton, but enough. We'll finally have enough for all of us, Matt. *Enough.*"

"When's all this going to happen, Mom?"

"Soon," she says, with a smile. "I'm not sure exactly."

He wonders how to let Jasmine know where her family has gone. Tack a message to the front door? Run a classified ad in the *Register* or the *News-Post* and hope she sees it? What are the chances that a kidnapped girl even sees a paper?

After dinner they spend a few minutes with Walter Cronkite, looking for Kyle on the snowy black-and-white RCA. This report comes from Cu Chi in South Vietnam. Matt watches with a clenched gut as two medics rush a soldier toward a waiting helicopter. The soldier's torso is wrapped in a bloody white bandage the size of a bath towel. His helmet is off and his face is a grimace. He looks enough like Kyle to send a jolt of adrenalin through Matt. His breath catches and his eyes are locked on the screen.

"It's not him," says Julie, digging her nails into his upper arm, hard. "It's not, Matt."

"No, it's not."

Heart pounding.

Laurel looks up at him with a pity that embarrasses him.

"Mom, Laurel and I are going to take the van and drive around before the Pageant. Look for Jasmine. I know it's a long shot but, well, she's out there somewhere. Somewhere close. We could use another set of eyes. You want to come?"

"You bet I do."

20

L aurel votes Thousand Steps. It's the last place she's seen Jasmine so why not? But, after going down all 219 steps, then all the way past the pools to the flooded cave, there's no Jazz and no artsy Camera Man or Robe Giant or Duffel Guy. No flock of pretty young people cavorting about with peace-sign flags, pink skateboards, or plastic sundaes. Brooks Street is a bust, so is Main Beach and Crescent Bay. No photo shoots; no Jazz, no late-model white-on-green VW vans.

Detouring from the Laguna Beach Festival of Arts grounds—and Laurel's gig at the Pageant—Matt putts through downtown and drives very slowly the same route he was walking last night when he saw Jasmine.

He describes the kidnapping in detail again to Laurel and Julie, pointing out his exact footpath, right down to cutting across Third and jumping the curb to keep from getting hit. Drivers are honking and shouting at him now, but Matt ignores them.

He details Jasmine's frantic, weakening run for escape, her billowing orange dress with the lilting wing-like sleeves, the sudden headlights, the tire-skid cloud and the two husky men—he remembers them now as husky—yanking his sister off her bare feet and carrying her toward the waiting van. He remembers also that both men were wearing dark, long-sleeved shirts, or maybe jackets. And curtains! The van had curtains with a pattern of some kind . . .

He tells Laurel and Julie his new memories. "Details are important," he says. "I'm remembering better now."

Matt parks in their driveway and Julie scrambles out.

"You two have fun," she says. "Nice to see you again, Laurel. Be safe and don't go anywhere alone."

After the show Matt takes Laurel and Rose out for sundaes at the Sunshine Inn. Watches a buck-fifty disappear. Drives them home, walks them to the porch, wants to kiss Laurel but the older sister seems to be daring him.

Laurel pecks him on the cheek and follows Rose inside.

Matt is turning to go when Laurel bangs back out, runs and throws her arms around him, kissing him hard.

Her pupils are large in the porch light. "Thanks, Matt. Jazz is close to us. I can feel her and she's going to be home soon. I'm sorry you're moving to Dodge City but it might be really nice out there. Rose is jealous that I like you so much. Bye-bye."

Then she's gone again and Matt is headed for the van, his heart beating hard and strong.

Too strong for him to go home and to bed, so he gasses up at the Union 76 on PCH and heads north to Sapphire Cove, where he makes a sweeping turn into the guarded entrance. He sees the same security guard, getting up to slide the booth window open. Pulls up to the lowered gate arm, concentrating on his story.

"Yes," says the guard. His nameplate says MALAPANIS.

"I'm Jim Sloan and I'd like to visit the Johnson family on Oceanfront, by the park." Mikey Johnson being a friend from school.

Malapanis sits back down, checks something on his desk, stands back up.

"You're not on the list. You can back up and U-turn out of here."

"Fred and Florence Johnson said I could visit anytime."

"Not without a call to me you can't. Aren't you the kid who flipped me off and crashed your bike last week?"

"I don't have a bike."

Malapanis sizes up the Westfalia. "Didn't we tow that thing out of here a few days ago?"

Matt hadn't thought of that. Shit.

"I still don't have a bike," he manages.

"You have the Johnsons call security if you expect to get in here. That's how it works."

Matt hands the guard one of the Jasmine Anthony missing-persons flyers, which he takes, examines, and hands back.

"You can't post it here without homeowner association approval."

"I don't want to post it. I want to know if you've seen her."

"She looks like everyone else."

"No, she doesn't."

"Back up and get out."

Matt punches the Westfalia south on PCH and back into town. It's after midnight and Laguna is quiet for summertime. He slowly cruises Mermaid and Third streets, and Forest and Ocean avenues, where the green van had outrun him last night. He's trying to deduce Jazz's starting point. She was running south on Third Street, toward home. Meaning she'd come from the north, and probably the east. Which left half a city from where she may have come.

He drives past Mystic Arts and Taco Bell. At the Sandpiper he shows the flyer to the nightclub bouncer, who won't let him in, and to the people coming out the decal-slathered front door. One young woman says the face looks familiar but she can't be sure. Looks a lot like her friend Jenny in Tustin.

Matt watches the cars go by and sees a VW van stop at the light. His hope launches like an Apollo shot, but he sees that it's not a late model at all, and it's white-over-blue, not green. And it's got batik-looking curtains, not the peace-symbol curtains like the van from last night. Yes, peace-symbol curtains—another image barging in from his subconscious-ness! He wonders if adrenalin preserves memories then slowly releases them as it fades. Like an iceberg melting in summer. Yes, he clearly sees the peace-sign curtains on the white-on-green van as it curves away from him, more or less pinned against the GTE building.

Back in the Westfalia Matt gets his sketchbook, sits on the bed, turns on the overhead light, and slashes in a new drawing of the white-over-green kidnapping van, making sure the curtains are detailed and accurate. Black peace signs on a white background. He tries to make the van look like it's going fast—for a hippie van anyway—coming at him then veering sharply into the U-turn.

The drawing is good. The zoom-like perspective makes the vehicle look closer than it was in real life. It's the drawing he'd give the *Register*, he thinks, to illustrate his eyewitness account of the kidnapping. If he defies the police and writes up his story for the paper. What could it hurt? People will read it and see the picture, then see the van and maybe even see Jazz, and call the cops. Though apparently only Darnell believes that he really saw her. Maybe believes. The rest think the whole incident was nothing more than stoned hippies having a wild night in Laguna, and a sixteen-year-old boy seeing who he wanted to see. He remembers the desk officer asking him if he was on LSD that night. Why should the *Register* believe him?

Five minutes later he's parked across from Patricia Trinkle's home on Diamond. He looks out at the wall of bougainvillea. Only the pitched roof of the Craftsman and its chimney show above the flowery walls. A hidden porch light sends up a glow in the damp night, as if something bright and valuable was waiting in that hidden front yard, an open chest of gold coins maybe, or bars of sterling silver.

He props his sketchbook on his knees and the Westfalia steering wheel, opens it to a fresh page. Draws the Trinkle house, trying to get the funny glow from the flower-walled yard. But he can't. So he touches up the peace-sign curtain van that he now thinks he'll submit to the *Register* for sure. It's still not a photograph, which newspapers prefer. And it's still kind of cartoony, he sees. When he looks at his latest Laurel from just a few hours ago, her proportions are all off and she looks more like a manatee than native maiden. He wonders if he'll ever get good at this.

Matt sets aside the sketchbook and lets his head rest against the cool window glass. He's wasting his time here and he knows it but he doesn't want to give up. Jazz was here once, not too long ago. Doing what he did earlier—delivering for MAW. Now it's two fifteen. He closes his eyes, feels his heart thumping away, and sees Bonnie on the rocks at Thalia, and Jazz running through the night on Third. He sees the orgy at Cavore's, and he knows Bonnie and Jazz have seen it too.

Then bright headlights behind him, almost blinding in the rearview mirror.

They do not approach. They are simply, suddenly, there. Mist rises through the beams as Matt watches Furlong climb out of Moby Cop, slipping his club into the loop on his belt.

Matt rolls down the window, wondering: doesn't this guy ever sleep?

urlong jangles and clomps. Gives Matt a long look. Lifts
his flashlight and beams it in.

"No adult with you? I hope you have more than that
learner's permit."

Matt works his wallet from his jeans and hands the limp, brine-
dipped license to the sergeant, who trains the flashlight on it.

"You just got this today?"

"Yes, sir. It got wet fishing."

"How'd you do?"

"Three calico bass."

Furlong hands it back. "Congratulations on getting your
license, Matt. But what are you doing here?"

"Looking for my sister."

"Seeing her two nights in a row would be nice, wouldn't it?"

"Sure would."

"I want to believe that you saw Jasmine abducted, Matt."

"Why won't you?"

"I think you saw hippie drug fiends. You know, having fun
on a summer night. I think with fog and a quarter moon, your
perceptions might have been a little off. And I think that,
given your involvement with Mystic Arts World, you might
have been high on drugs that night."

"You don't want to believe me because it happened right in
front of the police station and none of you even saw it."

"That is correct. No cops and no witnesses reported seeing
such a thing. Other than you."

Something in Furlong's tone makes Matt wonder if the cops

know something about his sister that they're not telling him. It's an ugly little thought.

Matt sets his wallet on the seat beside him. "I know my sister when I see her."

"But do you know whose house that is?" Furlong nods toward the Craftsman hidden in the bracts.

"It belongs to Patricia Trinkle."

"Do you know her?"

"I've never met her. I delivered a book to this front porch today. Well, yesterday now."

"Let me guess. From Mystic Arts World?"

"Yes."

"But why are you here again at two thirty in the morning? Not making another delivery, certainly."

"Why are *you* here and not looking for my sister?"

"I can't devote every minute of my night shift to her."

"I'm here because Jazz delivered books to Patricia Trinkle. I'm looking for a connection. A certain connection to her. It's . . . hard to explain."

Furlong turns off the flashlight and slides it onto his belt, gives Matt a long frown. To Matt his eyes look cold and unemotional. He's so big his uniform is tight.

"What book did you deliver?"

"*The Tibetan Book of the Dead.*"

"Sounds exciting."

"I haven't read it."

"Isn't that part of Tim Leary's LSD sales pitch?"

"The book has to do with living, not dying, Leary says."

"Grail and Christian Clay both have criminal records by the way."

Matt knows all about Christian's. "Christian got busted for a roach in Oregon. The cops beat the shit out of him and threw him in jail for nine months."

"A light sentence if you ask me."

Furlong steps closer, puts his nose past the window frame, breathes in.

"Step out, Matt."

Matt swings open the door and gets out. Moves away to let Furlong lean in with his flashlight again. Watches the beam traverse the tight interior. Furlong climbs into the driver's seat, shines his light into the ashtray, glove box, side pockets.

Then he squeezes between the seats, and into the back of the van. Matt hears him opening cabinets and drawers, sees the light beam through the bongo-drum-and-palm-tree curtains sewn by his mother for the Westfalia's many windows. He stands up close to the glass, charting Furlong's search. Wonders if Furlong will plant evidence, as he'd heard cops do all the time. Nine months for a roach.

It takes Furlong nearly ten minutes to finish. He throws open the big side doors and hops to the street with a muted clang of gear. Holsters the flashlight.

"Nice van," he says. "They don't make them like they used to. Come here, Matt. Sit."

Matt sits on the open door's frame. When Furlong sits down next to him, Matt feels the Westfalia take his weight.

"I need a favor."

Matt is too astonished and suspicious to even answer. First Johnny Grail needs a favor. Now Furlong?

"I'd like to know what's really going on at Mystic Arts. Half the people who run the place are criminals. I'm talking about the Brotherhood, now. Addicts. Street fighters. Burglars. You walk in there and it's all tie-dye peace and love, baby, get enlightened, get happy, get in touch with your inner child. But I think there's more. For one thing, Laguna Beach is being flooded with LSD—Orange Sunshine, Purple Haze, Window Pane. You can buy it mixed into air fresheners and eyedrop bottles. One drop in each eye or a spray in the crook of your elbow, and you're high for a whole day. High enough to jump out of a window or off a roof. Or, just maybe, to go for a late-night swim in an ocean that wants no part of you. We know that a lot of that LSD is coming in through Dodge City. That's in addition to the new hash balls covered with opium. Someone's taking a lot of risk to smuggle them in from Afghanistan, where the poppies grow. Now, we took down twenty-five *hundred* hits of Orange Sunshine, heading into Dodge City just a few days ago. Matt, the coroner found drugs in Bonnie Stratmeyer they can't even *identify*. But what's the Brotherhood and Mystic Arts doing about these little problems? I'll tell you: selling books and bringing in Harvard psychologists to tell people *how to use LSD*. Selling everything that has to do with dope except the dope itself. Or, wait a minute. Are they doing that too? Are they distributing?"

Silence, then: "I just help in the art gallery."

"But you're a smart young man, Matt. You've got a good brain, good eyes and ears. I want you to tell me what you see and hear at Mystic Arts World. I want to know the Brotherhood, as if they were my best friends. I want to know what's happening and where. And what's going to happen next."

"What about your narcs and informants?"

"Narcs get rolled up sooner or later, and informants lose their balls."

Matt shakes his head and sighs. "I can't do that. Christian's a good artist and a good friend. He's not BEL."

"Then leave him out. Free pass. There are plenty of others."

"You mean, just rat out people I don't even know?"

"It's not ratting. It's using the truth to give criminals enough rope to hang themselves. You can't make anybody talk. But you can listen."

Matt leans forward, places his elbows gingerly above his kneecaps, thinks about all this. He can't argue that any of what Furlong has said isn't true. He's seen the drugs and read the stories. Bonnie. The girl who thought she could fly across Coast Highway. He already knows his answer but, strangely, doesn't want to disappoint the big, bear-like Furlong.

"Would you look harder for Jasmine if I work for you?"

"We're already doing everything we can. In spite of what you might think. I want her back and safe as much as you do."

"Believe me you don't."

"So what do you say to my offer?"

"No, but thanks."

"Why not?"

"I don't think I'm on your side."

"Oh boy."

"No, I don't think you're pigs, or want people to kill cops or anything like that. I like Officer Darnell. You seem okay. But leave me out. I don't want to be a part of your team. No."

"Well said, Matt. Well argued. And I'm going to give you one more chance to explain what you're doing outside this house right now."

"I told you."

"But you don't know who owns this house?"

"Patricia Trinkle."

"No. The man who owns this house is Marlon Sungaard. And Marlon Sungaard is one of the richest men in Southern California, Matt. This is only one of his homes. He has others, in Aspen, New York, and Macau. He's got a jet and lots of important friends."

Thus his twenty-dollar tip, Matt thinks.

"Wow. Where's Macau?"

"Across the Pearl River Delta from Hong Kong."

Matt looks out at the bougainvillea-wrapped Craftsman.

"Did Sungaard give you any type of compensation for your delivery, Matt? Cash, a gift, anything at all?"

Matt evades with ease. "I never saw him."

"Let me know if he offers payment of any kind."

"I told you I can't do that."

"This is different. He's not a criminal. And remember Matt, it doesn't hurt to support your local police. It's your duty."

"Okay."

"When's Kyle getting home?"

"July twenty-sixth."

"Not long. Well, say hello to your mom."

"I won't rat on her either, Sergeant Furlong." Matt smiles.

Furlong actually smiles, too. "You're okay, Matt. Think

about what I said. I can bring a little money your way. I know things can be kind of skinny on a waitress's take-home and a newspaper route."

Matt noses the bait. "How much money?"

"It depends what you give me, and how good it is, and how often."

"What's an example?"

"Something decent I can use? Five bucks. You come up with three a week and you're into some good cash."

More money a week than my paper route, Matt thinks. He has a brief vision of Christian's face when he finds out that Matt has ratted out a Brother.

"But then, no info no pay," Furlong says.

Matt considers. "Why did you come up behind me with your lights off?"

"Basic cop procedure."

"It scares people."

"Then they do something stupid and I've got them. But you didn't, Matt. We're cool. Now, if this was a school night, it would be a whole different story."

"It bothers me that my sister's been kidnapped and you're spending all your time recruiting me to rat out people I don't even know."

"Drugs are eating this country alive. You of all people should know that. I refer now to your mother."

"I'm referring to my sister, who is eighteen and got dragged into a van."

"I believe you."

"I know you don't. None of you do. Maybe Darnell."

"You help me and I'll help you."

Matt considers Furlong's brow and his strange tan eyes. Considers the money versus the betrayal.

"No."

"You'll regret this."

"No. I hope not."

22

Officer Darnell has placed three black-and-white photographs on the table, facing away from her. Matt sets his hand-sewn, emblem-emblazoned backpack down and takes the same bolted-to-the-floor swivel chair he'd sat in for the missing-person report.

Detective Lance McAdam, whom Matt heard just minutes ago telling reporters that the death of Bonnie Stratmeyer is now being investigated as a homicide/suicide, sits across the table from Matt.

McAdam is trim and young looking for an older man. He wears jeans, a paisley tie, a white shirt, and a loose brown sport coat. Maybe forty, Matt guesses. His eyes are brown and unusually large behind his glasses. He looks like a college English teacher should look.

He hands Matt a copy of the Los Angeles tabloid weekly *LA Moves*, with its black-and-white cover photo of a pretty girl in a bathing suit slung over the shoulder of a large muscleman wearing dick-hugging briefs. They're on a beach, rocks in the background. Two more bikini-clad young women kneel at his feet, smiling up at him.

"Do you recognize anyone in this picture?" asks the detective.

Matt hears that low whooshing in his ears again, the one reserved for bad news, danger, for things going wrong. Like when he saw Bonnie on the beach at Thalia. This time it accompanies another intersection between his sister and that very girl.

"That's Bonnie Stratmeyer," says Matt. "Hanging on the Robe Giant."

"Robe Giant?" asks McAdam.

Matt looks through the tabloid as he tells McAdam, and Darnell, again, about the Thousand Steps shoot and his nicknames for some of the people. Among the many photos in *LA Moves* he sees other Thousand Steps shots—there's one of the girl with the phony sundae, one of the guitar boy. And one of pretty Sara, the Skateboard Girl. McAdam makes careful notes.

He asks Matt question after question and before Matt knows it, a full hour has gone by. He checks his Timex again. It won't be long until Tommy drops off his papers and a new bag of rubber bands.

"We're almost done," says McAdam. "I hear you're a busy young man."

Matt doesn't like the idea of cops talking about him behind his back. He trusts Darnell, barely, but not the others. He wonders what Furlong says about him. Do they all know that he's refused to inform for the sergeant?

Darnell points to the photograph of Robe Giant. "His name is George Williams but his stage name is Equus."

"He's an actor?" asks Matt.

"He makes pornographic movies," says McAdam.

Matt remembers Teddy's "cruddies." Does not look at Darnell.

"And your Camera Man, here, is Hollywood film director Rene DeWalt," says Darnell, tapping a glossy portrait. "This head shot came in the press packet for one of his films, *Secret Heroes*. It's a love story about a young French widow and a Nazi soldier. DeWalt was born in Switzerland and came here when he was young."

Matt wonders why a Hollywood director would be doing *LA Moves* shoots using amateur models. He's also never heard of the *Secret Heroes* movie.

"And the man you call Duffel Guy is Amon Binder, DeWalt's assistant," says Darnell. "He's an up-and-coming porn director. He pled guilty to conspiracy to distribute obscene materials through the U.S. Mail. Did time."

"Matt," says McAdam. "Did you see any minors at Thousand Steps that evening? As part of the shoot?"

"I don't think so, but it's hard to tell."

"Under eighteen is a minor," says Darnell.

"I just can't say for sure. Most of them seemed older than me by a couple of years. Maybe more."

"So there could have been seventeen-year-olds as part of this photo shoot?"

Matt nods.

"Matt, take Officer Darnell and me through this event at the Vortex of Purity. Something to do with evolution. After that, you're free to go."

Counting Q&A it takes Matt almost another hour to describe the ceremony, the characters, the campus. McAdam asks him three different times if Williams, Binder, or DeWalt were present at the Vortex that night, which they were not. McAdam is particularly interested in Mahajad's physical contact with his followers. Of which Matt saw none.

"In your conversation, did Om acknowledge that some of his followers appear in the *LA Moves* sex mag?"

"No. We didn't talk about that. I don't know if he knows."

"Hmmm." McAdam sits back and glances at the wall clock. "Brigit? Anything more?"

"No, but thank you, Matt. You've been a big help."

"Can I say one thing?"

"Of course," says the detective.

Matt digs his sketchbook from the backpack at his feet, shows them his sketch of the van into which his sister was forcibly thrown two nights ago, describes Jasmine's abduction in brief, clear, unemotional detail.

"It happened," he says. "Just about fifty yards from where we're sitting. You can see the skid marks on the street. I want you to know that it's true and it was my sister and it was a white-on-green VW van, late model, with peace-sign curtains. I want a kidnapping investigation. Not a missing person, a *kidnapped* person. You need to make Jasmine as important as Bonnie."

"Matt, by law she's a missing person until we get a ransom demand or can prove otherwise," says McAdam.

"I with my own eyes prove it otherwise."

"Our department is putting its full weight into finding your sister," says the detective. "The fog was heavy and there was very little moon. So far as skid marks go, drivers miss that Third Street stop sign because they're watching for traffic coming down the hill. Last minute, they lock up and skid. It happens a lot."

They'll never believe me, thinks Matt. "Officer Darnell, Detective McAdam, I want to give this sketch and a written description of what I saw two nights ago. To the *Register*."

"Absolutely not, Matt," says McAdam. "If what you say happened really did happen—and I'm not saying it didn't— then you'll be putting the kidnappers on high alert. They'll destroy the curtains and ground the van. They'll be extra careful, instead of carelessly happy to get away with a felony. It's often the chance remark, the loose lips that lead us to the shitheads who do things like this. Pardon my French."

Matt stuffs the sketchbook into the pack and stands. "Jazz can't wait for a chance remark. She's been missing over a week. And what if the shitheads have stashed the van and the curtains already?"

"Detective McAdam is right, Matt," says Darnell. "I believe you saw Jasmine kidnapped two nights ago. I do. But all you'd accomplish with the press is help the perps get away with it. I *want* that green hippie van with the peace-sign curtains out on the street. Right where I can see it and pull those shi—those *people* over."

"Shitheads," Matt corrects.

"Shitheads," says Darnell.

Which leads Matt to Thalia Street and Joint-and-Martini Man's weather-beaten beachfront home. Matt walks a rope-railed wooden gangplank to the front porch.

It takes two knocks and two waits but the man finally opens the door. In daylight Matt sees he's older than he'd thought. Same long gray hair and potbelly. No joint or martini.

"I talked to you last week about the hippie van," says Matt. "You saw it parked right down there, the night before they found Bonnie Stratmeyer. I want to know if it had curtains."

"I remember, kind of." Same gravelly voice. "Come in."

"No, thank you. I've got papers to fold and deliver."

The man steps outside but leaves the door open. "A bike route?"

"Yes, sir."

"I had one. *The St. Louis Post-Dispatch*. The afternoon edition, so I did it after school."

"What kind of bike did you use?"

"It was a Schwinn Heavy-Duti."

"So's mine." Matt waits. "Curtains?"

"Curtains? Yeah. But there was fog, and reflection of the streetlight. I couldn't see inside very well. Except the two guys in the front, sitting really still. Why do the curtains matter?"

"The cops are calling it either a murder or suicide and I'm trying to help."

"That's awful. She was what, eighteen?"

Matt nods and waits again, trying to draw out the man's memory. The man closes his eyes and taps his forehead with his fingers. "They were light colored. Yeah, I see those two guys just sitting in the dark but not moving. And the van was a newer one. I noticed that."

"And you said they were all over Laguna now, those vans."

"You see them a lot. Different colors."

"And the curtains?"

"White with dark circles. Oh, of course—they were peace signs. Pretty sure, peace signs. Perfect for a hippie van, right?" The man opens his eyes. "I'm Myron Kandell."

"I'm Matt Anthony. My sister has been kidnapped by the men you saw, in a late-model white-on-green VW van with peace-sign curtains. I witnessed it with my own eyes."

"Holy shit, Matt."

"The cops don't believe me. I want you to tell them what you saw."

"I already did."

"But not the curtains. The peace signs are important. They're critical evidence, Mr. Kandell."

"You mean go downtown to the cop house?"

"I'll drive us. I know which cops to talk to."

Brigit Darnell takes Kandell's statement in the same interview room Matt has just left. Matt waits in the lobby. Detective McAdam strides through, gives Matt a surprised look with his big magnified eyes, keeps going out the door.

When Matt drops him off at Thalia, Myron Kandell invites him in for a smoke again.

"I've got papers to deliver."

"Good luck with your sister."

"Don't say anything to anybody about the curtains. The cops don't want that getting around and tipping them off that we know. What you saw is very important."

"I'll guard our secret. Porch those papers, Matt."

And porch them he does. His legs are strong, his scabs are thick and healing, the delivery bag feels light. His aim is true. Ozzie, the German shepherd on Wilcox, doesn't charge, and Jamaica, the cocker spaniel on Los Robles, is chained to a magnolia tree. Old Coiner cheerfully waves at Matt as if he's never seen him before.

When he gets home, his mother is loading boxes into the Westfalia.

"You're just in time, Matt! Our Dodge City home is ready early and I just gave Pedley notice. Help me load this in, and I'll show you your new place. God, I hope you like it."

23

Matt drives because his mother's feeling a little spaced. A touch of the flu, she says, nothing serious.

Matt steers out Broadway, passing the pageant amphitheater on his left, then picks up the Laguna Canyon frontage road. Putts past the new Sawdust Festival, where Christian is selling his psychedelic paintings and his bodacious wrought iron sculptures of desert animals. Makes a right onto Woodland Drive and a left on Roosevelt.

The houses here are small and old, some stucco but most of them the same wooden clapboard as the Third Street bungalow. Their front doors and windows are mostly open and the smell of dope rides the air. The streets are dirt, with cars parked chaotically. Long-haired young people stand around smoking, eyeing Matt and his mother. Children and dogs. Matt sees a skinny black monkey chained to an oak tree in a brown front yard. And an aviary that takes up half of a vacant lot, filled with bright red macaws and green parrots. A bunch of barefoot boys in swim trunks run alongside the Westfalia, lunging up toward his open window, for what reason Matt does not know. He slows to a crawl to avoid running over someone's foot.

Matt knows from his mom that this area—made up of Woodland Drive, Fairwood Lane, Roosevelt Lane, Victory Walk, and Milligan Way—had been a black neighborhood until the hippies and dealers and artists took over. Cheap rent, walk to town and the beach. A few of his schoolmates live out here. Christian told him Johnny Grail had started calling it Dodge

City because of all the cops raiding and hassling him and his Brotherhood of Eternal Love, chasing them around with guns drawn.

"There, Matt! The red one."

It's a small barn. The paint and white trim are faded and he can see space between some of the slats. The sliding door is open, chickens fussing in the sunshine. Matt has always liked barns. His Grandma Mae and Grandpa Elmer lived on a farm near Dayton, Ohio, and Julie took all three kids there one summer for two weeks. He remembers that barn clearly, from the rusted hand-crank corn husker that had taken off a man's hand in 1921, to the pigeon feathers wafting down in the dusty light, to the livestock-and-hay smell of it.

This barn sits on its lot, weirdly angled and somehow apart from the other buildings on Roosevelt Lane. Like it's been dropped here. Matt thinks of Dorothy's house in *The Wizard of Oz*, the way the tornado just picks it up and sets it down.

Like most of Dodge City, the barn looks a little long in the tooth.

"Do you like it, Matt?"

"I'm not sure. It's bigger than Third Street. What's the rent?"

"Less than Third Street! Plus I've got some canning and kitchen work."

"Kitchen work?"

"It's kind of communal. You'll see."

The boys tear into the barn ahead of Matt and his mother. There's no walkway or porch or entryway, just a footpath that leads through the dead-grass barnyard to the sliding door.

Inside, it's an odd mix of barn and home. There are enough windows to let in some sun, but not a lot. Matt stands just inside the door, his mother beside him. There are no stalls or pens, tractors or tools. Rather, a main room with a beaten linoleum floor with a white-on-purple fleur-de-lis pattern. In the center of the room is a large, upturned wooden utility spool with six mismatched bar stools around it, some with backs and some not. Against the rough slat walls are a wooden chair and three thrift-store sofas that look like they've supported generations.

The kitchen is spacious, with a four-burner stove, a stainless-steel sink, and an oven. Two refrigerators: a bulbous white Frigidaire with a Grateful Dead poster of a skull smoking a cigar, and a newer one with hundreds of surf stickers and peace signs on it. There's a wood-burning stove for heat. The barn smells of woodsmoke and skunky marijuana.

The boys peer down on them from the hayloft, point and laugh and disappear into the darkness. Matt looks at the stairway and the handwritten DO NOT ENTER sign hung across the handrails with twine. Suddenly the boys come flying down the stairs, jump the twine, and pound across the old linoleum and out the door.

"Welcome!"

"Welcome!"

"Butts!"

Through open doors, Matt can see a "master" bedroom and three smaller ones. He steps into each momentarily, because a moment is all it takes. They all have mattresses on their linoleum floors, defeated dressers, and saloon-y wooden furniture that reminds Matt of *Gunsmoke*. Each room has one window and a sink. The master has an old-fashioned clawfoot bathtub and a toilet. Matt, skinny and prone to his garage drafts, feels a shiver just imagining this place in February.

"There's no shower."

"Right next door, Matt—Don and Connie Schwartz—the owners of this place. They're Brotherhood. And they're hardly ever home. At least Don isn't. He travels a lot."

Smuggling in hash from Afghanistan, Matt assumes. "And we share our kitchen?"

"With one other family only."

"Is the rest of it ours?"

"The barn is all ours! Except the kitchen, sometimes."

Matt can't stop himself. "I hate it. I'd rather have the old garage and my own kitchen and a decent shower. Your room at home is better than this one. And we'd freeze here. The canyon's *cold* in fall and winter."

"But warm in spring and summer. Except for, you know, the June gloom . . ." A tear rolls down Julie's cheek and she brushes it away. A catch of breath. Then another tear.

"Why are you doing this, Mom?"

"I thought I could . . . you know . . ."

"No, I *don't* know."

"I feel very sad inside."

"Why? You weren't sad before."

"It gets a little bigger every day. And the things I have and love and look forward to, they get smaller."

"Do you have cancer?"

"Oh, no honey, *no!*"

"Is it what happened with Dad?"

"Maybe what happened to all of us."

"But Kyle's going to make it home alive. And we're going to get Jasmine back. And Dad's gone for good. Don't dwell on him."

"I know."

"Maybe it's the dragon balls, then."

Julie shakes her head but avoids Matt's eyes. "No, certainly not. What do you know about opium?"

"The hash you smoke is laced with it. From Afghanistan. The Brotherhood smuggles it in by the pound. It's how they finance the LSD and the Happenings."

"But what makes you think that I smoke that stuff?"

"You left a dragon ball in the silverware drawer and I found it. Wrapped in foil."

She looks down, takes a wavering breath. Her voice is softer. "If you're ever tempted to try it, don't. It will make you care less about the things you love. So all you'll want is more of *it*."

"That's happening to you."

"I'm fighting hard. I love you so much and I don't want

anything bad to ever happen to you. You are my baby forever,
Matt. My last and in some ways my first."

"First what?"

"My first and only you."

More tears, chin trembling.

"We need to stay on Third Street, Mom."

"No. This is where I need to be. This is where I make my
stand. Where I started. When I was young and brave."

Matt's anger spikes. He pities his mom but she infuriates
him too.

"I'm staying at Third Street until Pedley throws me out,"
he says. "I don't like it here and Jasmine needs a home to
come home to. I can't believe you're ditching her when she's
in some living hell we can't even imagine."

"I need to be here, Matt. I need to save myself so I can save
my daughter. You can have the van."

Half an hour later they've finished unloading the boxes.
There is mostly silence between them, and a heaviness in the
air.

The first thing she takes from a box is the countdown calendar for Kyle's return from the war. She's already filled in
today's magic number: thirty-six. She's packed the tape in
the same box, so the calendar goes right over the skull on the
Grateful Dead poster on the fridge.

"Can I bring you anything from home, or town?" he asks.

"Everything I need for today is here. I got it all. Thanks
for your help!"

She gives him a hearty hug and a beaten smile. Matt can
feel her desperation.

He drives down Roosevelt Lane to Milligan, loops back
around into view of the barn and parks again. Leaves the engine running. Sees that the big barn door is now closed.

Notes the thick plume of smoke drafting out of the master
bedroom window.

24

With the house to himself Matt calls Laurel but her mom says she's out with Rose. He eats two Husky Boy burgers and fries in front of the TV, watches the Huntley-Brinkley Vietnam coverage for yesterday—one of the deadliest days in the entire war. Most of the segment is from an address by President Johnson, who urges the American people to be patient with the war: we are winning but it is costly. He suggests that TV is turning America against the war. There is grim footage of metal coffins being unloaded from a huge cargo plane at a military base in Maryland. Kyle could be in one of those, Matt thinks. The military is supposed to notify you as soon as it happens, though, so families don't get shocked to learn it on TV. He read about a dad who died of a heart attack when they came to his door. Matt thinks of how scared Ernie Rios is of getting drafted, even though he's not eighteen yet. Kyle was number 353 and enlisted anyway.

He half watches *The Flying Nun* with the sound off. So stupid a show, with all the bad things in the world, he thinks. Then stares at the street outside where they'd bagged his sister. He wonders what she's doing right exactly now. Are they feeding her? Is she being tortured or raped? He feels like hitting someone, maybe the damned nun. Or how about the men who took Jazz? Or whoever sells that shit to his mom?

He looks again through Jasmine's room for some hint or clue to her whereabouts. With his mom moved out, Matt misses

Jazz more than ever. Leary looks back at him. As do Aretha and the Beatles. Maybe the Beatles had her kidnapped.

And Jazz loves her music. Which reminds him of the *Advanced Ukulele Hits* book he got for her birthday, and the lyrics she scribbles inside the back cover and in the margins. Maybe there's some clue in her songs.

He takes it off the shelf and leafs through, but no luck. Just phrases and lines and chords written over them. Feels some of his mother's desperation, the good things getting further and further away.

He gets her diary and sits on her bed. It's got a black leatherette cover and gold-edged pages of heavy, lined paper.

Opens where the marker is, and reads:

When I graduate it all changes. But into what?

She's always liked birds. Writes about migrating warblers the size of a woman's thumb. Millions of them flying at night. How if they get tired over large bodies of water they fall from the sky and drown.

I can see the beauty in his body and hear the beauty in his music but there is something missing in him. I think he has dedicated part of his soul to having success and this makes him a driven, relentless striver . . .

Matt thinks of the carelessly vain Austin Overton, guitar strapped over his muscles, entertaining Dana and the other girls on the patio of Big Yellow. How Overton remembered sleeping with Jasmine but not much else about her. Again, Matt wonders at his sister's brittle arrogance, how she's superior and self-doubting at the same time. How she likes the singer and is repelled by him, too. Matt traces this to his father and mother, the way that, between them, they stoked pride in their children one day, followed it with belittlement the next.

I want to live in a village in Mexico. On a beach, in a clean little cabana with tile floors, where I can feel the beach sand under my feet and play my uke.

She told Matt that a year ago. He said he'd go too, fish and draw and paint.

He fans back a few pages.

Neldra says that her scene isn't for everybody. She said I might be able to visit sometime, but she didn't invite me directly. There is a secrecy about what goes on there.

Matt feels sneaky, reading these words that were never meant for him. Jasmine's handwriting changes with her moods: angry, sad, playful, curious, confident. He hears her voice in the words. He reads a few more entries, but finds nothing to point him in her direction. In any direction at all.

Then he's back in the dimming light of the small living room, looking out the window through the lank avocado tree to the street and the hulking GTE building. He realizes this may be one of his last nights here, and it surprises him how unhappy this makes him. This is a crummy place by Laguna standards, a barely affordable rental, small, drafty, and shadowed by other buildings. The landlord is annoying, stingy with his avocados, and looks at his mother creepily.

But this has been Matt's home for his last four years—two of middle school, and two of Laguna Beach High School. The artists, he thinks. Like Christian. And Gauguin. This clapboard box with the groaning pipes and the flickering lights is a big part of what he is. He's really kind of loved it.

From here on Third, he's fished with Kyle, listened to Jasmine play and sing, had long talks with his mom about her growing up on that Ohio farm, the small school, Julie being the high school valedictorian for a graduating class of twelve, Julie and her friend Dee spreading out a map of the United States on the floor, closing their eyes and Dee dropping a Chinese coin onto it. The coin had a square opening cut into its middle and this square was to frame the city where fate told them to go—to find jobs and begin new lives in a world that might offer more than endless flat miles of corn, tiny towns, few people and little opportunity. The coin landed in New Mexico but there was nothing in its square window. On the next drop it landed way up in New Hampshire but again there was no town or city. Third try, Dee flipped the coin high and it landed in California. And when Julie and Dee leaned in close, they saw the small empty square framing letters *Lagu* . . . where his mother and Dee, aged eighteen, had begun their new lives in 1946, in rooms for rent on Victory Walk, and where they had learned to dance up in Newport Beach and to swim in a rich lady's pool in Emerald Bay.

His mother's lucky Chinese coin had made this place on Third Street in Laguna possible. Inevitable?

So yes, Matt will miss this house, and the hard garage that's been his lair for two years. All the sketches he's done there, all the music he's played on the rinky-dink Motorola portable stereo with the pop-up lid and the needles that get dull every few months. He'll miss lying back on that mattress and imagining what fish he might catch the next day, and how to make better time on his paper route with smart short-cuts, and picturing Laurel Kalina, the girl he's been furtively admiring since fourth grade and now has told him, *I like you so much.*

Again, spurred by fears for Jazz, hounded by images of her in pain, Matt drives to Laguna's beaches—Thousand Steps, Brooks, Main, Crescent Bay—hoping for a glimpse of his sister . . .

The evening is cool and breezy. Scores of young people walk the shores, trailing smoke and laughter.

But no weird *LA Moves* photo shoots, no Jazz.

At Diver's Cove the sun has just set when three girls come over and ask him where's the nearest party. They're older than him, maybe Jasmine's age: one with a red satin cape over leopard-print leotards, another wearing a long rainbow-pattern duster, and a barefoot redhead in shorts and a mac- ramé sweater with beads woven in. The redhead has a joint going and they all three huddle in close to him, and she offers it to Matt, who declines, but the girl takes a big hit and aims her exhale into his face, leaning in close, lightly kissing his lips. Her kiss is pungent and warm and it sends a lightning bolt of lust through him.

"Michoacan," she whispers. "You ought to try it."

Suddenly there's a hand on his crotch and Matt almost jumps out of his shorts.

"You *sure* you don't want a hit?"

The hand still moving on him.

"No, thank you."

By the time he realizes what they're doing, Red Cape is handing off his wallet to a muscular guy in jeans and biker boots who has appeared from nowhere, and he hands off the wallet to a little guy who turns and runs like a rabbit toward Coast Highway. Then from the dark comes a third man, fists up and ready to fight, joining his muscular buddy to corral Matt from the escaping rabbit. The girls dance around Matt, a swirling circle of cape and coat and sweater, the redhead shaking her tangle of curls into his face.

"Come on girls," says Muscles. "Kid, you stay the fuck right there. The wallet will be in the trash can."

"*Longton! Move it, man!*"

Laughter trails into the night.

A few minutes later he's driving toward home, hands shak- ing and stomach muscles locked. He's got his wallet, license, student ID, and not one dollar. His incredible twenty-dollar tip from Sungaard is gone. The dollars he had before that windfall are gone too. All of which could have fed him for weeks, bought him a new sketchpad and some used clothes from Fade in the Shade, paid for ice cream sundaes and dinners for Laurel. The loss is almost what he makes in a month delivering papers. Eighty-three fucking cents left in his pocket.

But his adrenalin won't let go and he really wants to fight, though he's only been in one fight in his life, which he lost.

Add those girls kissing and rubbing him—which makes Matt feel depraved and deprived and wanting Laurel—and he doesn't know *how* he's supposed to feel. He screams out the open window into the PCH traffic, just a scream, no words.

Making it all even worse, Matt has suspected since he last saw Jasmine two nights ago that it's basically useless looking for her like this. As if she'll appear again, running crazily free, and he'll magically be there to rescue her. It's futile.

Flattened by tonight's sorry events, this futility hits him like a wave breaking over the rocks where he fishes. He feels angry and stupid. He has been robbed by hippies.

"This is idiotic, Matt," he says. "You are an idiot."

25

He gets to Mystic Arts World before it opens, waves through one of the onion-dome windows at Johnny Grail. Grail is feather-dusting hookahs in the head-shop section of the store.

Two Jasmines stare back at Matt from the middle of the weirdly shaped window. Matt is seeing her all over town now, and every time she confronts him, his emotions swing from sadness and frustration over Jazz to anger at the cops for how damned little progress they appear to be making, if they're making any at all. Zip, is his guess.

Grail lets him in. Without customers and music, the store has the feel of a counterculture museum—all things foreign, subversive, and mystical. Grail leads him back to the hookahs, some of them large enough to sit on a floor and be smoked standing up, some no larger than a coffee mug. There's a replica of Emperor Jahangir's jade hookah in New Delhi for $25, brass *shisas* from Egypt, copper-alloy *Qaelyans* from Persia, and a few featuring ceramic chillums made by a local surfer-craftsman named Greg Nichols. Matt has seen him speeding around Laguna in his raised, four-wheel-drive F-150 with the custom gray paint, his longboard racked on the top.

"Any good news about your sister?"

"None. The cops aren't doing much. Much that shows, anyway."

Grail shakes his head and resumes his dusting of the exotic hookahs.

"These ceramics draw like a dream and keep the water

cool," he says, tapping the top of a large, floor-standing Nichols with his duster. "And this one holds an ounce and a half of hash."

"That's a lot."

"Why are you here so early?"

"I need money. I wanted to make some more deliveries if you have any."

"Interesting."

"I got ripped off down at Diver's Cove last night. My own fault."

"I can loan you some."

"No thanks, Johnny. I want to earn it. I have enough to get by for now." Eighty-three cents, he thinks.

"You and Jazz have been good to the brotherhood, Matt. Let me make some calls. You stay here."

Grail hands Matt the duster and heads out through the meditation room. Matt hears a door close, then takes up dusting the beaker bongs with the psychedelic paint jobs, the bubble-based vapor bongs, the double-recyclers, the dab-rigs, quartz bangers, and the Gandalf pipes. He picks up a beaker bong and examines the paint job, sees he could probably do as good with the right materials. It's beautiful—red roses on clear glass. Wonders how a mini-tableau of Laurel and Rose in the Gauguin would look. The smoke would swirl around behind them like fog and you'd have a werewolf kind of trip. Then he carefully dusts the comedy bongs and pipes: a red-and-white candy cane, a clear cobra, a vanilla ice cream cone, even a frosted-glass hand-grenade pipe with a swiveling pull-pin.

Matt is craving the organic breakfast muffins in the health food bakery when Grail returns. He's carrying a ream-sized box.

"This is like totally unreal that you showed up here today, Matt. Talk about Karma. Okay, there's two hundred and fifty of these things. Enough for every business in town, and some left over. They need to be delivered by tonight, and my prior arrangements just fell through. They're invitations to our Summer of Eternal Love Experience a week from Sunday. You can save me lots on postage. Just take you a few hours. I'll pay you five dollars when you're done."

Talk about the nick of time!

He opens the box and hands a sheet to Matt. It's a hot fuchsia background with dizzying Day-Glo green psychedelic letters. A bright orange quarter-sun beams its rays down from the upper left corner, like in a child's drawing:

EXPERIENCE THE SUMMER OF ETERNAL LOVE

Sycamore Flats, Laguna Canyon
All Day/All Night

THIS INVITE IS YOUR ADMISSION

Free Food, Free Live Music, Free Love

SPONSORED BY THE BROTHERHOOD OF ETERNAL LOVE

THE WORLD IS WELCOME!

"Nice graphic," Matt says. "It actually makes my eyes hurt."

Grail gives him a grinding little laugh. "Exactly. I designed it myself to take the eye into another dimension. Like seeing a double-helix that keeps rolling over and over while being lit by a strobe. Plus that incredible sun up in the corner."

"Free food and live music? Sycamore Flats will be packed."

"We hope."

"Does Furlong know about this?"

"Make sure he gets his invite, Matt. All the pigs are welcome!"

Matt loves the idea of this easy money. And the idea that the flyers will take him into the heart of the city where—

somewhere—Jasmine's abductors must be holding her. He might see her, hear her, sense her. Find the connection he needs. She has to be out there, right?

"Okay. I'll deliver. It's what I do."

"Don't use the mail slots or the *federales* will come after me. Just slide them under the doors or into the jambs, under the welcome mats, wherever. So cool of you do to this, Matt. So out-of-this-world, boss-Karma cool."

"You're welcome, Johnny. Oh, I'd like two of those organic poppy-seed muffins and a small milk."

Grail goes behind the counter, picks up the pastry tongs. "Yesterday's stuff, so I'll discount it," he says.

Matt sets the coins on the glass, thirty cents, but the muffins will be worth every penny. He's hungry enough to eat ten of them. He still has fifty-three of his last eighty-three cents, with Johnny Grail's five dollars coming sometime soon.

And an idea hits him.

Brigit Darnell seems suspicious of Matt's motives, but she radios Furlong about Matt Anthony's request to see the sergeant immediately on a matter of "some importance."

They meet in the gift shop of the Laguna Art Museum on Coast Highway. Matt's idea. He has spent some hours here, lost in the plein air oils that Laguna is famous for—landscapes and beach scenes, pastoral and pleasing. The watercolors by Millard Sheets and Rex Brandt are terrific too. His sketchbooks are filled with earnest attempts to copy some of this art, though the one he now holds in one hand has only recent drawings.

Furlong leads the way to the upstairs gallery, jangling with each step.

As Matt intended, they're alone up here.

Furlong speaks quietly. "What."

Matt hasn't rehearsed this, so it all comes tumbling out: Diver's Cove looking for Jazz, the hippie girls blowing smoke in his face and kissing him, the grope, the three guys and the warning and his wallet in the trash, minus his money. He tells Furlong it was close to thirty-five dollars of paper route earnings—not mostly a gift from one of the richest men in Southern California.

"Describe the perpetrators in detail, Matt."

He does, right down to the red satin cape and the tie-dye duster and the beaded macramé sweater.

"And, that's not all." He made one good sketch late last night, of the girl who blew the smoke in his face. He opens the sketchbook and shows Furlong.

"Hmmm. Darnell can take a report and we'll BOLO them. But there are a lot of drugged-up hippies out there."

"BOLO?"

"Be on the lookout."

"I actually was hoping you'd pay me for this information and drawing. This was a robbery on a city beach. I'm an eyewitness victim, and I've made a good drawing of one suspect. And—this is important—I know the last name of the man who threatened me."

Furlong waits, looking down at Matt, his bigness amplified in the cool, clean light of the gallery.

"You said five bucks for good information you can use."

"About the Brotherhood."

"These guys had drugs alright. From Michoacan."

"I'm after bigger fish, Matt."

"I've even half identified one of them. Longton—the leader."

"If they had a weapon I wouldn't hesitate."

"If you pay me for this, I've got something else. It relates directly to the Brotherhood."

"No, Matt. That's not how it works. What happens is you give me your best information, all of it, and I decide whether it's worth my money or not. We don't negotiate first."

"Then I'll need to consider this."

Matt walks away to the stairs, looks down into the stairwell. Then stands before a dazzling triple-perspective Wayne Thiebaud painting. Someday. Then comes back to Furlong, opens his sketchbook again and hands the sergeant one of Grail's fuchsia-and-Day-Glo-green Summer of Eternal Love invitations.

Furlong stares at it. "Where did you get this?"

"Mystic Arts."

"I knew nothing about it until now. An *experience*?"

"I think the invites are going out today."

"How?"

"The Post Office, I guess."

"Offers of free sex through the U.S. Mail?"

"It says free love, not sex." Matt knows he's digging a hole for himself but all he can do is hope Furlong doesn't see it.

"What else do you have for me?" Furlong asks quietly.

"That's it. An authentic eyewitness victim's account. A sketch of one perpetrator, and the last name of the leader. And an invite to a BEL event in Laguna Canyon you didn't know about, at which drugs will be all over the place. I lost almost all the money I had last night, Sergeant."

Furlong gets out his wallet and hands Matt two fives. "Take the sketch to Darnell. I'll keep the invite. Later today I want a list of the streets you ride on your route, delivering the papers. Leave it with Darnell with the sketch. I may want to find you."

Matt likes that idea not one bit, but he likes the ten dollars a lot. "Alright."

Furlong taps two fingers to his lips, which becomes a brief salute.

Late that night Matt finishes delivering Johnny Grail's flyers. He's tired and hungry. But Johnny owes him five bucks and Furlong's ten dollars are in his wallet. He's had nothing to eat since a skimpy peanut butter and jelly burrito for lunch.

But worse than hunger is his failure to come so much as one inch closer to Jazz, even after delivering those hundreds of flyers all over town. He hasn't found the elusive connection. Had he actually gotten close to her? He had not sensed her.

What's she doing right now? Does she have enough to eat? Are they hurting her?

Putt-putting toward the Hotel Laguna in the van, he asks himself a difficult question: If what you're doing doesn't work, if you've looked everywhere and don't find what you're looking for, what do you do?

One, he thinks, you look again.

Two, look somewhere else.

Three, learn to see in a different way.

Mahajad Om had said something like that at the end of the Evolution ceremony. How exactly do you see in a different way?

Luckily, Ernie is working tonight.

Matt sits in the folding chair, hidden from management between the walk-in and the shelves of foodstuffs. His stomach growls and churns. Ernie delivers half a prime rib that may be the best thing Matt has eaten in his life. The horseradish stings his sinuses and brings tears to his eyes. Also on the plate are two halves of two different potatoes, one drenched in sour cream and the other in butter. And a slab of chocolate cake the shape and size of a peaked SS cap, which Matt suspects is a non-leftover Ernie has lifted from the desert rack.

Ernie sits. "No Jazz?"

"Eight nights."

Matt tells Ernie about Jazz running down Third Street Tuesday night after the Leary show at Mystic Arts, the guys in the green VW van with peace-sign curtains, grabbing her out of the fog and stuffing her into the vehicle like she was a doll. He knows he's not supposed to talk details like this, but the idea that the Laguna cops aren't doing their best for Jazz comes jumping up at him again, like an ugly little jack popping out of its box.

"I made out with Laurel," he says.

"Woah, that's been coming on awhile."

"Like forever."

"How was it?"

"She's choice. I really like her."

Matt goes to work on the cake.

"I read the Bonnie Stratmeyer article in the *News-Post* today," says Ernie. "Now they say she could have been murdered."

Matt thinks of big-eyed Detective McAdam briefing the reporters the previous morning. "Yeah, I heard."

Ernie gets an unusual look, shaking his head. "Unbelievable that a guy can have the total hots for a girl at school and she gets murdered. Out of all the girls. Out of all the girls in all the high schools in the world, and Bonnie gets murdered. And the article said the FBI still hasn't figured out what drugs were in her. And how they got there. And she drowned but not there at Thalia. Not in salt water. The cops say the contusion cracked her skull."

"Suicide is still a maybe," says Matt.

"Bash your own head in?"

"Right. No."

"A weird thing is, I saw her months before she died, and I had this really strong emotion to talk to her. Even though she was out of my league, by a lot. And now I realize that if I had just gone up and talked to her, then maybe this wouldn't have happened."

"I don't get that."

"Well, just think. Say she *was* murdered. That means someone had to come across Bonnie at just the right time to get away with it. The right time to hit her, or shoot drugs into her, or drown her. But if I had just talked to her for even one minute, months earlier, that would have changed the timing of everything that followed. Meaning that whoever killed her might not have met up with her at all because of the one minute she talked to me. Get it?"

"I do," Matt says. "Even just a few seconds could mean a whole different reality."

Like Mahajad Om talked about, he thinks.

"Exactly," says Ernie.

Matt finishes the cake. He never knew Ernie was so keen on Bonnie. "Where was she that last time, when you could have talked to her but didn't?"

"March. I was at the Vortex for Sal Proetto's Evolver graduation. And she was one of them. An Evolver."

Like Sara, Matt thinks, who had seen Jasmine at the Vortex. Or was pretty sure she had.

Bonnie, Jazz, and Sara. *LA Moves*. The Vortex of Purity.

Now comes that rushing in Matt's ears again, his early warning system, his oracle. He has two important questions for Mahajad Om.

26

Matt is surprised to see the Vortex of Purity auditorium bustling this late. The marquee still has the beguiling golden Hamsa flickering in its center, but the message is different now:

> *THE VORTEX OF PURITY*
> *INVITES YOU*
> *FEAST OF THE SPIRIT*
> *TONIGHT 7–10*

Matt pauses at the marquee, just as he did before, drawn to the eye in the middle of the hand—the Hand of the Goddess, he remembers—which glitters gold and crimson, like the robe of Mahajad Om.

Inside, both the lobby and the auditorium proper have been set up for the feast, with food-heavy tables up front and scores of folding chairs set up before the stage from which the swami had delivered his Evolver welcome. The air is heavy with the smell of curry and rice, sautéed mushrooms and bamboo shoots, and of course incense. Having walked all of downtown delivering invites to the Summer of Eternal Love Experience, and having finished the prime rib, potatoes, and the immense piece of cake well over thirty minutes ago, Matt suddenly feels hungry again.

No sign of Mahajad now, just an auditorium of hippies and other young people eating and chanting between swallows as the same sitarist plays her shimmering notes.

He slides on his backpack, loads up a plate, and goes outside.
Sits and eats and watches, as he did before. Hears the generators humming. It's a different crowd tonight, not the eagerly
beautiful young people but a more streetwise hippie bunch,
many of them stoned, who seem more drawn to the feast than
the spirit, but he can't blame them for that.

He demolishes dinner, gets the sketchbook from his pack.
Touches up his sketches of McAdam and Johnny Grail and another new one of Laurel as Laurel—not part of the Gauguin—
just a dark-haired girl in a faded flannel, tilting her head as
she kissed him on her porch that night.

Time warps when he draws. When he looks up again the
last of the feasters appear to have left, and the women in the
lobby are rolling dish-laden carts toward a Vortex walkway.

"Matt Anthony."

Startled, Matt turns around to see that the swami has arrived from the darkness behind him on silent bare feet. Again
he wears his crimson robe with the upswept shoulders, and
his usual unidentifiable expression, almost buried in his gray-
black hair and gray-white beard and mustache: amusement,
curiosity, eagerness?

Matt stands quickly, the sketchbook in hand. "Swami Om.
You surprised me."

"It is I who am surprised. Are you okay? Is your sister
okay? Why are you here?"

"She is not okay." He blurts to Om what happened on Tuesday night in the fog, right outside their Third Street home.
"Now, I have two questions. One, are you sure you never saw
my sister Jasmine here at the Vortex?"

"I am sure!"

Matt detects no falsehood on the swami's face, just astonishment.

"*They placed her in a van and drove away with her? While you
pursued on foot?*"

"The police don't believe me."

"I will speak to them."

"They won't listen to you, either. My second question is, do you know that criminals who run a tabloid called *LA Moves* are publishing suggestive pictures of Bonnie Stratmeyer and Sara and others who follow you?"

"My Evolvers? My Enlightened and Ecstatic?"

"I'm sorry but, yes."

"Walk with me. Tell me more."

Matt follows the slow padded steps of the swami down a walkway. Tells him about Detective McAdam, and the three men who run the Laguna Beach photo shoots. And that McAdam is now calling Bonnie's death suicide or murder.

"Then these men should be questioned."

"I'm sure they will be."

Under a walkway light, Matt shows Mahajad his sketches of Rene DeWalt, Williams, and Amon Binder. The big swami holds up the book to study the pictures point blank, and Matt realizes how bad his eyesight is.

"I do not know them. They would not be welcome here."

Matt wonders how close Mahajad would have to get to a person in order to see them clearly. Wonders if, in his eyes, Jazz was too blurred for him to remember. Can you remember what you can't really see?

With a heavy exhale, the swami closes the book and hands it back. "The Karma of this murdered girl brings a shadow over my heart. I will call the police immediately if I see those men."

Matt gets out one of Jasmine's missing person flyers. Hands it the swami, who studies it.

"I have a third question for you, swami."

Om's black wet eyes study Matt from within the tangles of his hair and brows. "Please ask it."

"I've looked everywhere. I've walked every beach and gone to every bar and nightclub and restaurant, asked all of the people I deliver papers to. Remember when you told the Evolvers that now they could begin to see the world in a new way?"

"Yes, it is essential."

"But can I? See differently? So Jazz comes into view?"

Matt stays abreast of Mahajad, who continues in silence with his short, quiet steps. The path goes downhill through a swale Matt remembers was once crowded with black mustard and kudzu and wild tobacco. Now it's a grassy meadow with a stand of recently planted oaks in the middle, lit from below.

"Swami, please tell me how to see the world differently. She's running out of time."

They stop and the swami looks out at the young oaks basking in the floodlights. "It cannot be done instantly, Matt. You must begin with meditation. Meditation is simple and easy. Come here to the Vortex any day between two and five, or go to the Mystic Arts World store on Wednesdays or Fridays from seven to nine at night. Wear comfortable clothes but not leather. My Enlighteners are wonderful teachers. You only pay what you can afford. You will learn to see differently, which is only a way of thinking differently. Maybe it will help you find your sister. When you have passed my Evolution and Enlightenment ceremonies, I will personally oversee your training. Come."

Back in the auditorium the women are waiting for their swami. The two sharp-eyed, white-suited security men are there, too, apparently flirting with them.

The men withdraw as Matt and Mahajad enter the lobby. Om pays no attention to any of them as he claims one of two foil-wrapped paper plates from one of the now empty food tables.

"Take this, Matt."

"Thank you."

"We who are always hungry must eat when we can."

The swami collects a second foil-wrapped plate, lifts it to his nose for a whiff.

"Aren't these both yours?" asks Matt.

"Let us call them loaves and fishes. You will find your sister, Matt."

"I'm going to have to. The police don't believe me and they have Bonnie and Johnny Grail to worry about. Here I am, the son of a cop who's not here to help his own daughter. In a town where the police don't give a shit. I'm pissed off. Sorry for the unholy words, swami."

27

In the fragrant Dodge City "packing house," Julie, wearing one of her mother's homemade dresses and a matching bonnet, hands Matt a mason jar. Matt thinks that, for the first time in his life, she looks like the farm girl she once was. The dress is beige and the bonnet ties at her chin. She looks like the label of a dairy product.

This warm morning, the packing house is dense with the smells of tomatoes, garlic, and onions.

"I've been checking with Darnell by phone twice a day," she says. "They haven't learned anything. I've talked to all the neighbors about Tuesday night but nobody saw it happen. Ten thirty P.M. and nobody sees a thing! I've called all of Jazz's friends' families again, just hoping that something might click into place to help the cops find her. I taped up another fifty posters down in South Laguna and Dana Point. I had a long talk with an old friend who used to be a PI. I'll be meeting with him tomorrow. I even meditated at Mystic Arts World with one of that swami's so-called Enlighteners, hoping I could make that connection to Jazz you keep talking about, you know, like cosmically. I didn't. But we're going to find her, Matt. And I'm going to find my own strength, too."

She looks serene, he thinks. Her skin is smooth, eyes bright, her dark ringlets bounce beneath the bonnet lid. Matt has prepared himself for a kimono-and-dragon-ball Dodge City Julie, not this. Is it all an act, possibly drug-enhanced?

"This is from Johnny," she says, pressing some bills into his hand. The five bucks for the flyers, Matt thinks: just in time.

She takes a mason jar off the table and hands it to him. "Check out the cool label."

The label shows on-the-vine tomatoes in hot blue, cinnamon, and yellow, with the words in loopy psychedelic tomato red:

LAGUNA SUNSHINE FARMS

100% ORGANIC STEWED TOMATOES

GROWN WITH PRIDE, CANNED WITH LOVE

"We grow them right here," she says. "Sell them out at the roadside stand. We deliver and ship, too."

The packing house is an old home on Woodland, gutted of most interior walls, with an exposed beam ceiling, skylights, and enormous windows. The windows have no glass, only screens, so the weather outside is the weather inside, which this morning is warm and humid. Looking up, Matt can see sunlight between the ceiling beams and bees clustered near the peak, buzzing lazily.

"So anyway, this is where I work. Me and Crazy Carol, who isn't crazy at all. Basically, it's one big kitchen, but with canning stations. Those are the water bath canners and jar racks. There's all my jar wrenches and lifters and funnels. And those are ladles and bubble removers. Those boxes are all mason jars, the good ones with screw bands and commercial sealers. All new. Carol and I are supposed to work about eight hours a day, but they're flexible. And we get as long a lunch as we want. She usually comes in later. So it's working out for me here, Mattie. I'm keeping all the bad things away. Most of them."

Matt sees the pasteboard boxes of Laguna Sunshine Farms canned stewed tomatoes stacked along one wall near the double doors. The boxes have enlargements of the mason jar labels stickered onto them. There's a conveyor belt running from the cooling table to cut down lifting the heavy boxes. The prep tables are piled with spices, blenders, chopping blocks, and cleavers.

"Anyway," she says, looking around inquisitively, as if she's just arrived here. "We compost the skins. But I had the most terrifying dream last night. That my skin was being composted too. It was my responsibility to peel it off before bed, and throw the rolls into the compost heap."

Matt sees that troubled fear coming back into her eyes. Senses her mood beginning to tremble, like a building at the beginning of an earthquake.

"Why are you looking at me like that?" she asks.

"Nothing, Mom."

"I'm sorry. It's Jazz. It's what I said to her that last night, before she left. I said, bring the damned van back with a full tank or don't come back at all. I can't support you your whole life. That's what I told my daughter."

The words hit Matt hard and he knows they would have hit Jazz hard too.

"Sometimes you blow up like that, Mom. She knows you didn't mean it."

"Love the ones you love, Matt, because you never know what's going to happen next."

Suddenly, the Dodge City dogs are barking, and Matt sees two of them tearing off toward Laguna Canyon Road. Then two more. He hears popping sounds, like firecrackers, then bigger explosions, like the shotguns he used to shoot with Kyle and his dad. A fire alarm rings loudly, cutting through the popping and booming.

"Cops again," says Julie.

Outside Matt sees Moby Cop lumbering down Woodland. The Dodge City denizens emerge from their homes and yards, dogs charge the vehicle, the same barefoot boys who had invaded his mother's barn scramble toward the van brandishing sticks. The skinny black monkey screams crazily, pulling at his chain like a prisoner. Smoke wafts, and Matt recognizes

the sulfur smell of firecrackers as a cherry bomb explodes on
the crumbling paved road and sends up a burst of paper and
asphalt that brings Moby Cop to a stop.

Furlong and Darnell drop out, slam the doors and advance,
firecrackers skittering and popping ahead of them, and the
dogs barking shrilly from behind.

"Hello, Dodge City hippies, artists, and drug fiends!" Furlong calls out. "I smelled smoke all the way out to Laguna
Canyon Road and thought I'd come see what you bad kids
are up to."

Fuck off, pigs!

Peace and love, brother and sister!

Fuck off, pigs!

We've got the Constitution on our side!

"For cryin' out loud, folks," Darnell calls out, her rope of
blond hair braided and pinned atop her head. "We're just here
on a friendly visit!"

A cherry bomb explodes in the air not far from her, and
Darnell flinches.

Bullshit!

The times they are a-changin'!

But the citizens mostly stay in their yards and on their
porches, tossing lit strings of firecrackers, launching their
words like artillery. The boys with sticks run off after each
other, shrieking. Some of the dogs lie down in the middle of
street to watch as Furlong and Darnell march toward the
packing house.

"This kind of stuff happens a lot," Julie says.

"Wow," says Matt, watching Johnny Grail walk to the middle of Woodland Drive, stop, and face Furlong and Darnell
like a Western gunfighter. Grail furtively jams something
into a rear pocket of his jeans.

Then he takes a few steps toward the cops and stops again,
ten feet away. Matt hustles closer for a better view, joins a
family of five, all wearing overalls. Grail raises both hands
high.

"Don't shoot. I'm innocent!"

"You don't look innocent, Johnny," says Furlong. "You look like a spaced-out drug pusher."

"My kids are around here somewhere, man. Don't go spreading lies about me."

"I don't have to lie. When I saw you smoking dope with them last week, that said it all. And I really don't like it when you run from me, Johnny."

"Well darn, Marshal Dillon, that's better than getting handcuffed and taken away."

"What's that in your back pocket?" asks Furlong.

Furlong and Darnell stride forward but Grail holds his ground. Then submits with a shake of his shaggy head as Furlong takes him by the back of his neck, marches him to the curb, and bends him over the hood of a dusty white station wagon. Furlong cinches up on Johnny's arm as Darnell pulls a baggie from his back pocket.

"What's this?" she asks.

"What's it look like?"

"Weed, to me."

"You have no probable cause for this search."

"Cause? Plain sight, Johnny! I watched you try to hide it."

With this, Darnell pulls open the bag and sniffs it.

"Funny, Johnny."

"Isn't dried dog shit still legal in Laguna?"

With this, the Dodge citizens laugh and scream and resume the firecracker-and-cherry-bomb assault, and the dogs spring into action and the tribe of boys comes screaming out from behind the mailboxes at the corner of Woodland and Victory Walk.

Furlong has his handcuffs out and he tries to get Grail back over the car hood but Johnny twists free and hauls ass down Woodland away from Moby Cop and into the steep, rough flank of Laguna Canyon.

Furlong digs heavily after him, Darnell too.

Go, go, go Johnny go!

Fuck you dog shit–sniffin' pigs!

Matt can see that the cops don't have a chance. Lithe Grail has already vanished into the dense canyon brush. Furlong and Darnell gamely pursue, burdened by equipment.

Four of the feral boys converge on Moby Cop, squat at the wheels and let the air out of the tires. Matt hears the hissing. They finish the job and are peeing on the wheels just as the cops come panting back into Matt's view, Furlong trudging and Darnell's braided ponytail dangling.

When Matt gets back to where he'd been standing with Julie, she's not there.

He finds her in the barn on Roosevelt Lane. She's in her bathroom and not visible, but the bathroom door is mostly open and its mirror throws her reflection to Matt, who has stopped in the living room.

"Mom, I'm here."

"Good, Matt. Sorry, I just couldn't stand all that."

She's in the bathtub, still in her prairie dress but the bonnet is gone. She's reclining as if in a bubble bath, her back to him. A thick cloud of smoke surrounds her head, rolling back over her shoulders like fog. It swells and sways as she lightly coughs.

"I'm taking a warm bath but I'll be out in a minute!"

"I know what you're doing."

He strides into her bedroom, slams the bathroom door on her, and rifles the room for dope. Finds a foil-wrapped dragon ball on the dresser, another in the nightstand drawer. She isn't even trying to hide them, he thinks. And she can get more anytime she wants out here in Dodge. Furlong told him that every person out here was a drug user or dealer or both. Told him that even the kids out here are users, burying joints and chunks of hashish in the ground where the adults won't find them. Maybe Furlong isn't a paranoid fascist storm trooper after all.

The kitchen sink has a garbage disposal. The balls go down in a roar and a stream of hot water. Foil in the trash.

"What are you doing in there, Mattie?"

"Nothing that fucking matters!"

Matt takes the van and drives home. Julie's opium addiction is his personal last straw. She looks dreamy and content on the outside but inside she's as thin as the smoke she lives on. He feels suckered by her, manipulated, discarded. Probably what Jazz felt. And Julie dares to warble on about finding her strength. All of which leads him to conclude that the Westfalia is now his. He can use it for lots of things. His useless stoner mom doesn't need it and she shouldn't be driving anyway.

He lets himself in and answers the ringing phone.

"Matt, it's Dad. Is Jazz home or not?"

"Not. I told you two men threw her into a van in front of our house. Right in front of me. Four days ago. She's been missing nine days, Dad."

"Can't you handle the problem?"

"I've been looking all over for her!"

"But it sounds like you're not handling it. So, expect me."

"I've heard that before."

His father hangs up.

28

He opens Kyle's letter as he sits on a beach chair in the Third Street driveway, waiting for Tommy to bring his papers. He's been sketching angrily. It infuriates him to be drawing his mother in her bathtub like she was, entombed in hash and opium, oblivious to the world around her. It also infuriates him that his deadbeat father can't show up to help his own daughter. It'll be a relief to hear about the war.

Kyle's penmanship leans hurriedly forward.

Hello Matt,

Corporal Kyle Anthony reporting for duty, bro. Another nasty week underground here in beautiful Cu Chi. Samarond got a bullet through his eye and it took a winch to get him out. Next day I heard a baby crying in the dark, softly, way down in the tunnels. At first, it's just elbows and knees for Rat 9. I'm strapped with a good headlight and have my .45 in hand. So, on I crawl on all fours, thinking about Samarond, and I hear the baby again. Sound doesn't carry well underground so I know it's closer now. Then I hear a little squeaky voice—a woman or a kid maybe. I can feel the claustrophobia trying to get me. I'm getting closer to the crying baby and all of a sudden the tunnel opens up big enough for me to stand and I follow the barrel of my .45 into a hospital room lit by a lantern. It's got stained beds and a surgery table. There's parachute material stretched tight against the walls to keep the dirt back. There's an IV drip stand with an empty pouch dangling. And crouching on the floor is a girl with a baby in her arms, and her face is just pure terror when she sees me with my gun pointed at her. Course I wonder what kind of trap this is, what's this girl doing down here with her baby. Then I realize she's just had the baby and the others have run off. Or maybe this girl was alone here.

"Khong."

"No," I tell her.

"Khong."

The baby cries again but not loud. It's wrapped in a bundle of parachute nylon and I figure it's fifty-fifty there's a pistol in there too. I wave my gun at the exit tunnel. Her eyes widen and she backpedals, staring at me. I know if she has a gun she'll turn away, then pull it. I've got my sights lined up on her forehead to save the baby. Then she turns and stumbles and catches herself and runs with her baby into the tunnel. I watch her in the beam of my headlight. And she's gone.

I'm forty-four days short today. It's weird, little brother. I feel like I'm standing on a bridge with a noose around my neck and waiting for someone to push me over. Sarge reminds me that the shorter you are the safer you are, statistically, since you've made it this far. Much better chances than the day you arrived, he says. But this isn't a statistical problem. It's war, which presses a man's fate into a smaller and smaller container. A young mother's too.

I can't wait to get home. Still got the route? Mom good? Jazz okay?

Love to All,
Rat 9

Matt is finishing his letter back to Kyle just as Tommy arrives with today's papers. In the letter, Matt does not mention Bonnie, just as he hasn't told Kyle abut Jazz. On half a sketchbook page, he dashes off a quick drawing of the house that will no longer be Kyle's home by the time he gets back. Matt thinks of telling Kyle about losing the house, but it might be distracting. Although not as bad as hearing that Jazz has been missing for nine days and that Laguna is papered with her police missing-persons flyers. He creases and tears off the drawing, folds it carefully and puts it in the envelope with the letter.

Welcome home, Kyle.

Matt tears through his paper route like a kid on fire. His ridiculous parents, his inability to find his sister, Furlong's dull disbelief, the growing probability that Bonnie was murdered, all fuel him. He pedals as hard as he can. His turns are tight and his skids are controlled. He treats the traffic with contempt. His accuracy with the papers is the best it's ever been. Checks his Skindiver: 2:47 minutes, a record.

He's dripping sweat, panting hard, and still angry by the time he's finished, way up in Bluebird Canyon, looking down on the houses and the descending hills and the heaving white-capped Pacific. A yellow biplane pulls a Coppertone banner slowly up the coast, south-to-north.

He thinks about his sister. He thinks about Om. He remembers telling Mahajad that he's looked everywhere for Jazz. Is there a different way to see? But wait a minute: how could he make such a claim? He has *not* looked everywhere.

He has not looked everywhere.

An idea begins to form in his angry mind.

That evening he's eating fresh-caught perch alone in the Third Street house when the phone rings.

It's Jazz, her voice a caged whisper.

"I can't get out!"

"Where are you?"

"In Laguna! I'm in the . . ."

Then the sharp crack and the muted ring of a bell. Then dial tone.

Ten silent minutes.

Thirty.

He pictures her in a cage. A cell. A dark garage.

He calls Darnell, who answers on the first ring.

"Do not leave that phone," she says.

They sit in the living room for the next hour, Matt telling Darnell what happened until there isn't one more question she can ask or one more answer he can give. He repeats Jasmine's nine words exactly. And how she said them: in breathless terror.

Matt stares out the window as Darnell's assuring voice fills the little room. It's important to know that she's here, says the officer. That she's close. That's the hope.

"Do you believe me now?"

"I believe you now."

"Furlong won't. McAdam won't."

"I always believed you. But maybe not quite enough."

"Belief plus doubt is not belief."

"I believe you now, Matt. One hundred percent."

Matt feels numb, but in a good way. He's too afraid of what's happening to his sister for nonsense, frivolity, or anything like pride to enter his mind. He feels purged. Pure. As if he's broken through to another way of seeing things. Another connection to Jazz.

Suddenly, it comes to him: the way to find her.

It has clarity and logic, simplicity, and a dose of can't-miss. Like certain moments fishing—timing the surge, then the cast, the pause, the retrieve—it's all perfect and you know, you know. You just know.

29

The next morning, the *Register* coast cities reporter takes notes as Matt tells his tale. The reporter's name is Steve Mitchell, and he wants Matt's portrait of Jasmine, and an LBPD missing-persons flyer to impress his editor. His office is on Coast Highway in Laguna, in the basement of a real estate brokerage.

Matt senses none of the skepticism he's gotten from the police. Mitchell agrees that a boy of sixteen ought to be able to ID his own sister from fifty feet away, fog or not. And know her voice on the phone. Mitchell says he'll have to talk to the cops for their side of things. Kidnapping is serious business, he says, and newspapers have a responsibility. Matt says nothing of Jazz's links to Austin Overton, Jordan Cavore's parties, *LA Moves*, or Bonnie Stratmeyer. He's trying to find his sister, not humiliate her. On Darnell's advice, he says nothing about the peace-sign curtains in the kidnap van that night.

Sitting beside Matt, Laurel takes notes of her own. They've agreed that written documentation might be important. There will certainly be lots of things to keep track of. And Matt knows how important another set of eyes and ears could be.

"I hear you're in the summer writing program at UCI," says Mitchell. "I'm impressed."

"Mom and Dad got me in," she says.

"But still, you must be pretty good."

"All I know is how hard it is."

"Next summer, come see me if you want to intern here."

"I'd love to."

"And one more thing," says Mitchell. "Nothing about this to the *Times* or the *Pilot* until after the story runs in the *Register*. Not even the *News-Post*. Get it?"

The quest begins half an hour later, way down in South Laguna.

Matt's plan, hatched with Laurel, is for them to go south to north, to every occupied residence in the city, knock on each door, and show each person who answers his sister's MISSING poster. According to the city planning department there are just over five thousand households in town. Most stops will be brief, Matt reasons, because most of Laguna's homes and apartments are occupied by married couples, young professionals, families, women, the elderly and retired. He and Laurel will quickly see if Jazz could even possibly be a prisoner there. If not, they'll be quickly on their way. If so, they'll go straight to the police.

And Jasmine will be behind one of these doors, Matt knows. She has to be.

It's a mathematical fact.

I can't get out!

In Laguna!

I'm in the . . .

And if he surprises her tormentors and actually discovers her, what will he do? Those men were strong, determined, and at ease with violence. He thinks of Kyle's .357 Magnum under the bed, knows how to use it, sort of, knows where the ammo is, too. But to carry that bruising cannon around Laurel, and into innocent homes, is both illegal and stupidly dangerous. For that matter, could he really shoot someone?

No. But if he finds her, he'll find a way to free her.

By the end of this first day—just half a day, really, after talking to Steve Mitchell—they've knocked on seventy-one doors and looked through six homes and three apartments.

Two people slam doors on them. But five others offer water, juice, and soft drinks.

Matt pulls the Westfalia into the loading curb in front of the Pageant of the Masters grounds. He and Laurel are quiet and hungry and she's running late for her hair, makeup, and costume. Ticket-holders stream in around them.

"This could take longer than I thought," says Matt.

"But it's how we'll find her."

"Do you think I'm an idiot for doing this?"

She smiles at him, kisses him briefly, reaches for the door handle. "You're a genius, Matt."

"Dinner after the show? It would have to be at my house in case the phone rings."

"I'd love that."

Waiting for Laurel, Matt showers thoroughly, shaves his chin, straightens up his old room, makes up Kyle's bed, puts a few stolen City Hall roses in vases in the living room, and splashes on some of Kyle's Hai Karate. He remembers the TV commercial warning men that they'll have to "fend off women" if they wear it. Hopes he hasn't put on too much.

Laurel drinks iced tea at the dinette while Matt makes dinner in the little kitchen. It's insanely stimulating to be here with her, without his mother.

He forgets the disappointments of the day. He can't stop talking and trying to make her laugh. He's spent more than three of Johnny Grail's five dollars on steaks and frozen French fries and a cake for dessert, and he's good with a skillet. Laurel gives him an appraising look when she learns that Julie is in her new digs tonight. He doesn't mention that he's got to be out of this house by next Sunday.

After dinner they sit close together on the lumpy couch and watch the old TV that Julie has bequeathed to her son. Laurel's TV at home is color. Nothing about Kyle on the late L.A. news. Another replay of Bobby Kennedy's railway hearse rolling along with all the flowers and his body inside and his brother and widow waving.

The windows of Matt's house are all open so it smells of steak smoke and nightshade blossoms. Through the window Matt keeps an eye on the exact place where they bagged Jazz last Tuesday night. Glances at the phone too often.

Then he takes a deep breath and kisses Laurel. He's pretty sure she likes it.

So he kisses her more ardently, but she pulls away.

"Let's go slow," she says.

"That's probably best."

"I like you, Matt."

"I'll wait as long as you want."

"Okay. But maybe just one more short one."

The phone doesn't ring and Laurel has to be home no later than midnight.

The next morning, after knocking on 157 doors with Laurel, Matt sits in the beach chair on his driveway, folding and banding his papers. He's spent the last half hour on the phone with the *News-Post* and *Los Angeles Times.*

Tommy now holds Matt in awe because of the *Register* story—front page and above the fold—about the brazen kidnapping of Jasmine Anthony. Tommy holds the paper open in front of him, reading the jump and asking questions.

"This is just freaky cool, Matt. You, a sixteen-year-old paperboy chasing kidnappers down PCH on foot!"

Matt doesn't know how to feel about the article, which treats him as a minor hero for running into the night after a VW hippie van containing his abducted sister. Wouldn't any brother?

Hearing Tommy read the story, Matt is reminded that it was smart not to tell the reporter the true color of the van—he said in the excitement he didn't notice—or anything about peace-sign curtains. The cops still have their secret evidence, he thinks.

"And they put in your sketch of Jazz really nice and big, and the police flyer, too," says Tommy. "Everybody in Laguna's going to see this and talk about it. It'll flush the creeps out into the open."

"That's the hope."

"They didn't run a picture of you because it might put you in danger."

Matt nods. "We decided that was best."

Tommy closes the paper. "You look different."

Matt figures it's his new celebrity, his new dangerous life. "Different how?"

"Your shirts are too small."

Matt looks down at his *Endless Summer* T-shirt. In fact, his shirts and pants have been tighter lately and he's felt heavier. No surprise, given how much he's been eating. And spending, mostly on food. He's anxious about money, although Grail's five dollars can go a long way *if* you're catching fish. He still wonders where he'll go after Sunday, which is both the Summer of Eternal Love "experience" in the canyon, and the last day he'll experience sleeping in this house. His last not-quite-fifteen dollars won't last long if he has to pay rent on anything but a campground spot.

Tommy slams the trunk lid of his white Chevy Malibu and tosses the paper through the open driver's window.

Then turns his head sharply toward the base of the Third Street hill. "That chick looks kind of like Jasmine. But shorter."

Matt bolts out of the beach chair and sees the pretty blond girl coming down Third Street. His heart jumps, though he sees not Jasmine, but Sara the Skateboard Girl and Evolver, carving down one side of the narrow street on her pink skateboard.

"That's Sara," he says.

Although Sara seems to be concentrating on her ride—arms out and legs bent—she also appears to be coming straight at them. Matt would wave but he doesn't want to distract her. She's coming fast and the cars are buzzing up and down Third and Sara looks small and smashable.

Hair flying, she casts a look behind her and pumps twice hard, angling across the street and into Matt's driveway. Stops with a wheelie flip and catches the board in midair.

"Hello, Matt Anthony."

"Sara."

"Sara *Eikenberg*."

"And I'm Matt's good friend and boss, Thomas."

Tommy offers his hand and she shakes it with a motion and

posture that, to Matt, reveal an upper-class, perhaps even royal upbringing. She's polite but dismissive. All of her attention is on Matt and Matt feels it.

She's wearing denim short-shorts, a black halter, and pink sneakers that match her pink-with-white-daisies board. Her temples are soggy with sweat and her shoulders shine golden in the sun.

"I came by to see if you want a well-paying job," she says. "It's on my parents' estate in Emerald Bay. It will be hard work. Mahajad told me you're always hungry and need money."

"Yes. I am."

"Dad wants it done tomorrow morning."

"Do you need two men?" asks Tommy.

"Just one."

"Well you got a good one," he says. "This guy chases kidnappers up and down PCH just for fun. Here, front page."

Tommy hands her a freshly folded and rubber-banded *Register*. Smiles at her, climbs into his car and drives off.

"I already read it," says Sara. "Unbelievable that Jazz has been kidnapped in Laguna, and that—according to her phone call—she's being held somewhere right here in town."

"That's why I'm door-knocking with Laurel."

A look. "What a huge labor, going door-to-door like that and dealing with people who may not want to help. Or even be polite."

"She's out there, somewhere."

"You will find her."

She tosses the unopened afternoon final into Matt's pile.

"If you live in Emerald Bay," he says, "why don't you go to Laguna High?"

"I go to Jokewood, up in Newport. With all the other spoiled rich kids."

Matt knows of it: Oakwood Academy. Jazz calls it Jokewood, too. Jazz and Sara Eikenberg don't just look kind of similar, he thinks. They have the same superior attitude, same sarcastic humor.

"Congratulations on evolving," he says.

"Thanks. It took a while. I'm not cut out for evolution but the others helped me along. Some of them are spaced out and weird, but mostly they're alright. At least they want to *improve* themselves."

"Did you know Bonnie Stratmeyer?"

"From the photo Happenings and the Vortex. I saw her a couple of times. And then, poof—she was gone."

"You call them Happenings?"

"The director calls them Happenings. That's Rene DeWalt. He wanted to call them 'Be-Ins' but Timothy Leary has that title all sewn up."

Matt looks into Sara's squinting face. There's something pugnacious about it when she's not smiling. An inner toughness. Jazz again.

"What kind of job is it?" he asks.

"We cut down twenty big eucalyptus trees on our property. Ground the stumps, too. Eucalyptus are shallow-rooted, so they blow over in Santa Ana winds, and they're a fire hazard. Dad hates waste, so he wants the log sections to line the driveway. The driveway is long and steep, and some of the log sections are, well, sizeable. He wants the biggest ones down at the bottom by the gate, for a dramatic welcome. Then, the smaller ones up top. Dad doesn't want a tractor chewing up the roses and groundcover. The tree crew was bad enough. He wants it done by hand. We have a wheelbarrow."

"Why me?"

"When I told Mahajad I needed a worker, he suggested you. Told me the hungry always work the hardest."

"How much?"

"Fifteen bucks."

"That's a lot of money."

"Not really. Dad can afford it. You've probably heard of D.L. Eikenberg Homes."

Matt certainly has. And everyone knows that Emerald Bay is one of the best and most expensive neighborhoods in Laguna. The job doesn't sound too hard, and he has a pair of decent work gloves.

"Sara, how old are you?"

"Sixteen and a half. Got my license six months ago and Dad bought me a new Porsche."

"I got mom's hippie van."

"I really dig those."

He's about to say she could drive it sometime, but the Westfalia is for him and Laurel, right?

Moby Cop comes to a stop in Matt's driveway and the driver's window goes down. Furlong studies Matt and Sara from behind his aviators.

"Stupid," he says to Matt. "You should never have talked to the press. Now those kidnappers—if that's in fact what you saw—will keep low and hide their van out of sight. You helped them."

"I didn't say the color of the van."

"Come here."

Matt goes to Moby Cop, checks the back for prisoners but it's empty. He looks up at the still-seated sergeant.

"You disappoint me, Matt. I give you trust and money and a way to do the right thing. I am concerned for your family, whether you know it or not. But you do this. After I order you not to."

"I think it was best, sir. For Jasmine. They threw her into that van like she was a toy. It was terrible and people in Laguna should know about it. But you don't even believe that happened. I have no patience left for you or your department."

"There are places for boys like you. You do not want to see one."

He looks past Matt to Sara, throws Moby Cop into reverse, and backs out.

arly dawn on Emerald Bay, the water not emerald at all, but a gray mirror in the new light. The morning is cool and the beach homes wait in fog, their windows throwing faint reflections back at Matt Anthony, who waits high on a hillside inside the Eikenberg gate.

He pulls on his leather work gloves. He's got coffee in a thermos, two donuts from Dave's in his stomach, a simmering anger at Furlong and at himself, for taking this valuable time away from his search for Jasmine. No sign of Sara, who buzzed him in through the intercom, but the wheelbarrow she mentioned is right here by the driveway gate. He wonders if he can even use it on a slope this steep.

Matt takes another sip of coffee, crosses himself like in the movies, and gets to work.

First order of business from here is to get the smaller logs to the top of the drive, and the big ones to the bottom. He picks up two of the smaller ones, and damned heavy they are, but he clinches one under each armpit and trots uphill. It's like carrying car batteries or cocker spaniels and his legs feel the weight before he's halfway up.

He makes it to the top.

Drops the logs, then works them upright into the dirt. Two down!

Then he pushes one very big log off its flat sawn edge, aims it downhill and gives it a push with his foot. It wobbles, then straightens, gravity kicking in, then Matt's chasing it down the slope, guiding it with short alternating kicks like a soccer player, dodging the Victorian streetlamps and log piles and barely keeping up with the solid, barreling thing. It's like trying to control a hog with your feet.

Nearing the gate Matt turns the animal with a strong kick and watches it angle hard right, skid downslope, stall, and stop. He brakes but catches his heel and goes down, sledding through a bed of eucalyptus leaves on his butt. He stands, panting. Still twenty feet to get that log into position. Advancing in a mood of combat, he squats and flips the log flat-end to flat-end, laterally downslope, and finally into place.

He stands over log number three as something conquered. He's breathing hard. His whole body feels used, just like it does high up on Bluebird every day, after slinging his last paper. But he knows he can't move the big logs downhill in this way, and not get hurt.

He takes a moment to look out at the Pacific, already a deep indigo blue in the weakening fog. Smells coastal sage and, of course, eucalyptus. Hears doves *hoo-hooing* in a sycamore tree and thinks how cool it would be if his mother and father were still married, and he and Kyle and Jazz could help them build a house right exactly here, where they could wake up to this every morning. He could fish down there where only the residents can go. Get a dog.

He loads the wheelbarrow with four smaller logs and grinds his way uphill on the smooth concrete of the drive. It's slow going, all back and legs, and he stops twice to rest. His legs feel heavy but powerful.

I'm doing this for you, sister, he thinks. Doing this for you.

He places the logs upright, gets them close to level, then confronts the next monster. He thinks he can clean and jerk it into the wheelbarrow, and he sees that it will have to land dead center or the implement will flip over. He guesses the log at eighty pounds. He tells himself the log is none other than Sgt. Bill Furlong. Stoops, wrestles it up, and—all legs and arms now—takes two steps, drops it over the edge, and in.

With its heavy cargo the wheelbarrow tries to take off

downhill, but Matt hangs on, gets it into a slalom like a downhill racer, left and right and left and right down the driveway, leaning back to brake, the log bouncing against the steel like it's trying to jump out.

But he gets there, delivering his prize just a few feet from his target, and wrenching it into place beside the first big section.

He stands in something like victory, heart pounding throughout his body.

Sun beginning to break through.

Thinks: You can do this, you can do it. Sees his next four logs waiting for him in a fragrant heap just a few yards away.

Loads and goes.

By seven he's moving slower, but there have been no disasters. Five round trips so far and twenty-five logs in place. The wheelbarrow is a godsend. So are his leather gloves. His sweat-drenched work shirt has been mauled by the big logs, and his stomach and ribs are abraded and on their way to raw. But, looking down from the top, he's proud.

He turns to see Sara Eikenberg coming down the walkway from the house, swinging what looks like a wicker picnic basket. White shorts and a brown top and flip-flops.

"Good morning, Matt!"

"Sara!"

"You look exhausted."

"You look evolved."

"Aren't you the funny one. I brought you some breakfast."

Matt upends a big log for her and one for himself, and another between them for a table. He knows he smells of eucalyptus and sweat but doesn't care. Sara's perfume is spicy but rich. Her halter is dark chocolate brown like her eyes.

"I only have five minutes," he says.

"That's too bad."

She opens the basket, sets out two foil-wrapped items that smell like bacon and eggs, two bottles of orange juice and two bananas. Napkins with little sailboats on them.

His bacon and egg sandwich goes fast. Banana too, then the orange juice for energy.

She's squinting at him in that way of hers, like she's not sure if she approves of him. Her hair is wavy and corn-colored, strands bleached by the sun.

"You give me odd looks," she says.

He wads and drops his napkin into the basket. "Sorry. But you kind of remind me of my sister, and when I think of her the situation just seems hopeless."

He can't believe he's said this. He knows his hope of finding Jasmine has been weakening by the day, but he hasn't admitted it out loud until now. Just yesterday he thought he'd be relieved when this endless, clueless searching for her was over. The knocking on doors for nothing. The disappointment. Which made him feel traitorous and ashamed and angry at himself. And he's angry again, right now, for eating breakfast with a pretty girl who's not even his girlfriend—if he really has a girlfriend—when he could be searching for Jazz.

She leans forward and places her hand on his knee. A puff of that perfume. "It's out of your control. You're doing everything you can and it will either be enough or it won't. It is my personal belief that you will find her."

"Belief based on what?"

"That I like you and want the best for you. And for Jazz, of course."

Matt's skin is burning under her hand. And he's surprised to hear this from Sara. This word, "like." Does she mean it the same way Laurel means it?

Then her hand is gone and she's nodding toward the logs. "How's the job going, Matt?"

"Twenty-five done, maybe another one-seventy-five left. It's harder than I thought. So I really have to get back to work, Sara. If I take too long, my papers will be late."

Now it's Sara who gives Matt the odd look. "Om says we die

but we don't end. That we evolve into something higher, to die and evolve again. I'm not so sure I believe that."

"You think we just die and that's it?"

"I think it's very possible that we die and that's it."

"Are you serious?"

"Why can't I be serious?"

"Because you have everything."

"Yes, and that's exactly the point. Every single *thing*. Life is more than matter. More than material things. If we only live once there has to be more to care about than the houses we buy and the cars we drive. There has to be more to *love*."

A ripple of darkness on her face. A hard glance at Matt, then a faraway stare to the Pacific.

She packs the breakfast wrappings and banana peels back into the basket, closes the lids. "I'll bring this back full when you're done."

A look and she's off. Matt watches her head toward the house, basket swinging.

32

He's home by two-thirty, perched heavily on his upended red bucket in the driveway, folding and rubber-banding the papers as fast as he can. His tree-trunk muscles feel huge and cumbersome, not so much painful as inflated.

Sara has paid him fifteen dollars and sent him home with the picnic basket restocked with two sandwiches, potato salad, and an apple, all of which he shovels down while doing the papers. She told him to hang on to the basket and fork and return them to her sometime.

He looks at the Schwinn Heavy-Duti standing loyally by, wonders if he'll have the strength to make up the hour and a half of delivery time he lost in Emerald Bay. Considers doing the route in the Westfalia but with all the stops and starts it would actually take longer. More complaints. Old Coiner on the rampage. Wear and tear on Mom's van. He mildly shudders at the thought of what she might be doing right now out in Dodge City.

He feels terrible about working for Sara when he could have been looking for Jasmine. But he needed those fifteen dollars.

So now, on his paper route, he strains and finds new strength. He thinks of his pain as deserved punishment. He gets the job done more or less on time.

On the way home he gets two meat burritos and a side of rice at Taco Bell with Sara's money. He puts the bag of food in the front basket and slogs for home up Coast Highway, every gentle rise feeling like he's on the Tour de France.

Grail and Christian are standing outside Mystic Arts World and Grail waves Matt over. "Matt!"

He pulls onto the sidewalk and stops, straddling the bike. His groin and hamstrings twang with pain.

Grail jokes about Furlong bringing him in for questioning but not having anything to arrest him for except possession of a bag of dog shit.

"That was funny," says Matt.

"I've got another easy delivery tomorrow if you're interested," Grail says.

"I can't," says Matt. "I'm looking for Jazz door-to-door. It takes time, and I did some extra work today that I shouldn't have."

Grail shrugs, purses his lips. "I'm bumming for you, man. I had no idea what all went down, until I read that article. She's here in town for sure. You'll get her back. I've got every brother keeping watch for her. We all like her. There's lots of us who care. It's not Jasmine's Karma to be treated like that."

"She is being treated like that. But I hope you're right."

A moment of silence for Jasmine Anthony.

"You look bigger," says Christian.

"I think I'm growing," says Matt.

Grail takes a look inside the Taco Bell bag in Matt's basket. "You know, Matt, about tomorrow, it's the same gig as last time, same book, same customer. Take about five minutes of your life and I'll go five bucks this time."

Matt considers, but not for long.

"That's different."

"Sound judgment. See you tomorrow."

Back home, Matt devours the Taco Bell, then showers before picking up Laurel for their evening hunt for Jazz.

Drying off, something feels wrong. Standing in his underwear in front of his mom's mirrored closet door, Matt looks at himself and sees a stranger who has a face like his own, but a taller, bigger body. Muscles showing, and more hair on his legs and chest.

On a wall in his former bedroom there are two columns where he and Kyle used to chart their heights, weights, and dates. He gets a pencil and a measuring tape, which put him at five feet eleven—he's grown two inches in six months. So, Dr. Anderson was right—those drastic, long-lasting aches in his joints were just growing pains.

On the scale he weighs in at 165 pounds, twenty pounds gained in those same six months.

Back in the full-length mirror he gives himself a critical once-over, then assumes muscleman poses. His stomach muscles are visible. His biceps bulge when he flexes. His neck muscles move under the skin and his always-too-big Adam's apple looks as if it's finally found the right person. He can't believe how sore he is, all those eucalyptus logs up and down and up and down, and the paper route, and the walking and knocking. He could sleep a week.

He tries to find pants and shirts that aren't too tight, but can't. Kyle's are still too big. Thrift shop tomorrow, he thinks, if he can find a few minutes to shop.

But he gets to Laurel's on time and they continue their quest, which for Matt is transforming into a somber duty. Being with Laurel makes him feel strong and good, but it's not enough to deflect his mounting doubt. His search for Jasmine makes him think of Kyle's tunnels in Cu Chi, where all you will find is either nothing, or bad. He wonders if he's just exhausted.

Before every knock Matt takes a deep breath and tries to jack himself up for a good presentation. *Sorry to bother you, but I'm Matt Anthony and this is Laurel Kalina, and we both live here in Laguna Beach. My sister has been kidnapped . . .*

He feels that he's betraying Jazz with his pessimism. And

maybe even belittling Kyle by comparing his search with Kyle's, descending underground to kill or be killed.

He thinks of what Bette Page—his sophomore mythology and folklore teacher—said about the delusional Don Quixote, who imagined himself to be a knight and attacked windmills he thought were ferocious giants with a flimsy wooden sword. She said the story was intended to be funny. Matt wonders if he's like that guy. Delusional. Funny.

No, he thinks: Jazz's monsters are real.

After the Pageant of the Masters and a late dinner with Laurel, Matt drives her home. She's been quiet since he told her at dinner that the job he'd done that morning was for Sara Eikenberg's father. Parked at the curb in front of her house they kiss tenderly and for so long that Matt's log-tortured abdominal muscles start to cramp and he has to draw back, upright into his seat.

"Is something wrong?"

"No, my ribs just hurt. It's from the logs."

A strange, low-grade ache comes over him.

"I feel like you're changing," she says.

"I'm getting bigger. Everything hurts right now."

"No, your heart is changing."

"I can't stop thinking I'll never see her again. We did fifty-nine houses today and I never had the feeling we were anywhere even close to Jazz. When that guy laughed in our faces about me chasing the kidnappers on foot, I wanted to kill him."

"Keep the faith, Matt. God will bring her back."

"Doesn't that mean he took her away?"

"Everything happens for a reason."

"I've never believed that."

"I do. It doesn't mean you always get what you want. I say a prayer for Jazz every night. You should too."

"Okay."

"Sara Eikenberg has kind of a reputation, you know."

"I really didn't. She's funny and honest about things. And trying to make herself better, at the Vortex."

"She's a Jokewood snob," says Laurel.

After making sure that lights are on and the front door is unlocked, Matt gets into his sleeping bag in the garage.

He hasn't felt this bad since the mumps when he was five. Waves of pain, dull and incessant.

He squirms within it, his mind serving up ugly half dreams: logs that turn into severed bodies and severed bodies that turn into logs. He envisions Jazz and what has happened to her and what might be happening right now. How could he have let her get away that night? Will that be the last time he sees her? He feels his irresponsibility in not even having a fucking driver's license so he could chase after her, of not being fast and strong enough to run down that van and pull her out. He feels the weight of so many doors in town still left to knock on, while Jazz waits. And waits. He wonders if he's abandoned his mother out in Dodge when she needs him most. He likes Sara but feels guilt for this, loves Laurel but feels her drifting away from him.

He turns on his stomach, buries his face in the pillow, and shakes.

33

He sleeps past noon and wakes up feeling better. Stronger, less pain, and ready for his labors.

First he calls Laurel and apologizes, tells her he really isn't changing—he's the same as ever—then goes downtown for more Taco Bell, then to the Fade in the Shade thrift shop for some bigger clothes. Shirts and shorts, two pairs of jeans, and one pair of black Converse All-Stars high-tops only a little too big—one dollar and seventy-five cents.

By one o'clock he's in the Mystic Arts World back office with Johnny Grail, who takes an enormous toke on his desktop hookah, holds it in a long time, finally exhales a cloud of fragrant smoke. Matt declines. Grail slides a plastic-wrapped *Tibetan Book of the Dead* across the table to Matt, who squares it up and runs his fingers over the heavily embossed letters.

"Thanks again," says Johnny, setting a five-dollar bill beside the book.

"Why didn't you tell me it was for Marlon Sungaard?"

"I try to respect the privacy of my customers."

"Well, thanks for the money."

A conspirative smile from Grail. "Matt? I'm going to give you more than money. I'm going to give you something you might need even more someday. Come."

Grail walks not to the door but to the far wall, which is lined with bookshelves. He pulls down a copy of the Holy Bible, and Matt thinks he's about to get preached at by the founder of the BEL who has more than once told him that Jesus is LSD.

Instead, Grail reaches into the space where the Bible had been, and turns to Matt.

"Button on the wall," he says. "Open, you door of perception!"

Followed by his dry cackle of a laugh, as the entire shelf swings inward, leaving an opening easily big enough for a man.

Matt follows him in.

"Lights to your right, shoulder high."

On they come, revealing another room, probably for storage when it was designed, now outfitted with old furniture, a refrigerator, four small beds, a small kitchen and bath. Two floor heaters. No windows. Psychedelic paintings on the wall, some Christian's and some Matt doesn't recognize. In the back are shelves of what looks to be MAW merchandise.

"This is where you come to hide," says Grail. "From people like, say, Furlong. We call it the Bat Cave. The kitchen is stocked and there are books to read. Nobody knows about it but us."

"Nice."

"I've used it more than once. Most of us have."

"Cool, Johnny."

Grail turns to him with his eyes gleaming and a smile on his elfin face. "Matt, the Brotherhood of Eternal Love welcomes you as a friend. Not a member of our congregation but as a friend of our church. But who can know? Life is Karma and Karma is life. Maybe someday . . . you'll want to join us."

"I feel honored."

"Obviously this is our secret. Tell no one."

"I absolutely will not. Ever."

Matt interrupts his paper route to deliver the second *Tibetan Book of the Dead*. It looks identical to Matt, beautifully bound in gold-embossed leather, wrapped tightly in heavy, clear plastic.

He pushes his bike into the bougainvillea-walled front yard, hears the chime of the bell as before, notes the three gurgling birdbaths on his way to the porch. The blue milk box is as before, but Matt sees, with a slump of sadness, no white envelope. He sets the book in the box, and the front door opens.

"Matt. I'm Marlon Sungaard."

"Yes, sir. I have your book."

Sungaard looks old, at least forty. Bushy gray hair and a tanned, lined, handsome face. Prominent chin and nose. He wears a black turtleneck and strikes Matt as foreign. Unusual music—rhythmic but mechanical—throbs lightly from inside.

"Come in."

"I'm on my paper route."

"For only a moment, please."

The foyer is arched and paneled in dark wood. There's a wrought iron chandelier. Sungaard leads Matt into the great room, which has a beam ceiling and a hardwood floor. Sunlight slants through the blinds. The walls are white and hung with large black-and-white photo portraits in steel frames, mostly beautiful celebrities. There are Persian rugs and funny furniture—all chrome, black leather, and pale wood.

Standing in the middle of the room is a beautiful woman in black jeans and boots, and a sleeveless green blouse. She's tall, tan, and flagrantly blond.

In a slat of sunlight that cleaves her shadowed face like a mask, she smiles. Matt recognizes that mouth. Unmistakable. He's seen it with his own eyes: Cavore's cohost at the Sapphire Cove orgy, the woman with the little black mask and the long lighter.

"This is my wife, Neldra. Neldra, Matt Anthony. Johnny's friend."

She strides to Matt, hand extended. Her grip is cool and surprisingly strong. She looks her husband's age and Matt sees nothing light or cheery in her face.

Then, a swoosh in Matt's eardrums and a thump of heart, as he remembers the line in Jasmine's diary:

Neldra says I might be able to visit some time.

"My pleasure to meet you, Matt," says Neldra. "So, you work with Christian at Mystic Arts?"

"Yes, I assist in the art hanging."

"I think the psychedelic paintings are absurd. I've browsed there but never bought."

"I guess you like photography."

"I love the simple drama of black and white."

Matt looks to her husband. "Here's your book, Mr. Sungaard."

"Marlon is just fine," he says, taking the book without a look at it.

Matt's gaze follows a curving wooden stairway up to the second floor.

"I read the article about you and your sister in the *Register*," says Neldra. "And yesterday in the *News-Post* and the *Times*. You were so close to rescuing her. And I think the police were wrong to have kept your story quiet."

"They're not happy that I went to the papers. I hope they do some good. The stories."

"How many doors have you knocked on in Laguna?" she asks.

"Three hundred and thirty-one."

"Have you considered the danger of actually finding her? What you would do against violent men?"

"I don't know," Matt says.

"Do be careful," says Neldra.

Matt thinks that Neldra Sungaard may well have invited Jasmine to a Sapphire Cove orgy. The van. The diary entry. The many pretty girls Jasmine's age that night. How did she react to all that sex? Did she laugh? Run? Join in? Was Marlon Sungaard there, too?

"I'll give Matt the grand tour," says Sungaard. "We've got a project to discuss."

Matt follows Sungaard up the stairs.

It's warmer and brighter up here. Three bedrooms with big windows and the odd leather-chrome-blond wood furniture.

"What kind of chairs and tables are these?" Matt asks.

"Danish Modern—Bauhaus meets the human anatomy. Some original Klint pieces, some Ole Wanscher and Juhi. Of course, the swan and egg chairs are Jacobsen."

"Are you Danish?"

"No."

The bedrooms look clean and unlived in. "What's this project you talked about, Mr. Sungaard?"

"Marlon, please. Let's talk in my office."

Sungaard's second-floor office is spacious and bright; the blinds are open and the air conditioner drones quietly. A very large steel desk dominates from the middle, dense with space-age gadgetry: three phones with what appear to be tape recorders attached to two of them; teletype and maybe telex machines, an IBM ball-typewriter like some of Matt's teachers have, a wire-service news terminal, and a glass-domed stock ticker like he's seen in movies. There's a Xerox copier so big it stands on the floor. A globe of planet Earth nearly five feet high glows, lit from within. Matt takes in the tall black filing cabinets and the walls lined with bookshelves. A black leather-and-chrome sofa and chairs surround a glass coffee table with bright magazines arranged in orderly fans. The bookshelves are full with what look like reference books.

Sungaard sits in a leather chair before a big blank desk blotter, gestures to a facing egg-shaped chair.

It's surprisingly comfortable. "A Jacobsen?" Matt asks.

A smile on the tan, lined face. He slides a small, square white envelope with M.A. typed on the front. "Ten dollars, for taking the time to deliver the book."

Making this much money, this easily, embarrasses Matt. Along with the five dollars Johnny gave him to make the delivery, he has just earned fifteen dollars for what, half an hour of his time? He does wonder how anyone can get rich enough to own houses all over the world.

"Thank you."

Matt also wonders if Marlon Sungaard knows his wife is

involved in for-pay sex orgies. How could he not? And why are
old people so hornily fucked up?

"Do you know Jordan Cavore?" Matt asks.

"No, should I?"

"Jasmine went to one of his parties in Sapphire Cove not
long after she disappeared from home."

Sungaard looks baffled. "And?"

"You must know a lot of rich people, is all."

"I certainly do. I manage fortunes. Some are considerable.
I invest money profitably and I take a percentage. I travel
constantly to meet with clients, educate them, show them the
way forward. They need to feel valued. The tools in this office help keep me one small step ahead of the markets, and
my competition. Small steps can mean big things. But I don't
know every rich man in America. Not this Cavore you asked
about."

"Sorry. I was just looking for something that isn't there.
Again. Everything I do to find my sister ends up empty."

"You're going to find her. She's going to come home."

"Everyone says that, Mr. Sungaard. I used to say that.
Now, not so much. I think she knows it, that I'm losing faith."

An almost silence between them, the air conditioner humming. Matt knows why he's confided something this personal
to someone he doesn't know. Something in Sungaard reminds
him of his father. Suddenly a teletype machine is on, clattering a band of printed paper into a basket.

"Your machines are cool," he says. "But I don't know what
most of them do."

"They all do the same thing. They transfer information
from one place to another, instantly."

"What's our project?"

"Matt, do you surf?"

"Only a little, sir. Why?"

"I have twelve surfboards I want picked up and brought to
a rental space here in town. They're a brand-new design made
up in Huntington Beach, called a fish. A shaper friend of mine

got the idea from the inventor in San Diego who never bothered to patent the fish. So, a very expensive mistake for that
inventor. My lawyers are close to securing the patent for me.
The fish will revolutionize surfing. Hundreds of thousands
will be sold, just here in the U.S., and millions throughout
the world. I'm going to be selling them through Stoke Sixty-
Six here in town. And seventy-five other surf shops I've lined
up, worldwide. Probably be closer to a hundred by the time I
can get them product. Millions of dollars over the years. Too
many millions to estimate."

"Cool. How's it going to revolutionize surfing?"

"The fish is a short, thick twin-fin with a swallowtail. The
combination creates incredible acceleration and speed, so you
can make almost any wave that's got power. It's for crisp
clean waves like New Break or Black's. But it rides well in the
softer stuff, too."

"Do you surf?" Matt asks.

"With passion."

Matt has been wondering just why one of the richest men in
the world wants to corner the fish surfboard market, and now
he has at least a partial answer.

He sees nothing wrong with this job, which he guesses will
take two trips, one hour each. He won't have to wrestle eight
thousand pounds of logs up and down a steep driveway. He
can fit six short boards into the Westfalia. If he can do it late
at night, it won't interfere with his search for Jazz.

"What does it pay?"

"Thirty dollars."

Matt tries to keeps the smile off his face. A fortune like
that, and he doesn't even have to take time away from his
quest to find his sister. Added to Sara's fifteen dollars and
the fifteen he's just made, this thirty dollars would launch
his net worth into the stratosphere. He's never had this much
money except for snagging that hundred of Johnny's that day
on Coast Highway.

"Okay, I'll do it."

"A good decision. Like I said, the fishes are short, so they'll fit in your van. Two trips. No surfboard racks. I don't want anyone even seeing them until they hit showroom floor. It has to be done tonight. I'll give you the storage unit number and key. And here's the thirty."

Sungaard hands Matt the second envelope of the last half hour.

"You knew I'd take the job," he says.

"I know I would if I were sixteen and delivering papers."

"I can only do it late."

"The later the better. Less eyes."

34

Matt leaves for Huntington Beach at midnight.

The traffic is light this late, Coast Highway an asphalt ribbon leading north through Laguna to Corona del Mar and Newport. Just a few stoplights, at which Matt listens to the rough idle of the Westfalia engine and wonders where he's going to go after Sunday, the last day of paid rent and utilities at Third Street. He refuses to live with his mother in Dodge City. He will not crash with Ernie or ask Tommy to put him up. He's got other friends but they're not close enough that he could just move in with them. Some are away on summer vacations, and he thinks about using their empty houses, but it seems uncool. He needs his own space, like when he moved out of his and Kyle's room and into the garage. He could sleep in the van and use the public restrooms, but the cops write tickets for that.

Then a long stretch into Huntington Beach, dubbed Surf City for great waves, surfers, and surf shops. He drives past the Golden Bear nightclub, where Dylan and Jefferson Airplane and the Dead have played. Sees Austin Overton on the marquee with Richie Havens.

Huntington Beach is not as fancy as Laguna. It's a sprawling, flat town that reaches inland for miles. Oil pumps and look-alike subdivisions. Matt finds the pickup house on a residential street off Brookhurst. The garage door is up and there's a light on.

The young man's name is Troy, a surfer for sure, dressed in canvas board trunks, flip-flops, and a muscle shirt. He has the knee knobs that surfers get from hours on their boards, and red-blond dreadlocks.

One of the fish surfboards lies belly up on a dirty carpet remnant on the floor. In the garage light, Matt studies its graceful design and quirky swallowtail and the twin fins. He's surfed just enough to know how hard surfing is. Kyle is pretty good. The cream-white fish has a stunning orange wave airbrushed and the "Stoke Sixty-Six" logo under the wave in red, yellow, and purple psychedelic letters. The board's logo alone is enough to make him want one.

Troy helps him load the fishes, carrying on a monologue about tomorrow's surf conditions. When they're done, he invites Matt in for some herb but Matt declines.

"One trip half done," he says. "I'll be back in an hour and a half."

Matt puts in Jazz's Aretha for the ride back to Laguna. Hopes the music can take him out of his funk over his sister, and the often inescapable thoughts of what she might be going through. He and Laurel might have knocked on sixty-one doors tonight, but Matt had never felt further from his goal. Aretha cuts through those ugly feelings with pipes and soul.

He loads the fishes into Canyon Store-It, a poorly lit commercial storage space not far from Dodge. The lock is a new Schlage but stubborn.

By two he's back in Huntington Beach, picking up the last of the twelve boards, and by two forty-five he's at Canyon Store-It again, fighting the lock once more. He opens it to the flatulent sounds of Harley-Davidson motorcycles, and sees the beams hitting the sectioned metal door as it rolls up before him. He turns to face four bright headlights. Dust rising. Behind the bikers a large white panel van lumbers to a stop.

He raises his hands.

Behind the bright lights, the bikers exchange gruff words and laughs. Two of them shut off their engines and tip their hogs onto kickstands.

One huge man and one skinny one are backlit by the brights and difficult to really see. Vests and jeans and harness boots.

The big one is a tangle of dark hair and beard; the skinny man has a beanie pulled down tight.

"You guys don't look like surfers," Matt says.

The skinny guy's harness boot drives into his balls so fast that Matt is down and gasping before he knows what's happened. He makes a drastic, sucking sound. He needs air but the pain extrudes through him with a weight that won't let his lungs draw. He looks up at a human shape within a dizzying constellation of stars.

"I'm Staich. Tell Johnny Grail to leave the money at the Main Beach lifeguard stand tomorrow night at one. Not one second before or after. No money, we will burn his store down with him in it."

Matt's voice is a high-pitched whisper.

"Okay."

"What did I just say?"

"Money. Main Beach lifeguard stand. Tomorrow night at one."

"How old are you?"

"Sixteen."

"You're a waste of skin. Okay, surf Nazis. Get the boards in the van."

Staich slaps Matt's face, grabs his hair and shirt and rolls him over. Empties his wallet and tosses it.

Matt stares up at the foggy night. The men are gone and the surfboards are gone but the pain remains, pulsing heavily. It feels like something that will never go away.

The pain is tactical, he realizes: because of it, he can barely remember their faces, or anything they said, except for Staich's orders for Johnny Grail. And he remembers that their patches said HESSIANS and their logo was a skull with a sword run between the eyes, same as the bikers at Mystic Arts.

When he looks up at the fog he's still seeing stars.

How will he explain this to Sungaard?

He's penniless again.

He staggers bent over to the van and climbs in.

35

Matt, Laurel, and Julie climb the canyon path from Dodge City toward Sycamore Flats on Sunday afternoon, where the Summer of Eternal Love is in full swing.

Matt has spent most of Thursday in bed, icing his aching gonads on the advice of Christian. Then Friday and Saturday traipsing the city with Laurel, knocking on what seemed like ten thousand doors. They learned not one thing about where Jasmine might be; got not a hint or sense of her. It felt more like she'd been beamed light years away, like in that stupid new TV show. Late last night, dropping Laurel off at home, Matt has grasped the terrible possibility that their mission will fail and he'll never see his sister alive again. Maybe at all.

Today Julie wears another of her mother's hand-sewn prairie dresses, this one a periwinkle blue, and her old lace-up granny boots with the low heels. Her hair is brushed into a mane of dark curls. Laurel has a tie-dye dress, *huaraches*, and a straw fedora for the sun.

Matt flops along in the black, slightly too-big Converse hightops and his new-used shorts, and a very cool T-shirt with a faded *Disraeli Gears* album graphic front and back. His nuts still hurt from the Hessians, but the ice has helped.

Not only that, but this morning's paper-route collection got him his twice-monthly twelve dollars and fifty cents, *and* four dollars in tips for good service! Food for days. And maybe a week or two of campground rent. No more financial worries for now.

He does feel gutless and guilty for coming to this BEL "experience" rather than pressing forward with his search for his sister. She's a prisoner and he's going to a party. He and Laurel still have hundreds of homes and apartments to deal with. Their search is going slower than he thought it would. He says as much to his mother.

She takes his hand as they walk. "I'm guilty too, Matt, but we can take this time for ourselves, and I'll tell you why. This event is supposed to be a celebration of love. Let's celebrate everyone we love, and keep them in our hearts, and prepare ourselves for the days to come. We're going to find her. Someone will talk. Someone will see her. Something will fall into place. Who knows, we might even get a miracle."

It might take a miracle, he thinks.

It's hot and the traffic on Laguna Canyon Road is jammed to a stop, with hundreds of cars parked in both directions as far as Matt can see. He hears Tim Leary's amplified voice, and the band tuning up, and the war protesters hollering *Hell no! We won't go!* over and over as police and news helicopters hover and circle.

People stream like ants along the trails leading up to the meadow, lugging blankets and pup tents and folding chairs and coolers. Many of them have their hot-fuchsia-and-Day-Glo-green invitations out and ready.

Julie has hers in her hippie bag and Matt's is folded up in his pocket. He doesn't know what to expect of this "experience," though Johnny Grail told him it would be mind-blowing.

Scampering up from behind them, a wild-eyed man with a Superman cape and a batch of invitations takes Matt's arm and whispers into his ear. He says that the orange suns in the upper left corner of the invitations have actually been dipped in pure Orange Sunshine LSD by the Brotherhood of Eternal Love, and when Johnny Grail says "do it now," everybody is supposed to tear off the corner and eat it.

"Really?" asks Julie. "How clever!"

"I can sell you three for ten dollars."

"No thank you, I've got mine in the bag."

"I just heard Dylan's on his way."

Superman races ahead. Matt sure hopes Superman is hallucinating because he, Matt, has delivered 250 of those invitations, making him guilty of felony drug distribution. Johnny wouldn't pull that on him, would he?

Sitting in the Mystic Arts World office that morning, Johnny Grail told Matt that the Hessians were a new motorcycle club that had just started up in nearby Costa Mesa. Very violent, uncool people. Grail knew some of them from his Anaheim street-fighting days. From before he saw God on his first LSD experience and decided to found a church where worshippers could take acid and hear God speak personally to them, too.

The Hessians had been trying to buy large amounts of Orange Sunshine LSD from him for weeks and he had refused. He could barely get enough Orange Sunshine for his congregation, let alone to sell in quantity to a biker gang.

Johnny had then given Matt a sly wink and a gravelly cackle of laughter. But he had turned serious when confiding to Matt that someone had betrayed the BEL *and* Marlon Sungaard, and that this Judas would be discovered and punished severely. And no, Johnny had not left one dime at Main Beach for the fucking Hessians. The Brotherhood would have four sentries staying at Mystic Arts World after hours, every day from now on until the Hessians backed off. Johnny said most of the brothers had guns and knew how to use them.

At Sycamore Flats the trails converge under a big archway of scaffolding and four-by-fours. A fuchsia-and-Day-Glo-green plywood sign announces:

SUMMER OF ETERNAL LOVE

By its enormity and the way the psychedelic letters seem to move with a life of their own, Matt can tell that Christian painted it. He sees Christian pointing up at it with a little crowd around him, maybe explaining how he did it.

Cops and deputies and plenty of scruffy narcs are clustered at the entrance. Patrol cars and vans and of course Moby Cop. Matt sees Furlong and Brigit Darnell, both in plainclothes.

Chain-link screens and K-rail barricades have been set up to funnel the crowd into the meadow. There are dozens of trash cans under Christian's sign.

Matt reads the notice as they approach the entrance:

WELCOME TO LAGUNA BEACH
ALL ALCOHOL, DRUGS AND PARAPHERNALIA
MUST BE SURRENDERED HERE
NO QUESTIONS ASKED

Matt looks into one of the trash cans, sees the ounce-bags and half-pound bundles of weed, scores of tablets of Orange Sunshine, squares of blotter acid with the cartoon of Truckin' Man printed on, foil-ball mysteries, red, yellow, blue, and two-toned pills, bottles of liquor and wine and beer, baggies of powdered and glistening black shit he can't even guess the contents of. The trash can is three-quarters full and it's only one of at least a dozen—maybe more. Around a freshly dug ditch short of the entrance, people are swilling alcohol, then pouring the remnants onto the ground rather than surrender it to the cops, and others toss pills and shake magic mushrooms and peyote buttons loose from baggies, while dogs lap up the concoction and the feral boys from Dodge City form drug-and-alcohol mudballs and throw them at each other.

"Twenty-five thousand idiot hippies here today, and you have to be one of them," says Furlong, straddling the entrance.

Matt shrugs.

Julie rifles through her bag with an air of annoyance and drops two fat joints into a trash can.

"Is that all?" asks Furlong.

He's got his aviator sunglasses on and he's wearing jeans and a yellow Hawaiian shirt with hula dancers. Matt sees the sidearm bulge.

"Oh, hi Bill," says Julie. "Groovy shirt."

"What else is in the hippie bag?"

"Just water and my invite and some apples."

She holds the bag open and Furlong looks in.

"What about you, Matt? Anything to declare?"

"I'm clean."

"Attaboy." Furlong lifts his dark shades and gives Laurel an appraising look.

"And you, Miss Kalina?"

"No drugs, no drinks. Is Dylan really coming?"

"I wouldn't bet on that. But I did hear that the Dead are on their way. If they live long enough to get here."

Furlong lowers his glasses with a puzzling smile and they pass into the crowded meadow redolent with the smells of coastal sage and marijuana. Julie stops and takes her son by the hand, then Laurel's too.

"I'd like to give you some good news, Matt. And you too, Laurel. My good news is no more dope. No more dragon balls, pills, nothing. I threw them all away. Everything but a little pot. I was having a problem will all that hard stuff, and now I'm better. I'm done. I'm clean."

This is news to Matt, but is it true?

He and Laurel trade looks and Matt sees optimism and belief in her. He wishes he had Laurel's sunny trust in people and belief that prayer works and things happen for a reason.

"Anyway, that's my news."

"It's great, Mom."

"And look at yourself," his mother says. "Inches taller and pounds heavier than you were just minutes ago! You are growing up beautifully. I'll remember this moment the rest of my life."

Laurel squeezes his upper arm.

He does, in fact, feel much taller with Julie and Laurel by his side. Thinks: I'm pushing six feet.

With this alleged good news from his mother, Matt feels a noticeable lightening inside too, the lifting of a weight. Which makes him feel even taller. The weight also feels like it could drop back into him, fast. Can she really beat opium?

He puts an arm around her shoulder, and the other around Laurel's, feels protective and proud to be here, towering over them.

Wishes in his unsettled heart that Jazz was here too.

Buddy Miles and his band are cranking a Hendrix song, and the sea of bodies sways. Beneath the sycamores that line the meadow's edges, Matt sees half-hidden smokers, needle-shooters, snorters, fondlers and fornicators in sleeping bags and under blankets; and wandering naked people, dogs, small children, and Superman, still hawking his phony LSD invites. A naked woman canters on a white horse, followed by air-brushed nudists in rainbow colors. Matt isn't sure he can trust his eyes but a writhing woman with a huge stomach seems to be giving birth while splayed out on a blue bath towel in the tan grass. Officer Brigit Darnell—in a yellow sundress, her hair freed from its restrictive braid into a single thick ponytail—kneels to help with the delivery. A biplane trails a banner for *Rosemary's Baby*.

When the band takes a break, Matt hears the protesters outside starting up their chanting again.

Hell no! We Won't go!

Make Love Not War!

Kill Hate Not Babies!

We Won't Fight the Rich Man's War!

Timothy Leary and Johnny Grail take the stage, leaning in close together and trading off amplified exhortations to the crowd.

"Feel God's love!" Johnny screams out, spreading his arms, smiling and squinting up at the sun.

It looks to Matt that almost everyone in the crowd is waving an invite in the air, some of them waving *handfuls* of them. Fuchsia and green flash in the hot, hazy canyon air. If Superman is right, Matt thinks, this is going to be one giant hallucination about an hour from whenever Johnny Grail says to *feel it now*.

Which he now does, loudly through the mic.

"Feel it now! Feel it now! Breathe the breath of God!"

Matt watches in disbelieving dread as thousands of people eat the Orange Sunshine corner of their invites. All around him he hears the sound of paper being torn and sees hands going to mouths. A canyon full of chomping mandibles.

Julie swallows hers with a swig of water and a guilty grin.

Johnny Grail is leading mass chants now, which rise loud enough to overcome the protesters near the barricades.

Buddy Miles starts playing distorted Hendrix riffs quietly, while Leary plunks himself down center stage on a small Afghan rug and begins meditating.

Through the back-feeding mic, Grail tells a long, rambling story about the time he stole his first LSD at gunpoint because he'd heard it was such a great trip, and later that day when he'd dropped "maybe like ten doses, I saw God and my ego was demolished and I saw wonderful shapes and colors and later I saw that the secrets of the universe were totally attainable through LSD, and that I would found a church to prove it!"

Matt watches as his mother falls in with a group of hippies headed toward the stage. All tie-dye and hair, they dance as they travel. Julie is graceful, her black hair rippling in the sun, and Matt tries to believe that she's going to be okay after all. The dancers head up the narrow trail toward a sandstone plateau called the Porch, a popular young persons' place to watch the sunrise. Matt has been there himself, with Kyle and Jazz and friends from school. The last hundred feet are a steep climb, but once you get up there it's a great view.

After about an hour of this, Matt senses that Superman wasn't kidding about the Orange Sunshine on the invitations. The general level of revelry hasn't just increased, it's taken on a strange kind of urgency. Leary is gone and Grail's story is finally over and a Black Panthers spokesman takes the stage

and tries to get a *Fuck Nixon!* chant going, but Christian
yanks the mic away from him and starts singing "Blowin' in
the Wind" in a good strong tenor, and the bands kicks in, and
most of the crowd knows only some of the words by heart so
the song dribbles into chaos after that.

Matt watches as three open-bed pickups wobble to a stop
just inside the chain-link, loaded with bags of food and plastic
half gallons of water.

When the crowd realizes what's up, they charge the trucks,
board them like pirates, and run off with whatever they can
carry.

"I've had enough of this," says Laurel, fanning herself with
the fedora. "Getting weird."

"I don't want to leave Mom here. She ate that paper sun,
whatever it was."

"You don't really believe it's acid, do you?"

"Laurel, I believe it really could be."

"She's almost there."

Julie is easy to follow in her periwinkle dress. She's in about
the middle of the group, arms out, dancing between the boulders as she climbs toward the Porch. Matt remembers the rattlesnakes sunning on the rocks in spring but today is too hot
for them. Probably.

"We can wait for her," says Laurel.

Another biplane cruises over the meadow, this one pulling a
banner for Sea & Ski tanning lotion.

Matt sees a rush of bodies down near the entry barricades,
like a mob surrounding a fight. But it's not a fight at all, as
two skinny, shirtless men emerge carrying a naked girl who is
either unconscious or dead. One man has her under the arms,
the other by her ankles. Out of Matt's sight, behind the scaffolding, a siren shrieks alive.

"My God," says Laurel.

"Probably overdosed," says Matt, trying to see the girl's
face through her hair, and thinking of the seaweed in Bonnie
Stratmeyer's hair down at Thalia that morning.

By then Julie and her band of dancers are swirling on the Porch. There must be thirty of them, Matt thinks, remembering the deep-cut rain furrows in the sandstone and hoping his mother won't turn an ankle.

The crowd swells. Most are on their feet, swaying in rhythm— or no rhythm at all—to the music. People are still pouring in past the drug-filled trash cans and the cops and the barricades, many of them heading straight for the crowded, trampled meadow dance floor. The band has segued into a dreamy jam that keeps changing melodies, then drifts away from any melody that Matt can follow, while the rhythm guys plunk away in a heavy groove.

Julie lifts her arms and pirouettes, the long prairie dress swirling nicely. Then another, and another and another, to the front edge of the Porch which, Matt remembers, is sandy and treacherous. He reads the caution in the cant of her head. Julie looks down at that edge, plants a boot, and leans back in retreat, but it looks to Matt that his mother's boot is the jackhammer that parts the crumbly sandstone, and down she goes.

In free fall.

At first her body descends in near perfect perpendicularity, like a kid stepping off a diving board and trying not to splash. Her dress billows and her hair lifts. But then she bursts into motion, arms and legs clawing at the air as she crumples into the boulders below. Some of the crowd realize what has happened and close around her.

Matt takes Laurel's hand and they run through the swaying acid-jam dancers toward the Porch.

36

Julie is wide-eyed and breathing hard, bent over a boulder, one granny-booted leg twisted at a terrible angle. She's babbling nonsense, apparently not aware of what has happened. No blood, Matt sees. Just his broken, LSD-tripping, getting-sober-from-the-dragon-balls, former farm girl mom.

It takes the Fire Department ambulance and cops nearly twenty minutes to show up. Two medics, with help from Matt and Laurel, get burbling-sobbing-laughing Julie onto a gurney then into the vehicle.

Matt and Laurel are about to get in too, when a hand clamps over Matt's shoulder from behind and he turns to face Furlong.

"You're under arrest for conspiracy to distribute controlled substances, public endangerment, and mayhem."

He spins Matt against the ambulance and handcuffs him. Laurel screams at Furlong and Julie breaks into "I'm a Believer," and the hippies hurl insults at Furlong while pelting him with fruit and sandwiches, much of which hits Matt as the burly sergeant drags him toward Moby Cop.

Matt sits inside with ten young people, most of whom seem to be overdosed on something, probably LSD, which makes them incoherent but peaceful. Two are kissing and groping rather heavily. The others stare at Matt as if he's an exotic zoo animal, or maybe an alien. It's hot in here and the hippies stink and so does Matt and he's furious at his mother when he hears the ambulance siren blare its way by.

Ten minutes later Furlong throws the back doors open. His

hair is wet and his hula girl shirt is stained and his aviators are glazed with liquids.

He points at Matt: "Out."

Matt climbs over the zoned-out hippies and the ardent couple and lands—still handcuffed—on the dirt in front of Furlong.

"Did Johnny Grail tell you what was on those invites? If so, he'll confess and you'll be processed into Juvenile Hall within twenty-four hours. If not, you're every bit as stupid as you look."

"No sir, he didn't," Matt says, furious at Johnny now, thinking *that fucker.*

"And I'm not as stupid as I look. I've been lied to and broken on by events. Like waves, broken on today." Furlong raises his opaque glasses. "Matt, how many sunny orange invitation corners did you eat?"

"None."

"And your pretty, bad-luck mom?"

Matt nods. "One I saw."

"They took her to South Coast Hospital."

"Thank you, sir."

Furlong uncuffs him. "Everybody gets broken on, Matt. It's what you do after that matters. You owe me."

Matt and Laurel sit in the waiting room as the doctors cast Julie's leg. She's got a broken left femur and a broken left tibia and two cracked ribs. The good news is she landed feet first so her skull and spine were spared. The leg fractures are very fortunately not compound, and will not require setting.

The bad news—carried by Dr. Caroline Hoppe, whose white coat is stitched NEUROLOGY in red cursive letters—is that Julie may have ingested enough LSD to incur lasting brain damage. The doctor has seen it before, the brain "literally rewired" by the powerful hallucinogen. Difficult to treat. Julie is neither coherent, nor aware of her surroundings.

Later, she is strapped into an ICU "overdose room" with barred windows and a door not openable from inside. No

visitors allowed, unless accompanied by staff. She's deep
asleep, snoring lowly through the painkillers and tranquil-
izers. Her leg is in a full-length plaster cast that rests on a
boom-mounted cushion.

The barred windows are large and overlook the twinkling
blue Pacific.

Matt sits with her for hours, absently drawing in his sketchbook.

As his hands and eyes work, he thinks of Jazz. It bothers
him that she doesn't know about her mother. And it bothers
him that he's the only Anthony still at home to deal with Julie
and her . . . well, what exactly was all that?

He gets good sketches of Marlon and Neldra Sungaard,
and of Johnny Grail telling him about the Hessians. A decent
Staich, and a Furlong throwing hippies into Moby Cop.

He stops and ponders how to depict his mother's fall/slip/
jump but can't bring himself to picture it again. It hurts to
imagine.

He has an early dinner at the Kalina residence, with Laurel's
parents and sister. Kai Kalina is a professor of sociology at the
new UC Irvine. Marilyn Doss teaches in the English Department creative writing program. She's published two novels
and a collection of essays. Rose is finished with her freshman
year at UC Santa Barbara, majoring in marine biology.

Matt sees that Laurel has her father's rich Hawaiian coloring and her mother's lovely face. Rose too. He wonders why
different races don't get married more, put together the best
traits of each in their children. He tries to listen and talk
through a thick haze of exhaustion and worry. He eats like
a bear, and after seconds and dessert, escapes with Laurel to
knock on doors before sunset.

After eighty-three more households, Matt pulls the Westfalia into the Kalina driveway once again. It's almost ten
o'clock.

"I'm going home to sleep," he says. That's a lie because he has to pack up and be out of his house by midnight.

"I'm exhausted too," says Laurel. "But please kiss me."

They kiss long and tenderly, with the hunger of the young. In his mind Matt sees the hippies making out in Moby Cop. His gonadal ache quickly returns. Laurel sets his hand on her left breast. It's heavy and living and her breath catches, which makes the ache worse, and when he knows he's about to explode he ends the kiss and hugs her.

"I love you," he says.

"You lust me."

"Yeah, I do."

"See you tomorrow. I'll be praying for Jazz and Julie tonight. And for you, too."

"Get us lots of blessings and miracles."

"Don't make fun of things like that."

"I don't mean to. It just comes out."

"You have a lot inside."

"First it was Dad. Then Kyle. Then Jazz. Now Mom. There's no one left."

"They're all alive and well, Matt. You'll see. You'll get them all back."

"I want to believe you."

"You have a true heart and I like you more than you know."

The FOR RENT sign is up and the living room light is off, not as he left it. Nelson Pedley has been inside.

Julie has already taken some of Jazz's things to Dodge City, but Matt takes a few more highlights from Jasmine's room and loads them into the Westfalia. Like a lot of beach cottages, this house was rented furnished, so the big stuff stays. He picks out some clothes and shoes he's seen her wear. Rolls up the Buffalo Springfield and Beatles and Tim Leary posters, loads a box of books and the jewelry from her dresser. Her diary. Her ukulele and the music book he gave her.

Kyle's room is easy because he gave a lot of his things to Goodwill before enlisting.

His mother's scant possessions are already in the Dodge City barn. It's sad to be in her empty room. It's like she's died.

Matt's own clothes, fishing gear, art supplies, books, sleeping bag, pillow, towels, and toiletries go in last.

He takes every last bit of food—jarred pimientos, a can of green beans, and a bottle of soy sauce—from the little pantry and puts them in the Westfalia refrigerator. Climbs the avocado tree and takes all five of the skimpy avocados he can get to. With sixteen dollars and fifty cents to his name, and soon to be no roof over his head, he'll need all the food he can take.

Last, he racks the Heavy-Duti on the back of the van, wondering where to tell Tommy to drop his papers after tomorrow. Hopes that Pedley won't happen by and charge him a day's rent for stealing avocados and using the Third Street driveway one last time. Matt briefly imagines picking up the landlord by the collar of his shirt and dropping him into the GTE dumpster across the street. He never used to have violent visions like this.

It's strange to lock the door and put his and his mother's house keys under the welcome mat. He feels heavy and regretful and responsible and guilty. It was a good house. What, exactly, could he have done to keep this from happening?

He backs onto Third and stops the van in the exact place he last saw his sister. Right here on this asphalt, being stuffed into a van like this by strong men. He hopes to knock on their door, free Jazz, and fight them. And has another angry vision, but more violent, with fists and blood and breaking bones.

He parks on Cliff Drive, carries a jar of peanut butter and a package of tortillas toward Heisler Park. It's a beautiful place, high on a cliff, the Victor Hugo Restaurant twinkling behind him and a sprawling rose garden beyond. Used to come here with his family when he was little.

Matt settles onto a pathway bench behind a thicket of red

roses. The garden paths are empty this late. He makes a peanut butter burrito. Over the rosebushes he sees the glittering
ocean and the sharp dark shapes of Rockpile, where it's dangerous to fish, but where he has fished, and done well.

He's surprisingly not afraid to have no home now. A year
ago, he thinks, he would have asked Ernie Rios or maybe his
mom's friend Brenda from the Jolly Roger if he could just
crash a night or two. There are some scary people out there.
Like Longton, the mugger. Matt thinks with his new muscles
he could maybe take Longton now, one-on-one.

But Matt hasn't asked anyone for a place to stay, and he
won't. He can get away with this. Just stretch his sixteen dollars.
Do his job, keep his paper deliveries on time, wait for a larger,
better-paying car route to come up. Continue his door-to-door
search for Jazz twice a day until he's found her. Take care of
Mom. Be good to Laurel. Fish when possible. Hit the Food
Exchange as needed. Meditate as the Enlighteners are teach-
ing him at MAW. Eat meals at the beach or in the parks. Use
the public restrooms and shower out at Mom's. After Mom
goes back to Dodge, sleep in the Westfalia, at a different spot
each night so the cops don't catch on.

He feels that a new chapter of his life is beginning. Nothing
is the same as it was, and never will be. He's having thoughts
and emotions he's never had. He's becoming large. He wonders who the new Matt will turn out to be.

Back in the Westfalia Matt heads for his mother's barn in
Dodge City.

37

The next day, Matt finishes his route and sits astride the Heavy-Duti up in Bluebird Canyon, breathing hard and looking down on his world.

Furlong pulls up in Moby Cop. He lowers the window and regards Matt with his blunt, bear-like curiosity.

"How's your mom? I called last night but the nurses were vague."

Matt describes her injuries and the possibility of irreversible brain damage. This morning she was dazed and distant, but able to remember much of the day before. She seemed embarrassed.

Dr. Hoppe asked a lot of questions and made notes. Julie said she was very sore, especially the ribs, but when offered pain pills she refused. This surprised Matt, her finding the strength to say no.

"Where'd you sleep last night?" Furlong asks. "I saw the for-rent sign on Third."

"A friend from school," he lies. "Thanks for not taking me to juvie."

"Where'd Julie go?"

"She moved to Dodge."

"Oh, Christ."

"She was starting over, really trying to beat the dragon balls. Now this."

"Starting over in Dodge City." Furlong takes a long look at Matt from behind his now clean Ray-Bans. "Why didn't you go with her?"

"I need freedom and I don't like Dodge."

A beat while Furlong considers. "Did you see her fall?"

Matt nods, sees her falling again. Tearing at the air like she's trying to climb it.

"Was it an accident?"

"I believe so."

Matt still isn't sure. There was that moment of deliberate commitment, like she was stepping into a pool and trying not to splash. Like this was something she had decided to do, until fear took over and made her fight for her life.

Furlong turns off the engine and surveils the street before speaking.

"I need a few things from you, Matt. And, now that your mother is a resident of Dodge City, one of them might be easier for you to get."

"Five dollars per item."

"First, I want a jar of Laguna Sunshine Farms canned stewed tomatoes. They have a groovy psychedelic label on them, all organic, and they're grown in the commune farm out there. I'll pay for them, of course."

"You can buy a jar yourself, at the roadside stand."

"I tried. They wouldn't sell to a cop."

Matt remembers the dog turd trick that Grail pulled on the sergeant. Stifles a smile.

Furlong continues: "I also want my own copy of that fancy book you delivered to Marlon Sungaard—*The Tibetan Book of the Dead*. And, also from Mystic Arts World, a box of the Languedoc Toffees from France."

"The Tibetan books are special-made gifts for Brotherhood church members and important customers," says Matt. "Same with the candy. They keep those things separate because they're not for sale."

Safe in the Bat Cave, he thinks.

"Which is why I need you," says Furlong.

"That would be shoplifting."

"I'll look the other way."

"The Brotherhood won't."

"They're criminals, Matt."

"Those leather-bound Tibetan books are expensive," Matt says. "Just buy a cheap paperback."

"I want the same edition you delivered to Sungaard."

"Why is this stuff important—the tomatoes and the candy and the book?"

"A little bird sang in my ear."

"I don't want to steal for you," Matt says. "We didn't agree to that."

"I need those things and I need them soon."

Matt says nothing. He knows he shouldn't do it and he's not sure he even can get away with it. Johnny Grail gives him work, shows him the Bat Cave, helps his mom find a place in Dodge, and a job. And Matt rips him off for the cops? Matt is still pissed at Johnny for the drug-infused Summer of Eternal Love invitations, which have potentially made him a sixteen-year-old felon. And possibly contributed to his mother's broken body and perhaps damaged brain.

Matt has also heard grim stories about Orange County's Juvenile Hall. It turns you into a worse criminal than when you went in. Crowded. No family. No friends. No fishing, no paper route, no Laurel. Just big hoods ready to kick the shit out of you like Staich did. Hamsa Luke at Mystic Arts World told Matt that juvie was worse than jail, and he'd been in both. The food was vile.

"Two people died out there at Sycamore Flats yesterday," says Furlong. "Overdoses. I saw one of them give up the ghost, flopping around in the dirt like a fish. But then, to balance the deaths, two women gave birth, too. A boy and a girl, born in their own drug-riddled Garden of Eden with an acid-rock soundtrack and Tim Leary droning away on stage. From what I hear they're healthy, too—the newborns."

"I missed all that."

"It happened after dark. Got crazy. Ten heat strokes for the day, two rattlesnake bites. Three officer assaults. We arrested a hundred and twenty-eight people. This morning I lugged nine of them off to the juvenile court in Santa Ana, which will process them into Juvenile Hall. Which is exactly where you'll be if you don't get me my things. Be smart. Be careful. The Brotherhood of Eternal Nonsense is not your friend, Matt. They're criminals, smuggling drugs into Laguna from all over the world and selling them to kids. Look what they did to your mom. Julie wouldn't have fallen, or jumped off that ledge, if she wasn't too messed up to think straight. You know that. So, do the right thing, partner."

"I'm not your partner."

"I'll expect your call tomorrow or sooner. I'm pulling for you and Julie. I wish she'd have stayed at the Jolly Roger."

"Me too."

"I busted Grail at Sycamore Flats before he could scamper away. He said there wasn't any LSD on the invites. Said the crowd hysteria was set off by rumors, fanned by the police. He said nothing that happened was because of acid. The violence was all from us. He made bail this morning. Cash. He's back in Dodge already."

"Well, you can prove if there was acid on the invites or not."

"We already have."

A hard look at Matt, as if to remind him of his standing as a possible felon.

"I don't like you trying to make me steal from people I know. You stand here trying to make me commit a crime while Jazz is out there, held by men doing who knows what to her."

"I need the tomatoes, toffees, and the fancy *Tibetan Book of the Dead*."

"What if I get caught?"

"Explain that you like candy and valuable books. I heard you're going door-to-door, asking about Jasmine."

Matt nods. "You should be, too."

"She'll turn up."

"Turn up like Bonnie?"

Furlong's casual tone angers Matt. He's not doing jack shit to find his sister. To Furlong, it's all Johnny Grail and Bonnie Stratmeyer. He doesn't even believe that Matt saw Jazz in the fog on Third Street. Or got a terrified call from her.

Another long look from the sergeant. What did cops do before Ray-Bans to keep you from seeing their eyes?

"Can you give me any more information on Bonnie?" asks Matt, expecting none, now that FBI is involved.

"The FBI still can't identify the drugs that were in her."

"How did they *get* in her?"

Furlong considers. "Through a fine gauge hypodermic needle between her toes. The Bureau has been pretty open with us. Their general consensus is that Bonnie had been recently drugged and restrained. The ankle bruises came from some kind of soft shackle. The ligature marks on her neck, too."

"Restrained, like tied up?"

"They're not sure what with."

Matt tries to process this new information. Add it to the fresh water in her lungs and the serious blow to the top of her head. Add it to Bonnie being with Cavore at Sapphire Cove, and with DeWalt at the *LA Moves* Happenings, and the Vortex of Purity.

These jagged facts seem like pieces from different puzzles.

And they're pieces of Jasmine's puzzle too.

"What happened to Bonnie and what's happening to my sister are related."

"That's a big stretch."

"There's a connection."

"We're doing our best on both cases."

"Do more. They're not cases, they're people."

"You help me, I help you," says Furlong. "Think about my offer. Oh, I saw your dad early yesterday, walking into the Jolly Roger."

38

Barreling downhill down Bluebird on his bike, Matt almost gets airborne. He's shirtless—as usual in summer—and the empty, sweat-drenched carrier vest billows and provides lift. And cools him like a radiator. Air-cooled, he thinks. Like the Westfalia but *faster*. He fishtails the Heavy-Duti north onto Coast Highway.

A moment later he kickstands the bike up in front of Mystic Arts World, runs his hands through his sweaty, really-getting-long hair, and walks in.

Busy. Neither Christian nor Johnny are there, but Hamsa Luke is, and he whispers to Matt that Johnny left something in the office for him. Matt feels the long shadow of Judas in his heart.

Luke raises his fist and the Hamsa eye studies Matt. The good eye that protects you from the evil eye.

"You look like something that just crawled onto dry land for the first time," Luke says. "Like that newspaper bag is the obsolete gills that your lungs have evolved from."

"No wonder I'm so hungry."

"Top drawer of the office desk," he says quietly. "Johnny said to go right in."

Matt reads the note from Grail:

Call Sungaard. He wants you to talk to some friends of his about the surfboards.

Matt puts it in his wallet and sits back down in Johnny's swiveling wheeled chair.

His heart speeds.

What he is about to do here—or not do—is more complicated than *thou shalt not steal*. It's not only about theft, it's also about betrayal, and about preserving himself and his sister and his mom. It's about contradictions and irreconcilable differences. He looks to the bookshelf, where the Holy Bible defends the button to the Bat Cave.

And he asks God, what do I do?

Waits. Waits more.

Tells himself there's plenty of time but he knows there isn't.

Then he's standing at the book shelf, the Holy Bible in his hand, peering through the shadows to the steel button within. He listens intently for Hamsa Luke.

Consult God himself, he thinks. Ask your question directly.

Again he asks what to do, then opens the Holy Bible to a random chapter.

Ezekiel:

"Son of man, when a land sins against me by acting faithlessly, and I stretch out my hand against it, and break its staff of bread and send famine upon it and cut off from it man and beast, even if these three men, Noah, Daniel and Job, were in it, they would deliver but their own lives by their righteousness, says the Lord God."

Not exactly sure if that applies, Matt thinks.

Kings:

"Now King Solomon loved many foreign women: the daughter of Pharaoh, and Moabite, Ammonite, E'domite, Sidonian and Hittite women . . ."

Matt doesn't think this is his answer either.

John:

"Truly, truly, I say to you, he who does not enter the sheepfold by the door but climbs in by another way that man is a thief and a robber . . ."

According to John I'm fucked, Matt thinks.

Philippians 2:

"Therefore, my beloved, as you have always obeyed, so now,

not only as in my presence but much more in my absence work out your own salvation with fear and trembling; for God is at work in you, both to will and to work for His good pleasure."

But that's a maybe.

He closes the book and presses the button. Bows his head while listening for Hamsa Luke, while waiting for God to just plain answer.

Waits.

Steps into the Bat Cave, hits the lights, sets the Holy Bible back in its place.

The Tibetan Book of the Dead volumes are shelved together and easy to see. The embossed gold letters glimmer even behind the plastic wrap. He'd forgotten how heavy it is. He drops it into the depths of his newspaper bag, rearranges the books on the shelf to close the gap. Then bags a box of the Languedoc Toffees from France.

In a blink he's back in the store, which is even busier than a few minutes ago. Luke is ringing up a handsome ceramic-and-bamboo Nichols hookah and five ten-packs of incense for an astonishing $39.

"Everything groovy, Matt?"

"Yeah, it's cool."

Customers are already heading into the meditation room for tonight's introductory meditation sessions guided by Vortex of Purity Enlightener Don Stanwood.

"Busy for a weekday," says Matt.

"Yeah, and still early."

A few blocks down at the Post Office, Matt uses the key supplied by Furlong to open the commercial-sized P.O. bin into which *The Tibetan Book of the Dead* and the Languedoc Toffees easily fit. He removes a handful of junk mail advertisements—an alibi supplied by Furlong—in case Matt runs into anybody he knows.

Next, he stops off at the GTE building on Third to use the pay phones. Sungaard gives him a time and place for tomorrow morning, right here in Laguna, be up at the water tower in

Bluebird Canyon, nine o'clock. Sungaard wants Matt to talk
to some friends about the Hessians. Take just a few minutes,
says Sungaard, an edge to his voice.

By seven Matt has pedaled to the Dodge City packing house
with the idea of buying a jar of Laguna Sunshine stewed tomatoes. Nobody around. Matt sets two cans into each side
of the paper carrier, tucks some money under a canning jar
wrench, then walks his bike to his mom's little red barn on
Roosevelt Lane.

He unslings his now heavier paper carrier and locks it in
the Westfalia. It's getting near sunset and there's a rosy glow
over Dodge City, and a fragrant scent of burning marijuana
and canyon scrub. Random cars and trucks up and down
Roosevelt, as usual. It's hot and stuffy inside so he leaves the
door open.

Water is running in his mom's room.

In the middle of the cable-spool table stands a liquor bottle.
Even from this distance Matt recognizes it as Bruce Anthony's brand of whiskey, Colonel Givens. Beside it are two white
take-out bags from Husky Boy.

A big suitcase stands behind one of the chairs. There are
two smaller carrying cases beside it. Matt recognizes them.

The water has stopped running, and Bruce Anthony walks
in from Julie's room.

39

It's been six years since Matt has seen his father, minus the four days when Bruce took the kids on day trips for four consecutive summers to Disneyland, Knott's Berry Farm, the Alligator Farm, Disneyland again, racking up thousands of truck miles only to vanish back into his world for another year.

"Good to see you, Dad."

"Thanks for keeping a window cracked for me. I don't deserve it."

They meet in a brief, stiff hug.

"Food and drink on the table, son. We have much to discuss."

He returns from the kitchen with two mason jars and they take bar stools across the spool from each other. The main room light fixture hangs directly above, throwing a warm incandescent light on them.

Bruce pushes a white Husky Boy bag across the table, then an empty mason jar.

"Pour some bourbon if you'd like."

"I've never tried it."

"You still like fries over onion rings?"

"Right, Dad."

Bruce pours some bourbon, lifts his mason jar to Matt, then sips.

"Son, I came here to find Jazz. What has happened to her here is absolutely predictable and unacceptable. I will not let my daughter become a victim of these times and this place.

And let her become a symbol of all that has gone wrong in our republic."

"No," says Matt. "We can't."

"She's been consorting with the scum of the earth. We're going to hose that scum into the sea until we find her."

Bruce Anthony sips his bourbon. Matt senses the hardness in him that has always been there. Hardness, and the conviction that he is right. Matt feels the anger coming off his father just in the way he moves the liquor to his mouth. It can get to be a roar, he thinks, the anger. Both the hardness and the anger seem stronger now, or at least more obvious. He wants to know what his father has been doing for the last six years.

Matt pours a finger of the Colonel Givens, feels the sharp reach of fumes as he brings the mason jar to his nose. Wow. Sets it down.

"Based on what I know, she's somewhere here in Laguna," says Bruce. "It sounds like we're up against at least three experienced individuals—the men you saw abduct her that night. Also, we have Jordan Cavore, Rene DeWalt, and Mahajad Om to consider, as possible vectors between Jazz and Bonnie Stratmeyer. If those connections hold, then we're dealing with murderers."

"How do you know what Jazz was doing, and Bonnie?"

"I still have friends in the sheriff's department. I've been in touch with Darnell and McAdam. Good people."

"Furlong?"

"Less so."

Matt has long assumed that his father knew of Furlong's rebuffed advances on his mother, but he's never directly asked and isn't about to. Furlong versus Father is nothing Matt wants to witness.

Bruce sips from his mason jar, eyes locked on Matt's across the spool table. His father's eyes are gray, set deep under hard dark brows. His hair is wavy and blond, like Matt's. It's surprisingly long now, much longer than Matt has ever seen it, almost to his shoulders. The hippies are winning him over, Matt thinks.

But not completely. Bruce's sideburns are long, wide and razor-straight at the bottom. His mustache has the Earp droop, Wyatt Earp being one of his heroes. The legendary lawman/gunfighter/gambler had actually lived not far from here, in San Diego, in his later years. Matt remembers his parents taking the family to the site of Earp's San Diego brothel downtown for Sunday brunch. Bruce and Julie had had cocktails and laughed and the food was great and Matt liked all the photos of the Earp brothers and Doc Holliday and Bat Masterson and the hard-faced ladies of the house. But the drive back to Laguna—parents up front in the Country Squire, Matt and Jasmine behind them, Kyle commanding the entire rear section—erupted in a brief but heated mom-and-dad screaming match. The radio got turned way up and Matt remembers little that was said, but he remembers Julie's bared teeth point-blank to Bruce's ear, and Bruce, ramrod straight in the driver's seat, both hands on the wheel, guiding the great station wagon north, slapping Julie on the cheek with his open hand. The crack. The radio-filled silence between Encinitas and home.

Now, eleven years later, looking at his father across the table, Matt repeats Bruce's favorite Wyatt Earp saying.

"Fast is fine, but accuracy is final."

Bruce smiles. "We'll get to that in a minute."

They eat the Husky Boy double cheeseburgers, Matt the fries, Dad the onion rings. Chocolate shakes. Matt sniffs the bourbon again. Bruce sips twice and pours another. He's wearing a white Western shirt with snap buttons, tucked in, sleeves rolled up. Jeans and boots. Sitting across the round spool table with the bourbon before him and the light directly overhead, he reminds Matt of a saloon gambler.

"What have you been doing all these years for work, Dad?"

"Oh, that. Well, as you know, I left this cutesy place for the

sheriff's department in Clay County, Texas. Which was somewhat on account of lovely Sharon in payroll having family
there. You never met Sharon. Just as well, we didn't get on.
Clay County and I didn't either, so I worked the Odessa oil-
patch boom-to-bust, then proceeded to the Tulsa PD. Talk
about a law-and-order city. I had me a sweetie named Betsy
but she turned out to be not so sweet after all. Then El Paso
PD. They had me buying heroin undercover from Mexican
poppy growers. That was one helluva scene."

Matt notes again the accent that has worked its way into
his father's speech. He can't tell one accent from another but
he likes them. They're subtle and invite you to listen. And not
just how they sound, but the phrases, too. Like "on account
of" and "didn't get on," and "had me a sweetie."

"After Tulsa came Abilene, Kansas, for skip tracing, which
some people call bounty hunting. Michelle. I tried. Then to
San Antonio with some old Air Force friends on the PD.
Annie, a Lipan Apache. Great gal and a bit wild. Then there
was Kansas City, Dodge City, Fort Worth. I liked the look of
Tombstone but couldn't find work. I went anywhere from my
outlaw books when I was a kid. Anywhere I liked the sound
of. Weird, kinda, for a full-grown man to wander around like
that. My hope was always to find work in the genuine West,
and a woman to make a life with after Julie. Somewhere I
could say my piece, carry my piece, and be good to good
people. Away from cute, fairy-tale places like this. Away from
phonies."

Matt feels very strange right now, talking to a man he has
barely known "after Julie." A cop in Tulsa? A bounty hunter
in Abilene? Mexican heroin?

It's like a deputy/gunman has ridden into his life on some
dusty trail from history.

Matt's got a million questions. "What's your work right
now?"

Bruce smiles, sips. "I'm in-between. A little money in the
wallet. I don't intend to budge from here until we find Jas-

mine. I rented your old Third Street place from that Pedley guy. You're welcome there. He told me you'd been living in the garage."

"That bedroom was never big enough for Kyle and me. He'll be home in twenty-five days."

"That makes me very happy."

"He's really worried, short like he is."

Bruce nods in silence. A moment between soldiers is how Matt reads it.

"I like what you told me on the phone about your knock-and-talks for Jasmine," Bruce says. "But it's too slow. So, this is what we'll do. We're going to skip all the houses with kid stuff in the front yards or porches. That means trikes, bikes, skates, skateboards, surfboards, Hula-Hoops, jump ropes, toy trucks, and horses—anything that signifies a family. And we're going to skip the old people, college students, and young couples, too. Just tell them we got the wrong address and skedaddle."

"That's half the houses here."

"Then we've made up some lost time already."

"I think we should knock another hour in the evenings, too," says Matt. "We've been stopping just after sunset."

"Absolutely. Tell me about the 'we' part of this."

He's happy to: Laurel Kalina, fourth-grade crush at El Morro, now in the Gauguin at the Pageant of the Masters, enrolled in a *college* writing program, really pretty and smart, dinner just last night with her family.

Bruce listens with a poker face that turns into a wry smile.

"Sounds like a terrific girl. Sex yet?"

"No, sir. Second base last night."

Bruce considers. There's a stony cut to his features and he doesn't blink much.

"Clear this table, son. You have an important decision to make."

40

Matt busses the spool, pausing to smell his bourbon again, but can't quite bring himself to try it. The fumes are like needles in his nostrils. From the kitchen he watches his father, kneeling next to his suitcase, setting aside neat stacks of folded shirts and jeans.

When they are both seated again, Bruce sets a padded fabric case in the middle of the table. It's roughly the shape of a shoe box, but flatter. He unzips and folds it open.

"This is my Smith & Wesson three-fifty-seven Magnum revolver. It's got an eight-inch barrel, stainless finish, and a light trigger pull. No aftermarket grips because I like the feel of wood. It's my everyday carry. A hand-cannon. If I expect trouble or need to conceal, I've got others."

The weapon catches the overhead light, gleaming dully.

Matt remembers it. It's like the one under Kyle's bed, now unloaded and hidden in the Westfalia. "Nice."

"I taught you that it is definitely not nice."

Matt nods, calling back from long disuse the basics of how to open the cylinder and check if it's loaded, how to never point at something you don't intend to shoot, how to handle the gun safely, how to aim, squeeze the trigger, how to empty and reload. He recalls now what Bruce said about revolvers as opposed to automatics: they're idiot-proof. Matt always believed that statement was directed at him. He remembers how heavy that gun is.

"Now, there's these," says Bruce, setting two gun cases onto the spool. Matt, leaning on his elbows, feels their weight.

The latches of the black case open in unison with one sharp snap. Bruce removes three handguns from what Matt knows is a green felt interior, and sets them on the table.

He does likewise with the brown case, for a total of six guns on the spool. He arranges them in a semicircle between himself and his son. Puts the cases back on the floor. Matt takes in the sweet smell of gun oil.

"I remember some of these," he says.

Bruce points out Matt's grandfather's Colt 1911 from World War I; a Bond-style Walther PPK; and a Colt Detective Special .38 revolver.

"Do you use these for work?" asks Matt.

"If I need to. My cop creds give me both open- and concealed-carry in some states. And here too, if the local jurisdictions reciprocate, which they have. I registered here last week with my old employers. Good to see some of those guys again."

He identifies the remaining three firearms on the spool table: a five-shot American Arms derringer; a Ruger Bearcat that used to be Julie's; and a .45-caliber revolver used by Wyatt Earp at Tombstone.

"Well, it's an Italian knockoff," Bruce says with a smile, taking another sip of bourbon.

To Matt the gun looks perfect for a gunfighter, except for maybe the long barrel. How long would it take to get it out of your holster?

"I haven't told you the prices because I don't want you to shop price."

"Shop?"

A look of amusement from his dad, as if he'd been expecting this answer.

"You're a man now, Matt. You can drive a car and make love to a woman, and you must buy a gun."

"For what?"

"To defend yourself and the people you love," Bruce says. "That's what men and guns do."

Matt has never wanted a gun. But could it do any harm to

take his father's offer, stash it somewhere safe, and just *have*
it? Maybe he'll actually need it someday. People in town were
still talking about the rabid coyote that attacked the girl up
in Top of the World last summer and her mom, who shot it.
Atticus Finch needed a gun. If the people around Dr. Martin
Luther King and Bobby Kennedy had had guns handy, would
they maybe be alive now?

"Consider each, son. Handle them if you'd like. Make a decision. They're all equally good at what they do."

"Why don't you just give it to me, like your dad gave you
the World War One gun?"

"He certainly did not. I paid a fair price for it."

"That seems strange."

"It's the Anthony way."

Still thinking it's strange, but intrigued by the lethal hardware before him, Matt works his way around the curve of
spool. Bruce watches him from his chair, elbows on the table
and his chin resting on his knuckles.

"They all come from different times in history," he says.
"And who knows, maybe one will step into history again, accompanied by you."

Matt has to think hard about these words to even partially
understand them. Worry stalks the edges of his understanding. His father's words seem to predict tragedy, or, even worse,
welcome it. This is how men think? Certain kinds of men?
Generals and soldiers? Kings and heroes? Outlaws? Assassins?
Did Oswald or Sirhan think like this?

"I don't care about history right now, Dad. I just want to
find Jazz."

"We wish never to draw the weapon."

"Okay."

"The taking of a man's life is no small thing."

"No, sir. But how does it connect to my search? Taking
life?"

Bruce clears his throat softly, then takes another sip of
bourbon.

"At some point we will find Jasmine. And we will be forced to confront dangerous men. Three, minimum. For that, we must be prepared, not just to *pay* the last full measure, but to *collect* it."

Matt studies the guns, one at a time. Takes a step to better assess.

"You might think I'm crazy," says Bruce. "But I'm not. I'm an earnest man who wants his family back."

"You do?"

"You're all I've thought about for six years."

"Really?"

"Almost."

Matt's thoughts blur like his bike spokes on a downhill, as he tries to catch up with six years of information he never had. He can't process it all. Ideas come crashing down like waves in a set.

He says: "I'll buy Wyatt's gun."

Bruce comes off the stool and they hug again, but this time is different. For the first time in his life, Matt isn't surprised by his father's strength, but by his own. The two strengths form a wall that neither chooses to move beyond. A few months ago, Bruce would have swung him around like a child. Now Matt feels he can match him, at least briefly.

"Well done, son."

Matt lifts the heavy revolver with both hands, sights down its endless barrel, his trigger finger riding outside the guard like his father taught him. He aims for a knothole in the barn wall, but even with his new strength the gun bobs and dips no matter how much he tries to hold it still.

"Keep it where no one will stumble onto it. Keep it loaded or it will do you no good when you need it most."

"There's a bunch of boys here in Dodge, they go in and out of the houses whenever they want. Get into everything."

"Outsmart them. The gun is twenty dollars. I'll throw in the soft case and some ammo. No tax. I'll take half now."

Matt sets down the Earp gun. Hands two fives over to his

dad with a strange and terrible disappointment in his gut. He's down to five dollars and change. He feels like he's being robbed again.

"You're welcome at my place on Third Street tonight, son. Any night, in fact."

"No, thank you. I'm glad you're home, Dad. It's confusing but I'm glad you're here."

"I am too. We'll get Jazz home. We'll put this sinful world back right."

41

At 9 A.M., Matt puts the stewed tomatoes in Furlong's business-sized P.O. box on Forest. He wonders what the sergeant plans to do with them.

Five minutes later he pulls into a wooded glade near the Bluebird Canyon water tank, where a vehicle containing Sungaard's friends is waiting. He's used this place to rest in the shade scores of times. There's room for maybe three or four cars but it's marked NO PARKING by the city. The eucalyptus stands high and dense, and the sunlight falls faintly to the seed-pod-and-leaf-littered ground.

Their vehicle is a very large Mercedes van, the likes of which Matt has never seen. It looks almost twice as high and wide as his Westfalia, and half again longer. No windows. It's painted a low-gloss gray, kind of military, Matt thinks.

Two doors motor open in opposite directions and four men step to the ground, black weapons holstered in the depths of their suit coats. Two are large, two slender and shorter. Behind them Matt sees the back of the driver's head, and two rows of seats, facing each other. There are luggage and storage racks above, and black rubber floor mats.

The men look foreign to Matt, in the same way Sungaard himself does.

"Mr. Anthony, I thank you for meeting with us. I am Bayott. We are friends of Marlon and friends of you, also."

Bayott holds up a leather badge wallet with a small gold shield and mug shot. Matt reads INTERPOL.

Bayott is slightly built, with curly brown bangs and two days' growth of whiskers. A prominent nose. His smile is thin but seems genuine. His handshake is gentle and brief.

"Please step into this vehicle. It will be private."

Matt follows Bayott's direction and climbs in first, the men crowding in behind him, the doors sliding shut.

Inside, Matt feels the engine idling and cold air hitting his face.

Bayott produces a tiny tape recorder and a notebook. Turns the recorder on and unsheathes an elegant black pen.

"We are sorry for your robbery and beating recently," he says. "Mr. Sungaard furnished for us some facts. Please describe to us what happened that night, from the time you received the first six surfboards in Huntington Beach to the time you were confronted at the storage facility in Laguna Canyon. No detail is too small, no impression too faint. Please . . ."

"Are you really Interpol?"

"How could we not?" Bayott says with a chuckle.

Matt wonders what his father would make of these guys. Or Furlong or Darnell.

He tells them the story as clearly and understandably as he can. Bayott writes fast, and on the empty seat directly across from Matt, the little tape recorder spools turn slowly behind the smoked-glass window.

If he had any doubts that these were real cops, Bayott's endless questions and checks for clarity erase them. Bayott is every bit as thorough and craving of details as anyone on the LBPD, even Detective McAdam.

One of the big men, a blond with buzz-cut sides and a very low fade, like an exaggerated Marine Corps cut, hands Matt an aluminum clipboard with an INTERPOL emblem on the clamp.

Matt looks down at a grainy black-and-white photograph of the Hessian emblem.

"That's it," he says.

"Please describe the colors," says Bayott.

Matt closes his eyes, tries to see it again. The storage facility had a decent security light up on the wall, although it was Matt's adrenaline-blitzed alertness that seared the emblem into his memory. And having seen it before, that night at Mystic Arts World when the bikers blundered into the Timothy Leary show.

"It was all black and white except for the handle of the sword and the MC letters, which were red. The skull was yellow."

Bayott takes the clipboard and notes the colors with his pen, then flips the page.

"The Hessians are new," says Bayott. "Just chartered as a motorcycle club. They have already engaged with the Hells Angels and are not afraid of a fight. They base their identities on German mercenaries who fought for the British against your colonies. Hessians were greatly feared. Many settled in America after the Revolution. This motorcycle gang makes what American police call bathtub speed."

"What do they want with surfboards?" asks Matt. "Mr. Sungaard told me about the patent. But what can twelve boards be worth?"

"They are only valuable as secrets," says Bayott. "Until Mr. Sungaard possesses the patent, he must keep the prototypes hidden. Or lose them to pirates who will sell the design for replication. Such as the Hessians. Mr. Sungaard has already received their ransom demand for the boards. It is very high."

Matt remembers Sungaard's prediction regarding the worldwide sale of fish surfboards year after year. *Too many millions to estimate.*

Bayott hands Matt the clipboard again, now open to the next page. It's a police mug of Staich, the man who groined him. He's not wearing a watch cap.

"The leader is Erik Staich," says Bayott. "Is this the man who kicked you?"

Matt nods, feels that pain, fresh in his memory. Erik Staich is a strange-looking man—a square face and a high forehead, a slender neck, prominent cheeks, and pale eyes.

"And what did he say to you, again?" asks Bayott.

"*You're a waste of skin. Okay, surf Nazis. Get the boards in the van.*"

"Do you know how they learned you were transporting the surfboards?"

"No," says Matt. "I was hoping you might come up with that."

"Did you talk to Johnny Grail or Luke Lucas about the surfboards—Luke is also known as Hamsa Luke, from Mystic Arts World."

"No. Johnny told me Mr. Sungaard had a job for me. So it's possible he knew it was the surfboards."

Matt has a small realization: how loose and trusting the BEL is. The lax things they do. Such as all the MAW employees sharing gossip about customers and each other. Such as Johnny dispatching young people like Jasmine and Matt to make home deliveries to one of the richest men in California, among others. Such as Johnny hiring Matt to deliver LSD-impregnated invitations—Matt is sure of it now, thanks to Furlong's update—not to mention Johnny giving Matt a way into the Bat Cave. None of that seems like high security to Matt. He thinks that this, here—a windowless van full of armed un-Americans—is high security.

More questions. The A/C is still on high and the big van idles smoothly.

Matt checks his Timex Skindiver because he's got doors to knock on with his father and Laurel. It's only nine forty but he can't be late.

"I have to go," he says.

"Thank you for your time, Mr. Anthony."

"I hope you catch him," says Matt. "You can kick him in the balls for me if you want."

The men murmur their approval and Bayott smiles his thin smile.

Matt climbs out, not quite believing that he just told Interpol its time was up.

42

Matt and his father pick up Laurel just after ten. The early morning is thick with coastal haze. Bruce wears a white straw Stetson, a snap-button shirt, a yoked corduroy sport coat, and a pair of suede cowboy boots. He sets a tattered leather briefcase at his feet.

Matt and his father have already discussed whether Laurel should continue to be a part of the revised quest team. Matt has argued well in her favor, and prevailed.

But the first thing Bruce says to her after she climbs into the Westfalia and Matt has introduced them is:

"You're a fine young woman, Laurel, but I don't think you should be involved in this."

"Oh, why not, Mr. Anthony?"

Bruce turns around in the passenger seat, holds open his blazer to show her the gun.

"This mission has taken on some complexity," he says.

"Good God, it sure has. Matt? Is this okay? A gun, and what you're doing?"

"I think it is, Laurel. Dad's former law enforcement, as you know. But *you*, Dad, do not get to give Laurel Kalina orders. You are not her boss. Or my boss, either."

Bruce drops his jacket flap.

"I am *one hundred percent* not your boss, Matt. Nor yours, Miss Kalina. I'm simply pointing out that sooner or later, we will find Jasmine, and very likely at least one of three physically powerful kidnappers. Things could turn. I don't want you in the middle of it, Laurel. An unarmed girl. You can get hurt, or worse. I can't let that happen. What would your parents say about you doing this?"

"She's great on the interviews, Dad. People let us in because she's intelligent and asks good questions. She saves time."

"Do you know how reckless and naive that sounds, son?"

Matt throws his brain into reverse and sees very clearly that his father is right.

"I resign," says Laurel. "I don't want to go. I'm not putting myself around guns for this. I have books to write."

"Good girl," says Bruce.

"Matt, Matt, look at me," Laurel says, tears forming. "I'm so sorry."

She climbs out and slams the van door and comes around the driver's side, where Matt has gotten out to say goodbye.

"Please don't cry."

"Okay, I won't cry."

Laurel kisses him loudly on the mouth and hustles through her front door without a look back.

Of course, the door-to-doors go nothing like the old days. Matt starts the first interview as before, which gets them inside, but refused a full walk-through. Bruce introduces himself as Matt's father, a detective, and flashes his Tulsa PD shield.

Matt starts his backup pitch about Jasmine being a songwriter and ukulele player, and her tireless volunteer work with Down syndrome children and the Laguna Food Exchange—somewhat exaggerated.

The occupant—a young man in a jeans and work boots and apparently on his way out—is explaining that he really needs to go, when Bruce simply walks past him, across the living room, and into a short hallway.

"He can't do this," says the man.

"He'll be done in just a second," says Matt. "Don't get him riled up."

"Is he really your father?"

"Yes, really."

"Get him out of here."

By then Bruce is striding back down the hall, grin on, hat in hand, and his cowboy boots clunking authoritatively on the old hardwood floor.

"Cute little place," he says.

"Get the fuck out of it."

Matt hears the anger in his voice.

"Gladly," says Bruce. "Come along, son."

Heading for the next house, Bruce says, "Let me do the talking for these next few. Just see how it goes."

Strangely to Matt, by the time they stop at one o'clock for his paper route, they've gotten more permissions to enter and done room-to-room searches than he and Laurel had ever managed in one morning.

Matt sees that Bruce isn't just tall, handsome, and obviously concerned for his kidnapped daughter, but he's fast. He swiftly charms and/or intimidates. The men his own age want to be peers, and most of the women seem to admire him, some openly. Homosexual men and women instinctively dislike him, Matt notes, though they're polite in their refusals.

Bruce just talks and walks past the reluctant citizens anyway, leaving Matt with the small talk.

They're in and out in no time.

They knock on the door of their old home at Top of the World. It's a nice little fifties ranch house with a large American flag hung from a pole in the middle of the front yard.

"The pole, Dad."

"Still standing."

Matt pictures Kyle and Jazz and him helping their dad pour the cement footing. And later, sneaking their thumbprints into it. He toes back the grass and sees the prints.

"I liked this house," says his father.

The owners now are a young couple with children in the den, watching cartoons on TV. They've both heard of Jazz and have been hoping for good news since reading about her in the papers and seeing the downtown flyers.

"Is the bomb shelter still here?" asks Bruce.

"It's a wine cellar now!" says the missus. "Have a look."

Standing amid the racks of down-slanted wine bottles, Matt pictures the old shelves with the alphabetized cans. His favorite canned food was the paper-wrapped tamales that tasted nothing at all like tamales, Dinty Moore stew a close second.

Matt remembers the time Kyle locked him down here for eating his birthday candy. Then ran. Matt was five. It was a hot day and upstairs his parents had the window-mounted air conditioner going full blast and nobody could hear him yelling. The insulation down here was incredibly thick, too, Bruce and his builder friends having done their best to harden the cellar against bombs, Russian MiGs, tanks, and small-arms fire. So the longer Matt yelled the more hoarse he got, and the longer nobody came to let him out, the more claustrophobic and afraid he became. He called his own number and got a busy signal. The rising panic was one of the worst things he'd felt in his five years. Didn't know what it was. Worse than nightmares. Worse than measles. It was Jasmine who missed him first, finally came down and found him, and Matt in that moment pledged that if Jazz ever got locked up, he'd find her and set her free. Then Matt had quit blubbering and wiped his humiliating tears. He found Kyle upstairs and hit him in the side of the head with his baseball glove as hard as he could. Kyle got Matt in a headlock and waited for him to say uncle, which didn't take long. Matt had held a grudge for weeks.

"We had it," says his father. "We had everything here."

"What do you mean?"

"Life."

"It seemed pretty good."

Bruce nods. "It's incredible how bad a man can fuck things up. Without even meaning to."

By the time they're heading back to Third Street, Bruce has calculated a record-breaking 212 searches. Combined with the many residences obviously home to children, the old and the infirm, they've done three times his best day with Laurel. Figuring conservatively, Matt realizes they've covered well over half the city.

"Check this, Matt."

From his briefcase Bruce removes a tablet of quarter-inch graph paper, sets the briefcase across his lap, and squares the graph paper tablet before him.

"Last night, I sketched a street map of Laguna onto twenty-four sheets," he says. "Which makes one quarter-inch square for almost every house in the city. It'll show us where we've been and where we still have to go. We made some real progress today."

Bruce uses the ride home to log one- or two-digit alphanumeric address references from Matt's and Laurel's interview notebook into the quarter-inch squares. His numbers and letters are perfect. Matt thinks he got his own smidgen of artistic aptitude from his dad. Years ago, Bruce told him he'd rather be an engineer or pilot than a cop. Guiding the Westfalia toward Third Street, Matt glances at the graph paper map and the man making it, realizing how much about him he does not know.

Matt sits on the red bucket to fold and rubber-band his newspapers in his former Third Street driveway.

Bruce sits in the beach chair with the maps and a pack of colored pencils, coloring each graph paper square appropriately:

Orange for search completed.

Yellow for search not warranted—meaning old people, the handicapped, women, parents with young children.

Blue for no answer or nobody home.

Red for call the police: warranted, suspicious, and denied.

No reds yet, Matt notes. There was a guy over on Catalina who seemed worried and untrustworthy. His dog was barking viciously from a bedroom as Bruce pled his case, but the man was dramatically obese and looked nothing like the men stashing his sister in the van.

Now Matt takes a minute to look at the big GTE building and the blue summer sky and its wispy clouds. He feels oddly wonderful to be sitting here in the driveway getting his papers ready, the Heavy-Duti gamely standing by, just as he's done for well over the last two years of his life. He didn't think he'd ever be here again. Didn't think he'd miss Third Street. He definitely never thought he'd be sitting here folding papers with his dad.

"I'll drive and you can throw," says Bruce.

The proposition catches Matt off guard, and so does his answer. "No, thanks, Dad."

"Why not?"

"This route is more efficient on the bike."

"And?"

"And it's something I like to do."

"Because you're the boss?"

"Because I'm good at it."

"That's a good reason to do a thing. I'm proud of you for that, son."

Matt hears the engine before the shiny blue Porsche whines past him down Third, hooks abruptly into the GTE parking lot, decelerates around its perimeter, and rumbles back onto Third, parking on the driveway behind the pile of papers. The top is down.

"Matt Anthony, where's my fork and picnic basket!"

Matt's up off the bucket. "They're out in Dodge, Sara. Mom got hurt. I'm living there for now."

"I've been calling but no one answers. I saw the for-rent

sign. Nobody at the Jolly Roger would tell me where you went. I get the feeling you've been *avoiding* me."

Matt approaches, a folded, rubber-banded *Register* in hand. "I wouldn't avoid you."

"Well that's a relief." She's wearing little round John Lennon sunglasses and a Chairman Mao cap. Her hair spills out from under it in a tangle.

"Mom broke her leg in two places, and two ribs, out at the festival on Sunday."

"Bummer," says Sara. "Some of my friends went, said it was horrible. Hippies mating in the bushes and people overdosing on LSD."

"Two babies got born."

"You take Laurel?"

"Yeah."

She glances at Bruce then back to Matt.

"Look, I need that fork and basket. But I also need to talk to you. I'll pick you up after your door-knocking tonight for Jazz. Say nine thirty?"

"Nine thirty is good. You're not going to make me carry logs up and down hills, are you?"

"You just be here and be ready, Buckwheat. I swear, you've grown in the last week."

"Two inches and twenty pounds in six months."

"Wear something nice tonight, and bring an appetite. That shouldn't be hard."

Matt watches the Porsche trundle down Third toward Forest.

"Be on time for that one," says Bruce.

Matt and his father have TV dinners in Matt's old digs. Bruce has brought a small color television with him and they watch the news.

Cronkite suggests again that the war is not being won and might in fact be unwinnable.

"Fucking communist patsy," says Bruce. "He's worse than Frontly and Pinkley."

He makes a gun-finger at the screen and fires.

That night they knock on 142 doors, get 120 invites in, and make almost that many full searches.

On their way back to Third Street Bruce thoughtfully flips through his twenty-four page Laguna residence map, framing the alphanumeric address references in the tiny quarter-inch cubes. Matt sees him make a quick calculation in a margin.

"Roughly thirty percent of Laguna," he says.

"Already covered?"

"Left to go, Matt. Left to go."

ara Eikenberg's favorite restaurant is La Cave in Costa Mesa. It's hidden underneath the spacious High Time Liquor store, and it really feels like a cave when Matt walks in behind her. His hardly-ever-worn Sunday trousers are tight but he keeps his back straight and his stomach sucked up and his surfboard-pattern Hawaiian shirt untucked to help cover his over-snug pants.

It takes a moment for his eyes to adjust: brick archways overhead, a central chandelier, dark walls hung with sconces and lanterns that look medieval. The booths are thickly padded red leather, the tables have white tablecloths and flowers.

Every table and booth is occupied. Matt's keenly aware of being watched, and of Sara being watched. He feels as if he's surrounded by people who notice things and keep secrets. Sara's father has an ownership share in La Cave, which means Sara has a table whenever she wants it.

The maître d' ushers them to a two-top tucked up against a brick archway with an iron wall sconce throwing faint orange light. He hands them menus and adjusts a standing tapestry for privacy.

"Very nice to see you again, Miss Eikenberg." A glance at Matt. "Welcome, sir."

"So great to be here," says Matt.

"He works for Dad."

"Then you work for the best. Would you like to see the wine list, Miss Eikenberg?"

"Of course, Marcus, thank you," and Marcus is off.

Matt knows that the moment has come to say something intelligent. Something about this place and what a privilege it is to be here with her. But his mind shuts down as he looks at Sara, the hair untangled and brushed back on one side, the sleek black dress, the plum lipstick, the dark brown eyes trained on him with such casual intensity.

"How come you asked Laurel to the Summer of Eternal Love instead of me?"

"She's my girlfriend."

A displeased glance. "Oh. So how did it go tonight, the door-to-door?"

Matt explains the new setup—Laurel no longer with him, Bruce stepping up in his larger-than-life manner, bulldozing or charming his way into home after home, leaving dozens of pleased-to-help, puzzled, admiring, and sometimes annoyed citizens in his wake.

To Matt's surprise, they had logged another eighty-five full searches and dismissed thirty-four houses because of bikes, skateboards, or other toys in the yards, driveways, and porches.

"Your dad sounds like quite a guy," says Sara. "He left the family six years ago, now he's just showed up out of nowhere?"

Matt explains his father's return as best he can. He's not sure what "wanting his family back" or "put this sinful world back right" really mean, and he admits he's not clear on who his father really is, and what he's trying to accomplish beyond finding Jasmine.

"I don't really understand him," says Matt.

That brown-eyed look from Sara. Same as Jazz: dubious and somehow ahead of things.

"Maybe it's that simple, Matt. He wants his family back so his world can be right again. What's so mystifying about that?"

"Nothing, when you put it that way. But he's hateful of all kinds of people, and he can be violent, too. He drinks a lot and went from woman to woman before Mom and after. So when he shows up ready to continue where he left off, I don't trust him."

"I wouldn't either—he abandoned you at ten years old. Your own dad. See, but that's the whole human deal right there: people change. We have to. We evolve."

Sara the Evolver, thinks Matt. He had no idea when he first saw her at Thousand Steps beach that day, with her pink skateboard with the white daisies, being photographed with a giant near-naked muscleman, that he, Matt, could possibly be sitting with her in one of the great restaurants of the world a few short weeks later. He feels like he's been beamed from Earth to another planet to confront an alien being so intense and smart and simply beautiful that she takes his words away.

Strong emotions, but he doesn't know what they are. He loves Laurel Kalina, and has told her so, though she called it lust. And although nothing about him is different except his physical size, Laurel has told him more than once that he is changing. Is he betraying Laurel right now, right here, this very second? It feels that way. Are feelings ever not true?

Sara orders a Beaulieu Georges de Latour wine from 1962 and Marcus is back soon, uncorking the bottle with a fluid brevity that Matt admires. When she tastes it and nods, Marcus leaves the cork and is gone.

"I can't believe my dad actually encourages me to drink wine here," she says. "Two glasses of this will put us nearly on our butts," she says. "Do *not* let me order after-dinner brandies. But I am going to break my vegetarian vow tonight. The steaks here are out of sight."

She asks Matt to drive home, a few side streets then a ten-mile run down Pacific Coast Highway to Laguna.

Matt knows the basic shift pattern from the Westfalia but he's completely unprepared for the thrust of the Porsche and the impossible acceleration. The gear shifts come up fast, but unlike the Volkswagen's, this clutch is deep and heavy and the transmission is decisive. It feels like every part down there is rounded and machined and polished perfectly—no edges or shearing rough spots as in the van. It's like riding an animal made of stainless steel and a little bit of leather to sit on.

Matt steers south in the dark.

"You're a good driver, Matt. But you do need some practice with the shifting."

"I feel like I really have to pay attention."

"Eighty feels like forty."

"Jeez."

"There's a place across from the Orange Inn I want to show you," she says.

Matt pulls into the right turn lane and gets off for the Orange Inn. It's closed now, well past midnight. The headlights rake the colorful little snack shop. They make a peanut butter chocolate shake that is, in his opinion, the finest shake on Earth. Sara directs him down the frontage strip to a rough dirt road that crosses beneath PCH, then climbs a hillock dozed flat at the top. There's room for four or five cars but they have the view to themselves.

Matt can see Coast Highway and the cottages of Crystal Cove in the distance, and the glittering black Pacific all the way to the stars.

"Look at that moon—"

Sara turns his face and kisses him deeply and firmly. Moves her hand to his chest and hoists her knee onto his thigh. Her leg is warm and heavy and it sends a jolt of electricity through him. She's wearing the same spicy-leathery perfume she wore that morning at Emerald Bay. He tastes wine and gorgonzola but mostly the great human life of her. Her temples are damp and he can feel her jaw muscles working.

She moves her hand down to his too tight Sunday trousers. Finds the embarrassing bulge.

"What's this?"

"Um, you know."

"I do know. So how about some shifting practice? Get your shift pattern down so it's natural?"

"Okay, Sara."

"Okay. First gear is just a short throw, pretty much straight out."

Matt winces with pleasure as she shifts him into first.

"Then, clutch in and straight down into second."

Matt feels helpless, like his willpower doesn't apply. Her fingers are firm and warm and his thoughts come fast but incompletely.

"Got it."

"Good. Now, third's a long one up and to the right, not sharp right but a smooooooth glide up next to where first was, but further. Give it a good firm push. There."

Matt gasps and Sara does too.

"Now, pretty much straight down into fourth, Matt. Good, I can feel you getting the rhythm. Just rest in fourth. Savor the moment and feel the speed. Okay, now let's put her into fifth and let this race car go."

She shifts from fourth to fifth gear and by then Matt's eyes are squeezed shut and he's breathing fast and loud. She keeps her hand on the shifter.

Matt feels the final urgent collapse of his self-control. Then the surge, wild, tidal, and warm. Time does a funny trick, either speeds up or slows down but he's not sure which.

"I like fifth," he croaks.

"You liked them all. You are so sweet. Maybe for our next test drive, I'll steer the hippie van and you can help me shift."

"Okay."

"I have to get you home, Matt. I've got crew at sunrise at the Bay Club. I'll drive now."

After Sara drops him off at Third Street, Matt drives the Westfalia south on PCH. There's no way he can sleep. He's more than just awake; he feels alive in new ways. He feels a new kind of energy moving through him, very strong and crackling in all directions at once. He wants to do everything he likes, right now, all at the same time.

So he pulls over at Calliope, digs Jasmine's eight-track *Disraeli Gears* from the shoe box on the seat, and plugs it in. He's really hungry, so he gets Oreos from the cooler, and a can of this new Tropic Surf soda, cheap because they're promoting it in the stores now. Actually, he would drink more wine if he had it. Tonight was the first time he'd had more than a beer to drink—two at the most—and he'd been told what a great buzz wine gives you because it's strong. A little bit makes him want more. Now he knows why old people drink all the time.

He also wants very much to go fishing right now, but night-fishing the rocks alone is dangerous and the waves today were big.

But most of all in this cluster of desires, he wants to experience tonight's test drive with Sara Eikenberg again, her heavy warm leg pressing against his own, her tastes and smells and the sweat on her temples and her hand and what she did for him.

He pulls onto Pacific Coast Highway and goes through the Westfalia's humble gears, remembering.

He drives up into hilly central Laguna, where he and his father will continue their search in the morning.

The van chugs up the streets and Matt scans the houses. Cream plays Matt's favorite, "Tales of Brave Ulysses," as he notices white curtains lifting on the breeze through an open window on Brooks Street, Laurel's window, her light on because she likes to write in bed at night.

I'm sorry, Laurel.

Then an hour of random streets, thinking about his sister, his heart turning heavy with the fact that she's been missing almost three weeks now. Anything can happen in three weeks. In three minutes. They re-kidnapped her in less than that. He can't help but feeling she's further away than ever. He tells himself that she's here in this town because he *saw* her here. If he can't trust his own 20/10 vision, what can he trust?

Two girls stride down the sidewalk toward PCH in lock-step, arms joined, laughing. One could be Jazz but isn't.

Suddenly tired and sad, Matt drives past Laurel's house once more, then heads for his mother's barn in Dodge City, wondering if Laurel will sense his betrayal.

He turns the news station up loud.

This just in to KFWB—a bloody garage in Huntington Beach, where three members of the Hessians motorcycle club have been found shot to death in what police are calling an execution-style triple murder. No arrests have been made and no suspects have been identified . . .

Matt turns up the volume even higher to catch the rest of the story, but that's it for now.

He has no trouble identifying suspects: Bayott and his In-terpol comrades.

Comrades of Marlon Sungaard.

44

Julie is out of the overdose room in the ICU and has her own ocean-view room on floor four. She lies painfully—it looks to Matt—with her right, full-cast leg raised on pillows, arms at her sides, palms to the mattress as if bracing herself.

It's early but Bruce has talked his way past the nurse's station with his story of having been married to their patient for the happiest days of his life, then driven thousands of miles to see her.

"Good morning, sunshine," says Bruce, a greeting that Matt remembers his mother rolling her eyes at when she'd come into the kitchen for coffee in the bomb shelter house.

She shakes her head. "Not you again. Hi Mattie. You're growing every day."

Matt holds up the hospital gift-shop flowers, extravagantly expensive but cheerful. Daisies and carnations. He's drawn a nice little sketch of his mom from an old picture of her with Gus, the family dog, and written "Get Well, Mom!" on it.

Julie's smile turns to a wince.

"The ribs," she says.

"Julie," says Bruce, "is there anything in the world I can do for you?"

"Find your daughter."

"I certainly will."

"Then uncrack my ribs and heal my leg."

"I would if I could. They have terrific painkillers."

"No, thank you. I'm going to stay off those things."

"Atta-girl. You're getting stronger. I can see it."

"When I sit up it feels like my ribs are cracking all over again. I can't look for Jazz. I can't put up posters or nag the cops at the station. I can't earn money to pay that PI. I'm burning up the hospital phone, trying to get the FBI and the *Los Angeles Times* to believe my daughter has been kidnapped."

Matt sees her strength returning too. She's got clear steady eyes now, not the dreamy dragon ball glaze she had before. And good color on her face too, must be from the Summer of Eternal Love.

He sets the flowers on the table and touches her forehead. Thinks of her on Sunday in her periwinkle prairie dress in free fall. He hates to see it again, that awful pirouette-jump-slip-fall down into the boulders.

"Such a sweetie, Matt. You're my man."

Which draws her a blank look from Bruce.

"Bruce," says Julie. "Can you tell me exactly what you're doing here? You still haven't answered me."

Bruce steps closer to the bed, Stetson in hand, a white shirt with mother-of-pearl buttons, new-looking Wranglers.

"I tried to tell you yesterday but you were kind of out of it," he drawls softly.

"I'm not out of it now."

Matt moves for the door but Bruce stops him.

"Julie, I came back to find Jasmine. Matt and I can do it, of that I am confident. But I'll be honest with you—as I was driving here, I realized I wanted to see you again. Very strongly and honestly and without expectations. You. I've had this feeling for some years but I kept it inside because of all the damage I did to you and the kids. I told myself it was not my privilege to see you again."

"But driving out here you wanted to see me why?"

"I'd realized my desire to return to you and this family. To begin the long, long trail back to being worthy of you all. I'm sorry to just spring it on you like this. I wanted to wait until we found Jazz."

"You can't keep a job, a long string of girlfriends dumps you, and now you're ready to try me again? I read your letters home to the children. I wanted to burn them. Bruce, do you know how pathetic you are?"

"Yes, truly." He sighs, turning the Stetson in his hands.

"Truly, Bruce, you should be taken out and shot."

"Are you certain?"

"You're not funny."

"But if that's your decision, to have me shot, then . . ."

"I see nothing in the future with you. If you want to come back to this town you say you hate, I can't prevent you. But I hope you can be something like a real father to your children."

"I will insist on it."

"I'll have nothing to do with you."

"I rented your house on Third Street," says Bruce. "I'll vacate immediately whenever you want it back. Whenever that might be."

"No, we don't want it, thank you. Matt, Jasmine, Kyle, and I will all be living in Dodge City. Where you're certainly not welcome. You'd hate it anyway."

"I sure would."

Julie stares at Bruce a long beat. Matt can see her naturally good heart battling it out with her anger at a man she once loved. Matt does not ever want a divorce. Maybe not even a marriage.

"Out damn'd spot! out I say!"

"You still make me laugh, Julie."

"I can't laugh 'cause the ribs. They got me on anticonvulsants, too."

Dr. Caroline Hoppe is making early rounds and she stops Matt and his father at the nurse's station across from Julie's room.

"She suffered a grand mal seizure yesterday," says the neurologist. "Followed by two petite mals, so I've put her on strong doses of Dilantin and Tegretol. With no history of

epilepsy, I suspect the seizures were brought on by the lysergic acid she ingested at the festival on Sunday. She told me she
drank some orange juice that was being passed around by a
young man. He had an orange airbrushed face, an Uncle Sam
hat, and Stars and Stripes shorts. He said the juice was nectar
from the gods. She said she was already feeling very strange
before eating the corner of the invitation—bright tracers in
her vision and geometric shapes floating around her. The seizures may prove temporary, but they could prove to be part
of her future. We'll discontinue the anticonvulsants for a week
and see if she seizes again. I can send her home tomorrow if
someone can be with her during her waking hours. A grand
mal seizure can be very dangerous. There are hospital volun-
teers who can come by."

Matt stretches his imagination for a way to take care of his
mother.

"I can't be with her all day, every day," he says. "I have my
paper route and my sister to find."

"I can fill in around you," Bruce says eagerly. "Happy to."

Something gut-level, protective and suspicious, jumps up in
Matt. "I don't think that's a good idea, Dad."

Julie's voice rings from her room:

"That's not going to happen!"

Bruce manages an embarrassed smile.

"We can keep her another day or two," says the doctor.

45

After the hospital, Matt and his father get donuts at Dave's. Bruce tells Dave to be a good boy and pour more half-and-half into that coffee. Matt can't wait to get back outside.

They trudge up and down the steep, winding streets of Laguna, east of Coast Highway. The morning is hotter than yesterday and the usual onshore breeze is barely moving.

By midmorning, Bruce has lost his charm. They're getting spooked looks, refusals, closing doors.

It's almost noon and they've only made eighteen full searches. They've come down a nearly vertical Upland Road to Pacific Coast Highway and are heading north for the next street up the hill.

There's a gaggle of war protesters up ahead at Moss Street, waving signs at the drivers, many of whom are honking back and flashing their headlights on and off.

Hey, Hey, LBJ, How Many Kids Did You Kill Today?
I Don't Give a Damn for Uncle Sam!
Another Mad Jew for Peace!

"Your mother is right. I'd hate it here. It's the new Sodom. Look at those people. Weak, materialistic. Plump, pleasure-seeking, end-of-empire Romans. Ignorant of the Soviet world threat, ignorant of Christian-American history. Ignorant of self-defense, oblivious to the responsibility of owning firearms. But they're against a necessary war they don't understand. Well, isn't that just great? Kyle over there in the tunnels and these pathetic hippie homos are waving signs before they head home to get stoned and watch *Let's Make a Deal*."

Matt sees his English teachers, Marybeth Benson and Londa Jones, raising their big signs up and down: *Draft Beer Not Students! Bring the Troops Home Now!*

"Look," says Matt. "My teachers are there! They want beer *and* Kyle to be home."

"That's an insult to a boy whose life is on the line."

"Would you rather have him home or in the tunnels, Dad?"

"Home *from* the tunnels, Matt! After killing every wretched communist he could find. And maybe a few extra. And if, in a couple of years, our country is still in this war—or some other war—I'd want you to be over there, fighting for freedom and America. I know you would. I think you would."

A sharp glance Matt's way, then Bruce tugs the brim of his Stetson down lower.

"That's what I would want for you, son. Your mother does not feel that way, as you probably remember from Kyle enlisting. Nor Jazz. You, of course, are entitled to your own opinion. I pray that it be an informed and patriotic opinion—not a product of this immoral time and city. The queers are of the devil, not God."

Matt doesn't know what to say to that.

For what seems like the hundredth time since last night, Matt thinks of Sara. He wonders if male homos ever miss girls. Probably not or they'd change. Can they change? Lesbians must not miss guys, either. Who knows what's inside you when you're born, or for that matter, what grows inside you over time? His sophomore biology teacher said people can be born with their sexuality different than their biology, and that some undergo surgery to change their gender. Not for me, thinks Matt, not after last night's drive.

"So, son, if you ever have thoughts like that, I mean along the lines of what we've just been discussing, please talk to a minister or other trusted adult. Based on Laurel, and your friend in the Porsche, I don't foresee a problem."

"God, Dad. Me neither."

"Look at these freaks. Public schoolteachers among them. Disgusting."

By then Matt and his father are surrounded by protesters as they wait to cross at Moss Street. Matt waves at Marybeth and Londa, who smile and aim their signs at him and his father. Bruce doffs his cowboy hat theatrically and flips them off, which draws a band of young people into a chanting circle around them, *John Wayne, You're a Pain! John Wayne, You're a Pain!* Bruce shoves a young man, sends him skidding onto the sidewalk. Marybeth and Londa pick him up and hold him back while Bruce strides across Moss, away from the crowd. Matt watches his father in stunned amazement—embarrassed and saddened. If it weren't for Jazz, Matt wouldn't want to be spending time with him at all. So much snarling anger in him, so much wounded pride.

By one o'clock, quitting time, Bruce's brusque requests have turned off many of the homeowners, only ten of whom consent to a full house search for Jasmine.

While Bruce searches their last home of the morning shift—a neat glass-and-beam modern on Gainsborough Drive—Matt talks to Arnold Service, a mild-mannered old guy of at least fifty.

Matt answers his questions about Jasmine and her abduction. The man has no idea a local girl has been abducted in front of her very own home.

"Jasmine is an unforgettable name," says Service.

Out of sight, Bruce clomps from hall to bedroom, bedroom to hall, calling out *hello!*

Service carefully studies the pictures of Jasmine—Matt's sketch, her senior portrait. He sheepishly admits to not following the news or even leaving the house much.

"And you say she plays ukulele?" Arnold Service asks.

"Yes, very well."

"I do, too."

"And she writes her own songs."

Service's pale blue eyes scan Matt's face. "You wait right here."

He goes into a small dining room, takes something off the top of a china hutch, brings it to Matt.

Who recognizes it immediately from his boyhood: a Little Wing. It's a paper airplane, one of the boxy, up-tipped-wing ones that float forever in any kind of breeze. It's got small, precisely folded elevators along the rear edge of the wings, which gives the nose lift. Bruce Anthony himself came up with the design after much trial and error. Taught his kids how to make them—simple really, he explained—the secret was getting the wings wide and long enough to sustain flight, but short enough for rigidity. The elevators were his innovation. The heavier the paper the better the glider, until the paper was too heavy. If a Little Wing got into a good breeze, like a canyon thermal or an updraft at the beach, it could go forever. An incredible paper airplane. Kyle's always stayed in the air the longest because he had a strong arm. Jasmine had named the aircraft Little Wing, long before the song came out.

But what is most interesting to Matt is obviously what was most interesting to Arnold Service.

"The paper is sheet music for ukulele," Matt says. "It's from *Advanced Ukulele Hits*."

"It certainly is."

Matt's heart is throbbing in his ears so loud he can hardly hear his own words.

He now holds in his hands the connection he's been searching for.

A potential miracle in the form of a paper airplane, designed by his father.

"Where did you get this?"

"It was on my front lawn a few days ago," says Service. "I thought it was so beautiful. And mysterious. A glider made of ukulele music from a book that I myself own? At first, I thought I was being hazed. Maybe I was, but I knew that something quite strange had happened. If you unfold it, you'll see the song is 'I Am a Rock.'"

Which Matt remembers as the song from the night he watched his sister around the campfire at Crescent Bay with the older teenagers, lurking in the background to not embarrass her, watching the flames throw orange shadows on her face, listening to the ukulele and her strong, emotional voice through the crackle of the fire.

Now his own voice carries strong emotion: "Exactly when? Exactly what time and day did you find this on your lawn, Mr. Service?"

"I can tell you."

He goes into a bedroom and comes out a moment later, almost knocking into Bruce, who's marching back down the hall. Service drops whatever it is he's carrying, then flinches when Bruce makes a reflexive fist. Bruce quickly apologizes and comes back into the living room with a hard set to his jaw. He looks at Matt and shakes his head just once.

Arnold Service follows Bruce back in with an At-A-Glance desk calendar and a pair of reading glasses in place. He glances worriedly at Bruce then consults the calendar.

"Last Tuesday," he says. "It was there on the grass when I got up in the morning. Around seven. It was damp from the dew."

The morning he labored for Sara Eikenberg's father, Matt thinks, or late the night before. Launched by Jazz as a call for help. Which means *there might be more*.

An idea forms.

"What's this all about?" Bruce asks.

"Mr. Service," Matt says. "Can I have this?"

"If it would help you find Jasmine, please, do. It's yours."

"What the hell is all this about?"

"A Little Wing!" Matt hands his father the delicate thing. Bruce turns it in his big hands then gives Matt a gray-eyed stare.

"I'll be damned," says Bruce. His face looks pleased and

proud. The airplane rocks on his big palm like it's just landed. "We folded scores of these things."

"And now it's going to help us find her, Dad. We'll show this to everyone we talk to. In the houses, on the street, down-town, at the beaches—*everywhere*. Jazz is launching these for *us*. There have to be more. Which means, if we know where and when they landed and figure in the wind, we'll know where they came from."

"Hold on, son," says Bruce. "Not so fast. This thing could have been launched from practically anywhere. You know how they just go and go."

"No, Dad!" Matt pinches the body lightly, holds the air-plane up for his father to see. "The breeze carried it here on a downward path. It's glider aerodynamics. Jazz's plane came from the hills above us."

"We can't even know that it came from her," says Bruce.

"It has to be her! Little Wing is a one-of-a-kind design. You taught her to fold it and she sent this out for *us* to find!"

In a long moment's journey Matt watches his father's ex-pression go from disbelief to doubt to bewilderment to a hint of possibility.

Near the end of the night's door-knocking, at sunset, Matt and his father find another Little Wing. It's made of ukulele sheet music from the same book. Matt holds it to the lamp-light in a small bedroom on Sleepy Hollow Lane.

Sleepy Hollow Lane is far north of Moss. The finder is a Japanese girl—Hinata Saito—who is staying in a vacation rental with her family. She seems proud to own something that Matt owns, too. Her English is good and she says she almost stepped on the glider, then picked it up off the street because she liked origami and wanted to know how the glider was folded.

In the lamplight of the small bedroom, Matt sees the car tire print across one wing of the plane, the paper pocked by nicks and divots made by a two-ton automobile. To him, it's a miracle there's anything left of it at all. Another miracle in a miraculous day. Possibly the best day of his life.

Matt, Bruce, Hinata, her mother, father, and two brothers, have all crowded into a cottage bedroom, where Hinata keeps the Little Wing in a small red bucket half-filled with seashells and bits of driftwood. She found the plane two days ago. One of the brothers shows Matt some shells in a plastic coffee cup of brine and his father orders him away.

"This plane was made by my sister, Jasmine Anthony," says Matt. "She's in trouble and this is her way of communicating with me. May I have it?"

Hinata nods and smiles, delighted. She's got shiny dark eyes and a wonderful face. Her family seems delighted as well. Hinata is happy to give Matt the glider, and if she finds another, he can have that, too. They are staying here all summer, Disneyland tomorrow.

Matt and his father head down the busy sidewalk toward the Westfalia. The night is warm and a faint band of orange lingers along the western horizon. Matt stops and looks east across PCH to the city, the houselights scattered across the hills like a tossed handful of diamonds.

He remembers what Jasmine said on the phone that night, the last time he heard her voice: *In Laguna! I'm in the . . .*

"She's launching these things from somewhere *up*," Matt says. "So an offshore breeze will take them down toward the ocean—like Moss and Sleepy Hollow. An onshore breeze will give them lift, and scatter them in the hills above town, or even the canyon, where there's thermals. Like where Kyle and me used to collect hawk feathers and camp out."

His father is quiet for a moment. "This is a real longshot, Matt. The planes tell us almost nothing, except that it *could* be Jazz who made them. I'm being realistic."

"Another ukulele player knowing how to fold a perfect Little Wing? That isn't realistic, Dad—it's ridiculous! This is the connection. Something you taught Jazz is going to save her life. It's a gift or a sign or a miracle or whatever you want to call it."

They get to the Westfalia and climb in. Matt looks through the windshield at the hills and the moon.

"Sorry I lost my temper today," says his father. "It won't be the last time."

"Maybe you could be easier on people. Everybody's different."

"I don't fit in, but this is my home now. Part of me wants to just hose Laguna off into the ocean. The hippies and the druggies and the bums and freeloaders. Just blast them away and start over. Like God and Noah and the flood."

"It's a good city, Dad. It's live and let live."

"I hope I don't mess things up."

46

Matt sits across from Furlong and Darnell in the LBPD interview room, both paper airplanes on the stainless-steel desk between them. He explains how he found them. He doesn't want to give them up but he knows he'll have to. Last night he folded three identical copies, using pages from Jazz's *Advanced Ukulele Hits*.

Last night he also thought of the *Register* doing a front-page story on these airplanes, with a picture of one, so everyone in Laguna who had found one could tell him when and where. He quickly realized that her kidnappers would know what she was up to and keep her from ever launching another one again. Or worse.

Darnell, her notebook open, is too surprised to write or speak.

Furlong touches the first glider with the button end of his pen. "Unusual design," he says.

"It's a Little Wing. My dad invented it when we were kids. Jazz named it. She was really good at folding them, see?"

"Those ailerons along the wings—"

"They're called elevators. If they're not perfect, the plane spirals and crashes. Dad worked on the design for months."

Furlong pokes the plane again with his pen. "Tell me the man's name and address again."

Matt repeats Arnold Service's name and address, explains that the man doesn't read papers or watch the news, didn't know that a local girl had been missing for almost three weeks.

Both police officers make notes. Darnell excuses herself to get a camera.

"I want to see you in the conference room after this," Furlong says quietly.

Matt's heart dives. He knows that the insatiable sergeant will want something else from him. Furlong has become a burden. Five dollars per each bit of useful information isn't worth the betrayal. Thirty pieces of silver. Not that Johnny Grail and the Brotherhood of Eternal Love are comparable to Jesus, but Matt wishes he'd never taken Furlong's damned money to start with.

Darnell comes back with a big heavy-looking camera, rearranges the airplanes, and fires away. The shutter clatters and the flash fills the tiny room.

"Are you going to look for more of these?" Matt asks.

"Why should we?" asks the sergeant. "We have no evidence that Jasmine folded or launched them."

"But if we find more planes, we can establish a pattern," says Matt. "Of where they came from. Of where she is!"

"Doubtful," says Furlong.

Darnell carefully places the gliders into plastic bags for their journey to the property room.

"Officer Darnell, if it was up to you, would *you* look for more?" asks Matt.

"Brigit does what I order her to do," says Furlong.

She gives the sergeant a sharp look.

"And you, Mr. Anthony, have some explaining to do. Come with me."

"*Would you,* Officer Darnell?"

"Matt, come with me."

Furlong seats Matt facing the others in the conference room, and makes brief introductions.

In front of Matt, seated around a three-table horseshoe, are LBPD Chief Norman Hein, Orange County District Attorney Mike Saffalo, Detective Lance McAdam, and Dr. Mary Hamilton. They do not look happy.

Furlong takes a seat near a large tape recorder and turns it on. Also on the table before the sergeant are a roll of paper towels, a baking dish, a wooden spoon, and a pair of shiny metal tongs.

These are some heavy hitters, Matt gathers. And they're here to talk to *him* on the Fourth of July. No wonder they're unhappy. He knows this can't be good.

Furlong states that Dr. Hamilton is the director of Orange County Juvenile Hall's Youth Leadership Center, describing it as "a residence and rehabilitation center for troubled youth with sentences of a year, or longer."

Matt feels a faint, dizzy rush. He hears in Furlong's voice the pleasure of inflicting fear. Dr. Hamilton is very large and looks very old—over sixty, Matt guesses—hair in a high black beehive, her face tight-lipped and heavy-browed.

In the loaded silence, Furlong reaches into a box on the floor and places a mason jar of Laguna Sunshine Farms stewed tomatoes on the table in front of him. Then a leather-bound *Tibetan Book of the Dead*. Then a box of Languedoc Toffees. The plastic wrap has been taken off the book and the candy. Furlong takes a moment to space them equidistantly. Matt wonders what catastrophe his theft has launched, and who it will land on.

"First of all," says Chief Hein. "Thanks to all of you for being here. I'm sure you all have holiday plans and I'll try to make this brief. Dr. Hamilton, can you start off by telling Mr. Anthony here what you do at the Youth Leadership Center?"

"Yes, thank you." Dr. Hamilton's voice is pleasant but firm. "Matt, the Center is designed for Juvenile Hall's most promising—and most serious—older offenders. We house sixteen-to-eighteen-year-olds with sentences of over one year. Their crimes range from drug dealing to assault to murder. Many of our youth are being held over for trial in the juvenile courts, which are crowded and slow. Others will be tried as adults and serve out their time in the county jail, the state prison system, or in work camps. We offer occasional furloughs and excursions. You—our youth—are allowed two hours of weekly visitation."

Matt feels like crying. He imagines Laurel and Sara sitting

on the other side of a juvie safety-glass window, taking turns talking to him on a phone. Two hours a *week*?

"I didn't do it," he says. "I didn't know there was LSD on the invitations. I distributed them for Johnny because he paid me five dollars."

"Matt," says Dr. Hamilton. "You are not on trial here. None of us in this room *wants* you to be tried. You are a good citizen and a good student. You are employed. You have no criminal record. You are being raised in a challenging environment of divorce, low income, and a single, possibly drug-affected mother."

"She kicked it, doctor. She's clean now."

Dr. Hamilton gives Matt a tolerant nod. Then she looks across the table at Furlong.

"Sergeant Furlong, what more can I do here? I think we've scared this boy half out of his wits and I have eighty-four Leadership Center partners to attend to. We call them 'partners,' Matt, not prisoners or inmates, although that's exactly what they are. Whatever you can do to stay out of my Leadership Center, do it. I urge you to cooperate. Please excuse me to my favorite American holiday, gentlemen."

Furlong clicks off the tape recorder. The men all stand and thank the doctor and shake her hand. She's as tall as Furlong and looks about as strong. Matt stands too. Chief of Police Hein shows her to the door. She stops and looks back at Matt.

"Good luck, Matt."

"Thank you, doctor."

"I hope to never see you again."

"I hope to never see you again, too, I mean—"

Everyone chuckles.

"I know what you mean," she says, then is gone.

"Okay," says Chief Hein. "Let's get to the heart of this proceeding, Bill."

"Yes, sir," says Furlong. "Matt? Sit. I'm going to show you some things and you're going to answer some questions."

47

When the four men are seated, Furlong turns the tape recorder back on and picks up the Laguna Sunshine Farms mason jar. He holds it label-out for Matt to see, like he's in a commercial.

"This is a jar of your mother's prized stewed tomatoes," he says. "Sliced. There are diced and whole available, too. She and another lady called Crazy Carol can these tomatoes in the packing house out in Dodge City. They sell some of them at a Brotherhood of Eternal Love organic produce stand on Laguna Canyon Road. Sound about right?"

Matt wishes he'd paid more attention when his mom was showing him the packing house. He already feels the need to defend her but he's not sure from what.

He also wishes these people were out trying to find his sister rather than tormenting him with their paranoia of the Brotherhood of Eternal Love.

"From what I know."

"They're supposed to be great tomatoes," says Furlong. "So, of course I had to try them out."

He unscrews the lid, smells the jar, and spoons two loads of the stewed, sliced tomatoes into the baking dish.

"These look pretty good. But what have we here?"

Furlong folds a paper towel and sets it in front of him. Then picks up the tongs, reaches into the mason jar, and pulls out a small plastic sheath dripping with red juice. He wipes it back and forth on the paper towel then lays it down.

"My first thought was, well, it's some kind of spice pack

that Laguna Sunshine Farms has told Julie Anthony or Crazy Carol to include in certain batches of the sliced tomatoes. Maybe recipes. So I read the jar label, but there's nothing about a spice pack or recipes inside, or a toy, like in a box of cereal. So, what is it? Let's see."

Furlong unfolds the clear plastic sheath with his paws and uses two big fingers to extract a red rectangle from inside.

"Of course," says Furlong. "Laguna Sunshine Farms includes a sheet of red paper wrapped in plastic in their canned, stewed tomatoes. Who wouldn't? However, it looks a little unusual. For one thing, the sheet of what looks like paper is sectioned off into five rows of four roughly half-inch squares. Twenty, total. Each square is delineated by perforations, perfectly, symmetrically made. And look, each half-inch square of red paper has a small black outline of the sun on it, like a child's drawing. Which looks very much like the childish sun in the upper left corner of the Summer of Eternal Love invitation you delivered to every business in Laguna. The invite that, ingested by twenty-five thousand low-IQ hippies and other drug fiends, led to dozens of overdoses and two deaths last Sunday. Not to mention hundreds of arrests and god knows how much brain damage."

Furlong levels a look at Matt.

"It's LSD, Matt," says Chief Hein. "From a BEL-financed lab in Oakland."

"It's going out in shipments all around the country," says Furlong. "Possibly the world. I hope to find some kind of sales data, or shipping logs when we raid Dodge City."

Matt sees what's shaping up here and he doesn't like it one bit. Feels his anger spike at everything these cops are *not* doing.

"How many jars do they sell in a month?" asks McAdam.

"Matt?" asks Furlong, with raised eyebrows.

"How would I know?" he answers. "I do know that my sister was kidnapped almost three weeks ago and you haven't come up with one solid lead."

Silence, dead but brief.

"Your mother pretty much ran the operation until she fell on Sunday," says Furlong.

"She just worked there," says Matt. "It wasn't an operation to her, it was just a job. It didn't pay very well."

Furlong lets that observation hang in the air.

Mike Saffalo, the district attorney, comes around the table for a better look at the perforated red paper. "They call it blotter acid, when it's on paper like this," he says. "It's lighter and easier to transport than tablets. It's also a federal offense if they're using the United States Post Office to ship these drugs across state lines."

"I can just about guarantee you they are," says Furlong.

"'Just about' won't cut much ice in court, Bill," says Saffalo.

Furlong looks at Matt. "We're working on that."

"Sergeant," asks Saffalo, "can you put a street value on this?"

"Sixty bucks—three dollars a trip. Times hundreds of mason jars. If not thousands over a year's time. But the BEL isn't doing this for money—they're doing it to turn the world on.]In other, words, for fun."

"Show him the high-dollar stuff," says Chief Hein.

Furlong sets the tomatoes and baking dish aside, picks up the *Tibetan Book of the Dead*, and opens the lavish leather-and-stamped-gold cover.

He holds the elaborate title page up to Matt—a picture of a Tibetan holy man, meditating. He's wearing a crimson robe, much like that of Mahajad Om.

"Nice title page," says Furlong. "But after that, the plot fizzles out. There's not another written word in the whole volume."

Furlong, still holding the book up, turns the title page to reveal the book's first page—a white sheet of paper, perforated similarly to the canned stewed tomatoes from Laguna Sunshine Farms. Matt, with 20/10 vision, can see hundreds of beaming little suns from where he sits. These *Tibetan Book of the Dead* pages are much larger than the mason jar inserts.

"Same blotter acid as in the tomatoes," says Furlong. "Same half-inch squares, white instead of red. But each sheet in this book is seven by nine inches, which gives you two hundred and fifty-two doses of LSD per sheet. There are three hundred and eighty pages in the book, which means one hundred and ninety sheets. The grand total is forty-seven thousand eight hundred and eighty hits of acid. At three bucks a pop, this *Tibetan Book of the Dead* is worth one hundred forty-three thousand, six hundred and forty dollars. Johnny Grail has a storage room full of these things at Mystic Arts, according to Matt here."

"Not full," says Matt. "I never said it was full. I only ever saw a few copies of that book. I also saw two strong men drag my sister into a van a hundred feet from this police station, in case you're interested. In case you're interested in kidnapping instead of a *Tibetan Book of the Dead* my mother has nothing to do with."

Hein sighs and Saffalo clears his throat.

Furlong shrugs, opens his hands. "Stay with me, Matt. Every book has almost forty-eight thousand doses of LSD in it. Do you know how many people could lose their minds forever on this shit? That's what I'm talking about here. The human cost. In brain cells. In suicides and addictions and accidents. I'm *talking* about your mother, Julie Anthony."

"Matt, is this the same book that you delivered to Marlon Sungaard?" asks Detective McAdam. "Two copies?"

Again, Furlong looks to Matt.

"I thought they were just books!"

He suddenly remembers that Jazz had done similar errands for Johnny Grail and the BEL. Had she been fooled too, or did she know? Had she done something to the BEL to get herself kidnapped? But how could Johnny Grail do something that evil, and what good could it possibly do him? How could Grail act like a friend if the BEL has Jazz?

Furlong loudly drops the book on the table. Pushes it aside and squares the box of Languedoc Toffees in front of him and lifts the lid. Tilting it up to Matt, he pulls away the dark brown bubbly wrap, revealing the big round candies inside. They're wrapped in gold foil and look the size of Ping-Pong balls. They look pretty damned good after his hasty peanut butter and jelly burrito for breakfast.

"Don't tell me," Matt says. "The toffee in the middle is really LSD."

Furlong shakes his head. "No. Inside, they're plastic-wrapped dragon balls, double-dipped in chocolate. They've got very high opium-to-hash ratio. The foil, plastic, chocolate, and box wrapping throws off the drug dogs' noses. These things are packaged in Afghanistan and smuggled into Laguna by the Brotherhood of Eternal Love. Each box is thirty dragon balls—worth about twenty-four hundred on the street. As you know, Laguna Beach is awash in Afghan dragon balls. We've got dragon ball addicts sleeping in the streets, on the beaches, in the parks. Look what these things did to your mom."

"She beat the opium, I told you."

"Matt," says Furlong. "I've talked to Dr. Caroline Hoppe at South Coast Hospital. Getting off the poppies isn't as easy as Julie makes it sound, especially on top of her spectacular acid overdose and near death. The pain she's in? And living in Dodge City, where she can get whatever dope she wants from those stoned-out hippies and dealers? So, we'll see about her kicking the dragon balls. But I certainly hope she can, because we'll need her to testify at Johnny Grail's trial. That's after we've arrested him for narcotics distribution, felony mail fraud, furnishing narcotics and alcohol to children, and second-degree murder."

"Murder?" asks Matt.

"The two overdose deaths at the Summer of Eternal Love festival," says DA Saffalo. "Grail could be looking at life in prison."

Matt tries to imagine life in prison. Minutes ago, he had broken into a clammy sweat at the idea of a year in the Youth

Leadership Center at Juvenile Hall. But the rest of his life in prison? That, he cannot imagine.

Neither can he imagine doing what Furlong asks him to do.

"You're going to help us set up and take down Johnny Grail," says Furlong. "Or we will be forced to arrest you and your mother for pretty much the same charges we'll bring against Grail and the Brotherhood of Eternal Love. Which will mean the Youth Leadership Center for you, and the new women's jail in Santa Ana for Julie. Nice place. Brand new. Set to open in a couple of months."

Matt sits, stunned.

The door opens and one of the police dispatch operators comes in. She's walking fast, leaning forward at the waist, casting furtive eyes around the room. Goes to Chief Hein, cups a hand to whisper something in his ear. He takes the news without expression. Nods slightly. Waits. When she's done, she leaves as quickly as she came, with a quick look at Matt.

Hein sighs deeply. "Laguna Beach PD has engaged a suspected drug supplier in South Laguna, just minutes ago. The officer fired in self-defense and the suspect died at the scene. He's a local man, Luke Lucas. They call him Hamsa Luke. You must know him, Matt. He worked at Mystic Arts World."

Matt can barely hear Chief Hein's words through the rushing in his ears.

He's terrified by this news, but not surprised by it. It had to happen to someone, didn't it?

He can bear no more. Something inside him breaks loose of its moorings.

"I need to use the bathroom," he says.

The chief looks to Furlong, who walks Matt to the station visitors' restroom.

"Matt, I'm sorry about your friend."

"I don't believe you. And he wasn't my friend but I liked him."

"I truly am. But listen—you're doing well in there. We're almost done."

"Okay."

"You're going to like my game plan."

A minute later Matt is pulling off a paper towel to dry his hands. He looks at himself in the mirror, which is not glass but stainless steel, because glass can be a weapon. It gives his face a funny lopsided shape. His heart is pounding and his breath is short. He takes in a big breath, lets it out slowly, then again.

He prays: *God, this is Matt. Let Furlong not be there when I go out, and I'll do anything you want, forever. Amen.*

And when he steps from the bathroom, Furlong is in fact not there. Matt looks down the hallway, sees the conference room door ajar.

Anything you want! Thank you!

He nods to the young desk officer on his way through the lobby, and tries to look casual on his way out.

Thirty seconds and he's pulling the Westfalia away from the Third Street curb—his heart racing and the exhaust pipe sputtering—headed for he knows not where.

Someplace they won't think to look for him.

He stops at a pay phone and digs out change to call Tommy Amici. Stands inside the hot glass booth, hands shaking. It seriously bums him out to have to give Tommy this news, but Furlong will be all over Matt if he tries to do his paper route today.

Matt has never been wanted by the cops. And he's never been threatened with juvie or by anyone as frightening as Dr. Hamilton. Combined, they give him a gnawing, knee-melting feeling. He won't be able to show his face for more than a moment in Dodge, or near his father's Third Street rental, or at Mystic Arts World, unless he uses the Bat Cave that Johnny Grail probably shouldn't have told him about. He can't do his paper route. Can't go to South Coast Hospital for more than a quick, paranoid visit with his mom. Can't park the Westfalia anyplace where Furlong would think to look for it.

And where will he sleep?

He's got just under five dollars to his name, the ten-dollar down payment on the Wyatt Earp revolver having cut deeply into his finances. A motel would empty his wallet quick. And what about food? Have to catch some serious fish to both eat and cut costs, he thinks.

But from his mouth come words he never thought he'd say:

"Tommy, I can't do the route for a few days. Can you cover for me?"

"*What?* You haven't missed a day in over two years!"

"I know. I'm sorry. Give me two days, Tommy."

Silence. "Is this about Jasmine?"

"Yes."

"Jesus! *Jesus.* Matt, I can cover your route today and tomorrow. I'll do that for you and for her. But if you're not back on your bike day after tomorrow, I'll have to hire a new kid. There's a waiting list, Matt. I can't keep a route open for someone who's not showing up. My boss won't let me. You've won an Outstanding Carrier medal two years running. Now this?"

"I appreciate it, Tommy."

"Have you talked to her again? Is she okay?"

"I heard from her, kind of."

"Two days, Matt—that's all I can give you."

"The cops killed Hamsa Luke."

"When? Why?"

"I don't know. South Laguna."

"There were rumors about him."

"There's rumors about everybody."

"He seemed like a cool guy."

Matt hangs up.

48

He parks the Westfalia well away from Moss Point, where Furlong might not look, squeezing into a shady spot between a dusty Fairlane and a pickup truck.

KFWB news says suspected narcotics kingpin Luke Lucas was one of several "high-level drug dealers" caught in a raid on a South Laguna home. Eighty pounds of marijuana confiscated. Five arrested.

Matt thinks of Luke at Mystic Arts telling Matt he looked like something that just evolved from the sea onto dry land.

Thinks of Luke telling him that the Hamsa tattooed across his knuckles protected him from the evil eye.

But it couldn't protect you from bullets, Matt thinks. Drugs might be fun and profit for the Brotherhood but to the cops they were deadly business.

Hamsa Luke dead for a few bales of grass.

Matt wonders if they'd shoot him too, what with Furlong's drug-riddled tomatoes and Tibetan books, French toffees, and acid-drenched Summer of Eternal Love invitations?

He turns off the news, sits for a moment looking out the window at the traffic on Coast Highway, down below. He knows that the key to dodging Furlong is to not be in one obvious place for long.

He secures his fishing rod, tackle box, sketchbook, and lunch to the Heavy-Duti. He's facing a risky half mile of exposure, but all he can do is hope Furlong doesn't guess he'll use one of his secret fishing spots to hide out.

He launches for Moss Point, riding close to the curb, stay-

ing away from the open asphalt. At PCH he times the traffic
and cuts right behind a speeding Mustang convertible blasting "Satisfaction."

Pushing the bike through the sand at Moss Point, Matt
sees that the swell is strong and from the south. He gets to his
secret spot, a patch of beach safe from high tide, surrounded
by big rocks and hard to get to—especially pushing a heavy
bicycle.

He arrives with great relief. The sharp black boulders are
the walls of a fortress. The sun is warm on his back. There's
an old fire pit outlined with rocks, with damp ashes and black-
ened bits of driftwood inside. He'd be folding his newspapers
right now, if not for becoming a fugitive. He liked *The Fugitive*
on TV more than he likes being one.

Matt kneels in the sand and bows his head and tries to clear
his emotions and understand why he's doing what he's doing.
He had no choice but to run away, right? They weren't kidding about Youth Leadership Center. They weren't kidding
when they shot Luke.

It comes creeping up on him now that he was wrong to
betray Johnny Grail and the rest of the BEL, even though
they suckered him into a possible narcotics distribution and
second-degree murder charges. But he'd been almost broke,
which made him afraid enough *not* to take Furlong's Judas
money. He'd been hungry and weak, and his home was about
to be rented out from under him. He had no idea there were
drugs in his mom's tomatoes, the French toffees, and the Tibetan Books of the Dead. He had asked God what to do and
God had ignored him. Though he had asked God to let him
escape Furlong and God had answered clearly.

But how do you make up for betrayal? He thinks. Well, you
try to do what's right.

He believes that he is right to free his sister from her tormentors. And right to help his mother recover. Right to help Kyle
when he comes home; right to keep his *Register* paper route;
right to fish, and to see Laurel and yes, Sara too. Maybe it's

right for him to help keep his father from doing something drastic in the name of Jazz, or in trying to clean up this "new Sodom."

You do what's right and the betrayal is made up for. It doesn't go away, but it's diluted.

He ties on a fresh Carolina rig—red plastic beads, egg sinker, swivel, leader, and hook—then walks the beach looking for sand crabs. They're plentiful in summer and he catches a few left exposed by the receding foam. Puts them in the pocket of his fishing shorts, feels them trying to dig out.

Back on the boulders, Matt sizes up the conditions. Heavy swell, high waves, and the tide rising. Today's *Register* told him the high tide would be at 2:55 P.M., still half an hour away. The last few minutes of an incoming tide is good, with hungry bass, perch, croaker, and halibut working the edges of the submerged rocks.

He's after the bottom-feeders. The crucial thing is not to let his hook get caught. He's lost more hooks than he can remember on Laguna's hidden reefs, but he's learned where the sandy slots between the rocks are, and to put the rig onto them. Learned to lift and mend as he feels the egg sinker dragging soggily over sand. When the line goes tight you've either got a fish or a rock.

He casts and lets the rig drift north. Picks his way upon the rocks, line tight, guiding the crab along with short turns of the reel, believing that a good fish will hit. The rocks are sharp and barnacle-encrusted and he trusts his Keds for grip. A sudden burst of spray hits his face. A pelican plummets into the water. Matt looks down at a jagged rock pool that is sometimes shallow enough to wade across, but sometimes not. Sea grass sways in the green-gold water, anemones glisten, and the crabs hold fast. He waits for the surge to retreat, then clomps across.

And so on, north up the coast, casting and trying to keep his rig free of the rocks and into the fish, but there are no fish. Within an hour Matt is half a mile from his safe little

patch of beach between the boulders and he's getting that awful feeling that the old man has in the Hemingway book that
Londa Jones assigned him, which he loved. The feeling of
being unlucky.

He knows that sometimes the sea is too rough even for the
fish. He lets the sand crabs go. By the time he makes it back
to his spot, he's tired and hungry.

He sits in the sand and eats his lunch, letting the sun bake the
chill out of him. The rocks shelter him from the world and the
waves send spray into the sky.

He falls dead asleep for ten minutes, awakened by gunshots
that turn out to be his own snoring.

Ready to change his luck, Matt ties on a big blue Krocodile
lure. Picks his way toward the farthest visible tip of Moss
Point, a slippery shelf barely showing above the water.

This table of rock is difficult to get to, but it's *the* place to
fish. Because, beyond its visible end, the shelf plunges steeply
underwater and ends in the sand, where big fish stage their
attacks on the rock dwellers. Sharks cruise this jagged edge.
There are occasionally big bass. Both species of halibut are
here—the most prized eating fish in these waters—ambush
predators, meaning they wait and watch. They are flat and
almost round and can weigh up to fifty pounds. Their mouths
are small, powerful, and lined with small, pointed razors.
They can hit a distracted perch or smelt before the smaller
prey senses that the halibut—a mottled brown-and-cream-
colored trash can lid set into the sand—is even there.

He takes slow, wide steps for balance, feels the strength
of the surge against his shins. Gulls bicker in the blue above
him. At the end of the shelf, which feels to Matt like the end
of the world, he casts far and slightly south and waits while
its weight takes the Krocodile to the bottom. He feels the
tumble of the lure in the sand, moving north with the current.
Lifts and pauses, letting it rise and fall. Reels it back to him

gradually, across the deep sandbar, through the deep water in which the big fish cruise.

Repeats. Repeats again.

His next cast is farther out and he lets the lure settle through the water column. The gulls overhead move farther out to keep their keen eyes on the action.

The Krocodile hits the bottom as before, moves along, then stops suddenly. Matt sets the hook. The fish is already off, a small one—maybe a calico or sand bass—but brave and hungry enough to attempt the big lure. Matt reels him in steadily, keeping the fish off the sharp, line-cutting rocks.

But he underestimates the bottom depth, and the fish digs in. A crafty little bass, no doubt.

He pops the rod tip and the fish is off again, but it has magically gained weight, a lot of it. Matt knows instantly that a much bigger fish has taken the smaller one. The new big fish runs west and down.

The line screams off the reel in a way that Matt has never heard: frantic, high-pitched, accelerating off the spool. His next calculation takes no time at all, just an admission that the fish is too big for his twelve-pound line, which will soon come to its end and snap, unless . . .

He jumps in.

No bottom. His Keds are heavy and the water is cold and the current takes him north.

He tightens the drag, treading water frantically while reeling up the line with rapid cranks. The chop is mean and the wind blows gusts of sea spray into his face.

Up the coast the fish pulls him. It is strong, dragging Matt along with unhurried ease. When it pauses, Matt gains some line back, but then the fish takes it again in a stubborn run. He sees he's down to maybe twenty of the one hundred yards of the good monofilament he put on in May.

Legs churning, Matt keeps the reel up and out of the water. If the spool binds in the sandy sea, his fish is gone. He's breathing deeply, teeth clenched against the inrush of brine.

He guides the animal toward shore. It is slowing, and Matt gets a quick forty yards of line back onto the grinding reel, scissor-kicking his way toward the shore, hoping he can land this monster on a soft sand beach and not lose him to rocks. His hands are clumsy with cold and he's shivering.

He wonders, but only briefly, what kind of fish he has. A shark would pull steadier, more back and forth. A big bass or a tuna would fathom and rest and then run again.

I will do this.

But now, without apparent effort, the fish turns and takes him west, heading straight out to sea.

Matt swirls in alarm and sees the sandy tan water chopping all around him, feels the rip current pulling him away from shore. He's numb with cold, loudly panting. He knows to swim at an angle toward the beach, to wait out the rip— easier said than done with a big fish pulling the other way and the heavy canvas shoes that Matt now jettisons toe-to-heel, toe-to-heel. His arms are locked at the elbows to keep the rod tip up and to fight the fish, but his bigger muscles are now cramping and his lungs burn.

The rip lets go of him far from shore. Matt guesses a quarter mile, not a problem unless you're half frozen, cramping, and fighting a fish that's stronger than you are.

But the fish has weakened too, and it rests long enough for Matt to roll over onto his back and begin kicking, the rod in one hand, the tip high. He sees sky, his face just barely out of the water. His ear canals fill.

And his feet churn, propelling him slowly, blessedly east toward shore. He's done this before, riding out rips while bodysurfing at Victoria and Brooks and St. Ann's, but always with good swim fins. This is slow going. He closes his eyes and repeats *I will do this*, trying to slow the words down and let the water bear him toward a clean sand beach. *I will do this.* Then he tries his secret mantra given to him by one of the Enlighteners on loan to Mystic Arts World from the Vortex of Purity, his very own mantra, a six-syllable sound that will

plug him into the universal subconscious like a jumper ca-
ble. So, chest heaving, kicking steadily, and feeling the dimin-
ished strength of the fish, Matt meditates shoreward. When he
opens his eyes he sees blue sky. When he gathers his energy
and turns to look where he's headed, he sees a yellow sandy
beach bobbing distantly.

Matt washes up in the whitewater like a clump of kelp.

ack in his private Eden, Matt cleans the halibut and cuts it into big steaks. He's still shivering. His knife is a good one, given to him by his father many years ago, and Matt keeps it as sharp as possible.

In minutes, he's bagged and packed most of the fish into the two baskets on the Heavy-Duti, two layers of upright steaks, tight as books on a shelf. The last eight go into two plastic bags that he hangs on the handlebars. The skin, skeleton, and head go into the sea. He rinses his knife and himself thoroughly and packs the knife back in his tackle box. Lashes his rod to the rear basket with the bungee.

Very slowly he pushes and pulls the heavy-laden Schwinn over the Moss Point rocks toward Coast Highway. Rests twice. Shivers again. His bare feet hurt. By the time he hits the steps he's too tired to get the bike up to the sidewalk, but a couple of kids help him.

"Your feet are bleeding, mister."

"Okay."

Finally, he's on PCH, pedaling weakly north for Dodge City and his mother's freezer, a good four miles away.

He's expecting Furlong to pull up behind him in Moby Cop, throw him and his bike and fish in, and haul them off to the Youth Leadership Center. Dr. Hamilton would get possession of him and his bike, and Furlong would take his fish and probably tell people he caught it. Again Matt considers the Bat Cave for hiding, but no: Furlong will be looking hard for him at MAW, and there's not nearly enough refrigerator freezer space for the epic halibut. No, he'd rather fight Furlong for his bike and his fish than let him claim them.

Matt lets himself into his mother's barn on Roosevelt Lane. Inside he feels the closed-up heat of summer so he opens the windows and leaves the front door wide and the screen door closed. Of course, her refrigerators are all but empty. The halibut steaks fill the entire Grateful Dead Frigidaire freezer and some of the other.

He looks for the dragon balls that his mother alleges to have thrown away and finds not one, not even a foil wrapping. Ashtrays clean. No pot or pills, just the old open pack of Benson & Hedges Julie kept as a reminder of her quitting cold turkey just after Kyle was born. And some Mateus in the newer fridge.

He takes a hot bath in the deep tub, the shivers melting away. Washes and shampoos twice to get the fish slime and blood really off him. Drains and refills the tub, and soaks again. The soles of his feet are crisscrossed with short clean nicks but done bleeding. If Furlong finds him here he'll be naked, defenseless, and unable to even run.

He hears the front door fly open and slam against the wall, and thinks: I'm busted.

Little voices and laughter.

The feral boys burst into the bathroom and stand around the tub, studying Matt. There are six of them. Dirty faces, swimsuits, and T-shirts. Sneakers and bare feet, a skinny redhead wearing suede moccasins that reach his knees.

"What do you little shitheads want?"

"You're naked."

"You should knock first."

"Sorry, mister. How's your mom?"

"Great. Dinged up a little from the fall."

"She's a stone fox," says the redhead. "I saw it happen."

"Liar," says another. "Me and Jason are the only ones that did. You drank all that acid orange juice and *thought* you saw it happen."

"Did see it."

"Have any food?"

"There are some halibut steaks in the fridge, but you have to cook them."

"My mom's a great cook."

"Mine's terrible."

"You can have one big steak each, but that's all. The rest are mine to live on."

"Where did you get them?"

"I caught the fish and cut it up."

"My dad surfs."

Matt briefly studies each face. They remind him of an old photograph, something black-and-white or sepia, the Old West maybe, or refugees at Ellis Island.

"Are there people in the Living Caves?" he asks the redhead. The Living Caves is local slang for the sandstone caves up near Top of the World. They're impossible to get to except on foot or a dirt bike. For decades they've been a stopover for hobos and vagrants, migrants and drifters, now hitchhikers and hippies.

"Some. The cops can't get up there without getting seen and everybody has noisemakers and firecrackers and dogs."

"How many people are there?"

"We can take you there if you want."

"I know where they are. I need a place to park my van where Furlong won't find it."

"We got a garage that's empty. Mom won't care. It's the brown house on Victory with all the surfboards on the porch. Mine's the red twin-fin."

"Thank you."

"We saw your mom's gun. And the ammo."

"You idiots," says Matt. "Did you touch it?"

"We passed it around and put it back. Is it loaded?"

"You're damned right it's loaded. Don't you ever come into this house again. Ever! You promise me right now, all six of you."

The boys mumble promises, some rolling their eyes, none looking directly at Matt.

"Good. Someone hand me that towel off the door and all of you get out. Don't say anything about me being here."

He dries off and puts a clean T-shirt and jeans on. The feral boys have moved on, leaving a refrigerator door ajar, and dusty footprints across the white and purple fleur-de-lis linoleum floor.

He finds the good skillet and cooks up the biggest halibut steak he can find. Blackens the outside and leaves the middle cool and dumps a jar of canned stewed tomatoes onto the plate to go with it. He sends the plastic-wrapped LSD "prize" down the garbage disposal, wondering how long it will take Furlong to track him down. Or just blunder into him. It's a small town.

He parks the Westfalia in the Victory Walk garage of Hallie Tingly, who says no problem and offers him a hit off her bong as she breastfeeds. Matt averts his eyes and politely declines.

Forty minutes later he walks into the campfire light and dope smoke at the Living Caves. He has surprised the dogs, which now circle him closely. He's got his sleeping bag, his backpack with sketchbook, charcoals, and a plastic jar of peanuts inside, and a canteen of water slung over a shoulder. Wyatt Earp's loaded .45 rests at the bottom of the pack like an anchor. He couldn't leave it there for the boys.

The hippies regard him without getting up from their beach towels and sleeping bags and their Mystic Arts World Afghan rugs. Flame shadows move on their faces and their cheeks hollow when they hit the joint. They're hairy and young and dressed for a different age—the Medieval maybe, Matt thinks—or maybe a whole different planet.

Two of the men are older than the others and they have sharp, un-stoned eyes. They remind him of Longton, his Diver's Cove mugger.

"I'm Matt. I'm going to sleep on that flat spot over there tonight. I don't want any trouble."

"Then just don't bring any. Basic Karma, bro."

"Hi, Matt."

"Peace, Matt."

"You look too young to be a narc, Matt."

"I am too young for that," he says. "It's been a long day. Good night."

He climbs a gentle rise and settles onto the flat spot. Unrolls his pad and sleeping bag and wads up a jacket for a pillow. He's got a good downhill view of the canyon and Dodge City and Laguna Canyon Road. He can see the cars backed up near the Festival of Arts grounds and the Irvine Bowl amphitheater and he thinks about how long ago it seems that he was perched in the eucalyptus tree, eating peanuts and gazing down on Laurel in her tableau. He knows she was crushed when his father removed her from the Jazz Anthony search posse that Laurel had helped create, but Matt couldn't see then—and still can't see now—how having her around Bruce and his gun and three probably dangerous kidnappers would be a good idea.

Turning to look behind him he sees the lights of Top of the World and the houses scattered on the upper flank of the canyon and the blue-domed bell tower of the Vortex of Purity rising well-lit in the night.

Matt hears a boom like artillery. A white firework rises into the western sky and bursts, reaching mightily into the black, then the million sparks arch and settle into the ocean. Another big *thump*, then a red explosion, suddenly overlapped by an enormous blue blossom that hangs in the sky for a few seconds before melting. Matt watches, wishing he could get some of that beauty onto his sketchbook but knowing he probably can't. Maybe someday, he thinks, when he's a master of color like Van Gogh, and has the best paints and brushes money can buy.

He lies back on the sleeping bag and adjusts the jacket/pillow. To keep his soaked wallet safe from nighttime thieves like the Longton-esque creeps around the campfire, he pushes it all the way down into the front pocket of his jeans. Since getting three gallons at the Chevron on PCH, his wallet now contains three dollars and sixty-five cents, his driver's and first fishing licenses, and high school grad shots of Kyle and Jasmine. He figures the pictures might be ruined but the rest will dry out in time.

When he closes his eyes he feels the rise and fall of the ocean he spent nearly an hour in today. Hears the whump and pop of fireworks. A cold eddy ripples down his back. He knows he was foolish to follow that fish but he's glad he did it and he'd do it again, though maybe not in the near future. He has enough fish to last two weeks, even sharing it with Laurel and his dad.

He thinks of Hamsa Luke, and if Luke was really a drug kingpin and even if he was why they had to shoot him. He was trying to escape? Don't they always say that? Darnell would know how it happened. She might tell him if he called. But how long can you talk to a cop before they trace the call and bust you?

He's more tired than he can remember. More tired than mumps. More tired than doing his paper route with a cold so bad he could hardly breathe, coughing in pain on a winter afternoon that was dark at five o'clock. More tired than hauling eight thousand pounds of logs up- and downhill eight hours straight for Sara Eikenberg.

Again he feels that great ocean lifting and lowering, inhaling and exhaling, and the pitch and roll of his body within it. Remembers from freshman biology that his blood is fifty-four percent salt water. He feels the wild fish inside him and knows he'll wake up strong in the morning.

Jazz.

Laurel.

Sara.

Mom.

Donuts with Dad at six.

Only a few more doors to knock on . . .

50

S ide by side on swiveling stools at Dave's Donuts, Matt and his father ponder the color-coded graph paper maps. Bruce's Stetson is on his knee. He has apologized to Dave for calling him a boy but his loud voice turns the apology into another embarrassment for the man. Dave's locals look at Bruce with silent superiority.

On the maps, Matt sees that most of the remaining houses are in the hills of central Laguna and downtown, a few in the canyon. South and north Laguna are pretty much a wrap except for a few "nobody-homes" and three "come-back-laters." Laurel has let him park the Westfalia in her garage, though she seemed less happy to see him than usual. She said the Pageant was beginning to bore her, and her writing was going poorly. Matt blames his test drive with Sara, but how could Laurel know?

With his van hidden away in her garage, they'll use Bruce's pickup truck, a dented black F-150 with Oklahoma plates. Matt wonders, if Furlong comes to arrest him, can his father, as a former lawman, protect him? And *would* he? Bruce isn't happy about his son running away from the law.

"A lot of these places are close together," Matt says.

"How are your feet?"

"Sore."

"I still can't believe you're dumb enough to jump in after that fish. Get us a couple more peanut-chocolates to go, Matt. I'll wait outside."

Bruce stands and tips his hat to a glowering young man,

then his boot heels sound on the hardwood floor and out.
Matt puts the graph paper maps into his folder, goes to the
counter, and orders the donuts. Dave rings him up in silence.
Matt wants to apologize for his father but knows it would just
make it worse all over again.

"These are the best donuts in the world," he says.

"Feel free to not come back anytime you like."

With Matt's paper route temporarily abandoned, he and his
father press the search straight through the afternoon.

Bruce is inspired and persuasive. And their increased rate
of skipping homes occupied by families, the elderly, and the
otherwise harmless speeds everything up. Bruce is fast about
the searches, too, clomping down hallways, throwing open
doors and slamming them shut, talking cheerfully to himself
or anyone within earshot the whole time, clomping back to
Matt with that let's-get-moving set to his jaw.

By four in the afternoon they've knocked on eighty-one doors,
gotten zero refusals. Which leaves thirty-two residential doors
unknocked-on in the whole city.

Only sunset—nearly four hours from now—can stop them.

"We can do this, Dad," says Matt, wondering if he's cheer-
leading his father, or himself.

They knock and talk and plead and search.

But for the first time since this plan took shape with Laurel,
Matt is catching whiffs of a real possibility that they'll walk
away from that last house without Jasmine. He won't quite
admit it, but sees that it's almost certainly going to happen
that way.

Meaning she's not in Laguna anymore at all, unless she's
stashed in the back room of someone's business.

Meaning he'll have to knock on every door in California,
America, perhaps the entire world.

In Laguna! I'm in the . . .

They leave house after house without finding Jasmine,

or even a hint of Jasmine. One man offers his condolences, saying a girl gone that long isn't coming back. His words hit Matt like a punch he sees coming but can't slip.

In the evening sunlight he consults the tattering map tablet.

"Eight more downtown, Dad. And that one in the canyon from yesterday that didn't answer."

The downtown homes yield nothing.

They make the long walk out Laguna Canyon Road, where, finally, exhausted and starved, Matt comes to the last unsearched house in Laguna.

It's the ramshackle wood-sided two-story on Sun Valley from yesterday, red with white trim, set against the creek. An enormous walnut tree keeps the entire house in shade.

Matt knocks. No toys or bikes or surfboards, just Neldra Sungaard, at the doorway with an annoyed expression.

"Oh. Matt Anthony, right?"

Matt is jolted by the sight of her, and even more by the memory of what she was doing that night at the Sapphire Cove orgy. *Neldra says I might be able to visit sometime.* Seeing her now is like facing a beautiful witch in the long nightmare Matt feels he is trapped in.

"Hello, Mrs. Sungaard," he manages. "This is my dad. We're looking for Jasmine."

"She's certainly not here. Just like she wasn't at my home on Diamond. You search the most unlikely places."

"May we come in and look?"

"Well . . . yes, of course. Jesus."

She holds open the door and closes it behind Matt. She's wearing shorts, a flannel, fuzzy bedroom slippers, and a miffed look on her face.

"I have a guest whom I do not want disturbed."

"We'll be in and out before you know it," says Bruce, hat in hand.

"Too late for that, Mr. Anthony. Let me tell Danielle what's going on."

The living room is a replay of the Sungaard house on Diamond—Danish Modern furniture, black-and-white celebrity photos on the walls, hardwood floors. There's a fireplace with a fluffy white fleece rug before it and the smell of woodsmoke in the room.

From down the hall Matt hears a soft knock, then voices. Muffled laughter.

Into the living room walks Neldra, followed by a sleepy, blond teenager, barefoot and clutching a pink blanket. Her calves and feet are suntanned. Matt can barely make out her features, hidden by her tangle of hair. She curtsies.

"*Je suis Danielle.*"

"I'm Bruce and this is Matt."

"Nice to meet you guys, I guess," says Danielle. "Peace, love, dove."

Then disappears back down the hall. Matt hears the door shut.

"Go search," says Neldra.

Bruce does.

Matt stands uncomfortably with the black-masked, red-lipped orgy hostess / art critic / millionaire and co-recipient of not one but two copies of the BEL's *Tibetan Book of the Dead*, stuffed with thousands of doses of LSD. He can't not see her again from that night, doing what she was doing amid all the naked writhing. The mask and her red lips.

"Do you live here and on Diamond, too?" Matt asks.

"We have three properties in Laguna," she says. "And others in different states. What's in the folder?"

"Oh, sorry, I'm not doing my job." He takes out the copy of Jasmine's Little Wing airplane, unfolds it into shape, explains its unique origin and design, and that Jazz has been launching them to signal where she is. He hears the hopelessness creeping into his voice. "So far, they've been found on Gainsborough Drive and Sleepy Hollow."

She takes the plane and examines it. Holds it at different

angles to the burnished evening sunlight coming through the windows. "Incredible."

"I'm hoping to find more."

"Where could she possibly be?"

"I've been asking myself that for over three weeks, Mrs. Sungaard. I think somewhere high. A hilltop or hillside. Maybe Alta Laguna, or Top of the World."

"I'm impressed you can deduce so much from two paper gliders."

"It's just wind and elevation."

"Why do you keep leaning from foot to foot?"

"I cut them fishing."

Neldra studies him openly, a judicial look on her face. "Would you like to sit?"

"No, thank you. Does Danielle live here?"

"For now. She's visiting from Vancouver. We like to open our homes to young people, Marlon and I. I'm unable to conceive."

"That's terrible," he manages. "I mean, I'm sorry." Again he pictures Neldra Sungaard from that night at Sapphire Cove.

Bruce clomps in with a defeated look on his face. Matt realizes again—fully and painfully—that they've just searched the last house in Laguna that might hold Jasmine.

It hits him like a boulder dropped from the sky. The hours and days and weeks. A nightmare that still hasn't ended.

"I'm sorry, Matt," Bruce says softly.

"I could have saved you some time and trouble," says Neldra.

"No trouble at all," says Bruce. "And tell Danielle we're sorry for waking her."

"You'll find Jasmine," says Neldra. "You will find her."

Matt badly wants to ask Neldra if she saw Jasmine at the Sapphire Cove party that Friday night, and if so, what happened there and where did Jazz go when it was over? Was she alone or with someone? Did she take a look around, turn up her nose, and split? Was she not allowed to leave? Did she participate? Was she forced?

Matt and his father walk toward Bruce's pickup truck. Sun Valley Drive is a gravel road and the rocks hurt Matt's feet. But it hurts much more to know the dream is over, the long dream of knocking on every door until he finds what he's looking for. The plan should have worked, but it didn't. The falling light ignites the canyon now—the eucalyptus and oaks stand green and vibrant, the flowering birds-of-paradise are the most pure and beautiful orange he's ever seen in his life—but inside he feels nothing but darkness and defeat. He wonders if seeing Jasmine forced into the VW van by two strong men in the fog that night was seeing her for the last time.

Fifty feet from her own front door.

"I'm sorry," Bruce says again. "It was a good plan. You can get back to your paper route."

"Furlong."

"He's going to catch up with you sooner or later anyway. Maybe you should hear him out."

"They got a cell in juvie all ready for me."

"And enough evidence to put you there?"

"Probably."

"Matt, you hang around those scummy Brotherhood hippies, you're bound to pick up their stink. They're vermin. Maybe you *should* help the police get rid of them. Clean up some of the rot in this town."

"I like this town."

But Matt can't begin to explain his unusual relationships with Christian Clay and Johnny Grail and the others at Mystic Arts World. Can't explain why Hamsa Luke getting killed killed something in himself.

He doesn't even try.

51

The next morning Matt, his father, and a hospital orderly get Julie out of the wheelchair and into the Westfalia. It takes a minute to get her arranged comfortably on the padded bench, especially with the long loose farm dress she asked Matt to bring from Dodge. Matt is all but silent, Bruce irritable.

"You two seem gloomy," says Julie, once they're moving. "Is there something you're not telling me?"

Matt drives the back roads out toward Dodge while his father explains the failure of their mission, their many hours of hope and exertion all crashing down into nothing.

Matt tells her about the two Little Wings they've discovered. Found within half a mile of each other, near PCH. He tells her they could only have been folded and launched by Jazz, using the same ukulele music he gave to her as a birthday present.

He tries to bring optimism to his voice, hears none of it. Isn't sure if he believes himself.

"I think we might have a miracle on our hands," says Julie. "I see no reason why paper airplanes can't show us the way."

"It's a long shot, Julie," says Bruce. "We know that."

The feral boys of Dodge City whoop like warriors and run alongside the van as it putts down Woodland. They've got feather headbands, plastic bows, and rubber-tipped arrows, some of which stick to the windows. Matt swerves left and sends them scattering.

They get Julie in her chair over the threshold of the little red barn and into the main room. In the middle of the room she raises a hand and Matt stops.

"I love my home," she says. "I want us to be happy here, Matt. You, me, Jasmine, and Kyle."

"Don't forget me," says Bruce.

She gives him a sad look. "I didn't."

Matt glances at his father's stricken expression, then stares at the dizzying fleur-de-lis pattern of the floor. He's sick to death of his mother and father, can't wait to get out of here.

He stands and leans over Julie, hugging her softly, counting the seconds. Are five seconds enough to signify warmth and sincerity?

"Welcome home," he says. "There's halibut steaks in the freezers. I'm heading out now. I got my route back as of today, so, it's business as usual."

Except for Furlong, he thinks.

Julie gives Bruce a frank look. "You can hit the road, too. I could use some time to myself."

Bruce skedaddles but Matt stays put. There's one thing he needs to know before he gets out of here. It's been eating at him since that day.

"Mom, when you got hurt out at the festival, did you slip and fall, or did you jump?"

When his mother looks at him, Matt sees the shame on her face.

"I thought I could fly. I'm so sorry, Matt. I'll never get like that again. Ever."

Matt nods. "No, don't."

Halfway to Third Street to drop off his father, Bruce breaks the silence.

"Come on by tonight after work. We'll stash the van in the garage, get drive-through and have a few drinks. I wouldn't mind some company."

"Sure, Dad."

"I don't blame her for hating me."

"She wants to believe you."

After dropping off Bruce, he hides the Westfalia in Laurel's garage.

Sore feet or not, he's relieved to be back on the Heavy-Duti again, delivering newspapers, doing something he's good at. It's nice to be earning money. His bigger muscles mean more speed.

Furlong lurks all around him, Matt knows, but something in his failure to save Jazz has lessened his fear. Furlong can throw him into Moby Cop and the DA can charge him and the judge can toss him into kiddie prison and Dr. Mary Hamilton can throw away the key. But they can't make him twice betray someone who has trusted him, given him work when he was almost broke, even given him a Bat Cave to hide in if he needs it. Given him discounts on day-old muffins and given work to Jazz, too. As weird and mind-blown and occasionally devious as Johnny Grail and his BEL might be, they've stood by him.

Matt porches Coiner's paper over the sprinklers that he knows the old fart turns on this time every day in order to mess with him. He out-pedals the slobbering St. Bernard, Hercules, down Oak Street, lofts the Reiten paper over the oleander and fires the Shostag afternoon final straight into the open garage where Mrs. Shostag wants it.

He's just not afraid of Hercules anymore.

Furlong either.

He finishes his route early. Leaving him three hours of daylight in which to find another paper airplane from Jasmine.

Little Wing is his chance. It's registered in his mind's eye. He can see it clearly and perfectly, same as he saw that behemoth halibut in the shallow water or Laurel Kalina's expression in the Gauguin tableau or Sara Eikenberg's doubtful brown eyes. Little Wing waits inside him, the shape of hope, waiting to be filled.

He cruises the central and eastern neighborhoods, to which

Laguna's prevailing onshore breeze would carry a paper airplane. His sharp eyes scan from trees to streets, rooftops to gutters, hedges to lawns. Sidewalks and gardens, car hoods and birdbaths.

Moby Cop trundles across the intersection of Thurston and Temple Hills so he quickly slides in behind a wall of Italian cypress trees that shelters a house from the street, lays his bike and himself down on cool grass. He watches through the front spokes, and waits.

Five minutes later he's ready to go, when Moby Cop comes up the street from behind him. Pure Furlong, to double back like that. Matt's heart beats against the ground as the van passes by.

He gives the cops another few minutes, then gets himself back down Temple Hills Drive to Rim Rock—watching, watching, watching for the neat pale rectangle that will be Little Wing.

Later, in the fresh new dark, he sees a white shape lilting on the street near the gutter. And something round beside it. He skids to a stop and looks down at the Sunshine Inn bag and the paper beverage cup nearby.

52

Matt and his dad finish their late Husky Boys at Matt's old Third Street home, the Westfalia stowed in the garage he's lived in for two years.

"Try this," says his father. He pours the Colonel Givens into the final ice of Matt's large soft drink cup. "To Jasmine."

They lift their cups and drink. Matt feels the fumes in his sinuses, the burn in his throat.

"Strong," he says.

"It can give you strength and take it away."

Matt tells his father about the bottle of wine he drank with Sara Eikenberg, how the alcohol stayed with him for hours and made him want more. Matt thinks of the gear-shifting lesson but says nothing of it. Bruce says that a restaurant serving wine to sixteen-year-olds is proof of California's moral rot.

"She must like you to take you out to La Cave. Pricey."

"Her dad's an owner."

"I imagine a successful home-builder owns a lot of things. I would like to have married rich but I married poor instead. I knew when I first saw Julie that she was the one for me. She took some convincing but I finally got her attention."

"How did you do it?"

Bruce smiles, takes another sip of Colonel Givens. "I used flowers and poems and restaurants. They say the shortest way to a man's heart is through his stomach, but I'll tell you, your mom can eat like a great white shark. Especially if you put something good in front of her."

"I've seen her," Matt says. "I cook calico bass in the skillet with butter and garlic, then bake 'em with bread crumbs. She'll eat three, four plates, plus tater tots and canned beets."

"And she never gains weight," says Bruce. "I have to say she's still the most attractive woman I've ever known."

Matt sips again but he can already feel the bourbon speeding up his mind, pushing his thoughts closer together.

"I like Laurel and Sara in different ways," he says.

"How so?"

Matt describes his sudden crush on Laurel while learning to write cursive in fourth grade, how *She's beautiful!* was one of his early original cursive sentences. How he looked at her when he thought he could get away with it, and talked to her sometimes, all the rest of that year and through fifth grade too. Then, how in sixth grade he started feeling different toward her, more than friends, serious and all like that, which made him afraid to talk to her for fear he'd spoil things. Same, all the way through middle school and into his sophomore year of high school. But this weird feeling for her, growing. Until just a few weeks ago when he ran into her downtown and he looked at her under the traffic light at Forest and PCH and had this crazy burst of like, energy that made him accompany her across the crosswalk. Then she invited him to see her in the Pageant and him climbing the eucalyptus tree to see for free, and this powerful emotion that grabbed him by his insides and wouldn't let go. And still hadn't.

"No sex though, you said."

"Yeah. No. We make out a lot. Used to. And she let me get to second, once."

His father takes another sip of Colonel Givens and Matt does too. Then launches into first seeing Sara down at Thousand Steps looking for Jazz, and Sara was being photographed with a huge oiled muscleman in these horndog poses where she looked like she was having some badass fun, the opposite of Laurel looking innocent in the Gauguin tableau. And how Sara invited him to her Evolution ceremony that night at the Vortex of Purity, then later gave him the job of moving twenty cut-up eucalyptus trees, eight thousand goddamned pounds of logs up and down her driveway with just a wheelbarrow. And how Sara took him out to dinner at La Cave, which is quite possibly the finest restaurant in the world.

"I'm sure it is," says Bruce with a knowing smile. "Sex after?"

Matt shakes his head, still unwilling to confess the test drive to his father. He's not even sure if that *was* sex. If not, pretty close.

"So," he says. "I like Laurel because she's beautiful and smart and nice. And I like Sara because she's beautiful and smart and brave."

"Brave how?"

"She rides skateboards and drives sports cars."

"You're lucky to have two nice chicks after you. Especially in this town, where drugs and perversion are tolerated. If not worshipped."

"Yeah, I dig it."

Bruce leans forward on the little living room couch where Julie watched her TV for years. It's more than strange for Matt—especially with the Colonel Givens surging through him—to see his father there. Matt's got the blue chair with the view of the street and the GTE building.

"Matt, what makes you think Mom wants to believe me, when all she does is ride me like a stolen bike?"

Matt has to think about this. He wants his parents to get along and maybe love each other again someday but look what Bruce did to her. The gap between that, and what he says he wants, seems too wide for Julie to cross.

"Has she ever said anything to indicate that to you? That she wants to believe me?" asks Bruce.

"No."

"Just all fire and brimstone?"

"She's protecting herself."

"From me."

"Yes, sir."

"I truly wish I could change her mind."

"You could try the flowers and poems and restaurants again."

"That's funny, son."

Bruce takes a swig and replenishes both cups. Matt drinks again too, his thoughts bursting like fireworks on the dark screen in his head.

"I could show you how to catch calico bass," he says, smiling. "To cook for her."

"I was never good off those rocks," he says. "Scared the hell out of me."

"I didn't know that."

"Dads put on shows for their children. I always wanted to be your mighty man."

They drink through midnight. Topics come and topics go. The Angels' sorry season, Cassius Clay, the war, guns, politics, assassinations.

"Mark these words, Matt—Khrushchev says they'll feed us little bits of socialism until America becomes communist. He says we *will fall like overripe fruit* into their hands. Son, anybody who doesn't see that Vietnam, civil rights, the riots, and assassinations are all parts of the world communist conspiracy is not a man. He is a naive boob. We have nukes for a reason. Moscow should know that. President Johnson just doesn't have the nuts to use them."

Thoughts swirling, Matt considers nuclear war. The mushroom cloud over Hiroshima. Bodies and gigantic sores and deformed babies. The duck-and-cover exercises at El Morro Elementary School. The Mystic Arts World poster: IN THE EVENT OF A NUCLEAR ATTACK, PUT YOUR HEAD BETWEEN YOUR KNEES AND KISS YOUR ASS GOODBYE.

"That's why we had the bomb shelter," Bruce says solemnly. "I'd build another one if I had anybody to look out for."

"That's why you want your family back?"

Bruce drinks and stands as if he's decided something. Then sits back down.

"Yeah, it's all linked together."

"I love you, Dad, but I don't think I want to live with you."

Bruce gives him a furrowed look. Matt's vertical hold is now on the fritz, like his mom's RCA every October for the World Series.

"But that doesn't mean I don't want you to have your family back," Matt says. "My thoughts are coming out of order. Sorry."

"Why don't you want to live with me?"

"Freedom."

"I was the same way."

"Did you kill a lot of people in Korea?"

"Not nearly enough."

Matt watches the GTE building blipping up and down and up again. "Man, I'm plastered."

"First time for hard stuff?"

Matt nods, takes a small sip.

"You'll learn to pace yourself. One good hangover is all it takes."

"I think I'll have one. The room is spinning."

"Maybe crash in your old room. If Furlong knocks on the door I'll steer him out of here."

53

Matt wakes with first light, throws up, showers. He looks in on his father, always an early riser, sitting up in bed and making notes in a small black book.

In the dark garage Matt starts up the Westfalia and backs it into the driveway.

A white sedan pulls in behind him, blocking his exit.

Furlong, he knows. Matt knew it had to happen. You can't vanish in a small town forever unless someone is holding you prisoner.

He curses, kills the engine, and climbs out. Leans against the van, trying to figure some way around this. He's too hungover to run, almost too hungover to stand. The ache in his head feels permanent and he wants to go back to bed for the rest of the week. But he will surrender with dignity.

The driver's window goes down on Brigit Darnell. She's in street clothes, Matt sees, probably on her way to work.

"Get over here," she says.

Matt shoves off the van, his brain sloshing in his skull, goes to the car window.

"I should arrest you."

"Okay."

"Don't be an ass, Matt."

"I won't."

"Lean closer."

He does, smells coffee, looks at her frowning, pretty face, then away.

"Have you found any more paper airplanes?" she asks.

"No, ma'am."

"I have. Cheryl Cruz, 242 Hillview. Her cat was pawing it in the backyard. She took it away, looked at it briefly, then wadded it up and threw it in the trash. Which was picked up yesterday. But she remembered the shape, and the print on the paper—musical chords and lyrics."

"This is important."

"I've been going door-to-door with the originals you gave us. In my spare time, while my husband and daughter wait for me to come home and make meals. While you hide from the police and drink God knows what. It's still on your breath."

"Sorry. It was a lot."

"I could lose a promotion for helping you," says Darnell. "Or worse. I'm in a cross fire at work, caught between cops who would pull out the stops to find Jasmine, and cops who think a missing runaway is as waste of time."

Matt doesn't know what to say. He looks at Darnell, feeling the tidal swoosh of the bourbon still in him.

"Matt, you shouldn't be here. The day shift is coming on now, and someone's going to spot you. Your sister is out there somewhere, Matt. Find her."

Matt's Sunday collections seem feverish and eternal. The Heavy-Duti weighs a ton. Hercules almost gets him. Matt grinds it out on willpower, water from his clients' hoses, and pit stops at two parks to use the heads.

The only good thing is no Furlong.

After a shower at Ernie Rios's and a quick change of clothes in the van, he picks up Laurel.

Even through the hangover, Matt's heart jumps when she comes out her front door. She's in that cherries-on-white sundress she wore the first time she had dinner at his house. With a smile she climbs into the Westfalia. It feels like the old days, when they'd walk the city before sunset, their arms just barely touching sometimes, knocking on doors and pleading with citizens in the innocent belief that they would find Jasmine.

"It's so good to be with you again," she says. Then delivers
a kiss to his lips. "But if you've knocked on all the doors with
your dad, what exactly are we doing?"

"Looking for a Little Wing."

She gives him a puzzled look.

"I'll explain."

But the search is a bust, and half an hour before sunset Matt
drops Laurel off at the Festival of Arts grounds in time to
get in costume for the show. She gives him a really good kiss
before she gets out, even though people are streaming by the
Westfalia's many windows and Julie's handmade bongo-drum
curtains are tied back so everyone can see in.

"I feel good with you, Matt."

"Me too. I mean with you."

"I don't mind if you get your words mixed up sometimes,"
she says, tapping his chest. "It's what's in here that counts."

Laurel smiles and closes the door.

He signals and waits to pull out of the loading zone, still
feeling her fingers over his heart, feeling strong and happy
again. The hangover is mostly gone.

There's just enough daylight left to see Laurel making her
way through the turnstiles. But when Matt looks into the
rearview mirror for a farewell view, all he sees is Moby Cop on
Laguna Canyon Road, hooking a U-turn toward him, lights
bright and siren blaring.

He pulls out, draws a long honk, and pushes hard on the
gas. The thirty-horsepower van sputters, then lurches. He
shifts into third and thinks of Sara. Traffic is thick but he
makes the light at PCH, leaving Furlong caught behind a clot
of tourist buses and stranded at the red.

He heads north, quickly gauging the Westfalia's chances of
outrunning Moby Cop on the long road to Corona del Mar.
The chances being none. So he makes a sharp right turn on
Cliff, which returns him to the crowded festival grounds in a
sneaky double back that will leave Furlong futilely gunning

Moby Cop up Coast Highway. It's a cool move, Matt knows, but his left turn onto Broadway will be illegal and perilous with the festival crowd.

He hits his brights and rolls onto Broadway without stopping. Broadway becomes Laguna Canyon Road. He yanks a turn against the traffic and barrels through the chorus of horns and the river of headlights, tires screeching, and vehicles stopping. A covey of crosswalk pedestrians flushes and he accelerates around them, and—with muscular cranks of the big, stubborn, non–power steering wheel—straightens out of the turn.

The Westfalia sputters past the festival grounds. No sign of Moby Cop behind him. It kills Matt to stop at a crosswalk for more tourists but he runs the light as soon as they're out of the way, drawing curses and raised fists. The traffic is much lighter heading out of town now, and he sees the comforting darkness of the canyon before him.

He knows exactly where he'll go and where he'll hide the van—Windy Rise—where he and Kyle used to camp and look for tarantulas and the bird feathers that collected on a forbidding swale of prickly pear cactus. It's a rough place and hard to get to. You can't drive there and there's no trail in. Not even the hippies will be there. There's a sandy wash, too, less cactus, and good for campfires and sleeping bags. Furlong has probably never heard of it and Matt can ditch the van in the brush out beyond Dodge City.

Just off a rutted dirt road in the canyon dark, Matt noses the Westfalia into a stand of black mustard. Loads what he needs into his backpack, then lops off some mustard branches with is fishing knife, draping them over the back end to hide it.

He slings on his backpack and follows a rabbit trail through the scrub brush and into the hills.

It's easy going at first and there's a waxing gibbous moon that throws good light. He's got enough in the pack to get him through the night. Tomorrow he'll take his chances at his mom's place in Dodge for food and a shower and then . . .

well, he really doesn't know. Furlong will be all over his paper route.

As he follows the trail up the hill, Matt feels free, kind of, and his mind wanders.

First, he thinks he could just surrender to Furlong tomorrow. Maybe a lawyer could get him off. But that would leave no one on Earth really looking for Jazz. No one to free her from the hideous men who threw her into their van like an empty dress. No one to free her like she freed him—terrified, imprisoned—from the bomb shelter when he was five.

Unthinkable.

Setting up Johnny Grail and the BEL for Furlong is unthinkable also.

Something very thinkable? Turn around right now, walk back to the Westfalia, take Laguna Canyon Road to the freeways, and just keep going. Freedom. Camp in the van for a couple of years on a beach in Mexico, catch fish, draw and paint, live cheap. Get Laurel to come down and write a book. You don't need a writing program to do that. Or maybe hit the Sierras or Yellowstone, where the campgrounds are cheap. Could finish up high school in a small town where nobody knows who you are, or anything about stewed tomatoes packed with LSD, or the Brotherhood of Eternal Love, or orgies in beachfront mansions or Bill Furlong or Moby Cop.

And let Jasmine rescue Jasmine?

Full circle, back to unthinkable.

The trail vanishes, the grade steepens, and a bank of clouds arrives off the ocean and hides the moon. He can see well enough to avoid the bigger buckwheat and toyon and sage, but the rough-edged groundsel and young thistles rake his bare ankles and calves. Itches like hell. He should have put on jeans for this.

He should have just told Furlong to go to hell the first time he'd offered his betrayal money.

He should have found his sister by now.

He gives wide berth to the meadow of prickly pear cactus,

darker than the scrub in the muted moonlight, and carefully picks his way to the sandy wash beyond. He remembers a loose circle of boulders where they used to pitch the tent but the boulders are gone now, likely washed downslope by last year's record rains.

He shucks off his backpack and rolls out his pad and sleeping bag. The sandy wash is still warm as he sits and looks out at the canyon.

From this part of Windy Rise he can see the hilly backside of Laguna: the fog-dampened lights at Top of the World, and Alta Laguna, and the long face of the canyon tapering off in the dark.

His world as a boy.

He thinks of catching tarantulas here with Kyle one hot September, and how angry Bruce got when they brought two glass mustard jars teeming with them back to Top of the World. Remembers hiking all the way back down here to Windy Rise to let the tarantulas go.

He makes three peanut butter burritos—not bad when you're starved—and chases them down with canteen water.

The fog bank lifts. By moonlight Matt sketches the night scene around him, the cool play of light on the prickly pear and the sandy wash and a big oak he remembers. Dashes off a quick one of his first look at the halibut suspended in the wave. He sketches the feral boys standing around him in his mom's bathtub, surprised Neldra Sungaard in her doorway, a bottle of Colonel Givens.

But neither boyhood memories nor drawing pictures can pull him out of his sense of doom. His options seem either bad or worse. He reviews: He can give up on Jazz and run away. He can turn himself in to Furlong and betray people who have treated him well, and go through the rest of his life as a snitch and a traitor. He can stay a fugitive and sleep here or at the Living Caves, use his mom's and dad's bathrooms, or the stinky ones downtown or at the parks. He could get a cheap camping place down at Doheny State Beach. He's got less than three dollars. He's got Furlong, who will arrest him, sooner than later.

And underneath all of that—running deeper and sadder than all of it—is Jasmine and his failure to help her, as she once helped him, locked in the bomb shelter. She is a prisoner of some dark enemy that he can't even locate, let alone defeat. He sees no method and is out of plans.

So he gets into the sleeping bag and looks up at the stars and prays:

God up there, Matt here. Show me what to do. I tried to find my sister and failed. Summer will be over and fall is cold in the canyon. The halibut will only last a few more days. Furlong will arrest me and I'll lose my job, my school, my family, Mystic Arts, Laurel and Sara, fishing and drawing. They'll lock me in a cage with a bunch of ugly, stinky, stupid teenagers who think they're tough. Maybe they are tough.

Show me what to do. I promised you I'd do anything you want if you let me get away from Furlong, and you delivered me from him and I now repeat my holy vow to do anything you want. But you have to show me what it is. I know you can help me. Since I was small I've asked you to make Mom and Dad not mad, and to help me catch lots of fish, and for Laurel to like me and for Jazz to get over the pneumonia and Kyle the mono. Sometimes you said yes and sometimes it was no.

Show me what to do. I'm tired of my fear and your silence. I need to hear you, or see a sign. It doesn't have to be a miracle. Don't let Luke go to hell even if he was a drug smuggler.

Amen . . .

By *amen* he's asleep, his snores part of the Laguna Canyon night.

54

He's up with the sun, heading for a boulder with two fresh-made peanut butter and jelly burritos in his backpack. The canyon smells lightly of sage and the ocean. The prickly pear cactus spines glow white in the sunlight. Some have blossoms, which mean fruit. Prickly pears are good to eat but hard to clean, even with a sharp knife. If the spines don't get you, the fine little bristles will.

He sits on the boulder, eats, and considers. God has not answered his prayer. What he'd hoped to wake up with is some new way to find Jazz. Something faster than Mahajad Om's new way of seeing. Something surer than hoping to find more Little Wings. Something bold and clever, like James West and Artemus Gordon would come up with on *The Wild, Wild West*.

But nothing. Nada. Only a feeling of time running out, and no way to stop it. Only the unfillable hole in his stomach.

Something out in the prickly pear catches his eye, a bloom likely. It's moving, like a big white butterfly warming in the sun. Julie always liked butterflies and he did a watercolor of one for her birthday once. Framed it with popsicle sticks.

He starts in on the second burrito, weighing his poor-to-terrible options and watches the big pale prickly pear blossom flutter with the breeze.

It's starting to piss him off, this particular bloom. The others are pink. The others are smaller. The others do not open and close like a large, prehistoric butterfly.

He finishes the second burrito and heaves off the boulder to check it out.

The cactus swale is a sea of green pads, pink flowers, red fruit, and spines illuminated white by the morning sun. Some of the cactus is taller than he is.

Matt carefully picks his way toward the lilting, annoyingly wrong-colored blossom. From twenty feet away he sees it's not a blossom after all, just a piece of paper caught on spines of prickly pear.

Matt high-steps through the thorny patches. He gets as close as he can and leans in and—cactus spines touching his T-shirt—unhooks the paper and lifts it out.

Sees the printed song lyrics. The graphic ukulele chords.

This Little Wing is tattered and faded, but her elevators are still in position, her folds straight.

Pulse fast, Matt picks his way along the game trail, going deeper and higher into the canyon.

All around him, the cactus spines are studded with vulture and hawk feathers because Windy Rise is where the big birds circle and hunt. Thanks to his biology teacher, Matt knows that on sunny days the heat rising from the dark green cactus forms thermal currents. He feels it now, that uplift of warm air, rippling the cactus blossoms as it rises hundreds of feet into the sky.

Matt climbs steadily, leaving Windy Rise below and following the cactus along the canyon side.

He has to circle a thicket of prickly pear but the detour brings him to another Little Wing, crucified at eye level. His fingers tremble as he works it off the spines.

With a paper airplane in each hand, he heads up the trail and rounds a tall outcropping of sandstone that brings him to a meadow west of Windy Rise, and gives him a view of the city.

Breathing deeply and sweating hard, Matt looks out at the houses on the flank of Laguna Canyon. Sees some of his paper-route homes, just barely identifiable at this distance, and the curves of Skyview Drive and Falling Star, and the steep switchbacks of Thermal Ridge Drive cutting up the canyon side like zigzagging scars.

He presses on, the dense prickly pear retreating into scattered patches, the game trail climbing more sharply through slippery sandstone and rough coast scrub.

Twenty minutes later he comes to what he can only interpret as a direct answer from God, finally, to his desperate questions of the night before.

A third Little Wing sits in the middle of the trail, much as if it has just landed. It's facing him at a slight angle, rocking in the breeze. Matt traces the angle of flight, which leads his eyes high and far, up the canyon side, to the Vortex of Purity.

Half an hour later he's at the Vortex's fenced eastern perimeter, looking through a chain-link fence at the chancellor's residence. The handsome Spanish Revival home sits on a hillock overlooking the campus, its adjacent blue-domed bell tower stately and tall. The central commons are spacious, studded with sycamores and oaks. He can see the lap pool and the gym in the middle distance. The generators hum dully. The fence in front of him is eight feet tall and topped with three strands of back-slanted barbed wire.

He takes a sip from the canteen and settles into the shade of a big sycamore. There's a fallen branch to sit on, big and soft with age.

On campus, followers traverse the wide gravel walkways, a few wearing Mahajad's crimson, others in yellow, white, orange, or street clothes ranging from flower child to golf shirts and plaid shorts. Mostly young. The girls are mostly pretty and the boys are handsome. They seem representative to Matt but he's not sure of what. Purity? He sees two of the sharp-faced men in the white suits he's seen here before. They're walking past the library, silent and watchful as always. He wishes he had binoculars.

At two o'clock a late model white-on-green Volkswagen van

pulls into a parking space outside the chancellor's residence. Then another. A tickle in his gut. They have Vortex of Purity emblems on the drivers' doors—big Hamsas with writing above and below.

They have curtains too—airbrushed rainbows—not the peace signs that Matt had seen on the kidnap van. And that Myron Kandell had seen on the white-on-green van the night before Bonnie Stratmeyer was found on the beach at Thalia.

Matt hadn't seen a Vortex logo that night, though he'd gotten a decent look at the driver's side of the van. Myron Kandell hadn't mentioned a logo. But Matt knows you can get magnetic signs like that for your car, put them on and take them off whenever you want. Tommy Amici has them for his Chevy because the *Register* logo makes him feel important.

Two older men climb out of the first van, dressed in slacks and long-sleeved dress shirts.

Two younger others—one white and one black, both sporting white suits and black T-shirts—get out of the second vehicle, the white one stretching his torso as if it's been a long trip.

Moments later the huge, military-gray Mercedes Interpol van arrives. Bayott emerges from the driver's door and pulls open the big sliding door for Marlon and Neldra Sungaard. Marlon wears a trim dark suit and a white shirt. Neldra is all suntanned legs and arms in a snug, sleeveless green dress, her white-blond hair bright in the afternoon sun. Just behind her is Danielle, the sleepy girl from Neldra's house on Sun Valley Drive, now in an orange dress that shows her good shape. She laughs at something with Bayott.

A whoosh of bewilderment goes through Matt. He knows what he's seeing but he doesn't understand it. He recognizes the players but their roles are not clear.

They gather on the portico of the chancellor's residence. To Matt they look like a tour group. The bell tower casts a shadow on the front lawn.

Mahajad Om emerges from the big double doors, his arms spread in greeting. Then steps aside and motions them in.

Matt remains on his log, speechless and alone. Eats the last of his tortillas, peanut butter and jam.

He gazes at the Vortex of Purity and knows that Jazz is there.

Wonders what Darnell would do.

Wonders what his father would do.

And what he should do.

It's a long hike back to the van and by the time he gets there he knows, exactly.

55

The Vortex of Purity parking lot is nearly full when they arrive, just after six o'clock. The evening is still, the eucalyptus trees sagging in the heat. To the north Matt sees the big birds circling in the thermals out over Windy Rise.

Matt and his father are in the pickup truck, and as Bruce backs into a reserved space near the auditorium, Matt reads the Hamsa marquee:

> THE VORTEX OF PURITY
> PRESENTS
> *A FEAST OF ENLIGHTENMENT*
> *TONIGHT 6:30–9*

"What's all this about?" asks Bruce.

"They have feasts when followers get to the next level of consciousness."

"Followers of who, Captain Kangaroo?"

A group of white-robed young people drifts across the parking lot toward the auditorium.

"What's with the robes?"

"The colors mean how evolved and enlightened they are."

"The enlightened children of Sodom and Gomorrah."

Matt looks down at his backpack lying in the bed. It's heavy and deadly. But what if he needs it but doesn't have it? He slings it over one shoulder as his father locks the truck.

Sara Eikenberg sits at the welcome table in a yellow-with-daisies sundress. Hair up and smile on.

"Hello, Matt," she says coolly. "And Mr. Anthony. Welcome to the Vortex of Purity."

She tears off and hands them each a feast ticket.

"Can you get Mahajad to talk with us after the program?" asks Matt. "In private?"

"What's up?"

"Nothing."

Her doubting look. "Of course I can. There are seats still open, near the back."

It's long dark by the time the Feast of the Spirit ends and Mahajad Om can talk with Matt and his father.

They cross the campus slowly—the swami in his crimson robe with the high collar and pointy shoulders. He's barefoot as always and eating from a plastic plate—followed closely by his mother-daughter assistants, and, farther back, four of the men in white.

"So, what do you say, Mr. Om?" asks Bruce.

"I say, if your daughter was a prisoner at the Vortex of Purity, I would know! But yes, please search it all. If you find her I will celebrate with you. I have the keys to everything."

He waves over the older woman, impatiently, as if he's hailing a cab. She comes to him and hands him a small steel ring with a few keys of different sizes attached. He puts them in the pocket of his crimson robe and looks at Matt, then Bruce.

"You follow me."

They start in the two-story library, which is unlocked. The shelves are mostly empty and Mahajad apologizes for the lack of books. It's open and there's no place for someone to hide or be held on either floor. There are windows all around, but not the kind that open. Nowhere to launch a glider.

"We are four years here, but not much progress on our library," says the swami. "Time flies."

The lecture halls and classrooms are locked but Mahajad lets them in and finds the lights. The rooms feel used to Matt, in a way that the library didn't. His footsteps echo on the stairs and floors and Matt gets a whiff of the desperation he felt as he counted down the last few unsearched homes in Laguna. What if the Little Wings are wrong? he thinks. What if God answered your prayer with still another riddle?

The chapel is dusty inside and laced with cobwebs. Boxes of cobalt-blue tile stand open in the vestibule. They walk the aisle to the altar. Matt sees rattraps under the pews, some set but most not. The chapel basement is cluttered with paint cans and ladders and used drop cloths.

He's beginning to feel foolish.

Again.

Om gives him that amused, curious look of his. "And next we have the dorms where some of our Evolvers, Enlighteners, and Ecstatics live and study in an ascetic, communal fashion. Many will be sleeping."

They cross the commons. Mahajad drops his plate and utensils into a trash can on the path. Matt turns for a look at the women, who smile at him demurely, and the four men in white, who gaze at him blankly.

The dorms are two facing arcades of apartments that Matt and Kyle used to play hide-and-seek in. They interconnect. Mahajad knocks on the first door, which is answered by a mop-topped young man in a swimsuit and an open white robe.

"Swami, what's up?"

"Have you seen the missing girl, Jasmine Anthony?"

"Who?"

"The girl on the many posters in town."

"I haven't been to town lately, Swami Mahajad."

"Sorry to disturb you . . ."

"David."

"Yes, Evolving David. Good night. See you in the morning when we Praise the Light."

"Yes, sir."

Some of the followers have been sleeping and it takes them a while to answer Mahajad's firm knocks. They are all young and nice-looking. Again, Matt wonders how alike they are.

Not exactly alike, but similar. Comparable. Bonnie and Sara and Danielle and Jasmine. And many of these others. The boys/men too.

None have seen Jasmine Anthony, though several remember her from early June, when the hippies and tourists were flooding in. One remembers Jazz as the ukulele girl from an *LA Moves* Happening.

She closes her door and Om turns to Matt and Bruce.

"Matt and father of Matt," the swami says. "You can go from door to door and talk to everyone. I'm going to sit here on this bench with my assistants, and rest. It's been a long day. When you're done, I'll be waiting."

It takes them twenty minutes to finish off both rows of dorms but none of the beautiful, fresh young people have seen Jasmine lately, if ever.

Matt and Bruce walk back to the swami, who sits on the bench between the women. The four men in white wait under a nearby sycamore, hands folded.

"I'm sorry," says Om. "But it's good you searched. An untaken path can be a torment to the soul."

"We'd like to see your residence and the bell tower," says Matt.

"Oh, Matt, that is where I live. I certainly would have noticed if your sister was spending time there!"

"It won't take long, Mahajad," Matt says. "We need to search these last places. Against the torment you just mentioned."

"You've searched everywhere in this city, haven't you?"

"Pretty much."

Mahajad sighs deeply, setting his dark hands on his big thighs. The women take his hands in theirs.

He looks at Matt with his usual forbearance and curiosity.

"Let us end your torment, then. I have houseguests, but come. It won't take long."

The swami's residence stands on a knoll on the far commons, bathed in moonlight. The bell tower presides beside it, lit from below, its blue dome shining. Matt hears the Vortex generators humming.

The barefoot swami climbs his porch steps, then turns.

"Give me a minute to prepare my guests," he says. "We were not expecting company this late."

"We'll help you," says Bruce, taking off his Stetson.

"You are very distrustful of your swami," says Om.

"We won't take long," says Matt.

"I hope not," says the swami, shaking his head sadly and opening the right-side double door. Matt holds the door for the women, then follows them in. He looks behind him for the white suits but they're gone.

The foyer is tile-floored, high-ceilinged, and dimly lit: white plaster walls with wrought iron sconces, its round archway framing a great room. Matt steps down to the hardwood floor, his eyes drawn to the enormous Persian rug in the great room's center, to the large river-rock fireplace filled not with burning logs but with burning candles and incense. Seated on the heavy rustic furniture are the Sungaards, Bayott, and Danielle. Two white suits now stand in the darker recess of the big room. Two of the four, Matt notes.

Bruce is already at it with the guests, hat in hand, introducing himself in his best loud drawl.

"And this is my beloved son, Matt, with whom I am well pleased. Just kidding, I'm not God, but I am proud of Matt, only sixteen, and we'll be out of here in a jiffy. I just have to make sure my daughter Jasmine hasn't stowed herself away in this fine place—which I'm sure her mother, my ex-wife, would have done at Jasmine's age. In a heartbeat. Anyway, we'll make this quick, you weird fucking people."

Matt sees the amusement on the Sungaard faces but they say nothing. Danielle shakes her head derisively. Bayott nods to Matt in recognition.

"My disciples in white must be with us at all times," says Mahajad.

"Disciples?" asks Bruce, unbuttoning his jacket. "Is that what they are?"

"We will be leaving now," says Bayott, standing with the Sungaards and the girl.

The women have disappeared. The second two white-suited disciples await them in the dining room.

Matt follows his father and Om into the dining area, passing a formally set table, where the silverware shines dully in the sparse light of an electric chandelier turned low.

He takes in the strange, dark, stuck-in-time home. He senses the disciples behind him but doesn't turn to look. He's aware of the heavy pack. When he thinks of what's inside it, his breathing tightens and his strong legs feel undependable. He wonders if this is really happening.

Outside, a vehicle starts up then crunches slowly down the gravel drive. Through a window Matt watches the gray Mercedes van roll away. He wonders why people as rich as the Sungaards would be hanging around a spiritual center. Especially this late, on a weeknight. With a teenaged girl. The Sungaards aren't spiritual. An orgy hostess and a money manager / surfer / bulk LSD purchaser? With their private squad of phony Interpol cops even the Hessians couldn't handle? What do they need with Purity?

And what have they done to his sister?

In the big and well-lit kitchen, Matt watches two stout women conversing in Spanish while they wash dishes. The smell of *carnitas* lingers in the air, meat and onions and chilis.

"*Buenas noches*," says Bruce.

"*Buenas noches, señor*," they answer together.

Matt, with four years of Spanish under his belt, listens closely as his father converses with the women. No, they know no Jasmine Anthony. They have not heard of a kidnapped girl. His eyes wander the room as he imagines the great meals they must prepare here. He eyes the pantry and wonders what treasures wait behind the closed door.

The downstairs master bedroom is spacious and richly furnished, the bath small.

A short hallway leads to three smaller first-floor bedrooms, all neat and empty.

Matt has that feeling again. Not quite hopelessness, but almost. He tries to banish it, make room for willpower and optimism. Pictures Jasmine, age seven, coming through the fortified security door of the bomb shelter to rescue him. And at the beach by the bonfire, singing for her friends. Brushing her mother's hair.

I can do this.

Back in the great room, Matt follows his father and the swami up the hardwood stairs. Bruce's boot heels pound and echo. Two of the disciples look down from the dark recess of the landing above.

Matt looks into the first room: children's bunk beds, two small dressers, Om shaking his big head as Bruce opens a closet door. Matt listens for the sound of the white-clad men but hears nothing.

Curious, he drifts back to the landing. Sees that the two disciples lurking upstairs a moment ago are now downstairs without having *taken* the stairs. He would have heard them. As he hears them now, clearly, as they stride into the great room from the direction of the kitchen, crossing paths with the Mexican cooks as they head for the front door.

"Adios, señors."

"A good night also to you."

Matt hears the man's accent, similar to that of his boss. The swami's mother-daughter assistants now sit by the cavernous, candle-filled fireplace, the mother on a chair and the daughter on the floor, legs crossed, meditating.

Then his father and the swami are back, and Matt follows them back down the stairs to the great room.

Om's smooth baritone is edged with annoyance as he orders the mother and daughter out of the house.

"You have insulted away my guests and employees," he says

to Bruce. "And it is getting late. I shall be happy when you go and the Vortex is pure again. I have seen the cold weapon at your back, Mr. Anthony. They are not permitted here."

"I need to see the bell tower," says Matt.

The swami regards Matt with a wet black stare. "It is a useless relic of Christian-capitalist excess. The bells are gone. We have long ago boarded the door. You can pull on the wood with all your strength and it will not open, Matt."

"I'll try."

56

S tanding at the foot of the bell tower Matt considers the two-by-six boards nailed horizontally across the door and into the heavy wooden frame. Seven of them, the lumber unpainted, and the nails rusty. The generators in the squat building beside the tower are surprisingly loud up this close.

He chooses one chest-high board, clamps his hands tight and pulls hard, then harder.

"I can see that's not going to budge, son."

Matt braces his feet on a lower board, bringing his body weight into play. His eyes close and his muscles quiver as he pulls with his arms and pushes with every bit of strength he has in his paper-route legs, the legs that moved eight thousand pounds of logs up and down Sara Eikenberg's driveway, the legs that kicked him out of a riptide and all the way to shore fighting a fifty-pound fish trying to pull him out to sea.

He throws back his head and screams.

But lands on his back, gasping and looking up at the stars.

"True strength is only achieved through purity," says Mahajad.

Matt sits up and crosses his arms over his knees. His breathing settles and his heart slows and his thoughts are clear. He feels the resurgence of hope.

"We need to see the basement of the house," he says.

"There is no basement," says Om. "Did you see stairs? No, you did not."

"There's an elevator. The security men and your women use it. It's how they come and go like ghosts."

"Yes, but the elevator only services the two floors. There is no basement. I do not want you back inside my home, Matt and Mr. Anthony. You must honor my generosity and depart. Right actions follow right minds."

"Give me a break, Om. Matt, where's that elevator?"

"It has to be in the kitchen," says Matt. "I didn't see it but it has to be there."

"Om?" says Bruce. "We're going back inside to confirm your no-basement statement, then we'll be on our way. Deal?"

"If you are not most rapid, I will have my disciples remove you. They are trained."

"We'll be most rapid. Come on, Matt."

In the kitchen, Mahajad Om scowls at them, arms crossed. His long black hair and gray-white beard glisten with sweat and Matt sees big wet rings on the satin robe. Two disciples look on from behind them, hands folded and feet spread. Two more appear in the dark periphery of the great room.

Matt surveys the big kitchen. Wonders if there might be a secret room like at Mystic Arts World. A moving wall or shelf. He opens cabinets in search of a button or a control of some kind. Tries the pantry and finds not foodstuffs or a secret room, but the elevator he predicted. It's small and old. But the swami was right, the wood-handled lever only has two positions: Floor 1 and Floor 2.

Nothing more.

However . . .

"No basement, as I testified," says Mahajad. "Now be gone, please. You are destroying my good spirits."

"Come on swami Om," says Matt, stepping into the elevator. "Help us find her."

Bruce headlocks the swami and drives him into the elevator car.

Matt slams the collapsible metal gate closed, pulls the lever hard, down past the Floor 1 setting, then pushes the worn brass button.

The old car shudders, and starts its way . . . down.

"Stop kickin', you hairy goddamned devil!"

In the scuffle, Matt pulls the swami's key ring from the pocket of his robe and stuffs it in the wallet pocket of his jeans.

The car lowers and bangs to a stop and the lights come on. Matt slides open the door. The basement is bigger than he expected. The main room is an office with two large desks that form an L. The chairs and wooden file cabinets look as if they were made back in the twenties, when the Vortex was still a seminary. The ceiling is low and the fluorescent tubes give off a jittery glow. Beyond the office is a kitchen and dining room.

Released by Bruce, Mahajad backpedals into the near desk, steadies his big body, rearranges his sweat-soaked robe. To Matt, he looks like a different man than the one he first saw at Mystic Arts World, and later here at Sara's Evolution, and later at the Feast of the Spirit. His eyes are furtive.

"Now, you have seen the basement. Call out her name. Jasmine Anthony! Your family is here to free you from the Vortex of Purity!"

Om's smooth, subtly accented baritone rings out, but only silence and the drone of the generators answer back.

"Why did you say you didn't have a basement?" asks Matt.

"So you would depart the Vortex. Your presence is an offense to me."

"How many of those disciple bodyguards do you have, Omley?" asks Bruce.

"As with everything, only what I need. Now, you will exit as you promised."

"Search, Matt. I'll stay with our gracious host."

Matt goes room to room. The doors are all open and the light switches easy to find. There are three bedrooms on one side of the hall, three on the other, all with small beds made with crimson bedspreads. Also, two bathrooms and a living room with couches and recliner chairs, a TV, and a cabinet stereo. It all looks ready, but unused.

Back in the office Matt finds Bruce telling the swami about the natural passivity of the Indian people and how the Ganges is the most polluted river on the planet thanks to the people letting their holy cattle shit and piss in it. Om sits in one of the old wooden office chairs, looking exhausted and defeated, his black eyes tracking Matt.

"Nothing, Dad."

Matt can hardly bear the disappointment on his father's face. "Okay, son. We tried. Sorry for the intrusion, Omar."

Matt feels the weight of defeat trying to take him down. He can't believe that Jazz's desperate airplanes have guided them here but not to her. He takes one last look around the big room. Walks disconsolately into the kitchen/dining area, flips on more lights.

And sees a door.

"Where's this go?" he calls back to the swami.

"To the generators."

The second key that Matt tries unlocks the door and Matt pushes it open to a wall of sound.

A long, dark hall extends straight ahead. He finds the lights. The power station is small and tight, the floor concrete but thrumming with horsepower. The generators, gleaming and large, hum loudly, vibrating Matt to his bones. He turns to see Bruce guiding Om into the room.

Another door waits behind the generators, roughly where Matt gauges the bell tower to be. But being underground it's hard to tell what goes to where—there's no perspective and no spatial logic, but as he studies it . . .

"It goes only to storage," says Om.

"No," says Matt.

The same key unlocks the door. He opens it and finds the switch. A nearly empty room, windowless and unfurnished. And metal stairs leading up from this noisy basement.

Bruce wrenches Om in by the peaked shoulder of his sweat-heavy satin robe.

"I told you, Matt—storage!"

Matt considers: plastic gas cans, cases of bottled water, hoes and shovels and concrete mix leaning against the walls.

But from under the stairs something else catches his eye: a brown paper shopping bag stuffed with a loose bundle of material that shows over the top.

Black symbols on a white background.

Peace signs.

Another connection.

"Where is she?"

"You have lost your beautiful mind, Matt Anthony."

"Jasmine!" he yells. "*Jasmine!*"

Matt flies up the stairs and out of the basement and into a small, round, plaster-walled room. It's the bell tower entrance. He sees the door he tried to open. And the stairway spiraling up into the tower itself.

He doesn't just sense her; he feels her.

"Jasmine!" Matt bellows, taking the steep stairs two at a time in a dizzying circular sprint. The iron steps thrum and vibrate with his weight, and Matt bellows her name again.

Her voice is faint. "Yes. What?"

"It's Matt! I'm coming!"

"Oh, good, Matt. Good."

He gets to the top and steps into the belfry.

Jasmine sits at a small desk. She wears a loose crimson gown. She's pale and her hair is long and combed out. Her eyes are calm and distant. She looks at Matt and smiles. She stands and comes toward him in uneven, labored steps, dragging an iron ball chained to her right ankle.

"It really is about time, Matt."

He kneels and tries to get the shackle off but it's padlocked around her ankle.

"Om has the key," she says evenly.

Matt's down on the floor again, trying keys on the padlock when Bruce and Mahajad barge in.

Just as Bruce looks to his daughter, the swami whirls and drives his open palm into Bruce's nose, then stomps hard on the side of his knee. Bruce collapses, hat rolling, nose gushing blood, gasping with pain as he tries to draw his gun. Om kicks him in the jaw.

Matt lunges for him, but Mahajad is already lumbering down the stairs on his thick padded feet, crimson robe streaming behind him.

57

The only way out of the bell tower is the way they came in. Bruce limps terribly back through the roaring generator room and the basement, followed by unchained Jasmine and Matt.

In the elevator car, Bruce orders Matt to get his gun ready. Matt digs out the long-barreled revolver and slings his pack back into place. With the Earp gun in his hand, his legs go heavy and his breath comes short.

The elevator stops.

Bruce throws open the metal gate, his face swollen and bloody, his voice a rasp. "I'll lay down cover if you need it. Zigzag to the front door as fast as you can. When you get outside keep going. Don't wait for me."

Bruce opens the wooden door and hobbles into the kitchen, gun raised.

Matt clambers past with the big revolver in one hand and Jasmine just behind him. No fire from Bruce but it seems like hours to the foyer, a dreamlike, slow-motion slog.

Once there, Matt turns to see his father following through the great room in a lopsided gait.

Then, movement near the fireplace, and on the second-floor landing.

Gunfire erupts in soft spitting bursts. Bruce crashes behind a sofa as bullets tear into the floor toward him, ripping through the chairs and walls, stitching a trail of dust on the huge Persian rug.

Matt points the heavy revolver at the disciple on the landing, who is firing a short, fat-barreled machine pistol. Matt's gun kicks hard. Twenty feet from his target, the stair railing splinters.

But Bruce rises awkwardly from behind the couch and shoots the man twice dead center, dropping him onto the stairs.

Then two more shots at the disciple by the fireplace, who falls backpedaling as a string of his bullets pock the ceiling.

Bruce lurches into the foyer behind his son and daughter, turning as a third disciple runs in from the kitchen, firing. Bullets snap past Matt and plaster flies off the foyer wall and he points the Earp revolver. Tries his best to steady the wavering barrel. Then the big kick, and the twang of metal somewhere in the kitchen. Bullets still zapping into the foyer walls.

His father moves toward the shooter, firing but missing twice. The disciple's next spitting burst sends Bruce to the floor.

Matt yanks off another round, then runs to his father, grabs him by his bloody coat and drags him to the front door. Turns and raises the revolver but the shooter is gone.

Jasmine is through the door and out.

Bruce has propped his back against the foyer wall, his head lolling slightly, the floor a bloody slick around him, the gun still in his hand. He's staring past Matt, out toward the great room. Kneeling, Matt faces him, takes the shoulder of his coat to drag him outside, sees the seeping little holes in his father's shirt and pants.

"Duck, son!"

Matt ducks and Bruce's gun roars twice, then clicks with a sharp metallic ping. The percussion deafens Matt but he feels the weighty thud of a body hitting the floor behind him.

His sneakers slipping on the bloody tiles, Matt and Jasmine get their father to his feet. Together they stumble out, cross the porch, and wobble cumbersomely down the steps to the grass.

Where the fourth disciple steps from behind the trunk of the big oak tree, raises his fat little machine pistol and pulls the trigger.

Nothing happens.

Matt dumps his father as the disciple struggles with the bolt to clear the jam. It takes a short forever for Matt to draw the Earp revolver, its endless barrel slowly clearing his belt. But he gets it out and tries to hold it steady on the white-clad disciple.

Matt's voice is high and his knees are shaking. "If you drop the gun I won't shoot. Where's Om?"

The disciple glances up, finally jacks the bolt free, which slams home with a fatal ring.

He raises the weapon and Matt blows him into the oak tree.

For a moment he looks down at himself, then up at Matt. He sags to the ground and rolls over, facing the branches high above. The tree trunk is splashed with blood.

Matt approaches slowly, not wanting to see but needing to see. The disciple is breathing fast. His eyes are open and his face caught in an expression of wonder. Matt goes around the tree and pukes mightily. When he gets back the man is still.

Woozy with nausea, Matt kneels over his father, using his pocketknife to cut pieces from his sister's crimson dress. Jazz plugs her dad's side and thigh wounds—small holes on the front and bigger, jagged holes out the back. Matt and his sister apply pressure. Bruce looks at them intermittently, dazed and eerily calm.

Matt looks up at the crowd drawn by the commotion, wide-eyed young people, most in the baggy white, yellow, and orange garments of the Vortex, some with their arms out and their faces to the sky, chanting.

Jasmine seems numb and detached, and when she speaks it sounds like she's talking to herself.

"They put the purity nectar in between my toes," she says. "Hide the needle tracks in a Purity Girl. I want more of that stuff."

"Purity nectar? Purity Girls?"

She looks through him. "Not now, Matt."

Some of the followers offer help. One has already called the

police and an ambulance. A girl folds a jacket and puts it under
Bruce's head. Two more kneel and place their hands on his
bloody body. A young man who seems to know what he's doing takes Bruce's wrist and times the pulse with his watch.
He tells Bruce he'll be alright: he can see Bruce's Karma in
his aura, and it is good. The others stay back on the moon-
shadowed grass, young and beautiful.

Matt and Jazz keep the pressure on the wounds. The fabric
plugs are soaked and sloppy. Bruce's breathing is shallow and
he tracks them with one watchful eye. Matt wishes the cops
would hurry. Wonders where Mahajad has gone. Can't believe
this has happened. Is happening.

He closely studies the faces of his sister and father. Knowing
Jasmine has been deeply changed. Knowing his father might
not live for long. Knowing that he himself has killed a man
who—in a way he only faintly understands—now belongs to
him forever.

Soft chanting while the sirens wail.

58

Two weeks later, Matt sits in the Laguna Beach Police Department for the eighth time this summer. First was for his and his mother's filing of the missing-person report for Jasmine, that distant lifetime ago. Most recently is now, yet another detailed statement regarding the events at the Vortex of Purity.

This room has become a sort of comfort to him. There are sometimes coffee and donuts. Since that night at the Vortex his mind tends to wander on its own, like a young dog off-leash, and this drab, familiar room allows for it.

Today is his third Vortex statement, and like the ones previous, it's being filmed because Matt is a minor and the film can be used in court without him being present.

They need to talk to him again because some important things have happened since the arrest of Mahajad Om—real name, Zeke Andrujic—in North Hollywood.

Things such as Marlon Sungaard's suicide by hanging in the Orange County Jail.

And Neldra Sungaard's sudden laying of blame on her departed husband.

Matt's got on his best new-used short-sleeved madras plaid from Fade in the Shade, hand-washed and ironed by his mom, as she deftly balanced herself on one crutch.

"Take it from the top, Matt," says Furlong.

Also present are Detective McAdam, Officer Darnell, a stenographer, and DA Mike Saffalo, who will personally try

Zeke Andrujic for the murder of Bonnie Stratmeyer and the
kidnappings of Bonnie and Jasmine Anthony.

"The camera and tape recorder are on," Furlong says.

It takes Matt just under an hour to retell what happened
from the time he and his father arrived at the Feast of the
Spirit, and the arrival of the cops and the ambulance. He
recalls most of it with a dreamlike detachment, but some
parts—hearing Jazz's voice, seeing her alive and imprisoned,
feeling his father's blood on his hands, killing the disciple
under the oak tree—he relives with terrible clarity and strong
emotion.

He finishes, aware of the quiet in the room, the traffic out
on Forest and Third, the smell of the donut on the napkin in
front of him.

"How's your father healing up?" asks Furlong.

Matt synopsizes: Bruce's remaining kidney is working well,
and the leg wound is draining. The soft tissue of his knee is
detached but operable. He can have knee surgery soon.

"And Jasmine?"

Matt takes his time before he speaks. The question is complicated, and the answer changes daily.

"Better. At first, I thought she was holding back some
things until she wanted to talk about them. But now I think
they're coming back on their own. The memories, I mean. She
has a lot of mental strength."

"It's unbelievable to all of us, what Andrujic and the Sungaards put her through," says Darnell.

"We'll be seeing her again later this afternoon," says Furlong. "Not here. At home, where she'll feel safe and comfortable."

Matt considers beefy Furlong. "I don't know if she'll ever
feel safe again. Don't make her remember things she doesn't
want to."

He tells them that the Anthony family home is now Third
Street again. Same drafty clapboard beach house, he thinks,

same GTE building for a view, same grumbling pipes and touchy electricity. His dad gave it to Julie in return for her place in Dodge City, when he leaves the hospital. Matt doubts his father will stay in Laguna for long.

"You don't have to go out to Dodge," Matt says with a small smile at Furlong.

He knows how much Furlong hates the place, and his smile's a dig on Furlong's continuing inability to ensnare Johnny Grail, or even make decent narcotics busts out in Dodge. Mostly, Furlong just gets lies and misdirection there—firecrackers and tomatoes thrown at him and his men, the feral boys trying to sell them more dried dog turds, and vandalizing Moby Cop and the LBPD radio cars.

But, as adversarial as Furlong and Matt have been, Furlong has still not arrested Matt for his transgressions with LSD and dragon balls on behalf of Johnny Grail. Or fleeing this very cop house and disappearing. Or reckless endangerment for Matt's perilous double back in the Westfalia against Festival of Arts traffic, and his terrifying of pedestrians in crosswalks. All of which was well witnessed and reported to LBPD.

But that crazy chase—the Westfalia versus Moby Cop—had been necessary, Matt thinks. More than necessary, critical. It had led him to his connections, to Windy Rise, to the Little Wings trapped in the prickly pear, to the Vortex, and to Jazz.

Just as importantly, Furlong has not again pressured Matt into a setup of Grail or anyone else in the Brotherhood of Eternal Love. But Matt believes it's coming. Just a matter of time.

"Matt," says McAdam. "Tell me again why you think Zeke Andrujic would allow you to search his home."

"A bluff. Hoping we'd find an empty house and give up."

"His whole life is a bluff," says Darnell.

They ask again about Andrujic's disciples, who said nothing that night that Matt had heard, except good night to the cooks.

The cops are interested in the idea that Om had trained and rehearsed such violence with them, which will establish conspiracy and give the surviving disciples—the Laguna cops have questioned two others—ample reason to turn state's evidence against their boss.

All Matt can say is that the silent disciples seemed to anticipate events, moving into, out of, and throughout the big house, using the elevator to mask their movement.

As did Andrujic's two assistants, Matt says. Whom, Chief Norman Hein told the *Register* last week, had been cooperating with the police. They'd known about Bonnie and Jasmine—and others, going back five years—all along.

"What exactly did Bayott Benir say to you that night?" Saffalo asks.

"Just that they all were leaving—the Sungaards and Danielle."

"I'd leave too," says the DA. "If I knew your sister was being held prisoner two hundred feet away and a hundred feet up."

Matt nods, picturing the bell tower lit at night. He hears the drone of the generators that drowned out her calls for help. Sees Jazz in her crimson gown—Om's color of purity, because he was pure and he wanted Jazz to be pure, too—dragging her iron ball and chain across the belfry floor.

Matt has heard a lot from Darnell over the last two weeks, some of it astonishing. Most of it part of Neldra Sungaard's plea deal: Andrujic was a small-time criminal drifter and con artist, and later a self-taught spiritualist who had modest success with the Garden of Earthly Delights, a meditation center / health food store / social space in the hills north of L.A. He was smart and ugly, a glutton and a sexual opportunist, but he had charm. Neldra told them that Andrujic had a "physical and spiritual craving" for the beautiful, pilgriming teenaged girls and boys who showed up weekly at his Garden of Earthly Delights. And he assumed that thousands of men throughout the world shared that craving. He sensed the money to be made if he could cultivate a "pure product" and offer it to refined and wealthy customers in a way that everyone would profit—even the pure young people who would be his merchandise. According to Neldra, when she and Andrujic met at a party in the Hollywood Hills one hot September night, they recognized one another as kindred spirits. A partnership began. Neldra was impressed by Andrujic's grasp of how to market popular culture. American youth and beauty for anyone in the world who could afford it, said Darnell. Barbie and Ken dolls for old men, Matt thinks. He remembers Gauguin's natives in the Pageant tableau, Laurel hopeful but Rose suspicious of corrupt invaders. Her eyes wary because she *knows* . . .

"Still with us, Matt?" asks Furlong.

"Yes, sir."

"Not daydreaming of Dr. Hamilton's Youth Leadership Center, are you?"

Matt shakes his head, never surprised by Furlong's eagerness to induce fear. Two weeks ago he had panicked Matt into running away. But now, Matt thinks, things are different. Now if Furlong threatens him, he'll just put out his wrists for the cuffs. Get a public defender, tell the truth, and hold on tight.

"What did you sense the relationship was, between the Sungaards and Danielle Huber?" asks Darnell.

"Hard to tell. That day in Mrs. Sungaard's place, they just seemed like friends sharing a house."

"And later, arriving at the Vortex that afternoon with Bayott and the Sungaards?" she asks.

Matt pictures Danielle Huber following the Sungaards toward the front porch of Mahajad's home, smiling and joking with Bayott.

"She seemed happy," says Matt. "Like she was looking forward to something. Her clothes were pretty and her hair was good and she had makeup on. You know how people behave when they're eager to please. Like that."

"And again, what color was her dress?"

"Still orange," says Matt.

"And still important," says McAdam. "The colors mean rank to Andrujic's followers. First, street clothes, then white, yellow, orange, and crimson. Lowest to highest. Danielle Huber was on the same path of destruction as your sister and Bonnie Stratmeyer. Oh, not a path to destruction—to *purity*."

This rings true to Matt in a way that makes his heart ache. Bonnie from high school, kind-faced and happy. The first dead person he'd ever seen.

"Last interview, you made it sound like Bonnie's death was an accident," says Matt.

"Caused by Andrujic," says Darnell. "The Vortex wanted its girls and boys to be physically strong and beautiful. So, weights, swimming, yoga, vegetarian diet. Neldra says Bonnie overdosed on their so-called 'purity nectar' during one of Om's exercise routines. They'd use the gym and the pool at night, keeping the other followers away so they wouldn't see. Bonnie, drugged up, dove into that shallow lap pool, hit her head on the bottom and knocked herself out—probably all by accident. Which tracks with the autopsy—the syringe marks between her toes, the drugs, the head blow, the fresh water in her lungs. Neldra says Andrujic decided to let Bonnie drown. Two of the disciples took her body to Thalia in one of the green Vortex vans we were looking so hard for. Carried her down the stairs and laid her out on the rocks."

As almost witnessed by Myron Kandell, Matt thinks. His tired mind's eye goes to Bonnie's pale cold body on the beach.

"Have you found out what's in purity nectar?" he asks.

"The FBI is still analyzing," says McAdam. "Mostly it's synthesized opiates and barbiturates, mixed with a heavy dose of LSD. Designed to keep you calm, comfortable, hallucinating out of your mind, and craving more. God only knows how much it must have disoriented Bonnie to make her dive into a shallow pool like that. Or what 'purity nectar' did to the other girls and boys we'll probably never see again."

"How many have there been?" asks Matt. He already knows last week's figure, courtesy of Darnell.

The cops all look at each other. Matt knows that they can't tell him everything. But he also thinks they owe him, considering how poorly they've handled things—from their initial disbelief that he really saw Jazz kidnapped that night in the fog, to their non-help in his difficult quest to search every home in the city, to their refusal to take the Little Wings seriously. Hadn't he cracked this case while living by his wits for a week while they did their best to run him down and throw him in juvie? Matt knows he's a star witness. Right up there with Jasmine.

"I think we can share this information after all he's done," says Darnell.

A beat, loaded but not long.

"Eight young people sold in four years," says McAdam. There's emotion in his voice. "Four girls, four boys. None from Laguna. Runaways from across the country, so we didn't see a pattern. Silence from you on this, Matt."

Matt considers. "I keep secrets," he says. "Just ask Sergeant Furlong."

Chuckles, even from Sergeant Bill himself.

For another half hour they pepper Matt with questions about that night, and beyond. They want to know more about the thermals over Windy Rise, the prevailing onshore winds and the occasional offshore Santa Ana winds, and how many paper airplanes Jazz launched through the bell tower slots. They seem impressed that Matt was able to estimate the varying Little Wing flight lines based on wind, but to Matt it was obvious. As a fisherman and occasional surfer, he'd been keeping an eye on the wind for years. There was some element of faith at work in his calculations, too. And desperation.

Furlong asks again about Sungaard and the twelve fish surfboards recovered from the Hessian murder house up in Huntington Beach. Matt has never told them anything about surfboards or Hessians, and he's not going to tell them now. Somewhat amusingly to Matt, the surfboards were never meant to be sold as such. Sungaard's "revolution" in surfboard design was just diversional fantasy. They were hollow and stuffed with canned, distilled hash oil from Afghanistan, worth ten thousand dollars per board. The cops discovered the oil when a young off-duty officer took one of the irresistibly beautiful boards out of the property room and went to Brooks Street beach to surf. He dropped into a nice five-foot wall and his foot went through the deck. Furlong suspects Johnny Grail and BEL involvement through Mystic Arts World, and he listens closely to Matt's calm evasions, making notes.

As before, the LBPD is especially interested in Bayott Benir and his comrades—definitely not Interpol—who haven't been seen since the night at the Vortex. Matt has little to tell them.

But he's heard that Danielle Huber does.

59

That afternoon after his paper route, Matt and Laurel Kalina walk south along Main Beach. It's a perfect day, a spangled ocean and a tan beach under blue sky. Three times already, people Matt barely knows, or doesn't know at all, have run up and congratulated him. They're all wide-eyed with astonishment, surprise and relief: *It's unbelievable, man, unbelievable.*

But right now, Laurel is another story. Matt has taken her hand twice since starting down the beach from the lifeguard tower, and Laurel has retracted it both times. She is subdued. She's been hard to get a hold of the last few days, busy with her writing and the Pageant and friends.

"Matt," she says, stopping and squinting up at him, then taking a deep breath. "I need freedom. Freedom to grow as a person and meet new people and to write. It's the most important thing in my life. To be a writer. I've started a novel that takes place in France during the grape harvest in Bordeaux. My professor is very positive but I know it's not very good. Yet. I have a chance to go there in late August, to France."

"You mean break up?"

"I mean to continue, as friends."

Matt feels as if the iron ball that hobbled Jasmine has been dropped from the sky and landed on his head.

"Okay."

"I knew you would understand and approve."

"I don't either of those, but it's up to you, Laurel."

"This is the hardest thing I've ever done."

"Is there some other way?"

"You mean and stay together?"

"Yeah, exactly."

They pass Thalia without a word. Matt thinks of Bonnie but more of himself. He's just been dumped by the first girl he's ever cared about. The first girl he's admired and liked and wanted to kiss and probably even loved. He looks at Laurel, sees a tear from under her sunglasses spreading down her cheek.

"I know you've changed, Matt. Inside and outside and it's good. You'll change again. So will I."

"We can change together," Matt says, having absolutely no idea if that's true. Julie and Bruce didn't. Two of his friends, their parents were divorcing.

"Then there's Sara," says Laurel, with a flash of pained hostility in her eyes.

Matt shrugs. "I don't think that was going anywhere."

"I've thought this through a thousand times," she says. "I talked to Rose and Mom and Dad and my professor. I prayed and prayed and cried. Matt, I'm very sure this is what I need to do. And I'm sorrier than I can describe. If I were writing this scene it would be the saddest scene of all time. That's how it feels to me."

"Me too."

Another gut-wrenching silence, this one all the way to Cress Street. Matt feels suddenly chilled, as if the breeze has changed from west to north but he knows it hasn't.

"Friends, Matt?"

"Yes, good."

"Do you mean that?"

"I really don't know. I'll try."

"I love you."

He feels the storm inside, the pressure in his ears, and the sting in his eyes. The painful lump in his throat. But he's got enough pride to tamp it all down. And enough anger to state the obvious.

"That doesn't add up, Laurel. All the stuff we did. Together and happy to be with each other. Now this."

"There are different kinds of love, Matt. Give it time. Please."

They stop and Laurel kisses him on the cheek. More tears as she reaches into her beaded macramé bag and hands Matt a thick, rolled-up tube of typing paper with a yellow ribbon around it.

"I tried to get it all in here," she says. "Yellow means friendship."

She runs back the way they've come, angling toward Brooks Street where she lives.

Matt heads north too, for his own home. Drops Laurel's gift-wrapped papers into a Main Beach trash can.

60

On this last Friday morning of late July, Matt's hobbled
parents sit quietly in the living room of the Third Street
house. Julie, in a long blue birds-of-paradise kimono,
has her cast propped on the wicker chest. The cast is crowded
with signatures and doodles. She's reading *I'm OK—You're
OK* and drinking ginger ale.

Bruce sits across from her, intent on the *Register* sports page.
His bad leg rests on the table also. He's wearing sweatpants
with one leg cut short, and a crisp white snap-button Western
shirt. His elaborately hinged postsurgical knee brace is black
and looks painful.

Matt's at the breakfast dinette, sketching the bouquet on
the table before him—chipper daisies, courtesy of Bruce—
and waiting for his sister.

The house is decorated for Kyle's homecoming. There's an
American flag taped to the wall above the TV, and a cake
with red, white, and blue frosting, and a red plastic tub filled
with ice, beer, and soft drinks. Food on the way.

"Come on Matt!" calls Jasmine, coming down the hall, slinging a bag over her shoulder. "Let's give these lovebirds some
privacy."

"We are not lovebirds," says Julie. "We are parakeets in
separate cages."

"You look like lovebirds to me," says Jasmine.

"I can't believe they call them the Angels," says Bruce.
"They take a five-run lead into the ninth and blow it."

Matt has noticed that, in the nearly three weeks since the

Vortex night, when his mother and father are together there is tension but few words. They seem to occupy separate but shared worlds. Whether here or in the red barn on Roosevelt Lane, Julie and Bruce maintain a truce. Occasionally, Matt catches his father looking at his mother the way he used to: pride of ownership. Julie looks at Bruce more and more often but her thoughts are less obvious. She's cautious and analytical, not quite friendly and not quite hostile. Matt gives his father fifty-fifty odds of staying in California more than two weeks. And his mother a fifty-fifty chance of throwing him out before that, finally and forever.

Today is about Kyle, though. Nothing bad will happen today.

His and Jasmine's daily walks are at eleven, so Matt has time to get his newspapers folded, banded, and bagged. Sometimes they walk the beach, but mostly they go downtown, then north or south to the galleries or the museum or Mystic Arts World, sometimes get a quick lunch. The purity nectar has been hard for her to kick. She gets nauseous and mean without warning. She sleeps a lot.

After almost three weeks of this, Jasmine has shed her crude disguises and is able to talk to the many locals who know or recognize her. Now she actually stops and converses. Matt steers her away when she gets tired, or is being asked too many or too personal questions.

He asks her almost nothing about the Vortex. She talks about it when she wants to, rarely but suddenly, in short sentences or phrases, as if she's just now remembering and wants to get it on the record quickly. As if she wants to forget. He's done some reading at the library on recovered memory and trauma-induced amnesia and selective processing.

I wouldn't let them touch me. They talked and studied me and brought gifts. Most spoke English and most were old. I tried to make them afraid of me. I strummed my ukulele and made up ugly, crazy songs. Om called me the crazy princess. Om said I was one he couldn't break. He said we all want to be broken. He said he knew he wanted me to become pure the second he saw me. He tried to pass this off as some sort of spiritual insight that he had. He said he was like the Hamsa, the eye that sees and protects. His price was twenty-five thousand dollars for a year with me. I would get twenty-five hundred when the year was up. No contract. No vows. No obligations except to be peaceful and available for travel and pleasure. That is what Om said. He also said his grandfather was a custom dollmaker in the old country, which stuck in my mind because of how Om was trying to make us into dolls.

They cross PCH at Forest toward Eiler Larsen—the old, unofficial Laguna greeter. He stands at the curb, smiling and waving, his big gray beard lifted to the breeze. When they hit the sidewalk, Jazz pulls Matt hard away from him.

"I can't look at another beard," she says.

The protesters have clustered on the boardwalk, shouting their slogans and waving their signs against the war that Kyle will be coming home from in just a few hours.

Matt can't wait to see him. He couldn't sleep last night he was so wound-up. Kyle beat the odds. Kyle made it. Kyle, back in his room and them fishing again! Matt has gotten Tommy Amici to come up with a sub for his route today so he can be there when Kyle gets off that Greyhound. Today will be the third day of work that Matt has missed in two years and four months. Tommy says it could hurt his chances of a third Outstanding Carrier medal but Matt hasn't been this eager for something to happen since knocking on doors to find Jazz. The last time he saw his brother, Matt was in the eighth grade!

Neldra was my groomer. Brought me clothes and makeup and everything for skin and hair. Expensive things. She thought she was counseling me. How to please a man. Her Sapphire Cove parties were where she scouted for Purity Girls. Others came from the LA Moves shoots at the beach. Neldra's husband trolled the gay places for Purity Boys. He was mostly that way himself, she said. They filled up the Vortex with good looking young people who could pay the tuition and were actually there for a spiritual journey. Or estranged and adrift. But they handpicked which Evolvers would be groomed and sold. I talked Neldra into getting me a ukulele and a book of sheet music. For my sanity, I said. Later I realized I could make Little Wings and fly them over town. I wanted to write "help!" or something but they wouldn't let me have a pen or pencil, like in prison. It really was a prison. I ran away after a fight with Mom, took a few things, got ripped and slept with Austin Overton. Couldn't really stand more than one night of those people. I'd been hanging with the LA Moves Happenings for weeks, and took up Neldra's offer to party at Sapphire Cove the next night. Disgusting. I tried to leave but they put me in a room and shot me with drugs. When I woke up I was in the bell tower. It was so windy. When the planes rose up with the wind I wanted to fly away too. I got out that night because Om left a door unlocked. He was very absentminded. After that they put on the ball and chain. I yelled until I lost my voice then gave up. The generators were so loud. I couldn't sleep at first then I slept a lot. The Vortex sleeping potion was powerful and not through a needle. I got used to the noise after a few days. Hypnotic. I used it like a mantra. People can get used to just about anything, especially when they're drugged. She told me she met you and her husband liked you but said you were not Purity material. I'm not surprised Neldra is betraying her husband for reduced charges. She's very manipulative and selfish. I met Danielle early on. I think she was supposed to be next, after me, like I was next after Bonnie.

"Why wasn't I Purity material?"

"You don't have enough imagination."

"Oh."

"Just kidding, Mattie!" She reaches out and flicks his ear with her middle-finger nail, a painful nip perfected in early adolescence.

Matt tries to get her back but she skips out of range.

When the Anthonys get to the Greyhound station on Broadway, the protesters have set up on the curb where the buses arrive. It's a bigger protest than the one that sent his father bonkers down at Moss Street a few weeks back. Louder too.

Matt sees that they're the usual protest crowd—mostly but not all young—lots of hair and beads and peace signs, all that.

He hopes not to see his English teachers among them because Kyle had them in school, too, and what would he think of them protesting him risking his life?

He feels the heavy pressure trip from these loud, sign-waving zealots, telling him what to believe. To take a side. Join us. Can't he honor his own brother *and* not want the war? They yell about killing babies, he thinks, but Kyle *saved* one in a tunnel! He scans the faces in the protest crowd, relieved that his teachers aren't here for Kyle to see.

Matt halts his mother's wheelchair well short of the crowd. Kyle is due on the 2:45 and it comes lumbering down Broadway just a few minutes late, swinging wide into the station.

The door hisses open and the passengers spill out, mostly hippies and tourists of all description, families and singles, old and young.

There's a pause in the exodus and Matt worries that Kyle changed his mind.

But a young serviceman gets off, then another, followed by Kyle Bruce Anthony.

Which is when the protesters come off the curb into the pull-out, signs raised.

Hey! Hey! LBJ! How many kids did you kill today?
No lies about Mi Lai!

The crowd surges toward Kyle and the other servicemen.

Kill hate, not babies!
Draft beer, not boys!

The lean, short-haired, smooth-faced young servicemen make it to the luggage bay, which the driver has already opened. The crowd closes around them and Matt pushes Julie closer, looking through the bodies. Suddenly, Kyle is coming toward him, his head down but his eyes up, one hand out for protection, the big oblong duffle heavy over his shoulder. He's got a growing-out buzz cut, pink cheeks, and a nervous smile, and he looks smaller to Matt, maybe even shorter too. Jeans and a T-shirt and combat boots. The shouting is louder now and the signs wave crazily and the protesters close around the servicemen again.

Kyle breaks through and Matt rolls their mother toward him. Bruce swings on his crutches toward Kyle too, but Jasmine easily outspeeds all of them and is the first to fly into Kyle's open arms.

Matt with Julie, caught in the swarm.

Baby killer! Baby killer!

"He's not that!" Matt yells. "He saved a baby! He's not that!"

Matt manages to U-turn Julie and gets ahead of Kyle and Jasmine, pushing the wheelchair forward through the noise and crowd, leading his brother and sister toward home.

An hour later, the party is in full swing. Friends of the family come by and the little house fills up. Matt picks the music and changes the LPs. Good rock, but not too loud because vets like peace and quiet, he has read.

Kyle is mostly smiles, thousand-yard silences, then smiles again. He's tremendously alert and his eyes dart. He smokes a lot. Matt stands close to him even when Kyle's talking with someone else. Feels funny to be almost eye-to-eye with his big brother. Kyle has lost weight, but Matt notes the sinewy muscles in his arms and neck.

Matt drinks a beer, then another. Watching his brother he imagines Kyle in the black tunnels of Cu Chi. A helmet light and a handgun. Matt sees that young girl running off with her baby into the safe dark. Then without warning, Matt sees the disciple at the Vortex breathing hard and staring up at the sky after he shot him. The blood on the oak tree. Makes his soul cry. Matt has pictured that man a thousand times, and knows he'll see him ten thousand more. A million, all the way to his grave. Part of his punishment for taking a life, even one that was trying to take his own.

Laurel Kalina calls, then comes over with a bottle of champagne for Kyle. Matt's not as happy to see her as he thought he'd be. She's lovely in a black dress with red roses and her hair is up, and it saddens him to see what he can't have. It's a bummer to be not enough. She radiates more than just beauty and every male eye in the room is on her.

Matt wolfs cake, pizza, hot dogs, potato salad, more cake. Sitting on the blue chair in the crowded, smoke-filled living room, he watches his mother and father, brother and sister. Really concentrates on them, one at a time. Draws them in his mind. Pictures them five years ago, then ten, then twelve or thirteen years ago, when his earliest memories start. Those years fly past him now in seconds but they're not gone, he thinks, just shelved, like books. Like drawings in a pad you can open and look at.

He ponders wholeness, as in being whole. An author was talking about that on Johnny Carson the other night. Matt knows he hasn't been whole since his father took off back in '62. Less whole when Kyle joined up, and less than that when Jasmine disappeared. Even less when his mother lost herself to Dodge and the pipe. Now, for the first time in all those years, Matt feels whole. Not like when he was ten but in a more complicated, weirdly less whole way, like maybe a man is supposed to be.

He's apparently the only one who hears the rattling knock on the front screen door and it breaks his thoughts and he answers it.

Through the screen it's Sara Eikenberg, a pink dress and granny boots, her hair up on one side.

Matt holds open the door but she doesn't move.

She gazes past him, taking it all in, skeptical brown eyes on assignment.

Her gaze comes back from the party to him.

"Go for a ride, Matt?"

He turns and looks behind him for a moment, catches Kyle's eye. Then Jasmine's. Now back to Sara.

"God, yes. Bitchen."

ACKNOWLEDGMENTS

A thousand thanks to Greg Nichols, Richard Lewis, and Larry McQuirk for giving up their time and stories of Laguna in the sixties.

And to my Laguna Canyon friends from way back—Larry and Nina Ragle; John Parlett; and Kathy, Mike, Megan, and Hallie Jones.

And hundreds more to all the many friends, neighbors, and strangers who offered me their tales of Laguna in my twenty years as a citizen there.

Artist, author, poet, and historian Dion Wright not only gave me some of his cogent observations, he wrote a terrific book about California in the fifties and sixties, *Tempus Fugitive*. He didn't just create art and write about that place and time; he lived them. He was *it*.

Also, many thanks to Nicholas Schou for his terrific account of the Brotherhood of Eternal Love, *Orange Sunshine: The Brotherhood of Eternal Love and Its Quest to Spread Peace, Love, and Acid to the World*. His book is not to be missed by anyone interested in this fascinating and resonant time.

Fond gratitude to my good friends Rick and Debra Raeber, who have welcomed me into the Laguna home for over thirty years. You guys rock.

In memory of Mike Schwaner, waterman and story lover. You are missed.

A thousand thanks to my agents, Robert and Mark Gottlieb

at Trident Media, and to my fine editor, Kristin Sevick, who shaped this book into what it is.

Last but not least, thank you, Laguna Beach, where I was delighted and shaped and learned to write. Always the place that formed me. I still love your Thousand Steps.

Turn the page for a sneak peek at
T. Jefferson Parker's next novel

THE
RESCUE

Available Spring 2023

1

Night in Tijuana, light rain from a pale sky.

Inside the Furniture Calderón factory and warehouse, the Roman follows his mongrel dog as it noses its way through the cluttered workstations, sniffing and snorting the chairs and sofas and barstools and bed sets in varying stages of completion.

The dog stands on its hind legs to smell the table saws and sewing machines, the measuring tapes and clamps and glue pots, then drops back to all fours again to sniff the fragrant bundles of hides and the colorful bolts of fabric piled high like treasures looted from a caravan. Between stops, it covers ground swiftly, nose up, nose down. Its short, four-count breaths draw the air both into its lungs and across the scent receptors packed within its muzzle.

The Roman is in black tactical couture all the way from his polished duty boots to the black ski mask snug to his face and

head. Black socks, a loose black kerchief for that band of neck
below the mask. The dog's black leash is bunched in one hand.
Behind the Roman are some of his business associates—four
militarized soldiers of the Jalisco New Generation Cartel, and
four men in humble street clothes instead of the khaki-with-
green-trim uniforms of the Municipal Police, their official em-
ployer. They all carry late-model automatic weapons, some
laser sighted and some with traditional iron sights.

Sullen and alert, these men trail the Roman and his dog,
respectful of their sizable skills and reputation as a cash- and
drug-detection team. The Roman has never told the men his
real name, only his nom de guerre, the Roman. So to them, he
is simply Román.

The dog's name is Joe, and he looks more like a common street
dog than a cash- and-drug-whiffing savant. Joe is a trim fifty-
five pounds, short haired, long legged, and saber tailed, with
rust ovals on a cream background. He is terrier-like and dainty
footed, but his gull wing ears protrude from what could well
be a Labrador retriever's solid head. To these heavily armed
men, accustomed to the burly German shepherd dogs, Mali-
nois, and Rottweilers favored by the DEA and Federales—and
the pit bulls adored by *narcotraficantes*—Joe looks amusing
and almost cute. The Roman, on the other hand, is simply *loco*.
But the Roman and his dog always find and deliver.

Joe's snorts sound softly in the still, cavernous factory. His
gently upcurved tail wags eagerly. He wheels and feints his way
through the river of smells. Cuts right, then left, then right
again, but moves forward, always forward. His ears bounce.
He loves his job.

The Roman, through his ski mask, also smells the leather
and the lumber and the faint dust-smoke of the incandescent
lamps above. He marvels once again at Joe's ability to experience not only these strong, obvious scents but also hundreds
of others that he, a mere man, can't smell at all. And not only
does Joe gather exponentially more than any human, he instantly distinguishes these smells from the chosen few that are

his purpose and his passion: fentanyl, heroin, cocaine, meth-amphetamine, marijuana, and currency.

And, of course, small animals.

Joe breaks toward a slouching stack of boxes, snatches a mouse off the floor, dashes it twice against the concrete—*rap, rap*—then looks proudly at his master.

Whispers and grunts and the metallic unslinging of guns.

"Joe, *down, you* sonofa*bitch.*"

Then laughter.

Joe plops to his belly, head up, ears smoothed back in sub-mission, staring at the Roman with eager penance. He doesn't know what *sonofabitch* means, but he knows what the Roman's tone of voice means.

"That's one of the reasons they retired him," the Roman says to no one in particular. His Spanish is good but accented by English. Learned in school, by the sound of it, not border Spanglish picked up on the job. "He's got a lot of terrier in him, and some things he can't control. Won't control."

"*¡Un perro terrible!*" says a policeman.

"*¡Muy rápido!*" says a cartel soldier.

"Come," orders the Roman. Joe bolts to his side and sits, looking up hopefully. "Steady, Joe. Steady, boy. Let's try this again. Okay, *find!*"

In the back of the vast warehouse, Joe alerts on a dented metal trash can overflowing with scraps of cloth and leather and wood.

He sits in front of his perceived find, as he has been trained. He looks first at the Roman, then at the trash can, but with a very different expression from his please-forgive-me-for-killing-the-mouse look. Now his ears are up and his eyes are fixed on the object of his alert. A quick glance at his master, then back to the business at hand. He's trembling.

Two of the policemen quietly tip over the container while a third, on his knees, rakes out the trash.

"*Ah . . . aha!*" he says, pulling a green steel ammunition box from the mound of trash, then another, and another.

The Roman can smell the gasoline that the ammo boxes have been wiped down with—a standard dumb idea for confusing a dog. He's seen hot sauce, cologne, mint-flavored mouthwash, cat urine, bleach, and antiperspirant used too. Most traffickers don't know that dogs don't smell the combined odors within a scent cone; they smell individual ones. They separate and register each component of the whole. A book of smells, each smell a word. So no matter how you try to disguise a scent, the dog is rarely fooled or repelled. The dog knows what's there.

The Roman knows the only thing that works against a good narcotics-and-currency dog is perfect packaging, but Joe has the best nose the Roman has ever seen. The much surer solution would be to keep your stash far away from dogs like Joe, maybe on another continent. Or to bribe the dog's handler, or the handler's handler. Money solves most problems.

A squat cartel lieutenant whom the Roman knows only as Domingo kneels and pops the heavy latch on one of the steel cases. It's a standard US Army–issue ammunition box—twelve by six inches and seven and a half inches high—and the former contents are stenciled in yellow on a lengthwise flank: 100 CAL. 50 CARTRIDGES.

As the rain begins to pound the metal roof high above, Domingo removes an open package of fragrant naphthalene mothballs from inside the box, then six neat vacuum-packed bricks of US twenty-dollar bills. The Roman knows that the old-school Sinaloans from whom he is stealing weigh-count the bricks to exactly one-half pound, which means this case contains $28,800. And he knows that $9,600 of it will soon belong to him and Joe, who is watching all of this with shiny-eyed pride. From one of the many pockets on his pants, the Roman gives him a cube of steak.

The other two ammunition boxes contain identical treasures, for a gross total of $86,400 for the Jalisco New Generation Cartel and the participating Municipal Police officers who have helped make this possible.

And $28,800 for himself, the Roman, and for Joe, man's best friend.

But the raindrops suddenly turn into footsteps, faint but fast.

The Roman and his little army dive for cover, machine guns chattering away at them. Domingo, closest to the loot, goes down with a cry and a wobble of blood.

The Roman calls Joe but the dog has vanished in the horrific noise. The compadres return fire, their bullets clunking home or twanging in ricochet. The Roman knows he's in a numbers game, and the noise actually sounds encouraging: four shooters, six? But this is the Sinaloans' warehouse and they know it better than he and his men do.

"Joe, come! Joe, *come!*"

The Roman draws his sidearm, a .40-caliber Glock 35 with a laser sight that holds twenty-two rounds and will not jam. He calls Joe again but the dog is gone. The gunfire subsides while footsteps land in the smoky silence. The Roman runs from his cover toward the rear exit of the warehouse. Then a volley and a high-pitched *yipe* from Joe. The Roman strides straight toward that yipe, shoots down a slender *sicario* in a white cowboy hat and a Shakira T-shirt, turns and center-shoots another man, twice—*boom, boom*—the bullets slamming into the far wall before his body plops to the floor. The Roman is a big man; he knows he might take a bullet someday doing shit like this.

But he loves it.

You wear the crown, you wear the target.

Joe whimpers to his left and the Roman charges toward the sound, zigzagging down a long aisle lined with mile-high shelves like a big-box store, and the Roman senses the enemy behind him, turns, and blows him down with three shots, the *sicario*'s machine gun clattering to the concrete.

The Roman and his employers press the running battle toward the rear exit and the loading docks and the street. The Sinaloans are fewer, just as the Roman had thought. They're running hard for the steel sliding door through which they entered; it is still cracked open. Two escape, but the Roman and his confederates cut down two others as they try to squeeze out.

Followed by Joe, who clambers over the bodies and limps crookedly through the door and into the night.

"Joe, come! *Come!*"

Outside, the Roman scans the dark barrio with his pistol raised, trying to watch the cars and the houses and the buildings and the street, trying to keep from getting shot, trying to see his wounded dog. The Sinaloans have apparently taken off. Two boys run down Coahuila Street, oversized athletic shoes splashing potholes filled with rain. Sirens wail and citizens stoically observe the Roman from behind windows and cracked doors. They've seen this before—their city is among the most violent cities in a violent country in a violent world.

The Roman calls out to them in anguished Spanish: "Where is my dog? Where is my dog?"

No one answers.

"Joe! Here, boy! Come!"

The Roman searches the sidewalks and beneath cars, under the festive furniture on the porches and the tiny front yards, even the gutters running black and throwing up wakes over pale sandbags that just maybe could be Joe.

The sirens force him away.

He's the last to pile into the white-and-green van parked on a side street. It's the one with the Ciudad de Tijuana Policía Municipal emblems on the sides and the orange light on the top and the three green cartridge cases on the floor beside the badly wounded Domingo. The driver runs the wet city streets fast, no warning light and no siren. Just the high beams. And the stink of blood and fear and gun smoke, and the pounding of the Roman's heart.

Five minutes later the van pulls into Superior Automobile Repair and Service, and the motorized wrought iron gate with the big sign on it rolls closed behind them. The compound is surrounded by an impregnable ten-foot concrete wall with broken bottles cemented to the top. A man in street clothes waves the driver in to the high bay and the repair stations inside.

Domingo has died, so the others climb over him and out. The Roman is first among them, carrying one of the three ammunition cases, his pay for the night's work. He loves the feel of $28,880 in his hand, but his heart aches with the loss of Joe.

Another man in street clothes walks the Roman to his car.

"It is terrible what happened, Señor Román."

The Roman has rehearsed a lifetime for what just happened. Which prepared him poorly for it. He's killed three men just now. His first, not counting war. He feels gutted and surprised.

"Fuck off, Amador."

The Roman's car is a green Maserati Quattroporte parked over a platform jack in one of the repair stations, as if to be worked on first thing in the morning. The Roman sets the ammo case in the trunk and tosses the ski mask beside it. Runs his hands through his short blond hair.

Behind the wheel now, he nods to the man, who throws a toggle on a cabled control box. The platform jack shudders and lowers the Maserati into the ground. The Roman looks at himself briefly in the rearview as the darkness claims him, blame and anger in his bloodshot gray eyes. Blame and anger. He thinks: *Joe. I'd go back and look for him if* la colonia *wasn't crawling with cops, some on cartel payrolls but some not.*

Five minutes and a slow mile through the dark underground tunnel later, the green Maserati rises from its grave, safe within the high spiked walls of Platinum Foreign Car Specialists in Otay Mesa, California.

The Roman waits as the gate swings open, then drives through it into the California night.

35 Days After the Shoot-Out . . .

2

Joe lies on his pad in the Clínica Veterinarea San Francisco de Asís, looking out from his ancient rock-and-iron-grated cell at the blustery winter day.

The clinic director, Dr. Félix Rodríguez, has named him El Perro Disparado, Shot Dog, because, well, he's been shot, and Tijuana street dogs don't have name tags, and he has to call the dog something.

Joe has named the doctor Good Man. He understands that Good Man brings the food. He understands that Good Man has done something mysterious to him. That he has a good face. That he scratches good—under the throat and behind the ears—like Teddy and Dan.

On his belly, head resting forward between his trim front feet, his saber tail curving along his hind legs almost to his chin, Joe watches and listens and lets the smells of the world drift past.

The clinic door opens with its clunk and long squeak. Through the rusting bars of his cage, Joe sees Good Man enter the row of kennels. With him is a Woman he has not seen before. From their expressions and bodies, Joe sees that they are not a Team.

Joe has no concept of luck, but the doctor knows that this animal is fabulously lucky to have been brought here by a boy, who, smeared with the terrified dog's blood and intestinal fluid, carried him over a kilometer in the rain.

But the doctor also knows that luck has two faces: Shot Dog's miracle rescue and touchy surgery have landed him at the end of his allotted thirty-day adoption period, which expires today. Baja California state policy, beyond the doctor's control. Shot Dog will be euthanized in the morning unless he is adopted before then, odds that Dr. Rodríguez knows are smaller than small. Not a single prospective dog owner has come by today, and the expected rain bodes ill for a late-hour miracle.

Last week, an elderly man was interested in Shot Dog but had no money. When the doctor offered to waive the modest adoption fee and give him a week's worth of food, a leash, and some good flea-and-tick pills, the man had promised to return the next day but never came back at all. Rodríguez turns away dozens of dogs every week because his clinic is 100 percent full. He's even got portable crates set up inside the hospital and lobby, but these, too, are full of yowling, hopeful, pathetic dogs.

It's been a long thirty-something days for Joe. No Dan. No Team. No work. No play. No meat treats. No sleeping on his couch in the living room or in Dan's bed when the women aren't there. No swims in the pool. Sure, his pain is mostly gone, and the itchy stitches, too, and so is the slobbery plastic cone once tied around his neck. But these are small things compared with the immense sadness that seems to run through every part of him. There are memories and there are dreams, dreams of memories and memories of dreams. They are one story. His dog mind is never fouled by time, beginnings, middles, and endings. He knows that Dan will return and they will be the Team again, but the long hours in the cell are wearing him down.

Good Man and Woman come down the walk between the

facing rows of cages; then Woman stops. Joe does not like women, because they get Dan's attention and sometimes even his bed. The Team Bed. The women are not part of the Team. The Team is Joe and Dan.

Now Woman plants a shiny, three-legged tree and screws a black thing onto its flat top. Joe is familiar with these. People have them all the time, mostly to talk to. Sometimes they make sudden strong light. People used to point them at him and Aaron, who was the leader of his Team before Dan. People used to point them at him and Teddy, his first Boy. Teddy then Aaron then Dan. His Teams.

Thirty feet downwind of the humans, Joe registers the familiar bleached-white-coat smell of the doctor, the leather of his new athletic shoes, his musky cologne. He smells the woman's flowery hair, her female sweat and perfume, and the strong, nose-quivering powder that Dan puts into his morning cup. All of these join the ambient river of scents that has flowed past him for thirty-plus days here at the clinic: car exhaust and street-vendor foods, trash and tire burns, diesel smoke, dog pee and feces and disinfectant sluicing down the walkway slot that runs between the cages, the restaurant food that makes his stomach growl, the climbing roses on the rock wall that separates the clinic from the auto repair shop next door. And much, much more.

Woman aims the black thing at Good Man, then stands beside him. Joe can see that the doctor is worried by the black thing, or it might be Woman who worries him. Not very worried, but a little. Dan is never worried or afraid.

Joe hears their words very clearly, and recognizes some of them, but not nearly enough to understand what they are saying. He never stops trying to understand. His ears are good and he listens to humans very closely. He watches their faces closely too. Woman's voice is calm. They talk the language of Dan, not the language of Good Man:

"Bettina Blazak here, with Dr. Félix Rodríguez of the Clínica Veterinarea San Francisco de Asís in Tijuana, Mexico.

Dr. Rodríguez, thank you so much for sharing your time with *Coastal Eddy*."

"I am happy to be here, Bettina."

"Tell us about the clinic."

"Yes, of course. Mexico loves dogs. We love them so much that twelve million of them run free on our streets and parks and beaches. They have no owners. No one cares for them. Without government sterilization programs, they breed. Many die of starvation and disease and, in my opinion, of sadness. We have a name for them, *perros callejeros*. 'Street dogs.' All these animals here come from our streets. Our purpose is to find for them a home. This is a great challenge because there are so many dogs."

"What exactly what is a Mexican street dog? What breeds do they comprise?"

"We like to say they are not a pool of genes but an ocean of genes! Terriers and retrievers of all kinds, collies, boxers, and German shepherds. Spaniels, huskies, Dobermans, Lacy dogs and vizslas, basenjis and pit bulls. Greyhounds, of course, because they race here and later are sold as pets, and what do they do when you get them home? They either sleep or run! There are many small and toy breeds especially popular in Mexico—Xolos, Chihuahuas, papillons, miniature dachshunds and poodles. Even the genes of the legendary Korean hunting dog, the Jindo, have been found in dogs here."

"What's the first thing you do when someone brings in a street dog?"

"Food and water. A dog starved once is always hungry. Then medication for fleas and ticks, and a thorough medical examination. Vaccinations. Sterilization is performed. Decayed teeth are removed. We bathe them so they are clean for a possible owner and a home."

"What do your examinations usually reveal?"

"Starvation and dehydration. Parasites, *Erlichia*, many viruses. Canine influenza. Skin disease is common. Some dogs have been on the street so long that their toenails have grown through their feet because of no trimming."

"That's awful."

Good Man nods his head and makes a sad face. Joe has recognized the words Dog, Beach—because Dan takes him there—Street, Food, and Water, and he thinks that the word *home* might mean Crate. Other than that, these two humans might be talking about anything. He understands from their voices that Good Man is serious, and Woman is becoming unhappy.

"It must be very expensive to do all this medicine on so many dogs," says Woman. "How does the Veterinary Clinic of Saint Francis of Assisi survive?"

"We are partially sponsored by a major North American pet company, and we receive a small amount of funding from the state and city. We ask for a donation when we place a dog for adoption."

"How much?"

"Whatever the person can pay. We recommend twenty dollars, which includes food, the collar they are wearing, a leash, and one toy."

"How many dogs do you rescue and place for adoption each month?"

"Adoptions are slow in January, February, and March because of the Christmas dogs whose owners have become tired of them. So they take them somewhere and let them go. No one wants another dog then. In September, when the hot weather is leaving, people want dogs. We place many dogs through December. As presents to make the children happy."

Joe has no idea what Good Man has said, other than Dogs, Dog, Dogs, and Dogs. The man's tone is not clear.

"How can our readers and viewers in the United States help?"

Good Man smiles and his tone of voice becomes happier. "There are two things they can do—send donations to us or come to Mexico and rescue one of our beautiful dogs. We take care of all the adoption paperwork right here, and send them home with all their shots. And the little things, the food and the toy. Your readers and viewers will receive a healthy, loving, and grateful rescue animal. They are intelligent, humorous, and very good learners."

"Dr. Rodríguez, can you introduce me to some of your dogs?"

"Yes, of course."

Woman removes the black thing from the shiny three-legged tree. They go from cage to cage. When Woman kneels down in front of one, a tan muzzle with a black nose appears through the bars and Woman makes high Woman sounds. She points her black thing at the cage.

"Oh, look at *this* little cutie!"

Again, her words are lost on the dog, but her meaning is very clear. And to Joe—as well as to his ancestors lying by the fires that first lured them into the world of men—meanings are always more important than words.

Now Good Man and Woman stand outside Joe's cage, looking down at him.

"This is Shot Dog."

"What a terrible name."

"It is more a description."

"How did he get shot?"

"I don't know. He was shot and a boy brought him in and I performed a dangerous but successful surgery."

Woman points the black thing at Joe as she talks: "A boy saved his life. A boy and you, Dr. Rodríguez. This dog has been very lucky."

"Some people shoot the street dogs for sport. Rather than feed or help them."

"My readers in California will want to know that," says woman, still pointing the black thing at him. "They'll be horrified. Could this have been an accident?"

Good Man's expression softens and so does his voice. "Anything is possible."

"Has anyone shown interest in adopting him?"

"An older man, but nothing happened."

"He's really cute. The way his ears stick out. How long has he been here?"

"More than the thirty days that I told you about."

Joe watches Woman lower the black thing. Her expression has changed. She looks at Good Man, then back to him. Her face is sorrow. She does not need words for Joe to understand that something very bad is happening.

"It breaks my heart, too, Miss Blazak. He is already past the limit. It is the policy."

"Just leave him where he is. In this cage. Simple."

"Injured dogs are considered bad luck."

"With all he's been through!"

The woman kneels near the bars. Joe smells the cinnamon and coffee on her breath and a spilled drop of hot sauce coming from the knee of her pants. He's used to finding valuable smells, but these are not valuable. He rests his head on his front paws and sighs.

"Excuse me, Doctor."

Woman walks briskly to the clinic building, turns, brings a hand to her mouth, and looks back at Dr. Rodríguez and Joe. Who understands that Woman doesn't know what to do. Dan always knows.

Then she's back.

"May I open the door?" she asks.

"Allow me."

Joe rises and stretches, then limps out of his cage and into the noose of the doctor's expertly dangled lead. Joe is long legged, long tailed, and concave like a whippet. He sits before the kneeling Woman and they are almost eye-to-eye, Joe's brown and Woman's blue. He reads her face for meanings as best he can. He can't understand them as he does Dan's, Teddy's, or Aaron's, or other people he has spent more time with. He has never known a Woman well, and never liked the way they take attention away from him. Away from Dan and him, the Team. Same as when he and Aaron were the Team, and when he and Teddy were the Team.

Woman is sad but Joe doesn't know why. The sadness began when Good Man said *thirty days*, but Joe doesn't know what those words mean. Dan is almost never sad. Dan is strong, and fast moving for a human. Sometimes angry, sometimes happy. But not sad. Joe smells her breath and body, under her arms, her legs, her feet and sandals.

She reaches out her stranger's hand slowly, palm down. Joe decides not to bite it. He has been sore and sad since coming here to the clinic, but his training is to bite only on command. He lets her pet him under his chin. He holds her gaze, and his eyes narrow at the pleasure. Then she strokes his throat, and behind his ears, and gently rubs the raised scar inside his ear flap. On her face Joe sees Woman's sadness change to something else: happiness. He smells her tear forming before it rolls down her face.

"Señor Rodríguez," she says. "I came here to do a story on your clinic and adoption center. It will be a good story. And I want to adopt Shot Dog. I will not let him die here. I want to help him heal and get him off these streets forever."

Good Man looks at Woman, his face filled with happiness. Joe knows that these two people have gone from sadness to happiness very quickly. He taps his tail once, looking at Woman. He thinks he understands what all this happiness means: Dan is coming to get him. They will be the Team again. What else could it be?

"Señorita Blazak, you have just done a wonderful thing for one of God's own creatures! You will be blessed forever by the Holy Mother."

"Let's do the paperwork quickly, before I change my mind. I have to be back in Laguna by late afternoon, and the border will be awful. I'll make a donation to your clinic, beyond the twenty dollars."

"I am a very happy *médico veterinario* and I know Shot Dog will be happy too."

"I'll probably change his name."

"This is your right."

"I need video of us together."

In the office, Joe lies under the big wooden desk, his leg

hurting but not badly. He's leashed at Woman's feet, her bag on the floor beside him. He smells the leather of her sandals, the woman skin of her feet, a medley of flowery smells flowing from inside the bag, and one of the very valuable smells he's trained to track. He listens to her making pleasant talk with Good Man, and scratching something on paper. From the man's side of the desk come the same sounds that Dan makes at home when he uses the black slab on his desk. Woman's hand descends and takes something from her bag on the floor beside him, and Joe smells the money. There isn't much. Dan would not be happy.

Two men walk in. From under the desk, and judging by their shoes, Joe sees that one is big and one is small. He knows people like these, their jangling metallic sounds, their commanding voices, their smells of leather and gun oil and solvent. They always do what Dan says. Joe does not like police, because they take Dan's attention away from him, just like women do. They are not part of the Team. So Joe stays where he is, listening, out of sight under the desk where Woman and Good Man sit. He understands none of their fast, unfamiliar language.

"What do you want?" asks Good Man.

"We are looking for a dog that ran away in the North Zone last month. There was a dispute and he was shot."

"Was it the narcos, or men just shooting dogs for fun?" says Good Man.

"It is under investigation."

"We have no such dog."

"We will search the kennels."

"Of course. Take your time."

When the police have clanked from the room, Good Man says strong, fast, quiet words to Woman. Dan sometimes gives orders in this tone. It means *now*. It means *important*.

Joe hears clunking on the desk, feels a firm tug on his leash, and follows Woman out of the clinic and into the bustling Tijuana streets.

He understands that his world has just changed.

ABOUT THE AUTHOR

Rita Parker

T. JEFFERSON PARKER is the author of numerous
novels and short stories, the winner of three Edgar
Awards, and the recipient of a *Los Angeles Times
Book Prize* for best mystery. Before becoming a full-
time novelist, he was an award-winning reporter.
He lives in Fallbrook, California, and can be found
at tjeffersonparker.com.